Dear Reader,

Once in a great while for an author, a book comes along that
she knows instinctively is somehow different from her usual
work, special in a way that she can't define, can only sense.

For me, my new novel *Dust Devil* is one of those rare books,
for a number of reasons. It's the kind of novel—a big,
mainstream, contemporary romance—that I've wanted to
write for several years but never had the opportunity until
now. It is an intricately interwoven story that, through its
heroine, Sarah Kincaid, touches on a number of issues that
affect all of us women in our everyday roles as lovers, wives,
mothers and daughters. And last but not least, its hero,
Renzo Cassavettes, is the one man who, out of all the heroes
I've ever created, I would most want to know in real life.

Renzo and Sarah share the kind of love that every woman
dreams of but is incredibly lucky ever to find. It is a once-in-
a-lifetime bond that endures forever and that for Renzo and
Sarah is symbolized by a butterfly that touches them both,
each in a special way. But like all things, there is a price to
be paid for their love, and the high cost is borne not just by
them alone, but also by the entire town in which they live. A
town whose secrets, sins and scandals threaten to tear the
two of them apart—and, in doing so, draw them together
irrevocably. For theirs is a love as deep and undeniable as it
is passionate and forbidden.

This is an epic story about the idealistic, the realistic and the
romantic, about the powerful, the ambitious, and the
corrupt, all of them swept up by catastrophic events that are
like a destructive dust devil blowing into their small, rural
town, changing it for always. But most of all, it is a story
about the triumph of the human spirit in the face of human
failures.

I am so thrilled and delighted that MIRA gave me the
chance to share this novel with you. I hope you enjoy
reading it as much as I did writing it.

All best,

Rebecca Brandewyne

Watch for
Rebecca Brandewyne's
next MIRA title in
the Spring of 1997

REBECCA BRANDEWYNE

DUST DEVIL

MIRA BOOKS

ISBN 1-55166-063-6

DUST DEVIL

Copyright © 1996 by Rebecca Brandewyne.

MIRA and the star colophon are trademarks of MIRA Books.

Printed in U.S.A.

For my agent,
Meg Ruley,
because she said all the right things—
and at a time when I most needed to hear them.
With much affection and appreciation.

Contents

Dust Devil

There is sweet music here that softer falls
Than petals from blown flowers on the earth,
Or sunbeams on still waters between walls
Of jagged old rock that once rang with mirth;
Music that gentlier on the spirit lies
Than summer breeze o'er tall grass sighs;
Music that brings passion's fire 'neath the blissful skies.
Here are cool mosses deep,
And honeysuckle vines that creep,
And on the banks the long-leaved willows weep,
And in the shadowed woods bluebottles flit and leap.

Rebecca Brandewyne

Now are we weighed upon with heaviness
And utterly consumed with dull distress.
Is there no rest from constant weariness?
From dreams that come on butterfly wings of night
And wake eternal yearning for those
Halcyon days of light
Long gone, like birds that soar in autumn flight?
From wild seed pain grows
And brings all our sorrows;
No surcease lies in slumber's holy balm,
Nor comfort in the inner spirit's prose,
"Seek refuge in the calm!"
Shall only emptiness haunt all our tomorrows?

No! for from the ever-winding road,
Hot wind brings a dust devil of forebode
To tear the past's dark veil aside
And sweep aloft all that would hide.
Full exposed to the sun's harsh blaze,
Secret sins must out, whether ill or fair;
The reckoning doth abide,
Lo! ever in the future's wake.
So comes the judgment, demanding full repair.
Now, again, music low doth spake
All its allotted length of days;
Night blossoms ripen in their ways,
Ripen and fade, wine-sweet, and fireflies spark
Like lovers in the silent dark.*

*Poem adapted from *The Lotus-Eaters: Choric Song* by
Alfred, Lord Tennyson

Prologue

All the Roads Run

Does the road wind uphill all the way?
Yes, to the very end.
Will the day's journey take the whole long day?
From morn to night, my friend.

Up-Hill
—Christina Rossetti

The Road Home

Like one that on a lonesome road
Doth walk in fear and dread,
And having once turned round walks on,
And turns no more his head;
Because he knows a frightful fiend
Doth close behind him tread.

The Ancient Mariner
—Samuel Taylor Coleridge

A Country Road, The Midwest, The Present

Once, a long time ago, he had thought that if only he ran fast enough, far enough, he could escape from the past, could leave behind in the dust, weary and defeated, what it was that chased him, and that then, turning to gaze back at it, he could laugh again, because finally, he would be free. But now, when all his roads were run, he knew the past was with him still, and always would be, because at last he had learned that no matter how long and hard you ran, the one thing in the world you could never outrun was yourself.

He crested the rise before him, and the old road—the one that had been the first and was now the last road for him—stretched ahead, narrow, wending and unpaved, its hard-packed earth as red-gold and sandy in the hot summer sun as he remembered. Time had dimmed many things in his mind...but not his memory of that road: the daunting sight of it unwinding interminably before him, the dusty smell of it in his quivering nostrils, the gritty taste of it in his parched mouth, the rough feel of it beneath the callused soles of his bare feet, the sound of it in his ears...a sound that had been the silence of aloneness and desolation, which he had already known so well when, his thumb uplifted in the hitchhiker's age-old gesture, he had first set his feet upon the road.

That silence, like the road, haunted him still.

Years ago, there had been no highway leading to the town that lay at the road's end. But although the state had long since built one—a two-lane blacktop now cracked from the heat of summers gone by, with a patchwork of light and dark macadam where potholes had been filled in—still, he had chosen to come this way, the long way, by the old road. He'd had to prove to himself that, finally, he could face it. That it was not, in reality, some monstrous, gaping-mawed snake, coils slithering and tangling as it lay in wait for him, as it did in his dreams, the nightmares from which, over the years, he had awakened in a cold sweat far more often than he cared to admit.

For a long moment, he paused on the rise, staring at the road, faintly incredulous at the sight of it, not quite able to believe that what had tormented him for so long was only an old, dusty country road, empty and forlorn, not much used ánymore. Then at last relief swept through him, and he almost laughed aloud at his foolishness, at the fear that had made his mouth taste as acrid as the fine layer of grime that clung to his wind-tousled black hair, his lean, bronzed face and his muscular, bare forearms, damp with sweat in the sun that had beaten down on him as he had driven for countless miles in the classic red roadster he had bought some years back and painstakingly restored.

It was hard now to believe that when he had fled from the town down this road, he had been the proverbial poor boy from the wrong side of the tracks, with the law hard on his heels, and nothing more to his name than the clothes on his back and a few dollars in his pocket. Sometimes, when he remembered that frightened, desperate young man he had been, it was as though he stood outside himself, watching his life unfold through the eyes of a stranger, as though it had been someone else who had lived those wild, bittersweet days of youth that would never come again. Those days might have broken a lesser man, but now he knew they had been the making of him. Whatever lay ahead for him, he was ready and willing now to meet it.

At the realization, sharp-edged anticipation rose suddenly within him, and with it, a rush of adrenaline that made his pulse race like the roadster's engine as he depressed the accelerator. Trailing a cloud of dirt that was like a dust devil in his wake, he abruptly bore headlong down the road toward the town that waited at his journey's end.

After more than a decade, Renzo Cassavettes was through running.

He was going home.

Book One

By Our Beginnings

Youth, what man's age is like to be doth show;
We may our ends by our beginnings know.

Of Prudence
—Sir John Denham

One

Love Lost, Long Ago

Though nothing can bring back the hour
Of splendor in the grass, of glory in the flower;
We will grieve not, rather find
Strength in what remains behind.

> *Ode. Intimations of Immortality from*
> *Recollections of Early Childhood*
> —William Wordsworth

A Small Town, The Midwest, The Present

"Alex, hurry up, please," Sarah Kincaid called up the steep, narrow staircase from the foyer of her old Victorian farmhouse for the umpteenth time that morning. She waited expectantly for a long moment, then sighed with both anger and exasperation when her son neither appeared on the landing above nor even bothered to answer her. "Alex, I'm going to be late for my hair appointment!

If you don't come on, you'll have to stay here." If her son heard her, he continued to ignore her. "Alex, if I have to trudge up these steps to get you, you're going to be sorry!" she finally threatened futilely, at her wit's end with the boy.

Every day, it seemed he became more withdrawn, more sullen, more difficult to handle. Since birth, he had never been a particularly easy child. But at least when he had been younger, smaller, there had been a child's inherent sweetness and curiosity in him. It had been easy to forgive him for his stubborn temper tantrums when, afterward, he had crawled up into her lap and laid his dark little head upon her breast, his big, thick-lashed, molasses-brown eyes fluttering shut as he had drifted to sleep in her arms.

But now that Alex was eleven years old, it seemed to Sarah that her son had become a stranger to her, that somewhere along the way, she had lost the child so precious to her that she had often lain awake at night listening intently to the sound of his breathing, her heart lurching with fear at the thought that he might die in his crib while she slept. She remembered all the times when, in the wee hours of the morning, she had crept to his bedside to check on him, to kiss his incredibly soft, chubby cheek and to marvel at his very existence. And it did not seem possible to her that these days, she frequently felt nothing but a sense a relief when his bedtime rolled around and she could spend the remainder of the evening alone, in peace.

At last, sighing heavily again, dreading the thought of yet another confrontation with her son, Sarah slowly climbed the stairs and made her way down the hall to Alex's room. Involuntarily, she shuddered at the sight of it. The place looked like a war zone, a disaster area, with dirty dishes stacked on the desk and equally dirty clothes strewn all over the floor, despite the laundry hamper that stood in one corner. Posters held in place with pushpins haphazardly jammed into their edges covered practically every inch of the walls. Unmistakable traces of Kool-Aid had dripped down the closet door to puddle on the hardwood floor. An assortment of colored felt-tipped markers, notebook paper, comic books, trading cards, action figures, stuffed animals and Nintendo games cluttered the room. Her son himself perched on the unmade bed, glued to his small television, a Nintendo controller in his hands, his thumbs quickly and expertly manipulating the arrows and buttons. On the TV screen, a parade of otherworldly warriors and humanlike creatures moved and leaped, all appearing to pummel and kick one another in a battle for supremacy.

Taking a deep breath, her green eyes flashing with vexation and determination, Sarah marched inside, picking her way across the littered floor as though it were a mine field. She deliberately snapped off the TV, then switched off the power to the Nintendo set, as well.

"Mom!" Alex wailed furiously, bouncing vigorously on the bed and stamping his feet on the floor. "I was almost to the big monster at the end!"

"I don't care!" Sarah retorted, struggling to master the urge she had to box his ears or shake him until his teeth rattled right out of his head. "Didn't you hear me calling you? You should have been downstairs thirty minutes ago! I woke you up in plenty of time to get ready, and I *told* you my hair appointment at Shear Style was at eleven o'clock this morning. You don't even have your socks and shoes on, and I know good and well that you haven't brushed your teeth yet, either! Now, do you want to go into town with me, to the Penny Arcade, or not?''

"Yes." The response was curt and disrespectful, and her son scowled at her in a way that enraged her further and at the same time wrenched at her heart.

Instead of rewarding him for his behavior, she should punish him, Sarah knew, by insisting he remain at home today and clean up his room. But that would only be stirring up already troubled waters, leading to further hostilities between the two of them. Denied his weekend trip to the Penny Arcade, Alex would either grow belligerent and rebellious or wholly uncommunicative, shutting her out completely. And at the moment, Sarah did not feel as though she could cope with any of that.

"Then get a move on," she finally ordered him tersely, steadily returning his glare, compelling herself to stare him down. "Because I'm leaving here in ten minutes—with or without you!''

After that, trembling from the force of her emotions, Sarah stalked from the room. Outside in the hall, where Alex could not see her, she leaned weakly against the wall, fighting to hold at bay the tears that welled in her eyes and pressing one fist to her mouth to stifle the sobs of anger, frustration and heartbreak that rose in her throat, closing it up tight, choking her. She loved her son deeply. He was all she had in the world, and she hated arguing with him. Worse, she had begun to grow more and more afraid that the townspeople who predicted he would eventually come to a bad end might be proved right. That fear gnawed deeply at her at times like these, when it seemed to her that Alex had slipped beyond her grasp and she would never be able to reach him again.

Unbidden, the thought that perhaps she *had* made the wrong decision about her son all those years ago crept into Sarah's mind, horrifying her. Of course she did not wish he had never been born! That she had given in to her parents and aborted him as they had at first pressured her to do. God forgive her for even *thinking* she had not done the right thing in having Alex, in keeping him instead of agreeing to sign the adoption papers that would have taken him away from her forever, as her parents had then strenuously insisted she do. It had been hard, so very hard, for her to stand firm against them, to hold her head high in the face of the townspeople's stares and whispers. Even now, after all these years, she could still hear the painful gossip that had rung ceaselessly in her ears back then.

"Did you hear about Sarah Kincaid? Seventeen, unwed and pregnant!"

"No! And she seemed like such a nice, quiet, studious girl. Who's the father?"

"Nobody knows. She won't tell. Hell, she probably *can't*. Most likely, she's slept with every guy in high school. She's nothing but coal-mining trash—and you know what they're like! Ought not to be allowed to associate with decent folk. Should have shut those mines down years ago and cleaned up all those miners' shacks...such a god-awful eyesore. But what can anybody do against a man like Nick Genovese? They don't call him 'Papa Nick' for nothing, you know. So as long as he owns those mines, they'll continue to operate, I reckon."

"Yes, to operate—and to breed more sluts like Sarah Kincaid! Still, who would have thought it of her? Despite her background, she just didn't seem the type."

"Well, you know what they say about still waters running deep. And no matter what, there's no denying the fact that she's baking somebody's bun in her oven! Otherwise, the principal wouldn't have expelled her from high school."

That was what had hurt and shamed Sarah worst of all—that because of her pregnancy, she had been promptly and inexorably expelled from high school, unable to graduate with her class, despite that she had been a straight-A student. It had been a real struggle after she had given birth to Alex, but in the end, she had managed not only to complete her GED, but also to win a prestigious scholarship to the local state university. Her mother had reluctantly cared for Alex while, attending classes by day, working nights as a waitress at a diner to pay for all the expenses the scholarship hadn't covered, as well as for her son's upkeep, Sarah had eventually earned her bachelor's degree in journalism, with a minor in art.

She had a good job now, as the advertising-and-promotions director for Field-Yield, Inc., which manufactured crop fertilizers, pesticides, and other farm products sold throughout the Midwest. Lately, however, most of her time had been spent planning the senatorial campaign of former governor J. D. Holbrooke, who owned Field-Yield, Inc. Why the governor had ever singled her out and taken such a shine to her, Sarah didn't know. But she was grateful he had. Except for Nick Genovese, J. D. Holbrooke was the richest man in town, with generations of old money and well-established roots behind him. In winning J.D.'s approval, she had at long last managed to put the scandal and social stigma of her past behind her. Nobody called her a slut these days—or if they did, at least it was behind her back and not to her face.

"Mom, are you all right?" Alex's voice startled her from her reverie.

"Yes...just a little tired, that's all." Sarah abruptly straightened up, wondering how long she had been standing there, leaning against the hall wall, lost in the past. She noted that Alex now had his socks and shoes on, and that his face was puzzled and shadowed with concern for her. His question was his way of apologizing to her, she knew. Although tall and strong for his age, he was still only eleven years old, she reminded herself, still young enough that the loving little boy he had once been lurked inside him—and worried for his mother. It was occasional glimpses of that little boy that gave her hope that her son was not yet wholly lost to her, that she still had time to find a way to reach him before it was too late. Her earlier anger dissipated. Perhaps their day together could still be salvaged. She smiled at him tenderly, reaching out to ruffle his tousled black hair. "Time's a-wastin'. Get your teeth brushed, and let's get going, pal. And when I'm finished at Shear Style, we'll grab some lunch at Fritzchen's Kitchen and maybe go shopping at Wal-Mart afterward. What do you say to that?"

"I say it's a deal," Alex answered, with more enthusiasm for her company than he had displayed in weeks. "Can I get a new Power Rangers figure while we're out?"

"May I," she corrected automatically. "We'll see. Hurry up, now. I don't want to be late for my hair appointment. It puts Lucille behind and throws off her entire schedule for the rest of the day. And that makes her so cranky that she's liable to scalp me instead of just give me a trim!"

Alex actually grinned at that, and Sarah's heart turned over with both love and anxiety. It seemed that with every passing day, he looked more and more like his father. She marveled that other people didn't see it and make the connection. But then, the boy's father was long gone, and there was no reason to think anyone except her remembered him. And she *did* remember, no matter how many times she told herself he was never coming back, and that he was best forgotten. He had been her first love...her only love. Foolishly, she still ached inside whenever she thought of him. Ached and felt a deep anger and resentment, too, that he had made love to her and then within hours had abandoned her, had left her behind that summer's day so many years ago when he had fled from town, with the law hard on his heels.

He was no good, had never been any good, the townspeople had declared afterward. He was the son of a small-time, big-city mobster. So what else could have been expected of him other than that he would take after his hoodlum father and commit a murder? Just like his father—if the law didn't get him first—he, too, would wind up dead in a ghetto gutter somewhere, gunned down during some violent gang war, they had direly predicted.

Only, he had fooled them all.

But it did her no good to dwell on any of that, Sarah reminded herself fiercely, giving herself another mental shake. There was no use crying over what might have been. Alex's father had never even once in all these years made any attempt to get in touch with her, as he surely would have done had he really loved her, as he had claimed. He was out of her life forever, and she should be thankful for that. He had taken her innocence and betrayed her trust, and she had paid dearly for her foolish mistake in believing his lies. It was only the fact that Alex clearly needed a man's strong but gentle hand that had made her think of his father today, had made her long wistfully that she were not a single parent. It was just so hard, being alone, trying to be all things to her son—and fearing desperately that she was failing.

Sarah wanted Alex to have better from life than what she herself had known. And while her job ensured that she was able to provide for him financially, in a way her parents had never been able to afford for her, she knew her son paid the price emotionally for that security. As a working mother, she wasn't always there for him when he needed her, so she had a tendency to spoil him in other ways to compensate for her guilt over her absence. And now that he was of an age to understand what it meant, he must endure the stigma of his illegitimacy, too. More than once, he had returned home from school to report that other children had started a fight with him, calling him a bastard.

But surely Alex could not doubt that she loved him, Sarah told herself, troubled. Surely by now, he must know how she had sacrificed and fought tooth and nail to hold on to him, that she wouldn't have done that if she hadn't loved and wanted him with all her heart and every fiber of her being.

Heading downstairs to the kitchen, she gathered up her handbag and keys, meeting her son at the front door. Despite everything, her heart swelled with pride at the sight of him. He was such a big, handsome boy, already nearly as tall as she, his T-shirt and shorts displaying tanned arms and legs sturdy with muscle. Only his still-round tummy reassured her that she had at least a few years left before she would be compelled to deal with a young man rather than a child. She tugged fondly at the baseball cap perched at a rakish angle on his head.

"All set?" she asked him, then, at his nod, said, "Well, let's be off." After she had locked the door behind them, they got into the Jeep parked out front on the circular gravel drive. She had bought the vehicle for its practicality both on country roads and in Midwestern winters. "Seat belt, Alex," she reminded him as she started the engine.

He obligingly buckled up, as Sarah herself did. Then she rolled down the vehicle's windows to let out the hot, stifling air. Although it wasn't yet noon, the day was already a scorcher.

The tires crunched on the gravel as she steered the Jeep down the wooded drive and out on to the country road lined with hedge-apple trees, which would take them to the blacktop highway into town. Except in winter, when the roads were snowy and encrusted with ice, the trip seldom lasted more than ten minutes or so, and Sarah never minded the drive. She loved the beautiful old white Victorian farmhouse and the acreage she had bought when

Alex was seven, when the previous owner, the Widow Lovell, had died. The property was close enough to town that Sarah didn't feel too isolated and yet far enough away that she had some privacy in a place where everybody always knew their neighbors' business.

The macadam was soft and steamy in the summer heat; along with the pungent aroma of the hedge-apple trees and the dry scent of grass and earth baking beneath the fierce yellow sun, the acrid smell of sticky, melting tar filled her nostrils as she drove. On the far horizon, a cloud of dirt rose, a dust devil shimmering and dancing in the sluggish, sultry wind that streamed into the vehicle, making Sarah long for the rainy grey days of spring that had, perversely, caused her to wish summer would come.

From the radio, the strains of some dreadful music reverberated as Alex tuned the channel to a station he liked. In an effort to keep up with her son, Sarah had learned the names of some of today's popular groups—Pearl Jam, Smashing Pumpkins and Red Hot Chili Peppers among them—but she couldn't have told one band from another. It made her feel strangely as though she were what the media sometimes claimed her entire generation was: adrift. But of course, she had missed out on any real social life in both high school and college—and had little time or inclination for one now. So she didn't even know what music people her own age listened to. Her own tastes were an eclectic mixture of jazz, blues and rock and roll.

By now, they had reached the outskirts of town and were gravitating toward its heart—a big, old-fashioned square with a grassy, tree-studded park and a large gazebo at its center. Dominating the west side of the square was the huge granite courthouse, which also served as the town hall. Shops, restaurants and business offices lined the other three sides. Meter parking was permitted along all four streets; instead of being parallel to the curb, as was common in cities, all the spaces were angled. Sarah thought, not for the first time, that the town looked as though it had long ago fallen under a spell that had caused several decades somehow to pass it by. She pulled to a stop in front of the Penny Arcade, already crowded with local youths.

"I'll be back to pick you up around twelve-fifteen, Alex," she announced as he unfastened and then shrugged free of his seat belt before opening the vehicle's door and hopping out. "Don't go off anyplace else. Do you need any money?"

"Nope." He shook his head, blowing a bubble with his gum, then popping it. "I've still got part of my allowance. Besides, I'm good at winning free games, Mom." Impatient to be on his way, he slammed the door and loped off before she could speak further.

Sarah watched to be certain he got safely inside, then drove on down the street to Shear Style, parking the Jeep out front and putting change into the meter. She glanced at her watch, sighing with relief. Two minutes to spare. Thank heavens she was on time, after all. She wouldn't have to worry about the hairdresser's temper and leaving the salon looking as though she had got her head caught in a combine!

"'Bout time you showed up," Lucille greeted her gruffly when she entered the salon. "I was beginning to think you were going to stand me up, maybe."

"Now, Lucille, you know I always call you if I can't keep my appointment," she replied soothingly as the woman promptly ushered her through the busy salon to one of the two shampoo stations in back. Sarah sat down in the black-vinyl, tilt-back chair, sweeping up her dark brown hair, which fell past her shoulders, so Lucille could fasten the huge, plastic cape around her neck.

"Well, there's always a first time for everything," the hairdresser muttered as she turned on the water and, after testing its temperature, began to spray Sarah's head, soaking her hair thoroughly. Fiftyish, stout, with a half-smoked cigarette invariably dangling from one corner of her mouth, Lucille was what many in town referred to as a "tough ole broad." If she were brusque to the point of rudeness with all her customers, however, it was mostly to conceal the fact that in her breast beat the proverbial heart of gold. Her hands, while strong, were gentle and sure, and she knew how to cut and style hair like nobody's business—which was why she knew everybody in town's business. "And I know you're having a hard time with that kid of yours. It ain't easy, being a parent these days—especially a single one. But I guess you already know that."

"Yes, I do. In fact, I was just thinking about it earlier this morning." Sarah sighed heavily. She guessed that not only Lucille, but also everybody else in town knew Alex was having difficulties, particularly since he was being compelled to attend summer school, to catch up on lessons he somehow hadn't managed to absorb during the regular school year. If he couldn't bring his marks up to snuff by summer's end, he was going to have to repeat the sixth grade, another depressing thought.

"A boy needs a father—and you need a man, Sarah," Lucille observed bluntly as she generously lathered her client's hair, massaging her scalp vigorously. "That being the case, when are you finally going to break down and marry Bubba Holbrooke?" J. D. "Bubba" Holbrooke, Jr. was the governor's son and managed Field-Yield, Inc. for his father. "I swear, the man's been after you for nigh on a coon's age now. Everybody in town knows it. Besides which, he's done practically everything but stand on his head to get your attention—and I imagine if he'd have thought that'd work, he'd have tried it, too."

"I know, but I—I just can't seem to make up my mind to settle down with him, Lucille. I can't explain it any better than that." How could she, Sarah asked herself, when she didn't even understand it herself?

Bubba Holbrooke was the biggest catch in town—rich, good-looking, a former high-school star quarterback, with a secure position at Field-Yield, Inc., and heir to the bulk of all his daddy's worldly property, to boot. Any other woman would have been thrilled and flattered by his interest, would have leaped at the chance to get his wedding ring on her finger. But not Sarah Kincaid. She knew the townspeople thought Bubba was crazy for wanting her, an unwed mother from coal-mining "trash," and that she was the world's biggest fool for keeping him dangling when she could have snatched him up on a moment's notice.

"Raise up now," the hairdresser instructed as, puffing on her ever-present cigarette, she finished rinsing Sarah's hair. Grabbing a towel, Lucille wrapped it loosely around Sarah's head, then escorted her to one of the styling stations. "Do you want my advice? No, you probably don't.

But I'm going to give it to you, anyway, since it's the only thing I give anybody for free in this shop. And for some unknown reason, I've got me a soft spot where you're concerned,'' the hairdresser declared as, after tossing aside the towel she'd used to prevent Sarah's hair from dripping, she picked up her comb, a pair of scissors and a couple of hair clips. ''I reckon it's because I never had me any children. But I always wanted a daughter of my own, and if I'd have ever been blessed with one, I'd have liked her to be a lot like you. So you listen to me now, Sarah, you hear? 'Cause what I'm fixing to tell you is for your own damned good, whether you like it or not.

''You've been alone for far too long. Now, that's maybe not so bad for a tough ole broad like me, who's had more 'n one man in her life, or even two—because believe it or not, I was something to look at in my salad days.'' Lucille smiled wryly, coughed hackingly for a long moment, then dragged on her cigarette again before she went on combing, clipping and snipping. ''But it sure as hell ain't no good at all for a pretty young woman like you, Sarah— being all alone, that is. So my advice to you is that you need to stop all this shilly-shallying and say yes the next time big, bad Bubba pops the question.'' The hairdresser paused. Then, after glancing surreptitiously around the busy salon, she lowered her voice and continued. ''Because I'll tell you what, Sarah. You're not getting any younger—or going to get any better offer, either. Your boy's father is long gone from this town—and he most likely ain't ever going to come back here.''

At Lucille's words, Sarah's heart seemed to lodge in her throat. In the trifold mirror mounted at the rear of the style-station counter, her wide, startled eyes met Lucille's shrewd, knowing ones.

She knows, Sarah thought, panic-stricken. *She knows who Alex's father was!*

"I—I don't know what you're talking about, Lucille," she lied, her heart pounding.

"'Course you don't," the hairdresser agreed affably, matter-of-factly, as she reached for her blow-dryer and snapped it on, effectively covering the sound of their conversation so they wouldn't be overheard. "I didn't expect you to say anything else, seeing as how—unlike some I could mention—you've kept your own counsel all these years. And don't worry. I may have an outspoken mouth on me, but it ain't a big, blabbing one—leastways, not when it comes to business that nobody's business but yours. But know this, Sarah—I ain't the only person in this town who's got sharp eyes in her head and a good memory. How long do you think you can go on concealing facts when that boy of yours looks more like his daddy every passing day? And why bother to hide 'em anymore, anyway? Alex, at least, ought to know he's got a daddy that made something of himself."

"Alex is mine! I bore him, and I reared him—*alone,* Lucille! With never a telephone call or a letter, not even so much as a single word from— I don't want Alex to know about his father!" Sarah cried softly.

"Is that it, Sarah?" the hairdresser prodded relentlessly, although not unkindly. "Is that *really* it? Or is the truth that you don't want the boy's father to know he has a son—a son you never told him about, a son you've kept hidden from him all these long years?"

Her face ashen, Sarah closed her eyes tightly, as though by doing so, she could somehow shut out the drone of Lucille's voice, as well. Because hadn't the hairdresser spoken the truth? If she were honest with herself, Sarah knew she must admit that.

"He's got no right to know," she insisted stubbornly. "No right at all."

"Sarah...Sary." Lucille's voice, low and raspy from years of smoking, abruptly softened as she spoke the old childhood nickname. "He was only twenty-two—and terrified."

"Don't you think I know that—now? Still, he could've taken me with him." Sarah's own voice was tremulous with emotion at the memory of that summer's day more than a decade ago, when the course of her entire life had been so suddenly and irrevocably changed. "I would have gone with him. I would have gone with him anywhere...to the ends of the earth! I loved him! He could've taken me with him," she repeated dully.

"You've got to learn that much of a man is his pride, Sarah. He had nothing to offer you back then. But he does now."

"I don't want anything from him—now. Or ever."

"Well, maybe you don't. But what about Alex? Think about him, your son. That's all I'm trying to tell you." Lucille turned off the blow-dryer and stuck it back into its holder. Then, taking her brush and comb, she parted Sarah's thick hair on the side, brushing it until it shone like dark, burnished oak, a mass of silkiness about the younger woman's shoulders. Handing Sarah the round mirror lying on the counter, the hairdresser spun her around in the styling chair so she could see the back of her head. "That's seventeen dollars you owe me for the shampoo and cut. The advice, like I said, is free."

Opening her purse and withdrawing her billfold, Sarah quickly, with a trembling hand, wrote out her usual check in the amount of twenty dollars, which included Lucille's tip. Normally, after booking her next appointment, Sarah would have lingered for a few minutes, chatting with the other clients in the salon and buying a Coke from the machine in the corner. Today, however, she couldn't wait to make her escape.

"I've got to run, Lucille. Alex is waiting for me at the Penny Arcade."

To Sarah's relief, the hairdresser only nodded and waved. Moments later, Sarah was standing outside the salon, fumbling in her handbag for her tortoiseshell sunglasses. Locating them at last, she put them on as she walked toward her Jeep. It was as she was inserting her key into the lock of the driver's door that her eye was abruptly attracted by a long flash of bright color over in front of the buildings on the south side of the square. At first, she figured it was just Jimmie Dean Thurley's brand-new pickup truck, which was fire-engine red—or, rather, what had used to be fire-engine red, since these days, fire trucks were generally a bright, hideous chartreuse. But then she realized the vehicle was some expensive foreign roadster, and she stopped and stared, just as everybody else in the square was doing—because nobody in town, not even Bubba Holbrooke, owned a car like that.

As Sarah watched, it pulled into a parking space in front of the local newspaper, the *Tri-State Tribune*. Then its engine died; its low door swung open wide, and like some predator awakening and stretching, a tall, dark man, lean and hard with muscle, uncoiled himself to get slowly out of the vehicle.

Like a lover's caress, the torrid breeze ruffled his long, shaggy black hair; sunlight glinted off his mirrored aviator sunglasses. Sarah could almost taste the salty male sweat that soaked his white shirt, its long sleeves rolled up to display his bronzed forearms, in its pocket a pack of cigarettes, which the man reached for as he stood there staring at the newspaper building. His movements deft and sure, he shook a cigarette from the pack and lit it with a lighter taken from the pocket of his black chinos. He inhaled deeply, then blew a cloud of smoke into the air.

I'm dreaming, Sarah thought dumbly, frozen where she stood, feeling as though she had just been struck a sickening blow to her head or midsection. She was suffering a nightmare or imagining things because of her conversation with Lucille inside the salon. That was it. That *must* be it! Sarah told herself desperately.

Only, it wasn't.

In that instant, it seemed impossible to her that it was just an ordinary summer day, with the bright yellow noon sun beating down on the small town, the humid breeze rustling the leaves of the tall old trees that dotted the grassy green square and lined the wide streets. With children playing tag and tetherball in the park, the townspeople strolling along the sidewalks, talking, laughing, calling greetings to one another. With traffic crawling along at its usual Saturday-afternoon snail's pace, impatient teenagers in a hurry to go nowhere blasting their car horns.

She should have had some word, some warning of what this day was to bring, Sarah reflected dimly in some dark corner of her mind. But there had been nothing. There *was* nothing. Nothing except the sweet, wild, unexpected rush of heat that rose from the core of her very being to spread throughout her entire body, so it was suddenly as though more than a decade had not passed and she lay naked again upon the wooded summer grass just beyond the old, abandoned quarry that had once served as the local swimming hole—and felt the man's warm, welcome weight pressing her down.

Feeling strangely as though she somehow floated somewhere beyond her own body, watching both herself and him from a distance, Sarah thought, *It all began with that old lunch box.* For she didn't know—she had never known—that for Renzo Cassavettes, it had begun long before that, in a rundown tenement of the big city where he was born, and with the butterfly that had shown him what, despite his harsh, inauspicious origins, he might someday become. . . .

Two

The Butterfly

I do not know whether I was then a man
dreaming I was a butterfly,
or whether I am now a butterfly,
dreaming I am a man.

On Leveling All Things
—Chuang-tzu

A Tenement, The Midwest, Twenty-Seven Years Ago

That Renzo Cassavettes should have witnessed the butterfly's emergence into the world was no more than the smallest incidence of chance—yet it changed his life forever, as he somehow knew even then it would, knew with a child's pure and simple faith. Had he been indoctrinated into the Catholic religion of his parents and grandparents, as some few decades earlier, he would have been, Renzo would have viewed the butterfly as a sign from God or, at the very least, a saint. But in the eternal rebellion of youth convinced it suffered as no other generation before it had ever done, his parents had cast off their Madonnas, their crucifixes and their rosaries as deliberately and determinedly as they had cast off all the rest of the teachings of their short lifetimes, along with the ever-too-tight, ever-too-far-reaching familial tentacles that had embraced, if not nurtured them. His parents had still been young enough then to be blissfully ignorant of the fact that no matter how long and violent the struggle to be free of that initial childhood bonding and imprinting was, escape was never truly and wholly possible.

There are some things that are with you always. They lie buried deep, perhaps. Still, they are there, the worm Ouroboros of the soul.

Renzo had only a vague, child's memory of his father, who had seemed to him to tower ten feet above him, a veritable giant of a man, long and lean and hard muscled, with mercurial moods, quick fists and a black, surly temper worsened by drink and drugs. In Renzo's mind, his father hovered always on that threshold between youth and adulthood, a bully boy playing at being a man—although no less awesome and frightening for that. It was only in later years that Renzo came to understand that beneath the facade of his father's preening and bragging, his laughter and wit, his shouting and bravado, there had lurked a child no less small, insecure and terrified of the world than Renzo himself had been. So it was that in the absence of any true religion, his father had been both god and devil to him, an Italian Adonis and Calabos rolled into one, blessed with dark handsomeness and bright charisma, cursed with dark hungers and burning ambition.

In Renzo's manhood, the suppressed memories of his father would sometimes come rushing to engulf him, so he would close his eyes tightly against the sudden onslaught and will them to retreat. Still, they would come—unbidden, irrepressible, triggered by the smell of cheap cologne or cheap wine; by the sound of a flimsy screen door banging shut in the summertime or of a car's souped-up engine revving and roaring in the street; by the sight of defiant young punks in T-shirts and blue jeans, a pack of cigarettes rolled up in one shirt-sleeve, bare arms sporting black tattoos, or of swaggering young Turks in cheap, jazzy suits, aflash with the gleam of gold chains and watches and rings. For all those things had been his father, a small-time, big-city hoodlum who had lurked on the fringes of organized crime, running drugs and numbers and women for what outsiders had always called the Mafia, but that was known to those within its own circle simply as *Cosa Nostra*—Our Thing.

Renzo's father had hungered to become a *capo,* a don more legendary than even the fictional Don Corleone, the Godfather of all Godfathers. How he had yearned to join the ranks of those who, in their long, sleek black cars, pulled up in the summertime before the sidewalk café in the elegant old plaza of the big city, causing a momentary but taut pause in the talk and laughter of the crowds who sipped colas and iced teas and other tall, cool drinks in the open air. Instead, Renzo's father had been gunned down by some equally hotheaded, ignominious rival in the meaner streets of the big city, ending his young, hard, fast life as no more than another Saturday-night fatality, a DOA statistic.

In his childhood nightmares, Renzo heard the shots, saw the bright, macabre crimson flowers that seemed to blossom in slow motion on his father's chest, heard the screams and the sirens wailing in response, saw the brilliant, incongruous blinking of the neon lights of the bars and strip joints that lined the cracked, littered sidewalk where his father lay, the cold, methodical flash of the lights atop the ambulance and police cars. In reality, Renzo had heard and seen none of what had happened that night two years ago. He had learned of it only afterward when, scared and hiding in the nooks and crannies of the tenement where he had lived, he had eavesdropped on the whispered conversations of its inhabitants.

He had been five years old then, tall for his age, but thin, his head too large for his slender neck, his eyes too big for his pinched face. But in later years, whenever Renzo gazed into a mirror, it was his father's handsome visage he was to see staring back at him: long, thick, shaggy black hair framing hawkish, strong features—high cheekbones and a hard, arrogant jaw; intense, molasses-brown eyes spiked with heavy black lashes and deeply set beneath thick, unruly raven's-wing brows; a finely chiseled nose set above a sulky, frankly sensuous mouth. A mouth that would mock him at those times, that would curve sardonically at the bitter irony that his own countenance should so constantly remind him of that other he had tried so hard to forget.

His father's face he bore. But not his father's name.

That had come from his Greek-Italian mother—Cassavettes, her maiden name, one of the few things she had given him, other than life itself. For like the butterfly that so unwittingly showed Renzo that day what he might become and, in so doing, set him on the road he was to take in life, Sofie Cassavettes was a creature who sucked the nectar from the heart, lush and beautiful in the way of belladonna. At one time, she had called herself his father's wife, although she had held no official claim to that title. But when Renzo's father had lain cold, bagged and tagged in the sterile morgue of one of the big city's hospitals, she had, once her initial, wild bout of weeping and wailing had ended, proved quick enough to resume the name that was her own and to bestow it, as well, upon her son, so the taint of his father's life and death would not cause trouble for them—although trouble of what nature, she hadn't said.

Afterward, his mother had resumed the frenzied, sluttish lifestyle his father's presence had only partially curtailed, taking a job as a cocktail waitress and dumping Renzo off at all hours at old Mrs. Fabrizio's across the hall. Into their own apartment had come a steady procession of men—each one "Uncle This" or "Uncle That" to the boy, although he had known instinctively that they were no real relatives of his. He had heard them at night, in his mother's room, in his mother's bed, grunting and groaning until she had cried out—a long, feral shriek that had embarrassed and shamed him, so he had clutched his pillow over his head in a futile attempt to shut out the terrible sounds.

A few weeks ago, awakening from the nightmare of his father's death and feeling afraid, Renzo had crept from the lumpy sofa bed in the shabby living room and sought his mother. Standing at the closed door of her bedroom, he had called out to her, but she hadn't heard. At last, impelled by his fear and by the sudden, overwhelming temptation of the forbidden, his heart pounding in his small chest, he had slowly reached out and turned the knob so the door had eased open a crack. His mother had sprawled naked on her bed, her dark thighs spread wide, her head thrown back, her mouth open and gasping. Uncle Vinnie had poised above her, a man-beast thrusting himself inside her, a part of her. At the sight, a small, choked sob had inadvertently escaped from Renzo's throat.

Afterward, the apartment had rung so with violent shouts and slaps and Renzo's bawling that the neighbors had banged angrily on the walls, threatening to call the police.

That was why he was being sent away.

"Some relatives of your father want you to come live with them, Renzo," his mother had announced, smiling brightly, brittlely. "They've got a house, a real house in a small, country town, and no children, so you'll have a bedroom of your own, all to yourself. Won't that be grand, Renzo? You won't have to grow up in the big city, breathing smog, listening to the rats and roaches at night, and hustling and scavenging just to make ends meet. You'll go to a nice school, too, where you won't have to worry anymore about being beat up and robbed of your lunch money.... Oh, it's such a wonderful opportunity for you, Renzo! It'll be great! Why, you'll be so happy that you'll wish you'd always lived there. Just you wait and see. And of course, I'll come down to visit you now and then, so you won't forget me...."

But of course, she wouldn't come. Somehow Renzo had known that instinctively, just as he had known she was secretly glad and relieved to be rid of him. He was a burden, a hindrance to the life Sofie Cassavettes had embarked upon even before his birth, a tie she itched to sever now that she no longer needed it to bind his father to her.

So it was that today Renzo perched dejectedly upon the broken, sunken, concrete steps of the old tenement that, despite its dereliction, was the only home he had ever known. He wore a new suit, tie, and socks and shoes—bought just yesterday by his mother and paid for by Uncle Vinnie—and he felt constrained and awkward in the unfamiliar clothes. The tie choked him, and the stiff leather of the tightly laced shoes had already rubbed a blister on one heel. Beside him sat a small, battered old suitcase dragged from beneath his mother's bed and into which she had crammed all his meager belongings, except for Teddy, the stuffed brown bear he clutched like a lifeline. It was several years old, ragged, dirty and one eyed, but a gift from his parents at his birth, tangible evidence that once, however briefly, they had welcomed and celebrated and loved him. So Renzo clung to it, his most prized possession.

"You mustn't be afraid, Teddy," he said quietly now to the bear, his lower lip quivering. "We're only going on a trip, you know, to a new home. And I'll take care of you there...really, I will! Mama says the Martinellis are nice people. Mr. Martinelli owns a newspaper. They live in the

country, with lots of trees and ponds, so we'll be able to go
swimming and fishing and—and... It'll be just like a real
adventure. It'll be great, Teddy... you'll see...." He echoed his mother's words to him before he buried his face in
the bear's scruffy fur, damp from his tears.

After a time, not wanting anyone to see he had been
crying, Renzo lifted his head and, with his sleeve, resolutely wiped his red-rimmed eyes and sniffling nose. He
must be brave, he told himself, like Batman and Captain
Marvel and all the other superheroes that peopled the
comic books he read, the imaginary world in which he
lived in his mind, so different from the world in which he
existed.

It was then the cocoon caught his eye. Once, long ago,
someone had planted a honeysuckle vine in front of the
tenement, and somehow it had not only survived, but also
thrived. So it was wildly overgrown, its tendrils running up
the grimy bricks of the building and snaking along cracks
in the badly settled sidewalk. Hanging from a small sec-
tion of the vine was the cocoon. It was an ugly thing, a
hard shell that harbored an equally ugly, wormlike caterpillar, Renzo knew, having broken open a cocoon once.
But even as he gazed at it, something wondrous happened. The shell suddenly split along one side, and what
gradually emerged was not the fat, grubby caterpillar he
expected, but a big, gorgeous butterfly.

Renzo watched, enthralled, as, free at last, the insect
slowly spread its fragile, gossamer wings and flicked them
tentatively, once, twice. For a fleeting eternity, it poised on
the cocoon. Then, without warning, it took flight, soaring up and away until it finally disappeared in the pale blue

sky. And in that moment, with a startling clarity far advanced for his tender years, Renzo thought, *Someday, I, too, will soar—because if an ugly caterpillar can change into a beautiful butterfly, who is to say what I may become, if only I try?*

Behind him, the front door of the tenement opened, then shut with a bang. He heard the brisk clatter of his mother's spiky high heels upon the concrete porch even before he saw them. Her shoes were bright red, like blood, and matched the color of the lipstick she had smeared upon her mouth and the polish with which she had painted her long, false nails. As he glanced up at her, silently pleading with her to change her mind and let him stay, Sofie Cassavettes smacked the gum she was chewing vigorously and fiddled nervously with one of her long, dangling earrings, refusing to meet his eyes.

"Come on, Renzo. It's time to go," she said tersely.

Even as she spoke, Uncle Vinnie pulled up alongside the curb. He was dressed in a new suit, too, and the top was down on his long, flashy, two-toned convertible, which Renzo knew the neighbors—behind Uncle Vinnie's back—referred to as "the pimpmobile." Smiling brightly, waving and calling out to Uncle Vinnie, her generous hips swaying in the tight leather miniskirt she wore, Sofie sashayed toward the waiting car. Feeling as though the weight of the entire world rested squarely on his small, miserable, hunched shoulders, Renzo followed more slowly, clutching his teddy bear tightly and lugging his suitcase behind him.

Without protest—because, like Renzo's father, Uncle Vinnie had a short, explosive fuse and quick, hard fists—

Renzo climbed into the backseat of the garish convertible. As they drove away from the tenement, he didn't look back. Instead, he forced himself to remember the butterfly, and he told himself fiercely that he wasn't leaving the only home he had never known. He was breaking free of his cocoon.

And at that, if only in his mind, he soared.

Three

Papa Nick

> I have seen the wicked in great power,
> and spreading himself like a green bay tree.
>
> *The Holy Bible*
> —The Book of Psalms, 37:35

It was a long drive for a little boy, despite the fact that Uncle Vinnie kept the pedal to the metal all the way, so it seemed as though the convertible flew instead of sped down the highways and dusty country roads to the small, rural town that was its destination. But finally, the car entered the town limits and slowed, nearly crawling along the old, shady, tree-lined, brick-paved streets, as though now, strangely, Uncle Vinnie were in no hurry to end their trip. Abruptly, he reached out and snapped off the blaring radio. Then he frowned at Sofie by his side, her short skirt hiked up to reveal her thighs, her blouse gaping where he had unbuttoned it earlier to fondle her dusky breasts as he drove.

"For God's sake, tidy yourself up, woman—and wipe some of that damned lipstick off your mouth, too, while you're at it!" he demanded irritably. "You look like a hooker!"

"That's not what you said when you saw me earlier, Vinnie," Sofie whined petulantly, her full, generous lips curving into a little-girl pout. "You thought I looked real good then."

"Yeah, well...earlier, we weren't just about to pull up in Papa Nick's driveway." Uncle Vinnie stuck a finger under his sweat-dampened collar and ran it back and forth, as though his tie were knotted too tightly around his throat. "And he won't like you looking thataway in front of Mama Rosa. Business is one thing, family's another. And whatever you do, don't mention the brat's father. Just let me do all the talking. *Capisce?*"

"Sure, Vinnie. Whatever you say." Sofie shrugged carelessly, smacking her gum loudly as she reached into her purse for a Kleenex and began obediently to scrub at her mouth. "But I don't see what you're so all-fired edgy about. Papa Nick's just a big, mean old spider who should long ago have crawled back into whatever hole he crawled out of in the first place. He's probably senile and bedridden by now."

"You're worse than a fool, Sofie, if that's what you think—and that's all the more reason for you to keep your goddamned trap shut this afternoon!" Uncle Vinnie growled, shooting her a sharp, quelling stare.

Sofie shrugged again. But she didn't speak, knowing from his glance that Vinnie was nervous enough to reach over and belt her a good one. She didn't want another black eye, like the one he had given her last week.

In the backseat, Renzo, too, was silent—and afraid. He had thought his mother had said the Martinellis were nice people. But if Uncle Vinnie were frightened, that couldn't possibly be true, because Uncle Vinnie wasn't scared of anybody. In fact, it was just the opposite. Most people with any sense at all were usually scared to death of Uncle Vinnie. He kept a big pistol in a leather shoulder holster underneath his suit jacket, and he had been known to pull it out and use it. One night at the tenement, when some young thug named Carlo had insulted Sofie and put his hands on her, Uncle Vinnie had without warning yanked out his gun and pressed the barrel right between Carlo's bugged-out brown eyes. Terrified, Renzo had huddled in a corner of the apartment, certain he was about to witness cold-blooded murder right then and there. But in the end, Carlo had apologized profusely, and the two men had finally laughed and clapped each other on the shoulders, then gone back to their drinking.

Now Renzo gazed with awe and fear at the huge, spike-topped, wrought-iron gates that swung slowly open to admit the convertible after Uncle Vinnie had pulled it to a halt before the barrier and spoken into a telephone box at the side of the drive. The car wound through stands of trees, up the long, serpentine drive until at last Renzo spied the tall, square, red-brick house that perched on the rise before them. He had never seen a house so large and imposing, and he quivered like a petrified rabbit at the thought that he was to live there, watched over by some horrendous, mean old spider of a man. Renzo felt as though he were going to be sick all over himself, or disgrace himself even worse by peeing his pants.

That would never do, especially since it was obvious from the number of cars parked out front of the house that some kind of party was in progress. After Uncle Vinnie eased the convertible to a stop, the three of them got out. Glancing at Renzo, Sofie pulled her Kleenex from her purse again and, with her tongue, dampened the tissue, using it to wipe a smudge of dirt from his cheek. Then she straightened Renzo's tie and smoothed his windblown hair, while Uncle Vinnie rang the doorbell. Presently, they were ushered by a man in a dark suit through the beautiful old house to a wide veranda out back.

There, long picnic tables covered the sweeping green lawn, on a strip of which a game of boccie was taking place, and the smell of barbecued beef and chicken wafted from the grill around which a knot of men were gathered, smoking and drinking. Gaily dressed women moved to and fro, laden with platters and bowls, carefully skirting the children who ran and played among the tables and benches. On a portable stage, a small band played, and young couples danced in the grass. The air rang with music, talk, shouts and laughter.

"Papa Nick," Uncle Vinnie said, greeting the hulking old man who sat and rocked silently in the shadows deep at the back of the veranda, a glowing-tipped cigar in his mouth, his powerful, age-spotted hands folded like claws over the ornate silver knob of a gleaming malacca cane. Vinnie bent and kissed the heavy gold ring on one of those gnarled hands. "How you doing? As prosperous as ever, I see. We brought the boy."

Then Sofie, too, greeted the old man, kissing his dark, weathered, fleshy jowl before she turned and dragged Renzo forward to present him. "This here's Renzo, Papa Nick," she said, tugging covertly at her skirt, as though only just now aware it was too short, too tight, and rode up vulgarly around her thighs.

Although he might have been anywhere from fifty to ninety, Papa Nick looked exceedingly ancient to a young boy, and Renzo saw at once why his mother had called the old man a spider. There *was* something spidery about Papa Nick, something dark and ominous that seemed to spin out from him like a web, something that was just as gossamer and chilling against the skin and made the fine hairs on Renzo's nape stand on end. In later years, he was to know it was power, lethal and immense, that he had felt emanating almost tangibly from the old man. But this day, he knew only that it was a thing to be feared. Papa Nick's hawkish, piercing eyes were as black as the coal that had provided much of his legitimate fortune, and they appeared to bore right through Renzo, making him shiver.

"Whadda they been feeding you, boy? You're not'ing but skin and bones. Looka more pitiful than a scarecrow in that new suit!" The old man's voice was deceptively soft, deep and deliberate, overlaid with a thick Italian accent, although it held a note of menace all the same. His black eyes burned like embers in his head. Suddenly, somehow, Renzo knew Papa Nick's anger wasn't directed at him, but at his mother and Uncle Vinnie, both of whom were sweating profusely, despite the wide-bladed fans hanging from the veranda's broad ceiling. With a sharp, contemptuous wave of one hand, the old man dismissed the two adults, then motioned Renzo closer. "You like candy, boy?" Reaching into his trouser pocket, Papa Nick drew forth a piece of gold-foil-wrapped chocolate and handed it to him. "Go on. It'sa yours. Take it," he urged when, still, the boy hesitated. "I wonna bite you."

At that, Renzo tentatively stretched out one hand and snatched the piece of chocolate from the old man's grasp, as though fearing he had lied, that he would, in fact, bite him. To Renzo's surprise, Papa Nick laughed then, long and loud, his big belly shaking.

"Go on now," he ordered gruffly after a moment, thrusting his cane at Renzo. "Go and play with the other children. Take that miserable jacket and tie and those socks and shoes off, and havva some fun for a change. You donna looka like you've had too mucha that in your young life. Joe! Madonna! Come getta the boy! Take good care of him! Fatten him uppa with some fine Italian cooking!"

A couple hovering nearby approached then, their plain, careworn faces kind, welcoming and anxious to please. They were, Renzo soon learned, much to his surprise and relief, the Martinellis, with whom he was to live from now on. Madonna, unable to bear any children of her own, knelt. Her eyes shone with unshed tears as she smiled and held out her arms to Renzo; and with that simple, accepting gesture, he somehow knew instinctively that here, at long last, was someone prepared to love him wholeheartedly, without reservation. Clutching the chocolate, he stumbled toward her, felt her arms enfold him against her plump, comforting breast; and in that moment, he understood, then and for always, that home wasn't a place—but a place in someone's heart.

Four

The Lunch Box

True love's the gift which God has given
To man alone beneath the heaven;
It is not fantasy's hot fire
Whose wishes, soon as granted, fly;
It liveth not in fierce desire,
With dead desire it doth not die;
It is the secret sympathy,
The silver link, the silken tie,
Which heart to heart and mind to mind
In body and in soul can bind.

> *The Lay of the Last Minstrel*
> —Sir Walter Scott

The first time Renzo ever saw Sarah Kincaid, he was twelve years old, and his life before he had come to the small, rural town, to live with Joseph and Madonna Martinelli, had faded so much that sometimes, when he thought of it, he imagined it had been only a bad dream.

There was nothing in the Martinellis' tidy white bungalow on Elm Street to remind him of the tenement in the big city where he had been born. Nor, since the day they had brought him to Papa Nick's imposing, red-brick house on the hill and left him there, had Renzo ever seen his mother or Uncle Vinnie again. After a while, they, too, had faded in his mind, to become no more than a memory so vague that he could no longer even recall his mother's face. When he thought of her at all, he remembered only her red mouth and nails, her high heels the color of blood.

Fueled by Madonna Martinelli's good Italian cooking, Renzo had in the past five years filled out, growing tall and strong for his age, so his body even now held the promise of a man's long bones and hard muscle. And if he resembled his dead father more and more with every passing day, he himself did not yet see that whenever he gazed into a mirror. He saw only the thick, unruly black hair, the dark brown eyes and the bronzed skin that marked him as being of Italian heritage and that had therefore caused to be erected around him a set of invisible boundaries in a town where everyone had his place—and was expected to keep to it.

It didn't matter that from his newspaper, the *Tri-State Tribune,* Joseph Martinelli earned as good a living as Fritzchen Mueller did from his restaurant, Fritzchen's Kitchen. In the town's social pecking order, Fritz's standing was higher than Joe's—because the color of Fritz's skin was white.

Few ever came right out and said that, of course. It was simply understood that that was the way things in town had always been—and were always going to be. It was, after all, the natural order of men.

Renzo had learned this lesson the hard way—by having it pounded into him at school by boys like Bubba Holbrooke and Skeets Grenville, Forrest Pierce and Drew Langford, Tommy Lee Archer and Clayton Willoughby, who were sons of the town's politicians, lawyers, doctors, bankers and merchants. So it was that when Renzo first spied Sarah, his initial thought was that he should get back on his bicycle and ride in the opposite direction as fast as his legs would pedal him. But for some unknown reason, his feet rooted him where he stood at the edge of the woods, fishing pole and bait bucket in hand, bicycle leaning against a tree.

She looked not like a little girl, but a fairy child, he thought as he watched her dance and whirl through the tall-grass meadow that was like a wide, shimmering green sea around her, rippling in the breeze and afoam with a profusion of wildflowers in every color imaginable. Her long, silky hair was as brown as the dark trunks of the towering old trees, whose leaves, rustling gently in the wind, matched the green of her eyes. Her cheeks were rosy, in beautiful contrast to her pale skin dusted with gold from the kiss of the Indian-summer sun that stretched even now toward autumn. She wore a shabby, faded pink sundress, and her small, delicate feet were, like his own larger ones, bare. As she skipped and leaped and pirouetted, she paused now and then to pick another flower to add to those she already clutched in one grubby hand; and she sang in a high, clear, sweet voice, some song about tallying bananas, because daylight was coming and she wanted to go home.

Renzo was mesmerized. He hardly dared to breathe, for fear she would notice him and, frightened by his presence, bound away like one of the startled fawns he had sometimes seen leaping through the woods in the springtime. So it was that he witnessed her grow suddenly still and silent as her eye was caught by a big yellow butterfly rising and dipping through the quiet air, skimming the undulating tops of the tall green grass. Slowly, enthralled, she dropped her wildflowers, which scattered in the breeze to strew the earth around her. Then she cupped her tiny, graceful hands and held them upward, as though in offering. In her piquant face upturned to the sun, her eyes closed tightly, her lips moved, and Renzo thought she might have been praying—or whispering a spell of enchantment. For just then, something miraculous, something magical happened.

The butterfly came to light in her outstretched palms.

At its feathery touch, she opened her eyes wide, her mouth forming an *O* of wonder and delight as she gazed raptly at the insect. For a fleeting eternity, it poised there in her grasp, its gossamer wings fluttering, she holding it carefully, making no attempt to capture and imprison it. Then, suddenly, she flung her hands up, spreading them wide and laughing aloud with pure joy as the butterfly took flight, soaring away into the boundless blue sky.

"Sarah," a woman's voice called from the distance, breaking the hushed drone of the summer air. "Sary, where are you? It's time for you to come home now. Sarah..."

Turning her head at the sound of her name, the child cried, "Here, Mama. I'm here." Then she began to run lightly through the meadow, toward the voice summoning her home.

In moments, she was gone.

Afterward, it seemed to Renzo that he was drawn inexorably to the place where she had stood in the grass and held the butterfly. Although he knew full well it wasn't possible, in his mind, he imagined that it was the very same insect he had watched emerge from its cocoon so many years ago at the tenement in the big city. The butterfly was, somehow, like a bond between him and the little girl, a secret they alone in all the world shared. Bending, he slowly picked up one of the wildflowers she had cast away. Its fragrance was as sweet as the summer grass; its petals were as fragile and ethereal as the child herself had appeared, and would be just as easily bruised.

Carefully, Renzo tucked the wildflower into his shirt pocket. Why he wanted it, he could not have said. He knew only that he did.

The second time Renzo ever saw Sarah Kincaid, she was standing on the school grounds, sobbing as though her heart would break. To her breast, she clutched a lunch box, and the way she held it reminded Renzo of how he had clung to his teddy bear that long-ago day at the tenement in the big city. In fact, it was only in the past few years that he had felt safe enough, secure enough, beloved enough to tuck Teddy away at last into the small cedar chest at the foot of his bed in his room at the Martinelli bungalow.

A butterfly. A ragged old teddy bear. A secondhand lunch box. Such small things they were. Yet because of them, unbeknown either to Renzo or to Sarah that day, his life and hers were to touch, to tangle like a honeysuckle vine—and forever entwine.

The lunch box was bright, colorful and still so shiny that it looked almost brand-new. Its metal was marred by only a few scratches and dents, the latter of which Sarah's father had told her he could pound out, so Wonder Woman's face wouldn't be squashed in anymore and the wing of her invisible spaceship would be straight again instead of crooked. Inside was a thin, hinged metal open triangle for holding a sandwich in place and a short, squat thermos capped by a cheerful, red plastic cup.

"You like it, Sary? I got it from Miz Holbrooke," Iris Kincaid said to her daughter, who sat at the kitchen table, gazing at the lunch box as though it were more precious than gold. "She was getting some things together for the rummage sale at the church, you know, and she told me I could look through 'em 'fore I left that day, see if there was anything I wanted." Mrs. Holbrooke was ZoeAnn, J. D. Holbrooke's wife. Iris worked as their maid. "I wasn't sure whether she meant I could take my pick for free or not, so I left fifty cents there on the table. That was the price she had marked on the lunch box. That were all right...that were the right thing to do, weren't it, Dell?" She glanced at her husband a trifle anxiously, now worried she might have done the wrong thing, after all.

"I 'spect it was." He spoke gruffly from behind the crackling pages of his newspaper. Smoke rose and curled from the pipe he puffed on, so it looked as though the pages had caught fire. "'Spect if it weren't, Miz Holbrooke'll let you know. She ain't never been the kinda woman to hold her tongue when she's got something to say."

"That she ain't," Iris agreed, shaking her head, relieved that if she had, in fact, done wrong, Mrs. Holbrooke would undoubtedly tell her so.

Sarah's parents went on talking, but she hardly heard them, she was so excited. A *real* lunch box! She was going to be able to take her lunch to school in a real lunch box now instead of just a plain old brown paper sack! Wasn't that something? Wasn't that fine? None of her friends had lunch boxes. The men who worked at Papa Nick Genovese's coal mines, like her daddy, and who lived with their families in what was commonly referred to in town as "Miners' Row," didn't have a whole lot of extra money for things as frivolous as a child's lunch box when a paper bag from the grocery store was always handy and the three or four dollars saved would buy a dress or a pair of shoes at the thrift shop, besides, and even more at a garage sale. Sarah knew that. Still, whenever she accompanied her mother to the local discount store, she couldn't help but run down the aisle to where the school supplies were displayed, to look at all the gleaming lunch boxes neatly lined up in a row on the top shelf, just beyond her reach.

The following morning when, bright and early, she climbed aboard the yellow school bus that picked her up and then later brought her home every day from Washington Elementary, Sarah carried the lunch box proudly and prominently in her right hand. Inside was a peanut-butter-and-jelly sandwich her mother's worn hands had carefully fixed earlier that morning, one of Mama's homemade dill pickles wrapped up in a scrap of aluminum foil and a shiny green apple from the Granny Smith tree in the backyard. Cold lemonade from the refrigerator filled the thermos.

"Sarah Beth Kincaid! You got yourself a lunch box!" Krystal Watkins cried, noticing right off the bat, much to Sarah's pride and delight.

The other elementary-school girls aboard the vehicle crowded around to look and make a fuss over the lunch box until the bus driver, a grizzled old black man by the name of Gus, ordered them back to the worn, rough seats, whose brown vinyl had split open in places over the years and been haphazardly patched with grey duct tape. On the beige metal back of one of the seats, amid all the other graffiti, somebody had scratched the words *The bus driver is an SOB*. Sarah didn't know what that meant. She had never seen Gus shed so much as a single tear.

"Y'all know the rules," he drawled sternly. "I cain't drive if'n y'all ain't in them seats."

Boos and groans greeted Gus's announcement. Sarah felt sure that when they reached the sharp turnaround at Junior Barlow's house, the kids would all rush to the far side of the bus in an effort to cause its wheels to slide off into the ditch alongside the road. Once, last year, they had actually succeeded, making the school principal, Mr. Dimsdale—whom everybody called "Mr. Dimwit" behind his back—so hopping mad that he had kept them all sitting in the vehicle for more than thirty minutes, lecturing them, when they had finally arrived an hour late at the grassy commons bounded on three sides by Washington Elementary, Jefferson Junior High School and Lincoln High School. But that had been small punishment compared to the time a bunch of the junior-high boys had, with a cherry bomb, blown up one of the bus's backseats. All the boys involved in that unfortunate incident had been suspended after Cheryl Kay Pendergast—because she had just *had* to go to the bathroom and couldn't wait any longer—had blabbed their identities to Mr. Dimsdale so he would let everyone off the vehicle.

In the end, Sarah was to think later, it was the lunch box that was ultimately to blame not only for everything that happened that day, both to the bus and to her, but also, finally, for the course her entire life was to take. For if not for the envious, excited stir caused by that lunch box, and Gus's subsequent admonishment, the kids might have stayed obediently in their seats instead of throwing their weight to the far side of the vehicle at the Barlow turnaround. The bus didn't actually topple off the road again. But one big wheel *did* slip off the soft, sandy edge into the ditch—to be punctured by an old, nail-ridden board that had fallen from Junior's tree house in one of the hedge-apple trees lining the verge.

The resulting leak was so slow that Gus didn't notice anything was wrong until the tire finally went flat. Having to change it was what caused him to be late in arriving to collect everyone from school that afternoon. And because Gus wasn't on time, Sarah was standing on the tree-shaded commons, a hapless target for Eveline Holbrooke's anger when she spotted her former lunch box clutched in Sarah's hand. Evie, the youngest child and only daughter of J. D. Holbrooke, was the most popular girl at Washington Elementary, so anybody who wanted to *be* anybody always went along with her, no matter what. Now, cutting sideways glances at her friends to let them know mischief was afoot and that they had all better fall in line for the fun, Evie, a martial glint in her eye and her friends backing her up, marched right over to Sarah to confront her.

"Hey, you. Yeah, you, Coal Lump Kincaid," Evie sneered, in a voice overloud and spiteful, causing a burst of appreciative snickers for the cleverness of her slur—even though the girls had all heard it before—to erupt from behind her. "Gimme that lunch box! It's mine! My daddy brought me that lunch box home from one of his trips out of town—and I want it back! You got no right to it. Your mama stole it out of our house."

"She did not!" Sarah cried vehemently, stung despite her abrupt apprehension into defending her mother loyally. Sarah always tried to steer clear of Evie Holbrooke, who despised her and teased and tormented her at every opportunity.

"She did so! Your mama's a thief! She's always stealing things from us—and now that I have proof of it, I'm gonna have my mama fire her. And once she does that, *your* mama won't ever be able to get another job anywhere else, because nobody wants a light-fingered maid working for them!"

Sarah's heart thudded with fear at the thought that perhaps Evie really could and would carry out this threat. The Kincaids needed the money Mama made by toiling for the Holbrookes, cleaning their house and washing and ironing their laundry for them. What would her family do, Sarah wondered, panicked, if Mama lost her job? Maybe Sheriff Laidlaw would even arrest her, based on Evie's mean-spirited accusations!

"My mama doesn't steal! Oh, she doesn't!" Sarah insisted desperately, tears now blinding her haunted green eyes, her lower lip quivering pitiably.

"Yes, she does. Now, you gimme back my lunch box!" Evie demanded, tossing her pale blond hair in haughty contempt, her ice-blue eyes narrowed and hard as, clenching her fists, she deliberately stepped in closer to Sarah. "Or I'll make you sorry you didn't, Coal Lump!"

Before Sarah, trembling violently, her tears spilling over now to stream down her cheeks, could reply, a low voice that came from somewhere behind her drawled softly, scornfully, to Evie, "Why don't you take a hike somewhere? Like off a steep cliff, maybe."

Shocked gasps of outrage and incredulity from Evie and the rest greeted this remark, while Sarah, startled and grateful, spun quickly around to find out who had come to her defense. As it had when the butterfly had alighted in her hands this summer in her favorite meadow, her breath caught in her throat. For although she didn't know him, she thought the boy standing there was the most beautiful creature she had ever seen. He looked as though he had stepped straight out of a movie, with his tousled black hair, his thick-lashed brown eyes and his bronzed skin. Dressed in a T-shirt, stonewashed jeans and a black leather jacket, despite the warmth of the autumn day, he was a rebel without a cause, with something dangerous and exciting in both his eyes and stance. He was older than she, but not yet old enough for high school. In junior high, then, Sarah decided, since she hadn't ever seen him around before.

"And why don't *you* pick on somebody your own size—like me, Renzo Cassavettes, you no-good, chicken-livered wop?" Bubba Holbrooke, surrounded by his cronies, jeered as he spied what was happening and leaped to Evie's aid. She was a prissy, pouty little pest—but she was his sister all the same, and Bubba was damned if he was going to stand idly by while some piece of Italian trash from the wrong side of the tracks got mouthy with her!

"I'll be more 'n happy to deal with you, Bubba Holbrooke," Renzo rejoined coolly, his eyes wary but hard. "If you want to go at it one-on-one for a change—like a *real* man—instead of ganging up on me with all those bully boys behind you to bolster your courage, you manure-sweeping, garbage-hauling piece of slime!"

Bubba's face flushed bright scarlet with fury at that—for everybody in town knew he had to earn his weekly allowance by doing minor janitorial chores at his daddy's fertilizer plant. It was humiliating! Him—J. D. Holbrooke's eldest son and heir—being forced to push a broom, empty wastebaskets and take orders from shiftless old black Thaddeus, the head janitor at Field-Yield, Inc. But despite Bubba's whining protests, his daddy had remained adamant: Bubba was going to learn the family business the same way he himself had—inside and out, from the ground up—not play around until the day he decided he was finally ready to sit his butt down in the big, cushy president's chair at the company's long, Honduras-mahogany conference table.

At Renzo's gibe, Bubba groaned inwardly, silently cursing Evie. Everybody from all three schools, it seemed, had flocked to the commons, and they were all staring at him expectantly, so he knew there was no way in hell to save face while simultaneously backing down from the challenge. A flicker of fear licked through him. He wasn't nearly so brave without Skeets Grenville, Clayton Willoughby and the rest of the "Rat Pack," as he and his cohorts called themselves, standing alongside, egging him on and covering his backside.

"Well, come on, dago! If you think you're big enough!" Bubba finally shouted, abruptly screwing up his courage and throwing his three-ring binder and schoolbooks down so hard on the ground that the colorful vinyl notebook broke open, scattering index pages, ruled paper and a *Playboy* centerfold Bubba had filched from his daddy's hidden collection at home and jammed into one of the binder's inside pockets. "I'm not afraid of you! I'll take you on alone, Renzo Cassavettes! I'll kick your sorry wop ass!"

"Bubba, no! You know the rules—if you get caught fighting on school property, it's an automatic suspension." Bubba's younger brother, Winston "Sonny" Holbrooke III, moved with quiet determination to stand between him and Renzo. "Daddy'll be fit to be tied if you get thrown out of school again—especially so early in the year."

"Not this time," Bubba growled, roughly shoving his brother aside, so Sonny tripped over the three-ring binder and schoolbooks strewn on the ground and fell, squashing Miss July. "Daddy don't hold with dagos not knowing their place—and not sticking to it!"

With that, the fight ensued. Both boys were tall, but Bubba was heavier, so that at first, to Sarah and the rest, it seemed he would easily prevail as he and Renzo went at it hotly, pummeling each other unmercifully, a flurry of flying fists and elbows, kicking knees and feet. But Renzo hadn't spent the early years of his life in a tenement in the big city for naught. And now that he wasn't grossly outnumbered, had room to maneuver and defend himself, he put to good use all the hard lessons he had learned from his father, Uncle Vinnie and all the other brutal men who had paraded through his mother's apartment. Amid the shouts and squeals of those watching, and heedless of his own bloody nose, Renzo blacked Bubba's eye, then rammed his head into Bubba's stomach, knocking him flat. Before Bubba could recover, Renzo was on him, straddling him, hands at Bubba's throat.

What would have happened next, nobody ever knew. For just then, his voice ringing out sharply with angry authority, Mr. Dimsdale appeared, accompanied by a handful of teachers. They forcibly dragged the two scuffling boys apart, then determinedly marched them away to Mr. Dimsdale's office.

By then, Gus had finally arrived. Deeply relieved, Sarah ran to the waiting yellow bus and climbed aboard, still clutching the lunch box tightly to her breast. Although the Holbrookes' big, white-columned house wasn't on the vehicle's route, so Evie rode a different bus to and from school, Sarah nevertheless sat down right behind Gus, coveting his protection. She spoke not a word all the way home, not even when some of the other girls who lived in Miners' Row tried to offer comfort. The boy who had come to her defense would surely be suspended from school for it, Sarah thought, and she felt terrible on his behalf for all the trouble she had inadvertently caused him. She had never even got a chance to thank him!

That evening, she told Mama and Daddy what had happened that day at school. The following morning, Iris Kincaid determinedly carried the lunch box back to the Holbrookes' house.

"I declare, Iris, I just don't know what to say," Zoe-Ann Holbrooke uttered coolly, without the slightest hint of fluster or embarrassment. "I thought Evie was tired of that old lunch box. Otherwise, I'd never have dreamed of putting it in that pile for the church rummage sale. Besides which, she mostly eats the school lunch, anyway. It's so important for a growing child to have a hot lunch at midday, I've always believed. But J.D. gave her that lunch box, and Evie's always set such a powerful store by her daddy. You do understand, don't you, Iris?"

"Yes, ma'am, I do," Sarah's mother replied tonelessly, her head held high.

"And of course, Iris, it goes without saying that I know you don't steal."

"No, ma'am, I surely don't."

"Well, now that that's settled, we'll just forget all about this unfortunate incident, shall we? After all, there's no sense in us becoming embroiled in a silly little children's quarrel, is there?" ZoeAnn insisted, her lips curving in a small, superior smile.

"No, ma'am, there isn't," Iris agreed, her face expressionless.

Afterward, when the lunch box was returned to her by her mother, Evie smugly shoved it away in the very back of her closet. Everybody who was anybody knew it wasn't cool to carry your lunch to school in a lunch box, that a plain brown paper sack was all the rage.

ZoeAnn Holbrooke kept the fifty cents.

Five

The Meadow

I was a child and she was a child,
In this kingdom by the sea;
But we loved with a love which was more than love—

Annabel Lee
—Edgar Allan Poe

Although, after that day of the lunch box and the fight at school, Sarah watched the commons alertly, ceaselessly, for the boy called Renzo Cassavettes, she never saw him. For his part in the incident, Bubba Holbrooke, she knew, had been suspended from school, and she worried that Renzo, lacking a father as prominent and influential as J. D. Holbrooke, had been expelled. The thought gnawed at her, for the boy would never have been in trouble had he not come to her defense.

But then at last there came an afternoon when she sought her favorite meadow in the woods beyond Miners' Row, the meadow that was like a vast green sea and where her daddy had built her a tree house in an old, spreading sycamore tree. That tree house was her own private little kingdom. There, at the meadow's grassy edge, she drew up short at the sight of Renzo Cassavettes reclining on the ground, as though she had wished him there, his back against the sycamore that was home to her tree house. His dark head was bent over a book, and he didn't notice her at first.

"Hey," Sarah called shyly from where she stood.

"Hey, yourself," Renzo replied, smiling as he glanced up and saw her. He closed the book he had been reading. "No more trouble over lunch boxes, I hope."

"No." Sarah shook her head forlornly at the memory. "I had to give it back. I guess Evie's mama didn't know when she put it in her pile for the church rummage sale that Evie still wanted it. So my mama returned it, even though she'd bought it and so it was really mine. My mama works for the Holbrookes, you see. She's their maid, and it would've gone hard on us if they'd got mad and fired her over the lunch box. But I want to thank you for helping me that day at school. I never did get a chance to say that before. I hope you didn't get into too much trouble on my account."

"Not much. A three-day suspension was all." Renzo's careless tone made it clear this was no big deal to him. "And it was worth it to have had a shot at big, bad Bubba. He and his buddies are always ragging me."

"I know what that's like. Evie and her friends are always picking on me, too. I try to stay out of their way, mostly. It was just bad luck that the bus was late getting to school that day and Evie realized it was her old lunch box

I had." At Renzo's friendliness, Sarah edged closer. She possessed an inherent appreciation for all beauty, and she couldn't seem to stop staring at the boy. More than ever, she thought he looked as though he had stepped from one of the movies that played at the town's Imperial Theater, which still boasted its original and now old-fashioned wedge-shaped marquee and its CinemaScope screen. Seeing a Saturday matinee there was a rare and thrilling treat for Sarah. Mostly, she had to wait until films were edited and shown on TV before she saw them.

She cast about for something else to say, her eyes lighting on the book in his hands. "That's an awfully thick book you're reading. What's it called?"

"*East of Eden*. It was written by a man named John Steinbeck and made into a movie that starred James Dean. He's one of my idols."

"Who? The writer or the actor?"

"Well, both, actually," Renzo declared. "I'd like to be a writer someday, when I grow up. I'd like to write a book that somebody might make into a film starring an actor like James Dean. There's no telling what roles he might have gone on to immortalize on screen if he hadn't been killed in a car crash."

Sarah didn't know who John Steinbeck and James Dean were. She knew only that she could have listened to the boy for hours. Even his voice was beautiful, she thought. Soft and low, with a melodic rhythm. She hadn't known, at first, that he was Italian. She'd had to ask Mama and Daddy what the words *wop* and *dago,* which Bubba had so derisively called Renzo that day on the commons, meant.

"You're Renzo Cassavettes, I know. I heard Bubba say your name right before the fight broke out. Your daddy owns the newspaper, the *Tri-State Tribune*, doesn't he?" she asked. "Is that why you want to be a writer when you grow up?"

"Joe's not really my dad. My real dad's dead. He died a long time ago, in the big city. That's why I live with the Martinellis. Joe's my real dad's second cousin or something like that. But, yeah, that's why I want to be a writer. I like the newspaper. I'm going to be a famous reporter one day—like Carl Bernstein and Bob Woodward. Maybe I'll even win a Pulitzer Prize. And then, after that, I'll write my book."

"It must be nice to know already what you want to be when you grow up, what you want to do with your life." Sarah finally grew bold enough to sit down beside the boy on the grass. "I like to make up stories myself, like fairy tales…and to paint pictures. I'm Sarah, by the way, Sarah Beth Kincaid, in case you didn't know."

"I do know. I asked somebody at school. And Joe told me your dad works at Papa Nick Genovese's coal mines. But I kind of figured that, anyway, seeing as how Evie called you 'Coal Lump' and all. That wasn't very nice of her."

"No, but I try not to mind. Evie's just a spiteful cat, that's all. My daddy's a good man—the best!—even if he *does* dig coal for a living. He says there's nothing wrong with good, honest, hard labor with your own two hands. Still, I know people in town call us 'mining trash' and look down on us, the same as they do Italians. It's not right. Daddy said those names Bubba called you were ugly and prejudiced, and Mama said she'd scrub my mouth out good with Lava soap if she ever heard me using words like that. Even so, it's awful hard sometimes, always being on the outside, looking in.'' Sarah's voice was wistful, her small face pensive.

"Yeah, I know what you mean. That was one of the reasons why I took up for you that day at school. I was just sick and tired of the Holbrookes acting as though they own the town.''

"Well, they do—a lot of it, anyway.''

"Maybe so. But that still doesn't give them the right to go around browbeating everybody else, treating us as though we're dirt beneath their feet!'' A muscle flexed in Renzo's jaw, which was taut with anger.

"No, that's true," Sarah agreed, sighing. "Daddy always says you don't rise higher in life by putting others down. But I guess there're a lot of people out there who don't understand that, who have to make themselves feel better by looking down their noses at everybody else. That's why I come here most of the time by myself. This meadow's my favorite place in the whole wide world. It doesn't belong to me, of course, or even to my family. A couple called the Lovells own that beautiful old white Victorian farmhouse not far from here and all the land around it, including the meadow. But they're retired and elderly, and they don't have any children of their own, so they said they didn't mind if I played here. They even let me have a tree house here. That's it up there.'' Sarah pointed toward the branches of the sycamore that formed a canopy above them, where the tree house nestled snugly, securely, and so secretly amid the leaves now turned the color of flames with autumn that Renzo hadn't noticed it before. "Daddy built it for me last summer, after the Lovells said he could. It's my own special hideout. But you're welcome to use it whenever you come here, if you want."

"Thanks, but I wouldn't want to intrude."

"No, it's all right, really. I'd—I'd like for us to be friends." Sarah stammered this last in a rush, her heart thudding anxiously, for fear the boy would laugh at the very idea, since, although he had been kind and had taken her part in the quarrel with Evie, too, he was still some years older than she, nearly a teenager, while she was still just a little girl. "But I guess you probably think that's a silly notion . . . I mean, with your being in junior high and all, while I'm only in the second grade."

"No, I don't think it's silly at all. I'm something of a loner myself, so I don't have a lot of friends," Renzo confessed, touched by her childish offer and thinking of the common bonds they shared—had shared since the day he had watched the butterfly come to light in her hands. "Will you show me your tree house? How do you get up there?"

"There're ladder rungs—nailed into the other side of the tree. Come on!" Smiling with happiness and excitement, her eyes shining, Sarah rose, brushing herself off, then holding out her hand. "There's a trapdoor, too, so once I'm up there, I either have to open it or lower the rope for somebody else to join me. Oh, you'll see it all for yourself in a minute. It's grand! It's just like sitting on top of the world! You can see forever, it seems, and the fields look like a great green-and-gold sea surrounding you. Sometimes I pretend my tree house is a kingdom on an island

and I'm a fairy-tale princess. You can be my knight in shining armor, if you like. After all, you *did* rescue me that day at school!"

"In that case, I suppose you'd rather I stand down here and wait while you go up. Then I guess you'll want me to shout out something like, 'Rapunzel, Rapunzel, let down your golden hair!' so you can lower the rope to admit me into your lofty kingdom, fairy princess," Renzo teased, grinning as he spoke and got to his feet, remembering the fairy tale Madonna had read to him, along with so many others when he was Sarah's age.

"No, really, you don't have to do that if you'd rather not." Sarah's beaming face grew crestfallen at the thought that he was making fun of her and her tree house and her offer of friendship, after all. "Besides, my hair isn't golden. It's only plain old mud brown."

To her surprise, Renzo reached out and gently tugged a thick strand of her long hair, which Mama had never yet permitted her to cut, so it hung down her back, past her waist.

"Now, where did you ever get a dumb idea like that?" he inquired, not missing the disappointment on her piquant face and determined now to join in her game, even if he *did* think it was girlish nonsense. "That hissing little cat Evie, I'll bet. Don't you believe it—not for one minute! Your hair's not the color of mud. It's the color of a dark old oak tree, and your eyes are the green of its leaves. You're a woodland fairy princess, as anyone with eyes in his head could see. So you go on up, and I'll wait here. And when you hear me call out to you from below, you'll know it's me, and that will be our secret password from now on."

"All right," Sarah said slowly, half afraid, nevertheless, that despite his words, Renzo intended to trick her, that he meant to run off, laughing at and taunting her for her foolishness, once she had reached the tree house. Still, she climbed up into the sycamore's spreading green branches, anyway, opening the trapdoor to the tree house and hoisting herself inside. "I'm here," she called timidly, now wishing she had never mentioned her tree house, had never told the boy of her secret daydreams. She waited nervously for the sound of his mocking laughter.

What she heard instead was her heart singing in pure joy when, from below, in response, Renzo shouted in his best knight-in-shining-armor voice, "Sarah, sweet Sarah, let down your oak-brown hair!"

Those years of Sarah and Renzo's childhood and early adulthood were turbulent ones for the world. For they were the years of the ending of the war in Vietnam; of Watergate and the resignations first of Vice President Spiro Agnew and then of President Richard Nixon; of the Grey Panthers and the Black Panthers—"Say it loud: I'm black, and I'm proud!"—and the trial of Angela Davis; and of the American Indian revolt at Wounded Knee. They were the years of ongoing wars between the Israelis and the Arab nations in the Middle East; of skyjackings and terrorist attacks and of metal detectors being installed at airports; of the oil embargo and the energy crises; and of the kidnapping of publishing heiress Patty Hearst by the Symbionese Liberation Army. The years of the continuing troubles in Northern Ireland; of Karen Silkwood and the Kerr-McGee plutonium plant; of the election of a grocer's daughter, Margaret Thatcher, to the British Parliament and then the prime ministry; and of the Israeli raid on Entebbe. The years of the birth of the world's first test-tube baby, Louise Brown; of Reverend Jim Jones and the mass suicide of his followers at Jonestown, Guyana; of the deposing of the Shah of Iran and the rise to power of the Ayatollah Khomeini; and of the Soviets in Afghanistan. The years of the deaths of many world leaders, among them America's Lyndon Baines Johnson, France's Georges Pompidou, Argentina's Juan Perón, Spain's Francisco Franco, Israel's David Ben Gurion and Golda Meir, and Nationalist China's Chiang Kai-shek and the People's Republic of China's Chou En-lai and Mao Tse-tung.

But of all this, only Watergate touched Sarah and Renzo in the quiet, small town where they lived—and only because the resulting fame of Carl Bernstein and Bob Woodward fueled Renzo's own dreams of becoming a journalist. Every day after school, he went to work for Joe Martinelli at the *Tri-State Tribune*. At first, Renzo did the very same chores for which he had ridiculed Bubba Holbrooke that day upon the commons: sweeping up, emptying wastebaskets and the like. But gradually, as the years passed, Joe began to let him try his eager hand at various journalistic endeavors: typesetting, copy-editing and writing headlines and obituaries to start. By the time Renzo had turned nineteen and been graduated from Lincoln High School for a year, he was cranking out real articles—hard news and feature stories both—under the daily deadline pressures of a small town. At twenty-two, he had nearly completed his degree in journalism at the local state university.

He never thought to question how Joe and Madonna, whose financial means were adequate but ran to only a few luxuries, had afforded to pay for his tuition and books. Just as he had never thought to ask how they had got the money for the secondhand but fiercely coveted Harley-Davidson motorcycle, either, which he had received when he'd turned sixteen and considered himself too old to ride the bus or his bicycle to school anymore. Later, he was to wish he had known the source of all the funds.

Hindsight is always a bitter teacher.

There would be other motorcycles—and cars, too—in his life. Still, that Harley was always Renzo's first love. It would someday be a classic, for it was a 1977 FXS Low Rider, a black-and-silver beauty with mag wheels, drag-style handlebars and special paint and engine treatment. He labored long and hard into the wee hours of his nights to repair and restore the motorcycle, until it was in mint condition and ran like a young man's dream. When he was spied wearing his black leather jacket and astride the Harley, the townspeople observed darkly that he looked and acted more like a hoodlum every passing day and was bound, sooner or later, like his rumored small-time, big-city mobster father, to come to a bad end. But Renzo took a perverse pride and pleasure in the gossip, telling himself that one day, when he was rich and famous, he would set the town on its ears.

Despite the five-year difference in their ages, which caused a temporary gap between them the older they grew, he and Sarah continued to meet in the meadow, their

friendship growing ever stronger and deeper, although, by
mutual, unspoken consent, they never mentioned it to
anyone. As young as she had been at the start of it, Sarah
had sensed instinctively, as Renzo had known for certain,
that the town would not only not understand their relationship, but would also, in fact, condemn it. At fourteen, she had begun to grasp the reasons why—that people
not only looked for dirt, but also delighted in finding it.
America might have laughed at Archie Bunker on television for years; still, that didn't mean there weren't many
who agreed with his viewpoints. There were. And rural
America was always the last part of the country to accept
change and progress.

In the small, prejudicial town that was home to her and
Renzo, he would, because of his Italian heritage, his pur-
ported mobster father and his bad-boy reputation, be suspected at the very least of contributing to the delinquency
of a minor where Sarah was concerned, and at the worst
of statutory rape, although he never even so much as
kissed her until her seventeenth birthday.

That was the day Sarah knew truly and fully, with all her
heart, that she had loved Renzo Cassavettes since that autumn afternoon at her tree house in the meadow, when he
had shouted out to her, "Sarah, sweet Sarah, let down
your oak-brown hair!"

She had never tired of looking at him, of listening to him
when he had spoken to her of his dreams as the two of
them had perched at the edge of one of the many abandoned quarries in the area, fishing poles in hand, captured catfish flopping in a nearby pail, bait bucket and
picnic basket sitting alongside. Or when he had read aloud

to her from the books he had over the years carried from the town library to the tree house, books not just by Steinbeck, but also by Faulkner, Fitzgerald, Hemingway and others. He had read to her the plays of Edward Albee, Eugene O'Neill and Tennessee Williams, too, and the poetry of Byron, Keats, Shelley, Tennyson and Wordsworth. In this way, Renzo had taught Sarah to love words as much as he himself did and had shown her how her imaginary worlds could be made real.

Sometimes she had taken her watercolors and brushes and paper to the meadow and had painted, while Renzo had read aloud or had sat quietly beside her, writing in the spiral-bound notebooks he had filled with thoughts and words of his own. Or he had wailed the blues on the saxophone he had taken up playing when he was thirteen. Or, in the cast-iron skillet Sarah had brought from home to the tree house, he had fried up the catfish they had caught that day. At other times, the two of them had done their homework together, then leafed through Renzo's collection of comic books, arguing over the virtues of Batman, Captain Marvel, and Wonder Woman, and which comics were more likely to escalate in value over the years. There had been long, lazy afternoons when they had waded in the shallow, pebble-bottomed creeks of the woods and meadows, too, or had gone swimming in the deep quarry that was the local swimming hole, or had run through the tall grass and wildflowers, laughing and chasing butterflies.

Sarah had flown upon the back of the Harley, too, along dusty country roads and across sweeping fields, her arms locked tightly around Renzo's hard waist, the rough grain of his black leather jacket and its silver studs pressing against her cheek, her dark brown hair streaming in the wind. And she had laughed aloud in sheer delight when they had sailed over hummocks and dashed through the woods, grass and creeks, shady water spraying coldly against her skin, the motorcycle engine revving and roaring.

Those were some of the happiest days of her life, she was to think years later, so much a part of her and of her youth that she was never able afterward to thrust them wholly from her mind, not even when Renzo was long gone and she was alone—and heavy with his child.

For it was inevitable that as the two of them grew up, they should turn to each other. Somehow they had always been destined for each other, Sarah thought that afternoon of her seventeenth birthday, as she sat with Renzo in the tree house and blew out all the candles on the chocolate cake he had bought for her at the Farmers' Market grocery store.

"So, tell me, what did you wish for, Sary?" he asked as he watched her slowly remove the still-smoking candles one by one from the gaily decorated cake, then, with the plastic knife he had also brought with him that day, slice two generous wedges from it.

Earlier that morning, Sarah had gone into town, to the Shear Style beauty salon, and had had more than a foot of her hair cut off, much to his anger and disgust. It was still long, falling below her shoulders. But this new hairstyle made her look different somehow—older, a young woman instead of just a child. She'd had her nails done, too; they were polished a pale shade of pink that matched the powdery blush on her cheeks and the gloss on her mouth. At her newly pierced ears, tiny gold studs glinted. They were her mama and daddy's birthday present to her. She was never going to be stunningly gorgeous, as Eveline Holbrooke was, but there was a quiet, arresting beauty about Sarah all the same. Renzo thought he had not misnamed her that long-ago day when he had called her "sweet Sarah."

As a result of all this, he was finding himself uncomfortably aware of the now cramped quarters of the tree house built for a child, of the softness and creaminess of Sarah's skin and of the delicate, honeysuckle fragrance of the perfume that drifted from it, of the way one strap of the blue gingham sundress she wore that warm spring afternoon had slipped from her shoulder and of her full, ripe, round breasts, which strained against the checked cotton.

"If I tell you what I wished for, then my wish won't come true," she replied lightly as she handed him a paper napkin holding one of the two big slices of cake. Grateful for the new side part in her hair, which caused the cascade of rich, shining brown to conceal her suddenly flushed face, her eyes unable in that moment to meet his own, Sarah pretended to concentrate on licking the chocolate icing from her fingers, oblivious of the effect this simple action had upon Renzo.

He wanted to grab her hands and suck the icing off himself. He wanted to jerk down her straps and suck her breasts, too. The sundress was cut in such a way that Sarah didn't need a bra for it, and Renzo was pretty sure she wasn't wearing one, that her breasts were bare beneath the gingham. He could just barely make out her nipples. His groin tightened at the realization; he felt himself growing hard. To cover that fact, he growled, "Well, *I* wish you hadn't cut your damned hair, Sary!"

"I'm sorry you don't like it, Renzo." She blinked back sudden, hot tears at his criticism, for she had wanted so desperately for him to like her hair, to understand what cutting it at long last had meant to her symbolically. "But Mama said I could style it as I pleased now, that I was a woman full grown today. And if you *must* know what I wished for, it was *that!* That you'd see I wasn't a child any longer, Renzo Cassavettes! That you'd—that you'd... Oh, just forget it!"

"No, I won't forget it!" Without warning, startling them both, he stretched out his strong, dark, slender hands, grabbing hold of her pale, bare arms and giving her a small, rough shake. His eyes blazed as he stared at her intently, searchingly, feeling as though he stood on the brink of some important discovery, that it mustn't slip away. "Tell me, damn it! That I'd *what*, Sarah?"

She glanced up at him then, and he saw the tears glistening in her wide, expressive green eyes, the trembling of her sweet, vulnerable, rosebud lips.

"That you'd kiss me," she whispered huskily, embarrassed and ashamed.

Renzo inhaled sharply at her words. "You think I don't want to kiss you? Is that it?"

"Well . . . do you?" The question was soft, breathless.

In response, his brown eyes darkened, glittered with a sudden, predatory hunger that both frightened and excited Sarah as she gazed at him raptly, her heart thudding so wildly that she was half afraid it would burst in her breast. In that instant, she was abruptly, acutely conscious of how cramped the tree house was, how near Renzo was to her, how potently male he seemed. At twenty-two, his dark, unshaven face was shadowed with a man's rough stubble. A small gold cross gleamed at the lobe of his left ear. The masculine scent of him—a mixture of soap, sweat and cigarette smoke—wafted from his white T-shirt to fill her nostrils, mingling intoxicatingly with the redolence of the greening sycamore tree, the sweet aroma of the chocolate cake, forgotten for the moment. At his glance, a violent shudder such as Sarah had never felt before ran through her, leaving her trembling with fear and expectation as, slowly, Renzo's hands slid up her arms to cup her cheeks, his fingers tangling in the strands of hair at her temples, tilting her face up to his.

"Sarah...sweet Sarah," he muttered hoarsely before his mouth took hers fiercely.

It was her very first kiss—but not his. She knew that instinctively, somehow. And the bittersweet pain of that knowledge pierced her momentarily before his urgent lips drove it from her mind and heart, scattering her thoughts as though they were no more than leaves torn from their boughs by the wild spring wind that whipped through the woods and bent the tall grass and wildflowers of the meadow. As Renzo's mouth moved on hers, his tongue insistently parting her lips to slide deep between them, to tease and twine with her own tongue, a mass of sensations erupted inside Sarah, new and tantalizing and terrifying.

She hadn't known it would be like this, as though she were being swept up and borne aloft by some dark, primeval force against which she felt utterly powerless. Of their own volition, her hands burrowed convulsively through Renzo's long black hair, tightening into fists as she clung to him, as though if she did not, she would be seized by the fearsome, unknown thing and hurled away to some equally fearsome, unknown place, as the tornado had hurled away Dorothy in *The Wizard of Oz*. In some dark corner of her mind, Sarah wondered dimly if when she at last opened her eyes, it would be to find herself standing upon a winding, yellow-brick road, lost and far from home.

She strove for air as Renzo swallowed her breath, kneeling over her, bending her back, pressing her down upon the floor, so the rough, worn wood of the tree house bit into her tender skin. But she scarcely felt the pain, was conscious only of the powerful electric shocks coursing through her body, so every muscle and nerve and sinew felt as though it were a live wire, hot and sparking and burning. A great longing for something unfamiliar yet instinctively felt and recognized wakened and uncoiled within her like an insidious snake stirring in the pit of her belly. She heard the sound of low whimpers—and realized dimly that they came from her own throat.

If her soft moans were as much in apprehension and protest as pleasure, Renzo closed his ears to that fact. He had waited so long—*too* long—for her to grow up, to realize she belonged to him, that she had always been his. While he had waited for her, there had been other women in his past, furtive couplings in the backseats of cars at drive-in movies, in the narrow beds of college dormitories and elsewhere. But none of those women had been Sarah, the other half of his soul. She tasted sweeter than Renzo had ever imagined she would. He wanted to breathe her in like cigarette smoke, to hold her inside him until his lungs felt as though they would burst with her, until his head spun and his blood throbbed with her, as it did from a nicotine rush. He wanted to savor her, to devour her, to explore every curve and hollow and secret place of her, to feel her body entangling with his own. He wanted to be inside her... deep inside... claiming her, impaling her, leaving his mark upon her for all time.

Groaning, Renzo tugged roughly, impatiently, at the straps of her sundress, pulling them down so her bare breasts abruptly came free, full and burgeoning with new-found passion, their nipples dusky, taut and engorged. His hands shook slightly with a young man's eager desire and excitement as he cupped her breasts, squeezed them, rotated his palms lightly over their sensitive crests. Sarah's sudden, swift gasp of shock and surprise and delight rang in his ears, spurring him on. He nuzzled her neck, trailing quick, feverish kisses down her throat before his mouth closed possessively over one pert, upthrusting nipple, sucking hard and greedily.

An exhilarating tide of feeling flooded Sarah's body, ripples of pleasure that began at the very center of the stiff, swollen bud he nibbled with his teeth, licked with his tongue, until the ripples became waves that pounded like a surf through her entire being, making even her toes curl. A strange, sweet, hot rush of moisture dampened the insides of her thighs, the inset of her panties, so the musky scent of her filled the air, mingling with the fragrance of her perfume, the leaves of the sycamore. Deep at the secret heart of her, a savage, scorching ache seized her. Instinctively, she sought easement, and as though aware of her need, Renzo abruptly crushed her to him, so she could feel his arousal hard against her mound, rubbing, taunting, speaking silently of both the promise and the menace of the unknown, the forbidden. She could feel his hand at the hem of her sundress, roughly shoving the material upward, his fingers tightening upon her naked thigh, moving ever higher.

In moments, he would be tearing away her panties, thrusting himself deep inside her, taking her innocence and filling her with his sex, his seed.

Sarah's heart leaped to her throat at the thought. She wasn't ready for this. It was too much, too fast, too soon. What if Renzo didn't love her as she did him? He had a bad reputation. What if he didn't respect her afterward? Although this was the age of the sexual revolution, she had been strictly reared, taught that a "good girl" saved herself for marriage, and warned of the trouble a young woman could find herself in otherwise. At the memory of those dictates, she began to struggle against Renzo, growing frightened and wild when it seemed that despite her objections, he would persist, would force himself on her. Even worse was the fact that she recognized that a part of her actually wished he would, so the decision would be taken out of her hands. But Sarah had also been reared to take responsibility for her own actions.

"No, Renzo! Please don't!" she cried, trying desperately then to push him off her, turning her head away when he would have kissed her deeply again to silence her demurring. "I want you to stop. Please. I'm—I'm not ready for this."

"You're ready," Renzo growled huskily, his breath harsh and labored, hot against her skin. "I can feel it in my bones. Come on, Sarah. You know you want this as much as I do. Let me. I won't hurt you, if that's what you're afraid of."

"No." She shook her head. "That's not it . . . not exactly. I *am* afraid, but not that you'll hurt me—at least, not any more than you have to. It's supposed to hurt, the first time, I mean, isn't it? That's what I've heard, anyway. It's just that . . . what if something goes wrong? What if I get pregnant, Renzo?"

"You won't. I've got something with me, in my pocket, to take care of that. So you don't have to worry about it. When the time comes, I'll protect you, I swear!"

Condoms. He was talking about condoms, Sarah realized. More than once, she had overheard the boys at Lincoln High School cracking jokes about them. Trojan was a popular brand, and as a result, several of the boys called themselves the "Trojan warriors." While she appreciated the fact that Renzo hadn't intended to use her heedlessly, without any thought or care about whether she would suffer any consequences from the act, that he had come prepared to safeguard her reminded her that, unlike her, he had undoubtedly done this before. The knowledge stung, wounded her in a way she would not have thought possible until now.

"I guess you've protected a lot of other girls, too, haven't you?" she said, her soft voice filled with hurt and accusation.

At that, with a snarl, Renzo rolled off her, sitting up and removing the pack of Marlboros twisted up in one sleeve of his T-shirt. Angrily, he shook out a cigarette and lit it, dragging on it deeply, while Sarah, fighting to hold at bay the sudden tears that brimmed in her eyes, fumbled to draw up the straps of her sundress to cover her bare breasts, now embarrassed and ashamed that she had let Renzo see them and fondle them so freely. No wonder he had thought he could have her, that she would be an easy lay. She had done nothing to make him think otherwise. Instead, she had practically thrown herself at his feet, had encouraged him from the start by asking him to kiss her. Both her sundress and Renzo's jeans were smeared with chocolate icing, she noted dully, as though the two of them had been wallowing in mud. The piece of cake on her napkin was squashed and crumbled, a victim, no doubt, of his pressing her down upon the floor of the tree house.

"Damn it, Sarah!" Renzo spoke at last, breaking the tense, uneasy, awkward silence that had fallen between them. "I don't have to answer to you for anything I've done in my past."

"I didn't say you did."

"No—but you might as well have. So, yes, I've had other girls. Is that what you wanted to know? Well, now you *do* know. But, Christ, what in the hell else did you expect? That I'd hang around forever, waiting for you to grow up? I'm a man, not a monk, damn it! Still, that doesn't mean those other girls meant anything to me, because they didn't. You're the only one who's ever mattered to me, Sarah—and you're a fool if you don't know that!"

Despite everything, she was in her heart secretly glad-
dened and thrilled by his words. "Do I? Matter to you,
Renzo, I mean? Really and truly matter?"

"Oh, Sarah, of course you do." His hard face and tone
softened. His dark eyes turned tender as he glanced at her.
"I love you. I've always loved you. Don't you know that?
That's why I want you so badly. I want to know you're
mine, only mine, that you belong to me and nobody else."

"You don't have to worry about that, Renzo," she assured him quietly. "There's no one else. Mama and Daddy
are quite strict, you know. I couldn't even date, really, until now... just outings with groups of boys and girls, not
even double dates. And the only guy who's asked me out
anyway is Junior Barlow—and I'm not interested in him.
I'm not interested in anybody but you, Renzo. It's you I
love, only you. I've loved you ever since I was a child, I
think. You must know that. Somehow I feel as though
we've always been intended for each other."

"That's because it's true. It's always been you and me
against the world. Here." He slowly withdrew the gold,
high-school class ring from his finger, sliding it firmly onto
her own. "I want you to have this, for us to go steady. I
don't want you seeing other guys—and now that you've
cut your hair, you're so grown-up and beautiful that they'll
be lined up around the block to take you out."

Sarah smiled shyly, blushing with pleasure at his com-
pliment and possessiveness as she gazed down at his class
ring, her heart hammering at all it symbolized. It was the
first step in a coveted trio: *class ring, engagement ring,
wedding ring*. It was heavy and too big for her finger, and
Daddy would hit the roof if he even suspected she was go-

ing steady, especially with a college boy like Renzo Cassavettes. But she had a gold chain at home, in her jewelry
box. She'd put the ring on that and wear it around her
neck, so it lay concealed beneath her clothes, between her
breasts and against her heart, thrilling and treasured, tangible proof of Renzo's love for her.

"You didn't need to give me this to make sure of me,
Renzo." She touched his class ring reverently, as though
scarcely daring to believe it was real, that he had placed it
on her finger. "Evie Holbrooke's the one with boyfriends
from one end of town to the other. But I don't mind, so
long as I have you. Does this mean you'll take me to the
junior-senior prom?"

"Well . . . I'd *like* to, Sarah. Really, I would. And I'll be
there, so you won't be alone. But I probably won't have
much time to spend with you," Renzo confessed. "And
I'm sorry for that. But you see, the high school's hired
Hard Road to play that night."

Hard Road was the band Renzo and some of his college
chums had put together to earn extra money on Friday and
Saturday nights. Nearly a decade after he had taken it up,
he knew now how to make his saxophone wail like that of
a young jazz great. He was at once the creative Coleman
Hawkins, the fluid Benny Carter, the toneful Johnny
Hodges, the tragic Lester Young, the lyrical Ben Webster,
the hypnotic Paul Desmond—and none of them. For
Renzo had a style and grace all his own, one garnered from
listening for hours on end to jazz, blues and rock and roll
as performed by the masters. Because she had heard him
play it, Sarah knew he did a version of "Take Five" that
was to die for, so sensuous and sultry that it seemed to

crawl inside her very skin, making her think of hot summer nights and cool white sheets and lying all tangled and sweaty with a lover, with Renzo.

She swallowed her disappointment. It was better, really, that he couldn't officially escort her to the prom, she told herself. Daddy would most certainly have had a conniption fit and forbidden her to attend with Renzo, anyway.

"It's all right," she said softly. "I understand. I know you need the money, Renzo. But you'll at least dance with me once, won't you?"

"Count on it."

They ate the chocolate cake then, washing up in the creek afterward, Sarah using an old rag from the tree house to scrub the icing stains from her sundress, so her parents wouldn't suspect she had been fooling around with some boy. It wasn't that she didn't want to tell them about Renzo. It was just that, somehow, she never had. Daddy was so obstinate about what was proper for a young lady standing on the threshold of womanhood, and Mama was so apprehensive about what could happen to an innocent, unsuspecting girl these days, that Sarah had always told herself there was no point in angering and worrying her parents over nothing. After all, she had known Renzo all her life. He would never do anything to hurt her. Hadn't he proved that to her this very afternoon?

She sang gaily to herself all the way home, a ballad about falling in love, Renzo's ring tucked carefully in her pocket, the secret love they shared tucked just as securely in her heart. She would never forget this day, she thought as she danced and whirled along, hugging herself tightly, exhilarated. She was in love—and the boy she loved loved her. It was a wonderful, glorious day, the first day of the rest of her life.

The first day of forever and ever.

Six

Stardust

Beautiful dreamer, wake unto me,
Starlight and dewdrop are waiting for thee.

Beautiful Dreamer
—Stephen Collins Foster

The theme that night of the Lincoln High School junior-senior prom was "Stardust," and the gymnasium, which normally hosted basketball and volleyball games, had been transformed accordingly. When Sarah spied it through the open doors from the linoleum-tiled hallway beyond, her breath caught in her throat at the sight. It was beautiful. Magical. The students in the art classes had worked for weeks on the decorations, and it showed.

Myriad silver stars, big and small, suspended on thin silver wires, dangled from the ceiling, from the center of which also hung a shining mirror ball. Gossamer lengths of white fabric twined with silver streamers and sprinkled with tinier silver stars draped three cinder-block walls.

Circular tables erected around the gymnasium were covered with stark white cloths strewn with silver glitter. At the heart of each sat a crystal vase filled with flowers and balloons and surrounded by crystal votives in which candles glowed. Between the tables stood tall, silver-painted replicas of old-fashioned streetlights, candles burning in their lamps, their posts bearing street signs with names like Blue Moon Boulevard, Milky Way, and Starlight Lane. Above the bandstand constructed at one end of the gymnasium, where Hard Road was now testing and tuning their musical equipment, hung a huge, silver crescent moon on which a stuffed version of the Lincoln High School mascot, Dandy, the Lincoln Lion, perched whimsically, appearing to swing against a night sky formed by the black curtain that ran the length of the wall. At the opposite end of the gymnasium, long tables set end-to-end boasted a starry ice-sculpture centerpiece flanked by a sumptuous buffet and two crystal punch bowls filled to the brim with pink-lemonade punch. The wooden floor of the gymnasium gleamed brightly from having been waxed and buffed earlier that day. Sarah hoped she wouldn't slip and fall in her new pumps, whose heels were much higher than she was accustomed to.

As though mesmerized, she walked slowly into the gymnasium, and it was then that, glancing up from the thick black cord, called a "snake," which he was taping to the stage floor, Renzo spied her. He inhaled sharply, hardly recognizing her, she looked so different, so grown-up, more beautiful than he had ever before seen her look. She had her hair swept up in a mass of curls threaded with white ribbons and tiny white flowers. And although the long dress she wore was only a simple, flowing white organza gown he knew her mother had sewn for her, it looked stunning on, molding her curves so sensuously that he marveled that her father had let her out of the house in it. Or perhaps, more likely, Sarah had pulled the short, puffed sleeves down to reveal her bare shoulders and an enticing glimpse of décolletage *after* she had left home. Around her neck was a gold chain that disappeared into her bodice and upon which hung his class ring, Renzo knew. Against her breast was pinned the corsage he had saved up for and sent her, a single, lovely, delicate white orchid—not one of the cheap, tough, tuberous kind to be found in the grocery stores around prom time, but a real orchid from a real florist. In the box, Renzo had enclosed a card upon which he had scrawled *From a Secret Admirer,* in case her father should demand to know who had sent the corsage.

Sarah would know.

She had spotted him now, Renzo observed, and the smile she gave him as she lightly caressed the orchid at her breast made his heart pound, his groin tighten with desire. Anger and jealousy filled him, too, at the way the high-school boys present glanced at Sarah, each doing a double take. Speculation and lust shone in their eyes, already aglitter from the booze they had sneaked in concealed flasks into the gymnasium. Renzo's mouth tightened. He decided that if any of those guys got fresh with her, he would flatten them.

A few minutes later, when the gymnasium was full to bursting at its seams, Hard Road launched into its first number of the evening, a lively rock-and-roll song that

quickly had the space for dancing crowded nearly beyond
capacity. Sarah sat at a table with some of the other girls
who, like her, didn't have dates, and watched Renzo per-
form, refusing the invitations to dance that she received,
much to her surprise. She had never been very popular, but
it seemed that suddenly more than one of the boys had
noticed her. Sarah could only attribute it to the dress
Mama had made for her, and she flushed nervously, guiltily, at the thought that Mama had never intended for her
to draw the sleeves down as she had, baring the generous
swell of her breasts. But Sarah had wanted to remind
Renzo that she wasn't a child any longer, so he would see
only her and not the other girls at the prom—especially not
Eveline Holbrooke.

Evie was so gorgeous that it was hard to imagine any guy
not wanting her, Sarah thought as she spied her on the
dance floor. Determinedly, Sarah swallowed down the knot
of fear that rose in her throat at the idea that Renzo would
be attracted to Evie, just like all the other boys in town,
even the older ones who attended college. No, of course he
would not. Still, Sarah wished desperately that Evie
weren't dressed in a long, tight, strapless, beaded white
sheath that was slit up to the thigh and fitted her like a
second skin. Sarah had seen the gown last month at the
trendy, exclusive Fashion Boutique, so she knew it had cost
over a thousand dollars. That day at the dress shop, she
had known, even before glancing surreptitiously at the
price tag, that she couldn't even begin to afford the gown.
She only went into the Fashion Boutique to dream, not to
buy.

Now for a moment, as she studied Evie, Sarah longed to run and hide in the girls' bathroom, certain her own dress was hideous and that everybody at the prom recognized that it was homemade, not store-bought. But then shame pierced her deeply. Mama had worked so many long, hard nights on the organza gown, tracing and cutting, pinning and basting, her gnarled, arthritic hands turning the fabric into a young woman's romantic dream. It didn't matter that the dress wasn't chic and expensive, Sarah told herself fiercely. Every seam had been stitched with love, and that counted for more than anything.

"Do you see that gown Evie's *almost* wearing?" Krystal Watkins asked, her eyes narrowed in her plain face. "Why, it looks as though she were poured into it! And she's practically falling out of the top of it, too!"

"I'm sure Parker is praying she actually will," Liz Tyrrell drawled dryly as, in the same tomboyish way she wielded a field-hockey stick, she tossed aside her prom program. Parker Delaney, quarterback of the football team, the Lincoln Lions, was the most popular boy in school. Liz was sweet on him, even though he and Evie were going steady.

"Well, if Evie's dress *does* come off, it won't be anything Parker hasn't seen already," Dorothy "Dody" Carpenter—people sometimes spitefully called her "Dodo"—declared firmly. "I overheard Evie in the girls' bathroom one day, bragging to a bunch of her friends about how she and Parker had gone all the way several times. Is anyone hungry? I know I am. I didn't eat any supper, I was so afraid I wasn't going to fit into my gown."

Everybody was too polite to remark on the obvious: that Dody was so heavy that it was a wonder she fit into *any* dress. She was always hungry, always eating, after which she had taken recently to retiring to the girls' bathroom, where she forced herself to vomit all she had consumed, in a futile attempt to avoid gaining any more weight. Still, at least the buffet offered a chance to escape from the sight of Evie in her tight dress, grinding her hips against Parker's as the sound of Renzo's wailing saxophone reverberated in the gymnasium.

"*I'm* hungry, Dody," Sarah announced abruptly, getting to her feet. "I didn't eat any supper, either."

She had been too nervous and excited to eat. The arrival of the delivery boy from the Flower Garden, bearing the box in which the white orchid from Renzo had lain, had thrilled her beyond words. Mama had got tears in her eyes when Sarah had untied the ribbon and opened the box to reveal the orchid, because Mama had fretted so about Sarah not having a date or even a corsage for prom night. Daddy had actually teased Sarah gruffly about her "secret admirer." Then, with his Polaroid camera, he had snapped several pictures of her, insisting she looked so beautiful that he was half afraid to let her out of the house, for fear she would inadvertently cause a brawl at the prom. She had nearly broken down and told her parents about Renzo. But Liz, having wheedled from her father her parents' car for the evening, had pulled up into the gravel drive just then, blasting impatiently on the horn, and Sarah's words had died unuttered on her lips.

Now, as she followed Dody toward the buffet tables, Sarah wondered if the rumors about Evie and Parker being lovers were true. From the way the two of them danced together, Sarah thought it appeared likely. She sighed heavily. She was probably the only seventeen-year-old virgin in the entire high school. In the entire world. No matter what Mama and Daddy said, it seemed everybody did it these days, even nice girls; that those who saved themselves for marriage were hopelessly old-fashioned. Or afraid. Or frigid. Sarah didn't want to be labeled any of those things. Or to lose Renzo because he thought she was.

At the buffet tables, she moved slowly through the line, lingering to pass the time as she filled a plate and accepted a cup of punch from one of the teachers serving as a chaperon. Even though the louvered windows of green glass set high into the walls of the gymnasium were open to admit the night air, it was hot and stifling inside. Sarah felt as though she were melting. Knowing it had been rumored that some of the rowdier boys planned to spike the punch, she sipped it cautiously, forced to admit to herself that she wouldn't recognize whether it contained alcohol or not. Daddy didn't hold with anybody younger than twenty-one drinking liquor, so the only booze she had ever tasted had been an occasional sip of the beer Renzo had brought to the tree house every summer since he was sixteen. The punch seemed all right, so she drank it in long swallows, grateful for its iciness as it slid down her throat.

Carrying her plate and refilled cup, Sarah returned to an empty table. The other girls had either got up to dance, had gone to the bathroom to repair their makeup or had sneaked outside to the bushes or the backseats of cars to neck furtively or indulge in a covert smoke. Even Dody had already finished eating and disappeared, probably to bring back up whatever she had downed. Sarah felt lonesome, awkward and conspicuous. She wished Renzo were beside her, that he didn't play in a band, that he hadn't had to be part of the prom's entertainment. She felt as though everyone were staring at her, whispering about her, making fun of the fact that she didn't have a date, was sitting alone, a wallflower. Rejected, the boys who had come stag and had asked her to dance earlier had now moved on to other, more willing prey.

For comfort, Sarah stroked the gold necklace around her throat and slid Renzo's ring back and forth on the chain, reassuring herself that she was loved. She ate her buffet supper. She whiled away more time by going to the bathroom herself, and then by pretending to study the prom program, a copy of which was placed at every seat. The program was bound in silver, with a braided, tasseled silver cord to hold the inside pages in place. Knowing it was meant to be taken home as a keepsake, she tucked it into the small evening bag Mama had lent her for the night.

"Now, what's the loveliest girl at the prom doing sitting all by herself?" a voice whispered in her ear, startling her. "No, don't answer that. It's my fault, and for that, I'm sorry, Sarah. I'll try not to be jealous if you want to dance with other guys. I know it can't be much fun for you, being all alone like this and watching everybody else have a good time," Renzo said soberly.

"It's all right," she insisted, smiling up at him. "I don't mind. Really, I don't."

"Well, I *do* mind. So I've arranged not to play this next song." He held out his hand to her. "Will you dance with me, Sarah?"

"Yes, oh, yes!" Her eyes shining, she laid her hand in his.

The guy running the band's sound and lighting equipment manipulated the controls on his board, and all the lights over the bandstand gradually turned a soft blue, except for the white light that shone on the now spinning mirror ball, so it seemed as though thousands of tiny stars were strewn across the dance floor as Renzo led Sarah toward it. From the band's PA system, the opening strains of Lionel Richie's "Truly" drifted into the darkened gymnasium, through the louvered windows and out into the night as Renzo took her in his arms.

In Sarah's mind, the two of them danced alone beneath a starry spring sky. She was oblivious of the other couples that crowded the dance floor, so there was barely room to shuffle in place to the music. For her, there were only she and Renzo in all the world, and the lyrics of the song told the story of their love. She felt so light on her feet that it seemed she floated in his embrace, his breath warm against her skin, his chest pressed against the sensitive tips of her breasts, rubbing the organza of her gown across them, the strapless bra she wore doing little to mitigate the erotic sensations. She thought Renzo, in his old, black leather jacket and matching trousers, looked more handsome than any of the other boys did in their smart, rented tuxedos. She wished she were really alone with him, that they danced together in their meadow instead of the Lincoln High School gymnasium.

But it was nearly summer, and soon there would be weeks of long, lazy days at the tree house, days during which the two of them would discover and explore each other in ways only dreamed of until now, deepening their love, growing closer than ever. At that thought, Sarah felt her heart well in her breast, as though it were unable to contain all the joy it held.

As though he had read her mind, Renzo tightened his arms around her. "Sarah. Sweet Sarah," he whispered against her ear, his lips caressing the strands of her hair, his hands roaming sensuously down her back. "Do you have to go home right after the prom is over, or can you wait for me outside?"

"I don't know. It depends on Liz. I came with her and some of the other girls, in Liz's parents' car. We said we might go to the Sonic for a shake and burger afterward, so I'm not expected home right away. If Liz isn't in any hurry to leave after the prom, I'll try to meet you outside."

"Try hard." He paused for a moment, then swore softly. "Damn! I should have just told the band I couldn't play with them tonight!"

"No, it's all right," Sarah insisted again. She knew the orchid he had sent her couldn't have been cheap and that the Martinellis, while not poor, were not rich, either. "It's enough just to dance this one dance with you, Renzo. Truly, it is."

"No, it's not. But by this time next year, you'll be old enough to get married without your parents' consent, so we won't have to convince them you're not too young to be tying yourself down, and then we'll have the rest of our lives together, Sarah. I promise you that. I love you. I want you. God, you don't know how much I ache to be inside you, to claim you as mine forever. I don't know if I can wait until next spring to have you." His eyes glittered as he gazed down at her hungrily, as though he would devour her right there on the dance floor. A wild thrill shot through her, making her shiver. Her heart leaped with happiness and excitement and apprehension. He wanted to marry her! He wanted to make love to her, to hold her naked in the darkness, to be a part of her for always. And he was impatient. That thought gnawed at her.

Was that how Evie held on to Parker, the most popular boy in high school? By giving in to his sexual demands? Sarah wondered, another shudder of fright and anticipation running through her at the idea of sleeping with Renzo. As they danced, she could feel the hard, strong muscles that rippled in his back and arms. She thought of him embracing her, entering her, enveloping her, and she knew that if she were honest with herself, she must admit she wanted that, too.

"Renzo. Oh, Renzo, are you sure about marrying me?" She glanced up at him earnestly.

"Surer than I've ever been about anything else in my life, Sarah."

Seeing that truth in his dark, intense eyes, she sighed deeply with pleasure and once more laid her cheek against his shoulder. This was where she belonged, where she had always belonged. There was nothing to be afraid of. Renzo loved her. Come what may, he would protect her and care for her for the rest of her life. She wanted . . . she *needed* no more than that. Her heart and feet had wings. She could have danced all night. But finally, the last strains

of the song died away, and Renzo was compelled, however reluctantly, to return to the stage.

With that, the magic he had wrought in the night dissipated for Sarah. The blue lights again became a kaleido-
scope of colors, and the tiny stars cast by the mirror ball
faded from the dance floor. She became abruptly aware
that far from being winged, her feet hurt from the unaccustomed high heels she wore, that her toes were pinched
and painful. Gingerly, she tottered from the dance floor,
relieved now to sit back down at the empty table, to slip the
torturous pumps from her feet and to watch, unsurprised
but wistful and envious even so, while Evie and Parker
were crowned prom queen and king.

The remainder of the evening passed for Sarah in a blur
of impatience and expectation, along with anxiety that Liz
and the rest would not want to linger after the prom, but
would want to head directly for the Sonic. Fortunately,
however, it appeared the other girls had struck up an acquaintance with members of the band sometime during the
evening. So they were in no hurry to leave after everybody
had sung the Lincoln High School alma mater and the
band had played its final number. Sarah wondered how
much Renzo had had to do with the musicians' interest in
her friends. But she didn't bother to ask once the two of
them were alone outside, hidden from prying eyes by the
shadowed, tall old trees, the sprawling honeysuckle vines,
and the spreading quince bushes that grew alongside the
exterior walls of the gymnasium, blooming flowers and
ripening fruit sweet and fragrant in the sultry night air.

Renzo's mouth was on hers—hot, demanding, making
her head spin as though the pink-lemonade punch had, in

fact, been spiked and she had drunk far too much of it. His tongue teased her lips, opened them, plunged deep between them, searching, tasting, savoring. Tentatively, Sarah touched her own tongue to his, unprepared for his swift, volatile reaction. He groaned low in his throat and pushed her up against the brick wall of the gymnasium, so the coarse stone abraded her bare shoulders. But she scarcely felt the pain, she was so swept away by the emotions and sensations now coursing wildly through her breathless body. Her heart hammered so fiercely that its pace almost panicked her. Her blood roared in her ears. Her breath came in harsh rasps. Her knees felt so weak and trembling that she was dimly surprised she had not fallen to the ground, had not melted into a puddle at Renzo's feet.

He had one hand roughly ensnared in her hair, tilting her face up to his for the kisses he rained upon her mouth, her eyelids, her cheeks, her ears. His teeth nibbled her earlobes. He muttered to her, words she only half understood, but that sounded sexy and forbidden all the same, that conjured up dark, misty images in her mind—thrilling, tempting, terrifying. He cupped her face, stroked her throat, slid his hands along her shoulders, pushed her sleeves even farther down her arms. She felt his palms at her breasts, fingers dipping inside her strapless bra to fondle her nipples, taut with fear and excitement. His sex pressed against her—hard, taunting, tantalizing. She wondered what he would feel like inside her. She was consumed by curiosity, haunted by the thought that she might unexpectedly die, never having learned what it was to know a man, to know Renzo as deeply and intimately as she could.

But Sarah was also just seventeen, young and afraid. She sensed she would be forever changed somehow by the act of making love, of becoming a part of Renzo, and he of her. She thought again that things were moving too fast for her, that she wasn't ready yet for what he wanted from her. The lifelong admonitions of her parents rang in her head, battling fiercely with the yearnings of her heart full of love, the desires of her treacherously eager young body, awakened and aroused by Renzo's increasingly skillful, unstill lips and tongue and hands. Every time he kissed her, touched her, he seemed to have found some new way of fanning the flames he had ignited in her the afternoon of her birthday and that now burned ever more hotly and brightly. He was handsome and potently masculine. The smell of him filled her nostrils, musky, male scents of soap and sweat, of cologne and cigarette smoke. The taste of him was sweet upon her tongue. Sarah was dizzily aware of his strength, of her own fragility in comparison.

"Renzo. Oh, Renzo," she whispered, gasping for breath as he took her mouth again, his tongue shooting deep, before his lips sought her throat, her breasts, bare now and burgeoning with passion.

It was the screech of tires upon the parking-lot pavement and the crunching of metal that brought them both up for air. Then someone shouted, "Renzo! Hey, Renzo! It's your bike, man! Some fool's run over it!" and at that, at last, he abruptly tore his mouth from Sarah's breast, flinging his head up. His eyes were dark with desire, momentarily drowsy and disbelieving as he struggled to regain control of himself and his emotions, to make sense of what was happening. "Renzo! Christ! You'd better get out here, man!"

"Sarah..." The conflict in his eyes was plain for her to see.

"Go on. I know how much that motorcycle means to you." She fumbled with her bra, her sleeves, panicked now at the thought that someone might come in search of him, that he and she would be discovered together—she half naked. What a shameful, embarrassing scandal that would be! "I'll be there in a minute."

Nodding his head, Renzo left her then, slipping through the tangle of bushes to emerge some distance away, giving Sarah time to compose herself and lessening the chance that she would be inadvertently found and exposed. She was grateful for that. She thought she must have been temporarily mad to have forgotten where she was, the fact that the teachers who had served as the prom's chaperons were still cleaning up the gymnasium and patrolling the parking lot, that they or anyone else might have come upon her and Renzo at any time.

Once she had rearranged herself, she crept unnoticed from the refuge she had shared with Renzo, everybody's attention now focused on the scene unfolding in the parking lot, near the rented U-Haul truck into which the band had been loading their equipment. Even before she neared the crowd that had gathered, Sarah could hear Renzo cursing and knew how angry he was.

"Damn it! Why in the hell didn't you watch where you were going, Holbrooke?" he snarled as she warily ap-

proached the throng, pretending as though she had come
from the gymnasium, in case anyone should notice her.

"Look, it was just an unfortunate accident, pure and
simple. I've apologized for the damage and assured you
my insurance will cover all the necessary repairs. What
more do you want from me, Cassavettes?"

"Your hide nailed to a barn door for a start. Do you
know how many long, hard hours I worked restoring that
bike?"

"No, but even if I did, I can't change what's happened
to it. It's dark...I've had a lot on my mind lately, and quite
frankly, I didn't see it parked there. I'm sorry." It was
Sonny Holbrooke who spoke, Sarah saw as she at last
reached the group clustered around Renzo's motorcycle
and Sonny's automobile. Sonny's Camaro was barely
scratched, but the Harley, lying beneath the car's front
bumper, was badly mangled. Sarah's hand flew to her
mouth to stifle her gasp at the sight, for she knew how
Renzo prized the bike, how furious and upset he must be
at its wreckage. His eyes were hard and narrowed, and a
muscle worked in his set jaw. It was all the two band
members who restrained him could do to hang on to him,
to prevent him from barging past Mr. Dimsdale, the principal, and taking a swing at Sonny.

"My bike was parked in the grass, Holbrooke," Renzo
ground out between gritted teeth as he strove mightily to
free himself. "Do you make a habit of driving over the
school grounds? Or were you just too drunk to steer
straight? Isn't that a flask in your pocket?"

"Is that right, Mr. Holbrooke?" Mr. Dimsdale asked
sharply. He stood between Renzo and Sonny, attempting

to mediate their quarrel and prevent it from turning into a fistfight. "Are you in possession of liquor on school property, young man?"

"Don't answer that, Sonny." Evie stepped forward to grab hold of her brother's arm when he would reluctantly but obediently have reached into his pocket to turn over the forbidden flask. "You don't go to school here anymore. You're not under Mr. Dimsdale's jurisdiction any longer."

"Everybody on school property is under my jurisdiction, young lady!" Mr. Dimsdale snapped huffily, incensed. "Whether a student here or not. And since you're not involved in this affair, I'll thank you to keep out of it and your mouth closed. In fact, all of you just break it up and go on home now before I call Sheriff Laidlaw out here and one or more of you wind up having to spend the night in jail. Mr. Holbrooke, you and Mr. Cassavettes will remain behind until this matter is sorted out to my satisfaction."

Sarah wanted desperately to stay, to stand at Renzo's side, offering her support in case there were further difficulties. But he must have sensed this, because he shook his head at her silently, warningly, but so imperceptibly that no one else observed the small movement. Still, she worried. It seemed as though, one way or another, the Holbrookes were always causing trouble for her and Renzo. She *was* startled, however, that this time the culprit had proved to be Sonny.

Of all the Holbrookes, he had always been the nicest to her. But he *was* a Holbrooke, even if he didn't precisely fit the mold. His father, J.D., doted on Sonny and referred to him as the Holbrookes' "golden boy." But behind J.D.'s back, people gossiped that his wife, ZoeAnn, must have slipped down to the Rest-Rite Motel when he wasn't looking and crawled into some out-of-towner's bed. Because although, like Evie, Sonny favored his cool, elegant blond mother in looks, his personality was as far removed from the rest of the Holbrookes' as a thoroughbred's from those of a herd of pack mules. He was quiet, thoughtful, studious and artistic. In his spare time, he wrote poetry and painted and played classical piano. Currently a sophomore in college, he attended Harvard back east. Home for the summer now, following the end of the spring semester, he had come to the prom as the date of one of Evie's friends, Veronica Grenville, who had been sweet on him for years.

Renzo must be right, and Sonny must be drunk, Sarah thought, or he would never have run over the Harley. Unlike his brother, Bubba, he just wasn't the type to have done something like that on purpose and then lied about it afterward. Surely it was all just an unfortunate accident, as Sonny had claimed. Surely Renzo would realize that, too, once he had calmed down enough to think things through.

"Come on, Sarah." Liz touched her lightly on the arm. "If we're going to the Sonic, we've got to be on our way. My folks want me to be home—with their car intact—by two at the latest. Krystal, are you coming?"

"No, I've got a ride." Krystal had latched on to the band's drummer and didn't seem to be in any hurry to let go.

"She's going to wind up pregnant or worse," Liz declared softly as they walked toward her parents' car. "She doesn't even know that guy. It was one thing to flirt with him at the prom. But going off by yourself with a strange boy is just asking for trouble."

"Yeah, especially since he's Italian." Dody spoke up, pronouncing it "Eye-talian." "Why, my daddy'd just skin me alive if I brought home a dago. He says they're all mobsters. He says there've been rumors going around the coal mines for years that the real reason the Feds'll never find Jimmy Hoffa's body is because after the Mafia whacked him, they trucked him out here, and Papa Nick had the corpse ground up at the dog-food factory."

"I thought Hoffa was supposed to be buried on the fifty-yard line of some football stadium," Liz drawled as she unlocked the car.

"Naw." Dody shook her head as she heaved herself into the backseat, stuffing another leftover cookie from the prom buffet into her mouth. "He was turned into a couple of cases of dog food...probably wound up getting fed to some old lady's poodle. That's why Daddy won't let me go swimming in the quarries, either. He says everyone in town knows that when the mobsters in the big city hit somebody, they send the corpse down here so Papa Nick can fit it with cement shoes and pitch it into one of the abandoned quarries."

"Well, I'm surprised your daddy continues to work at the coal mines if that's what he thinks about Papa Nick and Italians, Dody," Sarah said stiffly as she fastened her seat belt. "They're not all like that."

Dody shrugged. "Sure they are. Why, they even assassinated JFK because he and his brother Bobby were going to blow the whistle on organized crime. Just imagine! Getting away with shooting the president! That's why Daddy don't hold with unions and all, causing trouble at the coal mines. He says that if the Mafia can get away with murdering the president, they can get away with anything. I guess if Daddy had his druthers, he'd rather work anyplace but the mines. But everybody's gotta work somewhere, don't they? And in this town, there just aren't that many jobs besides those at the mines and at Field-Yield, Inc., and Daddy said he guessed he'd rather shovel coal than shit."

Sarah didn't answer. And although she felt guilty for being so mean-spirited, she was secretly glad when, on the way home, after downing two cheeseburgers, three orders of onion rings and a chocolate shake at the Sonic, Dody moaned that she felt awful queasy and begged Liz to pull over on the side of the road so she could throw up.

"If I were Dody, instead of worrying about Italian hit men, I'd be more concerned about choking to death on a plain old ham sandwich, like Mama Cass Elliot did," Liz remarked coolly as she lit a cigarette and exhaled a cloud of smoke rings. "Hey, Dody!" she hollered out the open door of the car, grinning wickedly. "I wouldn't go too far out in those bushes if I were you."

"Why—why not?" Dody gasped, groaning and clutching her stomach as she stumbled along the dirt road's dark verge, wildly overgrown and as yet uncut because of the spring rains.

"You might trip over Jimmy Hoffa's decaying corpse!"

A spasm of retching greeted this announcement.

"You're bad, Liz," Sarah observed, shaking her head at her friend's antics. She had always liked Liz. Of everybody in town, Liz was the one, Sarah thought, who would understand about Renzo.

"Yeah. I'd be the perfect gangster's moll, don't you think?" Liz struck a glamour-girl pose in her seat. "Diamonds dripping from my naked body—and one of those little pearl-handled guns in my evening bag. What do you think my chances are of making Al Pacino an offer he can't refuse?"

"Al Pacino's an actor, Liz, not a mobster."

"Oh, well, a girl can't have everything, I guess." Liz paused for a moment, then inquired archly, "Do you suppose Dody goes to bed every night expecting to wake up beside a bloody, severed horse's head in the morning?"

Seven

The Quarry

O Love, O fire! once he drew
With one long kiss my whole soul thro'
My lips, as sunlight drinketh dew.

Fatima
—Alfred, Lord Tennyson

That summer following her junior year in high school altered the course of her entire life, Sarah was to think afterward, bringing both pain and joy, destroying something infinitely precious to her—yet giving her something equally as precious in return. And in the end, that was, perhaps, a fair trade.

It was a scorcher of a summer, the kind in which the bright yellow sun shines so fiercely, burns so relentlessly and endlessly that the trees wither, the grass parches, and the earth bakes hard. Only where there was water was there also life—in the town itself and in the woods, where the shaded creeks had not dried up and the old, abandoned quarries were still full of water born of the winter snows and the spring rains. It was one of these quarries that the bolder and more reckless of the town's youth frequented as a swimming hole.

The town did boast a public swimming pool, but it was small and old, its Gunite coarse and cracked, its paint flaking and peeling. It reeked of the chlorine that was employed in such strength that it turned hair green and eyes red. Its two brick-and-concrete bathhouses smelled of mold and mildew, and the white towels provided were dingy and scruffy from usage. The rules posted were strictly enforced, so there was no horsing around. For all these reasons, the public swimming pool principally attracted elderly couples, young mothers with toddlers, and children not yet old enough to swim without the supervision of a lifeguard.

Those in high school and college scorned the public swimming pool in favor of the quarry. It was off the beaten track, surrounded by woods and meadows, a long, deep, jagged scar in the earth. From it, coal and stone had once been gouged, but once they had played out, the quarry, like so many others in the region, had been forsaken, the earth left to recover as best it could from Man's invasion. Tall grass and wildflowers covered the quarry's high banks; cattails and willows clustered at its edges, long leaves and weeping branches trailing in the cool, murky water. At one end, a series of rugged, exposed chunks of rock, remnants of what had years ago been hewn away by huge machinery, rose, forming natural platforms for diving. It was these that made the quarry so exciting, dangerous—and forbidden. And so of course, everybody between the ages of fourteen and twenty-five went there.

Periodically, Sheriff Laidlaw or Deputy Truett drove out to the quarry to issue stern warnings and run everyone off. But this chore proved about as successful as waving away flies from a garbage can. Every summer, the town's young people flocked to the quarry, and every summer, the town's old people predicted darkly that it was only a matter of time before somebody was killed out there—which was exactly what happened that summer, although not quite in the way anyone had ever expected.

Sarah awoke that morning to what she thought would be a day like any other, having no inkling of how, in a matter of hours, her life was to change so drastically. In later years, she was to recognize that dreadful things often had their roots in ordinary beginnings. But at seventeen, one is both invincible and immortal—or so one thinks. She was too nervous and keyed up to eat any breakfast and, after finishing her chores, instead spent her morning showering, dressing and grooming herself carefully. She was to meet Renzo at the tree house, and he had told her yesterday that upon her arrival, he would have a surprise for her. He was going to take her someplace, he had said, so she should look her best. He had also instructed her to bring along her bathing suit and beach towel, so he and she could go swimming afterward.

Despite how she had teased him, he had refused to give her any further clues about what he had planned for their day together, so the mystery added to her excitement. Once she was ready, she slipped from the house, waving goodbye to Daddy, who was mowing the yard and so, to her re-

lief, didn't question where she was headed. Mama had
gone into town to do the weekly grocery shopping. Sarah
knew they both would believe she was spending the day
alone at her tree house, writing and sketching, as she so
often did. She bit her lip guiltily at the thought. Soon she
must tell them about Renzo, make them understand,
somehow, the fact that she was going steady with him, that
she and he planned to get married next year. Her parents
were bound to be upset, which was why she kept postpon-
ing telling them her news. They wanted her to attend college, to obtain her degree so she could get a good job and
have a better life than they had. They would fret, too,
about Renzo being five years older than she, and about his
bad-boy reputation and background, the fact that his father had been not only a mobster, but also one who had
been gunned down on the mean streets of the big city. It
would take time to convince her parents that Renzo wasn't
following in his daddy's footsteps, but rather in those of
Joseph Martinelli, who had reared him and who had, in
truth, been more of a father to him than the real father he
had hardly known had ever been. Still, although strict, her
parents were fair. Surely once they came to know Renzo,
they would realize he was nothing like what the gossip that
circulated about him proclaimed. They would see how
hard he worked and how much in love he and she were,
Sarah reassured herself.

With that thought to lighten her spirits, she sang as she
tramped along the dusty path she had worn over the years
from her home to the tree house. And she swung gaily at
her side the big straw bag in which she had packed her

bathing suit and beach towel, her notebook, sketchpad and paints, and some fruit and cookies.

"Whenever I hear that song, I always think of you," Renzo, who was already at the meadow, said in greeting, his eyes glinting with both desire and pleasure as they took in her appearance. She had arranged her hair in a French braid, tying it with a green ribbon to match the green sundress she wore, which made her green eyes stand out startlingly like glowing emeralds in her face.

She smiled at him brightly, in a way that made his heart turn over, his groin tighten. "I like it. It's a happy song, I think. Daddy used to sing me to sleep with it." Reaching into her straw bag, she drew forth a banana, tossing it to Renzo. He caught it deftly. "So, Mr. Tallyman, get busy. Daylight's coming, and I want to go home."

Peeling and eating the banana, he sauntered toward her. "Now, is that so?"

"No. . ." she breathed as, tossing the banana peel over his shoulder, he took her in his arms and kissed her deeply. "I want to stay here with you, forever and ever."

"Hmm. I'd like that." He kissed her again, lightly this time, then reluctantly drew away. "But today I have a surprise for you."

"So you said yesterday. Are you going to tell me now where we're going?"

"Yeah." He paused for a moment, his eyes turning serious as he gazed down at her in his arms, which he tightened about her. "I'm taking you home with me, Sarah, to meet my folks. We're going to have lunch with them."

"No!" she exclaimed softly, abruptly a nervous wreck. "Oh, Renzo, are you sure? Oh, this is just terrible! Why didn't you warn me instead of springing it on me like this? Whatever will I say to them? What if they don't like me? What if they think I'm not good enough for you? I'll just die if they do, if they think I'm nothing but coal-mining trash! Oh, I—I should have worn something else, dressed up more—"

"Shh. You look fine... better than fine. You're beautiful, Sarah. And this is exactly why I didn't tell you sooner—because I knew you'd be anxious and upset. But you've no reason to be. My folks aren't snobs. They've been victims of prejudice themselves too often in the past for that. They're going to love you, the same as I do. So relax. They're not ogres, and they won't bite you, I promise. In fact, they're very nice people who're just as nervous about meeting you as you are about meeting them. Mom asked me at least a dozen times what you liked to eat, and Pop had already changed his shirt three times before I even left the house!"

"You're probably just saying that to make me feel better," Sarah said wryly.

"No, honest, it's the truth. Cross my heart and hope to die," Renzo replied, grinning as he made the age-old gesture.

"All right. So your daddy didn't throw you out of the house and your mama didn't scream and faint dead away when you asked them to invite me over for lunch. That means there's still some hope for me, then, right? What—what did you tell them about me?"

"Nothing much, really, except that I wanted them to meet you. I didn't have to say anything else. I've never brought a girl home before, so they know I'm serious about you. That's all that's important. That's the only thing that matters.''

Although Sarah was thrilled by the knowledge that Renzo had never taken any other girl home before, she was still tense and apprehensive. "But...what if they hate me, Renzo?''

"They won't. But even if by some extremely remote chance they do, it isn't going to change anything between us, Sarah, I swear. I'm a man and you're a woman, and in the end, we have to make our own decisions, to do what's right for us, no matter what our folks or anybody else thinks—even if it winds up being just you and me against the world, sweetheart. You know that. You feel it in your heart, just as I do, don't you?''

"Yes, you know I do.''

"Then there's no reason for you to be scared, is there? You'll do fine. So give me a smile and a kiss, and then let's go, okay? I told Mom and Pop we'd be there at noon, and I don't want to be late. Mom's probably already thrown out two batches of spaghetti by now, thinking they weren't good enough to serve to you, and burned up a couple of loaves of garlic bread, besides, *she's* so worried that you're not going to like her and Pop!'' His arm wrapped comfortingly around her waist, Renzo led Sarah toward his motorcycle, which he had parked off to one side.

"You got your Harley fixed!'' she observed.

"Up and running,'' he corrected. "It's still got some problems, things I haven't had time yet to repair, but at least it gets me where I want to go now. It's been a real hassle, not having it. That rental bike Sonny's insurance company had to spring for was a hunk of junk. And I still

have doubts about whether his hitting my own bike that
night at the prom was an accident.''

"Oh, Renzo, surely it was. I know how horrible Bubba
and Evie are, but Sonny's not like his brother and sister.
He's different. Half the time it's hard to believe he's really even a Holbrooke."

"Yeah, I guess you're right."

Renzo climbed onto the Harley, Sarah settling herself
behind him, the rope handles of her straw bag secured over
one shoulder, her arms fastened tightly around his waist.
He started the bike, and in moments, they were flying from
the meadow, en route to the Martinellis' quiet white bungalow on Elm Street. Once or twice in the past, when she
had managed to borrow her parents' car for an hour or
two, Sarah had driven by the house. But this would be her
first time inside it. Despite her nervousness about meeting
Renzo's parents, she was honest enough to admit to herself that she was curious about how he lived and what his
bedroom looked like.

But from the moment the Martinellis opened their front
door to her until sometime later, when they closed it firmly
behind her, Sarah sensed instinctively that they were startled and disappointed, flustered and distressed by her appearance. They smiled, they chatted, they tried hard for
Renzo's sake to make her feel welcome. Still, there was an
awkwardness to it all, and she knew she wasn't what they
wanted for their only child.

Sarah was deeply hurt by and sorry for that, not only
because she loved Renzo with all her heart, but also because she truly liked the Martinellis and felt she could have
been happy in their bungalow. Inside, it was cool and dark,

the shades drawn against the blistering summer sun, the two window air-conditioning units, one upstairs and one down, humming briskly. The furnishings were lovely, plainly, even to Sarah's untutored eyes, family heirlooms that had been handed down from one generation to the next, obviously treasured and cared for. Old-fashioned antimacassars protected the stuffed sofa and chairs in the living room; Italian whatnots and tables had been polished until they gleamed, and Capidomonte bric-a-brac was dusted and displayed just so. Renzo's bedroom was a young man's haven, boasting a comfortable double bed, a desk, chair and lamp for studying, a chest of drawers, and framed pictures of jazz greats on the walls. He had his own small bathroom, too.

"It looks like you," Sarah declared upon seeing his bedroom. Then she turned and clutched him anxiously, whispering, "Oh, Renzo, they don't like me! I can tell!"

"That's nonsense, Sarah," he responded quietly. "They like you just fine." But despite his words of reassurance, he knew deep down inside that she was right. He just didn't know why.

The lunch, served in the dining room, was excellent, and Sarah did her best to do it justice, sensing intuitively that Madonna Martinelli's feelings would be hurt otherwise, that she enjoyed food and equated its rate of consumption with approval of how good it tasted.

Still, "You should eat more, Sarah," Madonna urged politely. "Growing girls need nourishment just as much as growing boys. You should have seen Renzo when he first came to us. Why, he was pitiful . . . nothing but skin and bones! But I soon fattened him up. Now he loves food, especially my manicotti and lasagna and spaghetti. Do you know how to cook Italian dishes, Sarah?''

"No," she admitted. "But I'm sure I could learn, Mrs. Martinelli.''

"Yes, of course you could. I didn't mean to imply you couldn't. I hope I haven't offended you, Sarah," Madonna said, flushing and glancing anxiously at her husband and son.

"No, you haven't, Mrs. Martinelli, not in the least.'' Sarah forced herself to smile as she spoke. She wished desperately that she understood what was wrong with her, why Renzo's parents disapproved of her. She could only think it was because Daddy was just a coal miner, while Mr. Martinelli owned a newspaper—even if Renzo *had* insisted his parents weren't in the least snobbish or prejudiced.

To Sarah's relief, once the meal had ended, Renzo announced they had to leave, that they had plans to meet friends later. The Martinellis pressed the two of them to stay, but Sarah could tell their hearts weren't in the invitation. She thanked them for lunch and said how much she had enjoyed meeting them. They replied that they had been delighted to have her and make her acquaintance. Then they waved good-bye and shut the front door solidly behind her. Sarah was near tears by the time she got outside.

"They hated me," she asserted.

"No, they didn't. Get on the bike and wait for me there, Sarah. I forgot to get the beer from the refrigerator." Despite his words to the contrary, Renzo knew his parents hadn't liked her. He was angry; she could tell by the muscle that flexed in his set jaw.

"Renzo, please." She laid her hand gently on his arm. "It's all right. Really, it is. Please don't start any trouble with your parents on my account."

"I'm not. I'm just going to get the beer, that's all. And stop saying things are all right, when they aren't! You're better than that. You *deserve* better than that! You're as good as anybody else in this town—including the Holbrookes! And I don't like you demeaning yourself that way, especially for things that are my fault."

"This wasn't your fault, Renzo."

"Wasn't it? They're *my* parents, Sarah, and *I'm* the one who invited you to lunch. No, don't say another word. I won't have this coming between us. Just get on the bike, and stay there until I come back."

With that, Renzo stalked determinedly back to the house. He had left the beer inside on purpose, so he could confront his parents without Sarah overhearing their conversation. He didn't know what was wrong, why his parents had disliked her. But he certainly intended to find out the reason. As he pushed open the front door, he could hear his parents talking, Madonna plainly upset, Joe trying to comfort her. At his entrance, they abruptly broke off their dialogue, looking startled and guilty, so he knew they had been discussing him and Sarah. After a moment, Joe cleared his throat awkwardly.

"What's the matter, Son? Did you forget something?"

"Yeah, the beer." Going wordlessly into the kitchen, Renzo grabbed the six-pack from the refrigerator shelf. Then he strode back to the front door, telling himself that despite his intention just minutes before, now wasn't the time to confront his parents. He started to open the door, then abruptly shoved it closed again, slamming his hand so hard against it that his mother jumped.

"Why didn't you like her?" he demanded, his voice low, harsh and throbbing with emotion. He pivoted to face his parents. "She's beautiful, thoughtful, sweet, shy, creative and intelligent, and she loves me. So why in God's name didn't you like her?"

"Renzo . . . Son . . . sit down a minute," his father urged kindly.

"No. I don't want to sit down. I just want to know why you didn't like her."

"It wasn't that we didn't like her," Madonna insisted, wringing her hands in the face of her son's anger and hurt. "She's everything you said, a very nice girl, in fact—"

"Then why? I don't understand."

"It's just that your mother and I . . . Well, we always hoped and expected that when you fell in love and got married, it would be to an Italian Catholic girl," Joe explained.

"Italian?" Renzo repeated dumbly, momentarily nonplussed. "Catholic? You mean you didn't like Sarah just because she's not an Italian Catholic? Jesus! I don't believe this! I don't believe I'm *hearing* this! And to think I told her you weren't prejudiced, that you'd suffered too often in the past at the hands of bigots ever to become like that yourselves. But I guess I was wrong about that, huh? All these years . . . all these years, I've been glad, I've been *proud* to be your son. But you know what? Today, *today,* I'm ashamed! Yes, I'm *ashamed,* do you hear?" Renzo's voice shook with emotion.

"Don't you dare speak to your mother and me like that, do you understand?" Joe said sharply. "We're your parents. You show respect! Now, it's not that we're prejudiced— No, hear me out, Son, because I'm telling you the truth. You're right. Your mother and I *have* been on the receiving end of bigotry too many times in the past ever to engage in it ourselves. But because of that, we also know what the world is like, Renzo, how people feel about mixed marriages, in particular."

"Please. Don't give me that crap! Times change, Pop. This isn't the Old Country, for God's sake! It's America! My generation isn't like yours—"

"Isn't it?" Joe asked. "Renzo...Renzo...despite that you've grown to manhood, you're still young yet in so many ways, too young to understand that every generation shares the same feelings, repeats the same mistakes of that before it. You're not the first young man to think your parents are just a couple of old fogeys, set in their ways, and who don't understand you or your entire generation. And you won't be the last to think that, either. Because you're right. Times *do* change, yes. The world forges ahead, progresses technologically as our knowledge of things like history, medicine and science increases. But *people* don't change, Renzo. Man's still the same creature he was when he first stood upright, took up a club and bashed his neighbor's head in over a piece of meat. Those emotions, good or ill, are an inborn part of us."

"Your father and I, we love you, Renzo," his mother declared. "We know what the world is like, and we just don't want to see you hurt, that's all. So it's not that we didn't like Sarah. It's not that at all. It's just that... Well,

life is just so much easier, so much simpler if you stick to
your own kind, Son. These feelings you have for Sarah—
they'll pass, you'll see. Because what you want at your age
isn't what you'll want in ten years, or even five. In time,
you'll understand that. That the best relationships grow
from shared roots, from common backgrounds, heritage
and religion. Just give yourself some time, Renzo. That's
all we're asking. Time to see the world, time to experience
life before you tie yourself down to any one girl. And when
you're ready for marriage, bring home a nice Italian
Catholic girl, one like Anna Maria Pasquale. Now, there's
a girl who knows how to cook!''

"Your mother's right, Son," Joe insisted. "It's what's
best—and that's all we've ever wanted for you, the best.
Try to remember that and not to judge us too harshly."

After a moment, Renzo nodded tersely, not trusting
himself to speak. He thought his parents were wrong—
dead wrong. But he also recognized that there was no point
in arguing with them. They *did* love him—and truly believed they had his best interests at heart.

"Look, Sarah's waiting for me," he said finally. "So
I've got to run. I'll see you later."

"Sure, Son. Have a good time," Joe replied, trying, as
he always did, to behave as though there had been no
quarrel, no unpleasant words exchanged in the Martinelli
household.

"And don't drink too much," Madonna admonished.
"Are you sure that motorcycle's fixed good enough for
you and Sarah to be riding it?" she inquired, deeply sus-
picious of all forms of transportation, since she was afraid

of traffic, of driving in a car and of motorcycles, in particular.

"Yeah, I'm sure. Bye, Mom. Bye, Pop."

"Bye, Son. Take care. Drive safe, and we'll see you at supper."

Sighing heavily, troubled, the Martinellis watched silently as Renzo strode down the front walk, climbed onto his Harley and rode away, Sarah perched behind him, clinging to him tightly, her head resting against his shoulder. They did not know as they watched their son disappear that many long years were to pass before they ever saw him again.

Renzo took Sarah to the quarry that served as the local swimming hole. They both knew it was off limits; they had both been forbidden by their parents to go there. Neither of them cared. It was hot, and they wanted to swim. Besides which, everybody in town knew that in addition to the rocks that formed the unintentional and dangerous diving platforms at one end, the other reason this specific abandoned quarry was so popular was because it didn't connect with any of the rest, which meant that its water was unpolluted by the kind of waste that oozed through the others. The municipal sewer system didn't extend beyond the town limits, so everybody who lived in the country and had access to the quarries ran their plumbing pipes into them, using them as septic tanks. No one with any brains fished in those particular quarries, either. The fact that whenever it rained or snowed, the contents of those quarries sometimes spilled over to seep into people's backyards was accepted as simply a natural hazard, and people actually cracked jokes about the swamp gas.

Even before they reached the swimming hole, Sarah and Renzo could hear shouts, laughter and music above the purr of the Harley. So, knowing a crowd had already gathered there, Renzo dropped Sarah off a little way from the quarry, so she could change into her bathing suit in privacy, away from the prying eyes of the boys who delighted in shamelessly spying on girls changing clothes in the woods.

"I'll meet you at the quarry just as soon as I get my suit on," she said.

Renzo nodded, frowning a little as he glanced down at the front end of the bike. The shimmy he thought he had repaired appeared to be returning. He could feel a faint tremble in the motorcycle, as though it were still out of alignment.

"What's the matter?" Sarah asked, fearful that despite all his reassurances to the contrary, the lunch with Renzo's parents and their disapproval of her had somehow made him think twice about loving her, about wanting to marry her.

"Just the problems with the Harley. Damn that Sonny! I'd like to wring his neck! I had this bike in mint condition, and because of his drunken stupidity, I've had to start all over again on it. But I'll get it fixed, sooner or later. See you at the quarry."

Gunning the engine, Renzo drove off. Sarah stared after him anxiously for a long moment. Then, biting her lower lip, she turned and made her way to a thick clump of bushes, where she quickly stripped and yanked on her bathing suit. She had bought it at Wal-Mart, with the money she had saved from her baby-sitting jobs, so Mama and Daddy wouldn't know. It was a bright, tropical-colored bikini that showed a good deal more of her than either of her parents would have approved. Now, as she gazed down at herself, she wished she had never worked up the courage to buy the bathing suit. If she were honest with herself, Sarah knew she must admit she had thought to entice Renzo with it, to drive him crazy with desire for her. Now she worried he would think she looked cheap and trashy in it instead. But there wasn't any help for it; she had brought nothing else to swim in. Folding up her underwear and sundress, she stuffed them into her straw bag, then headed toward the quarry.

There, cars were parked all around, their doors hanging open, their trunks popped, a couple of radios, all tuned to the same popular station, blasting away in the muggy summer heat. Blankets and beach towels were strewn over the ground, peopled with near-naked bodies smeared with suntan lotion or baby oil, and soaking up the hot rays of the sun. Girls sprayed their wet hair with Sun-In or lemon juice to lighten it. Ice chests packed with beer and soft drinks sat in trunks, on hoods and beneath the shade of the trees. Empty aluminum cans and long-necked bottles littered the earth. Somebody had brought along a small, portable grill, and the smell of charcoal burning and of hamburgers and hot dogs cooking permeated the air. Water splashed as the bolder swimmers dived from the rocks or slid from the old tire swing suspended by a stout rope from a sturdy tree branch overhanging the quarry.

Sarah spotted Renzo standing with some of the members of his band, along with Krystal, Liz and a couple of other girls she knew, so she had an excuse for joining them. Renzo had changed from his jeans and tank top into a pair of cutoffs, and she couldn't help but admire his hard, lean body as she approached the little group. He was much more muscular than a lot of the other guys, his chest matted with fine black hair, his belly flat and firm, his hips narrow, his right forearm sporting a big, intricate black butterfly tattoo, which he had got the summer he was eighteen. A gold chain with a St. Christopher medal hung around his neck, glinting in the sun against his dark, bronzed skin.

"Hey, Liz, Krystal!" Sarah smiled and waved.

"Sarah!" they cried in unison. "Come join us."

They introduced her to the others she didn't know, while Renzo unobtrusively handed her a beer and made sure she wound up standing by him.

"Damn it, Sary!" he muttered in her ear, his eyes smoldering dangerously, like twin embers about to burst into flame. "Were you deliberately trying to drive me mad with lust and jealousy, coming out here in that suit you're wearing?"

"You—you don't like it?"

"Like it? I *love* it! What I *don't* like is all these other guys seeing you in it! The next one who looks at you with his tongue hanging out of his mouth is going to feel my fist in his face, I swear!"

"Shh!" she hissed nervously, at once thrilled, excited and horrified at the prospect of him really carrying out this threat. "The others will hear you!"

"Well, frankly, I don't give a damn! I'm tired of sneaking around, Sary. Tired of acting as though the fact that you and I love each other is something to be hidden, to be ashamed of. I don't care anymore what people will think. I want these guys to know you're taken, that you're mine."

"How can you say that—especially after what happened at your folks' house? After what they thought, seeing us together?"

"Do you honestly think your own folks are going to be any different, that they're going to accept me any better than mine accepted you?"

"No," she confessed reluctantly, "although before today, it wouldn't have occurred to me that my folks would object to you because you're an Italian Catholic, but only because you're five years older than me, and in college. Now, I find it terribly ironic to think they might disapprove of you because you *are* an Italian Catholic, while your own folks disapproved of me because I'm not!" She sighed heavily, pressing her arm against Renzo's. Even tanned, she was lighter than he, but what difference did that make? "What's wrong with people, Renzo? Why should the color of anybody's skin be so important? It's an accident of birth, that's all. It doesn't make you any smarter or stronger or better. And why should it matter that you're a Catholic and I'm a Protestant? Don't we both believe in one God, the same God?"

"You know what I believe, Sarah. So you're asking me questions to which I haven't any answers. And this is really too heavy a discussion for such a hot, humid afternoon. So what do you say we just forget the rest of the world for today, concentrate on each other, have a couple of beers and go swimming or something?'' His eyes roamed over her slowly, appraisingly, love and desire gleaming in their depths. Then he grinned at her insolently.

''Well, I guess that depends on just what the 'something' you have in mind is,'' she teased, vastly relieved that his earlier dark mood appeared to have dissipated.

''Let's go swimming first, and then I'll show you.''

They swam. They drank a few beers. They ate a couple of hot dogs. Then they swam some more—and drank some more, until Sarah realized dimly that she was more than just a little tipsy when Renzo at last pulled her from the cool water, wrapped her beach towel around her and led her toward the shelter of the woods, away from prying eyes. There, drawing the towel from her slowly, trailing it over her shoulder and down her arm, he spread it on the grass. Then he pressed her down upon it, amid the wildflowers, honeysuckle vines and cattails beneath the green canopy of the trees.

In that moment, as she gazed up at Renzo, it seemed to Sarah as though all her senses suddenly, strangely, metamorphosed, expanding in some directions, contracting in others. All the clamor surrounding the quarry faded so she could no longer hear the shouts and laughter, not even a single note of the blaring music. The place where she lay was hushed, as though it had been enshrouded by a cocoon—and she was the caterpillar inside it, on the brink of transforming into a gossamer butterfly and breaking free of her confines. She was vividly conscious of the white clouds in the sky, of the sunlight slanting down through the boughs of the trees, weaving delicate patterns amid the leaves and dappling the earth so it seemed magical, a fairyland. In her dazed, lethargic mind, the droning bluebottles flitting among the wildflowers were, in reality, fairies who danced and sang in the summer stillness. The summer heat upon her body, soaking into her skin, made her feel as though she were on fire, bathed in a golden glow. The sweet fragrance of the green, cool woods, tinged with the tang of still water, filled her nostrils. Most of all, she was aware of Renzo kneeling over her, his thighs imprisoning her own, the butterfly tattoo on his forearm appearing to flutter its fragile wings. He had never told her why he had got the tattoo, only that it meant something special to him. He stretched out his hands, tugged the band from her French braid. His fingers worked patiently, as though he had all the time in the world to loosen and untangle her damp hair, to spread it like a fan beneath her head. His palms cupped her face tenderly.

Slowly, inexorably, he lowered his mouth to hers.

A soft sigh escaped from Sarah's parted lips before she closed her eyes and drank him in. Her mouth was an unfurling bud, his tongue a hummingbird that tasted the nectar at the heart of her—so quick, so light that she instinctively hungered for more. She reached up, her hands tightening in his hair, drawing him down to her. She opened her lips wider to his, pliant, yielding, eager for the taste of him. Her own tongue darted forth to twine with his, a dance like that of the bluebottle-fairies, wings brushing, flicking, lingering, a mating ritual as old as time.

"Oh, Sarah," Renzo breathed against her mouth before he lay down beside her, his body half covering her own, his hand at her breast, one leg riding between hers.

They had never before lain together like this, nearly naked, flesh pressing against flesh. The heat that suffused Sarah's body deepened, spread. It was as though the touch of him seared her very being, melted her as the sun melted ice. He licked her throat, a feathery stroke so delicate that she would have thought she imagined it, if not for the shiver that ran through her, the sudden tautening of her nipples, so they strained against the fabric of her bikini top. Renzo's palm glided across them; his fingertips circled them, teased the sensitive tips before sliding sensuously down her belly. His hand slipped between her thighs, rubbing her lightly, as though he sensed the painful tightening that gripped her there, that made her arch against him as she instinctively sought easement.

Of their own accord, her palms glided down his back, stroking, kneading, tracing the strong planes and angles, the hard curve of muscle and sinew, so very different from her own softness. Male. *Forbidden.* And so, like the quarry, dangerous and exciting. At the thought, alarm bells rang in Sarah's mind. She ignored them, pushed them away, told herself dizzily that they were only wind chimes hung in the trees by the fairies whose place this was, stirring faintly in the sultry air. Renzo kissed her mouth again, this time more deeply, more demandingly, his tongue questing, stabbing her with its heat. Her breasts swelled against him, aching to burst free of their constraints, to press against his naked chest, to feel the fine mat of dark hair that covered him there. Her fingertips stroked the soft pelt, drew tiny circles amid the curls, outlined his own nipples, as hard as hers.

The clasp of her bikini top gave way at his swift, sudden yank; the spaghetti straps brushed her arms. And then the scrap of material was no more than a splash of bright color upon the grass, and her breasts were bare, full and upthrusting, begging to be fondled, imprisoned by his hands and lips, seized by his teeth and tongue. Groaning, he captured them without a struggle, pressed them high, buried his face between them. His mouth caught one dusky nipple, sucked fervently, until it was distended and engorged, and waves of electric shocks were radiating through her body. After what seemed an eternity—an eternity in which she could no longer think, could only feel—Renzo released her nipple, lifted his head. His eyes, dark with desire, pierced hers so intensely that Sarah could not bear to go on meeting his gaze, but shyly turned her face away, flushing. One hand ensnared her hair, compelling her to look at him; the other found the nipple he had teased, thumb and forefinger taking hold of it, rolling and tugging gently. Tightening his grasp in her hair, holding her still, deliberately watching her all the while, he slowly lowered his head again, took her nipple between his teeth, laved it with his tongue until she whimpered pleadingly, writhed beneath him, burning, aching, desperately wanting something more.

"You like that, don't you, Sarah?" Renzo muttered hoarsely.

"Yes," she whispered helplessly. "Yes . . ."

His hand crept downward once more, this time finding its way beneath the elastic band of her bikini bottoms, his lips and tongue stilling her demurring. She was soft and hot and wet, and not just from swimming, either. He stroked her, fingers parting the trembling, burgeoning petals of her, rhythmically sliding up and down the mellifluous seam of her, finding the hard little bud she had not until this moment known existed, but that now seemed to be the very center of her being. Sarah had never before felt the sensations that assailed her as he rubbed her there, lightly at first, then harder and faster as she opened to him, pushed exigently against his hand, straining toward whatever it was she suddenly knew with certainty that she must find or die. She clutched Renzo fiercely, her nails digging into his back as she sobbed against his mouth, at once terrified and tantalized by the terrible, unbearable thing that had seized her with sharp, inescapable talons, that squeezed at her determinedly, relentlessly, until she was certain she would explode.

And then she did, the waves of pain turning abruptly into a flood of pleasure that was so agonizingly intense that she thought she would faint from it. She stiffened, gasping and crying out, not understanding that the magnitude of her delight could be heightened still more until, without warning, Renzo drove his fingers deep inside her, thrusting them in and out of her frantically as she rode the tide of ecstasy.

She wasn't even aware of how, with his free hand, he fumbled at his zipper, jerked his cutoffs down and impatiently kicked them away to free himself. Her head still spun, her body still pulsed with the aftermath of her climax as he grabbed hold of her bikini bottoms, swiftly hauled them from her, so that before Sarah even realized what was happening, she lay sprawled and naked before him, his hands at her thighs, spreading her wide. Her eyes flew open to see him kneeling over her, as naked as she, his sex hard and heavy, poised to pierce her. His own eyes were open, too, dark with passion, glittering with hunger and triumph. She wanted to protest. But as though he sensed that, Renzo bent over her, his hand around his turgid member, guiding it to her, pushing it against her, rubbing and exciting the key to her pleasure again, so her objection died, unuttered, on her lips.

Moments later, with a low groan, a calling of her name, he plunged into her, swift and hard and deep, conquering the frail guardian of her innocence, penetrating and invading her. Sarah's breath caught in her throat at the shock and pain of it, and then she cried out. But with his mouth, Renzo swallowed the soft, stricken wail, his tongue silencing her, mimicking the movements of his body as he withdrew, then thrust into her deeply once more. His hand was upon her mound, kneading her as he took her, so the unendurable pressure built within her again and she knew nothing but him, the feel of him throbbing inside her, stretching and molding her as his body quickened urgently, feverishly, against her own. She clung to him tightly, instinctively wrapping her legs around his, arching her hips to meet each powerful stroke as he once more drove her over the edge of consciousness into the brilliant, bursting abyss of blind sensation. As she fell, Renzo, unable to hold back any longer—surprised he had managed to contain himself as long as he had—shuddered convulsively against her, his head buried against her shoulder, his breath coming in harsh rasps, his heart hammering against her own as he spilled himself inside her.

Afterward, although he half expected Sarah to cry, she didn't—not even when he abruptly realized that in his uncontrollable desire to have her, he had forgotten to protect her, had, in fact, left his package of condoms in the pocket of his jeans, which he had earlier rolled up and stuffed into one pouch of the saddlebags on his bike.

"What if I'm... What if I'm pregnant now, Renzo?" she asked quietly, tremulously, as they lay together in the afterglow of their lovemaking, he kissing and stroking her, already wanting her again, she utterly overwhelmed by her mixture of emotions, what she had just experienced in his arms.

"You aren't," he murmured reassuringly. "So don't worry about it. You have to do it a lot for that to happen. You're safe if it's only a couple of times, especially in the beginning, when you were a virgin." He kissed her mouth, silencing her fears. "Christ, but you're beautiful! You don't know how badly I've wanted to see you naked like this, to make love to you, to be a part of you." His eyes and hands roamed over her boldly, possessively, as though he had every right now to look at her, to touch her whenever and however he pleased. The effects of the beer she had drunk earlier were beginning to fade, and she was shy of him, but Renzo only laughed softly at that. "We're going to be married, Sarah, and I'm not going to be the kind of husband who lets his wife hide from him under the cover of a nightgown, bedsheets and darkness." He took her hand in his, wrapped it around his sex, taught her the motion. "Open your legs for me, Sarah," he demanded 'huskily. "You're mine now, and I love you. I want you ... like this ... and this ... yes, my love, yes...."

He enfolded her, sank into her, urgent in his desire and need as he once more hurtled them both into the kaleidoscopic void.

Eight

The Fall

There's no such thing as chance;
And what to us seems merest accident
Springs from the deepest source of destiny.

The Death of Wallenstein
—Johann Christoph Friedrich von Schiller

The partylike atmosphere at the quarry was still going strong when Sarah and Renzo finally dressed and crept back to join the others, knowing it was doubtful their absence had been noticed amid the crowd and noise. They were by no means the first couple ever to slip away into the woods. Still, feeling as though, like Hester Prynne, she had a big scarlet letter on her chest, proclaiming her sin to the world, Sarah kept her beach towel wrapped tightly around her and lived in fear that someone would suddenly point at her and announce she had slept with Renzo. She could smell the musky, male scent of him on herself, feel his semen damp between her thighs. She wanted desperately to go home, certain her face bore such a guilty expression that anybody looking at her would know what she had done. And that anybody looking at Renzo—his drowsy eyes raking her lazily, a satisfied smile curving his mouth— would know who she had done it with, as well.

But everyone was drunk enough by now that they had embarked upon the dangerous dare for which the quarry had for years been notorious, and before Sarah could voice her thoughts aloud to Renzo, he was dragged away by his friends to join in the dire contest. Although she would have done anything to stop him, Sarah knew instinctively that Renzo wouldn't back down from the challenge, not even for her; that, like the rest of those reckless enough to be involved in the terrifying game, his male pride was at stake. So she could only watch helplessly, silently, biting her lower lip anxiously as, powerful muscles rippling in his bare arms and back, he boldly climbed the first of the abandoned quarry's infamous rocks.

While even Sarah herself had dived from the lowest level, to go beyond that was considered both perilous and foolhardy, because nobody knew for certain how deep the quarry was—and what *was* known was sufficient to give anyone with any common sense at all pause. When excavated, the quarry had been cut at odd angles, so that beneath the water's surface, craggy stones jutted out jaggedly from the wall, in such a way that the higher one dived from the platforms, the greater the risk of hitting one of the treacherous rocks that lurked in the turbid depths.

So that, of course, was the fiendish dare, with the person who dived from the highest point winning. Most of the girls rash enough to take part usually chickened out after the second level; it was the guys who brazenly continued upward, steadily winnowing out their meeker or more sensible opponents. But Sarah, sick to her stomach with certainty, knew Renzo would not be one of those to drop out. Her mouth went dry; her heart thudded horribly in her breast as he ascended each subsequent level, only to fly from it like an arrow shot from a bow, arcing through the air to vanish beneath the water. And each time, feeling as though she would vomit, she thought he would not reappear.

With nerve-racking intensity, the contest dragged on, until it became clear to even the drunkest of spectators that something beyond the terrible dare itself was at stake. Sonny Holbrooke—being a good deal more conservative and levelheaded than his brother, Bubba, and so having in the past always retired from the game after the third level—had this afternoon instead gone on to the fourth and was even now hauling himself up to the fifth. It was equally plain that the cause of this was Renzo. Although the music from the car radios was so loud that no one below could hear what he was saying, it was obvious from Renzo's derisive, flashing smile and the angry, fiercely determined expression on Sonny's face that Renzo was taunting him, goading him ever onward. Nobody present had to think any further back than prom night, when Sonny had run over Renzo's Harley, to guess the reason for Renzo's behavior.

He and Sonny dived from the fifth level, and then the sixth. Panting hard, they crawled from the water to lie upon the grass, each attempting to catch his breath. Then, after a long moment, Renzo dragged himself to his feet and stood there, bent forward, hands on knees.

"Scared yet, Golden Boy?" he jeered at Sonny, grinning mockingly. "Ready to give up? Or have you got guts enough to go on, after all?"

"Don't listen to him, Sonny!" Forrest Pierce said sharply, scanning the crowd for Bubba, wondering why he hadn't stepped up himself, either to take Sonny's place or to put a halt to his foolishness. But there was no sign of Bubba, or of Evie, either, for that matter. They were probably off in the bushes, banging their respective companions, Forrest thought. "Even Bubba won't dive from the seventh level. Cassavettes won't either. Nobody will. He's bluffing you, man. Call it a draw and forget it."

"That's right, Sonny." Drew Langford spoke up. "You don't have to prove anything to Cassavettes or anyone else here. You've deep-sixed the sixth, buddy! And that's more than most of us can say. Leave him alone, Cassavettes! You know good and well he didn't mean to run over your damned bike!"

"Well, I've got ten bucks that not only says he did, but that Renzo has guts enough to do the seventh—and that chicken-livered Golden Boy there don't," Dante Pasquale, Anna Maria's brother and Hard Road's bass player, drawled insolently. "Everybody in town knows it's big, bad Bubba who got Old Man Holbrooke's brass balls. It sure as hell ain't sissy Sonny! So what do you pansy, 'Rat Pack' Anglos say, huh? Either put up, or shut up. That's the Italianos' motto."

"You're on," Sonny said quietly, struggling to his feet.

"Don't be a fool, man!" Skeets Grenville snapped. "Only an idiot would take that bet, and the last time I checked, you had a lot more brains than Bubba! It's like Drew said—you don't have to prove anything, Sonny, especially to a bunch of sorry Dagotown dirtbags. So why don't you scum get lost, go do your diving in whatever toilet bowl you ever crawled out of!"

Dante's hands clenched into fists at his sides. He took a threatening step forward, so it seemed for a moment as though the argument would erupt into an all-out fracas, with blows being exchanged right and left. But then, realizing he and the other Italians present were largely outnumbered, he evidently thought better of it, restraining his hot temper and forcing himself to laugh scornfully.

"Talk! That's all you Anglos ever do. Talk, talk, talk. You know what I say to all your big talk? Big deal, man! That's what I say." He flicked his fingers under his chin, a rude Italian gesture. "I'm a man of action myself. Ten bucks. Are you taking it or leaving it?"

"We're taking it," Sonny insisted, roughly shaking off his cohorts, who would have held him back as he started resolutely toward the rocks.

Shooting Dante a hard stare, Renzo followed slowly after Sonny, knowing Dante had only mixed in the affair to cause trouble, because Renzo wouldn't date Anna Maria. She was always ragging her brother about it, giving him grief. He had simply taken this opportunity to get a bit of his own back against Renzo, pushing matters to the breaking point. Renzo hadn't intended that. He had meant only to yank Sonny's chain, because of the damage to the Harley. He was amazed Sonny had kept on climbing and diving. He blamed himself for his own temper, for not recognizing sooner that just because Sonny wasn't a blowhard like Bubba didn't mean he lacked courage of his own—the kind of quiet courage Sarah had. Still, Sonny had to be scared now. Even Renzo himself was afraid. What Forrest Pierce had said was true—no one had ever dived off the seventh, the uppermost level.

For one thing, it was a single rock, smaller and more rugged than the rest and set at an awkward angle, so anybody diving from it would need to push out really hard to miss the other jagged platforms below. Besides which, Renzo thought as he scrambled atop it and gazed down at the cloudy water, it was a long drop. Although heights didn't bother him, he still felt giddy for an instant, as though he suffered from vertigo.

"Look, Sonny, this really isn't what I had in mind."

"Well, then, I guess you should have thought about that before you started all this, Renzo." Sonny's voice was stiff and clipped, his expression still set, determined—although his face was ashen. "It was an accident...my running over your bike."

"I know. It's just that, well, I truly *did* work awfully hard to restore it, and now, I'm having to do it all over again. It made me mad, that's all. But not mad enough to make me risk my life over it, that's for sure. And I don't think you want that, either. So why don't we just forget this, go on back down, have a beer, eat a hot dog?"

"Actually, that sounds like a pretty damned good idea to me. Onward, Watson."

"Right, Holmes."

"Good Lord, you've read Doyle!" Sonny exclaimed, obviously surprised.

Renzo nodded. "Among several others—most of the classics, anyway. Being an Anglo doesn't give you a lock on scholarship, you know."

"No, I suppose not. Still, not many guys our age read at all these days. It would be...nice to discuss literature with somebody who was interested in it, who actually understood it, for a change." Sonny made this observation tentatively, not certain, under the circumstances, how it would be received.

"Over espresso and cigarettes? I never have liked carrying on deep dialogues while perched precariously on top of a rock!"

"Tomorrow afternoon, then, at Fritzchen's Kitchen?"

"Done."

In agreement, each startled but intrigued at this strange prospect of if not friendship, at least friendly acquaintance and intellectual conversation, they turned to make their way down.

Far below, those watching had fallen uneasily silent, so that now the only sounds at the quarry were those of station K-104 on the FM dial and the loud report of Junior Barlow's thirdhand clunker backfiring as he drove up. Hearing the gunshot-like noise, Sarah, her heart lodged in her throat, knew that for as long as she lived, she would never forget it. She would never forget, either, Stevie Woods's voice belting out from the car radios that you could try, you could try, but you just couldn't win 'em all. That he could learn how to fly, but it was just too far to fall as, without warning, Renzo and Sonny plunged from the rock.

Hers were not the only screams that echoed shrilly above the pounding music as the two young men fell, seeming to drop forever, turning and twisting in a macabre mockery of Olympic high divers, before they each struck the water, disappearing into its murky depths. Tears streamed down Sarah's cheeks as she ran toward the quarry, passed by Forrest and Dante and the others who were racing toward it, too, one after another leaping into the water, vanishing and reappearing, in frantic search of Renzo and Sonny.

At last, after what seemed an eternity, Renzo surfaced, coughing and choking, to be dragged by the rest to the bank.

Sonny never came back up—at least, not alive. He had hit his head on one of the submerged stones and broken his neck. No one knew whether that was what had actually killed him, or whether he had drowned when his body had got entangled in a mass of snarled tree roots that stretched into the quarry, deep beneath its surface. They knew only that by the time he was finally cut free, he was dead.

"Goddamn you! Goddamn you! May you rot in hell, Renzo Cassavettes!" Evie screamed hysterically as she fell upon him, beating him so violently where he lay that it took Bubba and her boyfriend, Parker Delaney, both to haul her off. "You saw!" she cried, glancing around wildly at the rest. "You all saw! Renzo Cassavettes *murdered* my brother! He deliberately pushed him off that rock! Killer! Murderer!" she shouted, kicking out at Renzo as Bubba and Parker fought to hold on to her. "You knew he couldn't dive nearly as well as you, that you'd manage to survive the fall, and so you pushed him! You *pushed* him!''

''No. No! It was an accident! A terrible accident, that's all!'' Sarah exclaimed from where she knelt at Renzo's side, dabbing blindly with her beach towel at the cuts and scrapes that seemed to have bloodied him all over.

''No, Evie's right! Renzo shoved Sonny!'' somebody said.

''He did not!'' someone else insisted.

''The law'll decide. Drew's gone for the sheriff.''

''Why wait? Get a rope, and we'll string the guinea bastard up ourselves!''

The fight that had brewed earlier erupted then, quickly escalating to riotous proportions as beer bottles were broken so their jagged necks could be used as makeshift weapons. Girls ran screaming in every direction, trying to reach their cars, to lock themselves in, to escape. During the melee, fearing for his life, believing that at the very least he would be charged with and convicted of murder in the small, biased town in which he lived—most of which was owned by the Holbrookes—Renzo stumbled dazedly to his feet, staggered desperately toward his Harley. His head throbbed horribly. He had struck it somehow in the fall, and blood seeped into one eye from the nasty gash on his forehead.

He never heard Sarah calling his name. Never saw her trying frantically to reach him, only to be knocked down and nearly trampled in the brawl. His only clear thought was not of her, but of getting away. Gunning the motorcycle's engine, he tore off, thinking he didn't dare return home. Sheriff Laidlaw was certain to head straight to the

Martinellis' bungalow, looking for him. Renzo thought he needed to go someplace where he could lose himself, someplace like the big city.

So once he was free of the woods and meadows, he turned the bike on to the dirt road that led from town, ripping along at such a furious clip, his mind and emotions in such a turmoil, that he completely forgot about the railroad tracks, didn't slow for the bad, uneven crossing with its old, peeling white warning signs, but hit at full speed the rough dip just before the steel rails. The violent impact blew out his front tire, and the Harley, unable to sustain this further damage, slid into an uncontrollable skid that left Renzo lying stunned and hurting in the ditch alongside the road.

After several long minutes, the adrenaline pumping wildly through his body got him shakily onto his feet. Clutching his ribs, he limped toward the bike and saw it was done for. Hardly thinking, he snatched his jeans and tank top from his saddlebags, somehow dressed himself, then forced himself to press on afoot. He was a mile down the road before he realized he hadn't put on his shoes, but had left them behind. Now and then, he glanced back, terrified, over his shoulder, expecting to hear the wail of the siren, to see the flash of lights belonging to Sheriff Laidlaw's patrol car. Renzo didn't know how far he had traveled when he did at last dimly discern the frightening sound of an automobile engine behind him. He flung himself down into the ditch, peering up over its edge. The oncoming car was long and sleek and black. It wasn't the sheriff's.

In desperation, Renzo scrambled from the ditch, stuck out his thumb in the hitchhiker's age-old gesture, knowing he couldn't walk much farther. He was in too much pain; he felt as though he were going to pass out. Still, he didn't know whether to be relieved or filled with apprehension when the automobile rolled to a halt, its back door was slowly opened from the inside, and then a low, thickly accented voice from his past ordered tersely, "Well, donna just standa there, boy. Getta in."

Nine

Strange Company

Misery acquaints a man with strange bedfellows.

The Tempest
—William Shakespeare

Renzo eased himself into the car's backseat, next to its passenger, closed the door.

"Drive on, Guido," Papa Nick instructed his chauffeur. Then, pressing a button, he rolled up the glass partition that separated him and Renzo from Guido. "Where you headed, boy?" he asked.

"The big city."

"Uh-huh." His gnarled hands resting on the silverknobbed malacca cane propped between his legs, Papa Nick deliberated on this piece of information. "Whadda you gonna do there?" he inquired at last.

"Get a job."

"Uh-huh." Papa Nick thought hard some more. "What kinda job?"

"One at a newspaper, if I can."

"Uh-huh," Papa Nick said yet a third time. He reached into his trouser pocket, drew forth two pieces of gold-foil-wrapped chocolate, handed one to Renzo. "I remember you like chocolate, from that first time I ever see you. Whadda scarecrow you were then! Eh? But even then, I know whadda fine man you gonna grow into someday."

They ate the candy, chewing silently, Renzo thinking that cracking his skull must have addled his wits. Or else Papa Nick was as crazy as a june bug, picking him up off the road, sitting there, not saying a word about the cuts and bruises and blood that covered his body, the fact that he looked as though he had been dragged through a combine backward, that his feet were bare and that he could properly be thought to be running away from home—even though he lacked even so much as the battered old suitcase with which he had years ago arrived at the Martinellis' bungalow.

But apparently, Papa Nick knew more than Renzo suspected, as was made clear when the old man finally spoke again. "You kill J. D. Holbrooke's golden boy, Renzo?"

"No. Yes. I mean . . . it was an accident. Why? How—how do you know about it?"

"I got my ways, and besides, news travels fast in a small town. You wanna tell me what happened outta at the quarry, uppa on toppa that rock?"

"Well, the truth is, I'm—I'm not exactly sure what happened. Sonny and I . . . we had decided not to make the dive, after all. We'd . . . ah . . . sorta patched up our differences up there, realized they weren't worth risking our lives over. We turned to head back down, and then . . . I don't know. I felt a sudden, sharp pain in my shoulder, like I'd been stung by a wasp or a bee. They're always buzzing around out there at the quarry. But it startled me, so I flinched. I lost my footing, bumped into Sonny, and the next thing I knew, we were falling. He wasn't nearly as good a diver as I am, so he couldn't get himself into position before we hit the water. He was twisted around all wrong. We struck the stones under the surface. I cracked my head, just a glancing blow, I think, or I'd probably be dead, too. But Sonny broke his neck, got all tangled up in some willow roots or something. He might have drowned, but I figure he was already dead by then. Are you—are you going to turn me over to the sheriff, Mr. Genovese?"

"Papa Nick, boy. Everybody calls me Papa Nick. And no, why woulda I wanna handa you to the sheriff? Do you t'ink I shoulda or somet'ing?"

"Well, no. I mean...Sonny's death...it *was* an accident. But Evie and the others...they were all shouting I'd murdered Sonny, that I'd deliberately shoved him off that rock, knowing he couldn't hack the dive, would probably be killed. They were going to lynch me, for Christ's sake! That's why I have to get away. Nobody in town'll believe me over the Holbrookes."

"I believe you."

"Yeah, but you're Italian."

"Whadda gave it away? I got spaghetti on my tie?" Papa Nick queried, then laughed heartily at his own joke, his big belly shaking as it had that day on his veranda so long ago.

Renzo forced himself to smile, but the mention of spaghetti had reminded him of Sarah. He was deeply stricken by the sudden realization that he had left her behind. Still, what kind of future could he offer her now, especially if he were to wind up being charged with murder, hunted by the law, a fugitive from justice? She deserved better than that, much better.

Papa Nick reached out, took hold of Renzo's upper arm, examining it intently for a moment. "That sure donna looka like no wasp sting to me," he observed of the gouge in Renzo's shoulder. "Looka like a flesh wound from a bullet, if you ask me."

"A bullet? No, that's impossible. I must have just scraped it going under."

"Uh-huh." From his shirt pocket, Papa Nick withdrew a business card. Turning it over, cupping it in his palm, he wrote something on it with a gold pen, then handed the card to Renzo. "There. Keepa that. Donna throw it away or lose it. When you getta to the big city, give the man whose name I've written there a call. Tell him I told you to contact him. He works for the *Herald*. If you're any good at reporting, he'll see you getta hired on there."

Renzo stared at the name Papa Nick had written on the card, abruptly shivering. He told himself he had been injured and was in shock, so it was only to be expected that he felt chilled. But deep down inside, he knew his shudder had nothing to do with his physical condition and everything to do with Papa Nick's shadowy, spidery web of power and influence. Instinctively, Renzo knew he didn't want to be beholden to the old man.

"Thanks, Mr. Geno...ah...Papa Nick. But even if it means I have to get out of your car right now and walk from here on out, I have to tell you honestly that I'd rather

.not be put into a position where you might someday come to me and say I owe you a favor."

"Donna worry. You're not. Hal Younger's not in the business. And I donna wanna not'ing from you—not'ing, except for you to make somet'ing of yourself, somet'ing to be proud of."

"I wish I could believe that—"

"Believe it. Besides, you already owe me. You just donna know it yet."

"What—what do you mean?"

"When Sofie, that slut who called herself your mother, wanted to unload you, who do you t'ink set it uppa for you to live with Joe and Madonna, eh? Who do you t'ink paid for that fancy motorcycle of yours, and your college education, among other t'ings? I did, that'sa who! You donna know alla this before, but I t'ink maybe it'sa time you know it now."

If the old man had suddenly reached over and whacked him on the head with that silver-knobbed cane, Renzo couldn't have been more stunned. He thought he must be dreaming, suffering a hideous nightmare that was delivering multiple jolts to his system. He told himself more than once to wake up. But to his dismay, he didn't suddenly find himself at home in his bed.

"What are you saying to me? Why would you have done all those things for me?"

"I got my reasons. You t'ink I just happened along this here road, out for a Saturday-afternoon drive or somet'ing? Well, I didn't. After he hauled you outta the quarry and realized Sonny Holbrooke was dead, Dante Pasquale hotfooted it uppa to my house, as well he shoulda, to tell me the bad news. I figured you'dda come this way, so I rode outta here to getta you."

"You still haven't told me why."

"That's because I t'ink maybe you ain't gonna like whadda I havva to say."

"Try me."

"All right." Papa Nick paused for a moment, as though gathering his thoughts. Then he asked quietly, "Do you remember your papa at all?"

"Only vaguely. Why?"

"He was my son. That makes you my grandson—just in case you're a little slow figuring outta the connection, due to that blow you got to your head."

"No! That's—that's just not possible!"

"No? Why not? You trying tell me your papa wasn't Luciano Genovese? Luke, he called himself."

"Yes. No. I mean ... I remember his first name was Luke. I've—I've forgotten his last name. When he died, Sofie said we mustn't use it anymore, that it might cause trouble for us. I was barely five at the time, and I didn't talk much. I guess I must have just blocked it totally out of my mind. I've always thought of myself as Renzo Cassavettes."

"That'sa the only favor that trash ever did you—changing your last name, so you donna got no connection to me and Luciano. She didn't have no loyalty whaddasoever, no understanding about family, although in the end, that proved a blessing. I never wanted him to take uppa with her, or to go into the business, either. But Luciano wouldn't listen. He ran off to the big city, got mixed uppa with Sofie, and with the Spinozas and the rest of that lot uppa there, and got dragged into their territorial wars. Broke his mama's heart and damned near killed her, him getting gunned down the way he did. He was our only child. But then we found outta about you, and it seemed we'dda been given a second chance. We were starting to getta on a little in years by then, but there were Joe and Madonna, with no children of their own. The rest you know. Now, maybe you donna wanna know me, Renzo. Donna wanna my help or not'ing else from me, either. Fine. Havva t'ings your own way. But this mucha you owe me—donna cut yourself off from Joe and Madonna. And send a postcard to Mama Rosa, your grandmama, now and then. That'sa all I ask.''

Leaning back and closing his eyes, Renzo said nothing for a long while, reflecting on all these revelations, but too tired and hurting, really, to absorb them properly. Far worse was the ache in his heart whenever he thought of Sarah. But then, finally, he spoke.

"I wrecked the Harley. It's lying in the ditch by the railroad tracks."

"I saw it. It'sa been taken care of. Anyt'ing else?"

"I had a girl…Sarah…Sarah Kincaid. Her daddy works for you, at the coal mines. Tell her…" What? That he loved her? That he hadn't been thinking straight when he had driven off without her? That she should wait for him—when he didn't know what his future held at this point, had nothing now to offer her? That it wasn't just his father who was a mobster, but his grandfather, too, and probably his great-grandfather, as well? That he came from a long line of mafiosi, so she should consider herself well rid of him? "Tell her…I'm sorry."

* * *

Guido drove Renzo to the big city, leaving him standing on one corner of its old, elegant plaza, to make his own way, as he had insisted, determined not to take any more from Papa Nick than he already had. But in the end, after knocking on the office doors of countless newspapers, magazines and even advertising agencies, and being rejected, Renzo at last broke down and telephoned Hal Younger, managing editor of the *Herald*, who actually proved to be legitimate—an old school chum of Joe Martinelli's—and who did, in fact, wind up giving Renzo a job.

Ignorant of what had happened back home after he had fled, whether or not he had been charged with murdering Sonny Holbrooke, Renzo didn't try to contact either Sarah or his parents for six months. When, finally, assuring himself that no one but his folks and Papa Nick knew about him and Sarah, he attempted to call her, he got a recording that announced that her number had been disconnected. So he was compelled to write her a letter. He also wrote to his parents, giving as his return address the post-office box he had acquired and signing only the initial of his first name to the missives, in case Sheriff Laidlaw should intercept them.

When Renzo's letter was delivered to Sarah's house, it was Iris Kincaid who opened it. Seeing the bold black scrawl, she sensed instinctively that it was from the faceless, nameless boy who had sweet-talked Sarah into lying to her and Dell, into sneaking around and deceiving them behind their backs. Sarah had foolishly surrendered her virginity to the boy, who had repaid her by leaving her pregnant and alone—and still, she continued to protect him, refused to reveal his name so he could be made to do the right thing by her! Worse, she was fiercely insisting on keeping her baby.

The entire affair had broken Iris's heart—and literally killed Dell. They had had such hopes, such dreams for Sarah! She had been a straight-A student, college bound—and she had thrown it all away for a roll in the hay with some irresponsible, disreputable boy! Dell had never got over the shock of her betrayal. Only last week, he had keeled over dead from an unexpected heart attack. Iris read Renzo's letter twice—and then she tore it into little pieces and flushed it down the toilet, from where it traveled through the plumbing pipes to the quarries, to rot with the rest of the waste.

When Renzo's letter was delivered to his parents' house, it was Madonna who opened and read it. Afterward, she sat for a very long time at her desk, staring out the front window and thinking hard about what she should do, what was best for her son. Then, finally, she picked up her pen, writing to Renzo that while Sonny Holbrooke's death had ultimately been ruled an accident, there was no reason for him to leave a promising job in the big city to return home—especially since three months after he had fled from town, his friend Sarah Kincaid had got married and moved away to parts unknown.

Book Two

The Prodigal's Return

When the blood burns, how prodigal the soul
Lends the tongue vows.

Hamlet
—William Shakespeare

Ten

Remember

White clouds on the wing;
What a little thing
To remember for years
To remember with tears!

Four Ducks on a Pond
—William Allingham

A Small Town, The Midwest, The Present

By the time Sarah finally managed to get her Jeep unlocked, she was shaking so badly that she dropped her keys on the street, not once, but twice. As she knelt the second time to retrieve them, she accidentally knocked her sunglasses from her face and was forced to fumble around for those, too. Her heart was racing as though, unbeknown to her, some mad scientist had inserted a motor into it, and her mouth was so dry that she could hardly swallow. She slid into the Jeep, accidentally shutting the door on her seat belt, and spent nearly a minute jerking frantically on the strap, too numb to grasp why it wouldn't pull across her body. The whole time, she prayed—the same litany over and over: *Please, God, don't let him see me!*

She finally figured out the problem with the seat belt, cracked open the vehicle's door, snatched the strap free and fastened it around herself, watching Renzo all the while in her rearview mirror. He glanced her way. Panicked, she flung herself down on the front passenger seat so he wouldn't see her. Despite her apprehension, she felt like a fool, crouched in her Jeep. What if somebody on the sidewalk strolled by and observed her through the vehicle's windows? She was a grown woman, behaving ridiculously, as though twelve years had not passed and she were still just seventeen. Even so, it wasn't until Renzo disappeared into the newspaper office that she at last rose up and started the Jeep. Her hands still trembled as she turned the key in the ignition and slid the automatic gearshift into Drive. Pulling out, Sarah nearly backed into Jimmie Dean Thurley in his brand-new pickup truck. She flinched, startled, when he laid on his horn and shouted crossly out his open window at her. Shooting him a faltering smile of apology, she drove on blindly down the street, her nerves jumping.

Despite her instructions to him earlier, Alex wasn't waiting for her on the sidewalk in front of the Penny Arcade, so she was forced to park and go inside to search for him. The place was jam-packed with shouting and laughing youngsters. Rock-and-roll music blared; the engines of electronic cars and motorcycles revved, and the *rat-a-tat-*

tat of electronic guns sounded from arcade machines; the bells of pinball machines dinged loudly. She would never find Alex in all the cacophony and confusion, Sarah thought with despair. And she simply *must* find him. She must get him out of town before Renzo saw him—because if there were one person alive who would see Alex and know immediately who his father was, it was Renzo Cassavettes.

What he would do if he ever found out about Alex, Sarah shuddered to think. Her deep fear was that, enraged because she had never told him about their child, Renzo would try to take Alex away from her. She wouldn't have worried, except that Renzo was no longer a poor Italian boy from the wrong side of the tracks, wanted for murder. Although many townspeople still insisted Renzo had deliberately pushed Sonny Holbrooke to his death, Sonny's killing had eventually been ruled an accident. And in the past twelve years, Renzo had, as Lucille had earlier this day observed in her salon, made something of himself to be proud of. He was now a renowned, admired and respected investigative reporter who had, just last year, won a Pulitzer Prize for his exposure and coverage of widespread political corruption that had involved participants ranging from mafiosi and drug lords to Capitol Hill congressmen and White House aides. The affair had quickly been dubbed the "Racket Club" by the media—a double entendre referring not only to the actual political corruption itself, but also to the exclusive, tony sports club where clandestine meetings had taken place in the steaming saunas. Both the Racket Club and Renzo's source, known only as Whistle-blower, had soon become as notorious as Watergate and Deep Throat, as the Pentagon Papers and Daniel Ellsberg.

Hungry for news of Renzo, despite how she had told herself time and again that he was nothing to her—and that she had never been anything to him—Sarah had nevertheless avidly followed his meteoric rise in the field of journalism. She had read every article he had ever written and that she could get her hands on, combing both the archives of the town's public library and the old metal shelves of the journalism department at the local state university, where newspapers from all over the country were stacked high. Regardless of the quiet rage and resentment she harbored even now toward Renzo, she had in her heart been proud of him and of what he had achieved. Despite his humble beginnings, he had, with talent and determination, made his boyhood dream come true. But because of his success and wealth, he was now a threat to her where Alex was concerned.

To her relief—for she had had some crazy, terrifying, half-formed notion that Renzo had already snatched her son away from her—Sarah spotted Alex at last. He was sitting inside an arcade car, his eyes glued to an electronic race track, his foot jammed on the accelerator, his hands spinning the steering wheel deftly. A wide grin split his face as he drove, and every now and then, he cried, "Out of my way, scum bucket!" and other similar epithets. Normally, Sarah would have been angered by the fact that he had either lost track of time or else had deliberately disobeyed her instructions and hadn't been waiting for her outside. But today she was so happy to see him that her only thought was to get him home, where he would be safe.

"Alex!" She hurried toward him, pushing her way past the youngsters who crowded the arcade. "Alex, it's time to go!"

"Ha, ha! Crash and burn, evil dweeb!" He grinned with wicked delight before braking. Then he stamped on the accelerator again, turning the steering wheel furiously.

"Alex!" Sarah said more sharply, tapping him on the shoulder.

Her son glanced up, startled, his concentration broken. With a screech, his electronic race car skidded on the track, then rolled over and over, smashing into one of his imaginary competitors' vehicles. GAME OVER flashed brightly on the screen.

"Mom!" Alex wailed with disgust, scowling at her. "Look what you made me do! I only had one more lap to go, and then I would have won!"

"I'm sorry, but it's time to leave now." Sarah didn't remind him that he was supposed to have been waiting out front for her. Renzo might have spied him standing on the sidewalk, and looking at Alex now, Sarah knew with certainty that for Renzo, seeing their son would be like gazing into a mirror and seeing himself as a boy again.

"Oh, all right," Alex said, climbing out of the machine. "I'm hungry, anyway. We're still going to Fritzchen's Kitchen and then to Wal-Mart, aren't we?"

"No, I—I thought..." What she had thought was that the two of them would go straight home. But what reason could she give Alex for changing her mind when she had promised to take him to lunch and then shopping afterward? If she broke her word, he would be hurt and hostile. She took a deep breath. "I thought we'd go over to the

Chicken Coop instead of to Fritzchen's Kitchen.'' The Chicken Coop was on the outskirts of town, not far from Wal-Mart, while Fritzchen's Kitchen was just down the street from the *Tri-State Tribune*.

Alex shrugged nonchalantly. "Sure, Mom. Just let me cash in my tickets first."

Sarah stood by anxiously while, at the glass counter displaying toys, games and other trinkets, her son traded the tickets he had won for a rubber lizard that, when wet, stuck to any smooth surface, and a yo-yo that lit up as it traveled along its string. She told herself she was being foolish, that there was no reason for Renzo to step foot inside the Penny Arcade. But it didn't help; she still fretted impatiently as Alex made his choices. When he had finished, she rushed him outside and into the Jeep.

"Gee, Mom, what's the big hurry?" Alex glanced at her curiously as he fastened his seat belt. "You don't have some other appointment or something, do you?"

"No...no. I guess I'm...just hungry, too," she lied, flashing him a tremulous smile. There was a lump in her throat as she looked at him and thought of losing him to Renzo.

She knew nothing about the law, nothing about her rights. Would it make a difference that on Alex's birth certificate she had listed his father as "unknown"? These days, there were DNA tests to prove or disprove paternity. Would Renzo, seeing Alex, insist on taking such tests? Would she and Alex be compelled to submit?

Undoubtedly, she was working herself up over nothing, Sarah tried to reassure herself. Renzo had no interest in her. He had never once in all these years attempted to get in touch with her. She didn't even know what he was doing in town, why he had come back. It was possible he was here only for a few days, to visit his parents, and that he would be gone before she knew it.

Still, fear gnawed at her. She could hardly choke down her meal at the Chicken Coop, the crispy fried chicken and Italian potato salad and coleslaw sticking in her throat. She carried most of it home in a doggy bag, only to wind up throwing it away later because it sat so long in the Jeep, in the summer heat, while she and Alex were in Wal-Mart. There, she bought him not only the new Power Rangers figure he had wanted, but also a water bazooka, a pack of baseball cards, a comic book and a bag of pogs. As she watched the clerk scan the items, then put them into a plastic sack, Sarah knew deep down inside that she was guilty of attempting to ensure Alex's approval and affection, in case his father should try to take him from her. She felt ashamed of herself and nearly insisted the clerk return everything to the store shelves.

Once home, she informed Alex that she had developed a dreadful migraine from the summer heat, leaving him to enjoy his new acquisitions in peace, while she retired to her bedroom. The lacy sheers at her windows and French doors were drawn against the brilliant light of the blistering sun outside, and the fan hanging from the ceiling turned, stirring the air. As though in a trance, Sarah slowly opened her jewelry box to withdraw from the very back the slender gold chain on which Renzo's high-school class ring still hung. Clutching the necklace in her fists, she lay down on her high tester bed in the cool semidarkness, closing her eyes and pressing the ring to her lips. Only then did she at

last acknowledge that it was not just panic about her son
that had assailed her when she had spied Renzo Cassavettes standing before the office of the *Tri-State Tribune.*

She still loved him.

Turning her face into her pillow so Alex would not hear,
she remembered her lost youth and innocence—and wept.

Eleven

The Tri-State Tribune

This news is old enough,
yet it is every day's news.

Measure for Measure
— William Shakespeare

The newspaper office was just as Renzo remembered it—
small, cluttered and old-fashioned in appearance—although sometime in the past twelve years, Joe Martinelli
had at least managed the transition from typewriters to
computers. As Renzo stood there just inside the doorway,
he was transported back to his childhood, when he had
used to come here with his father, fascinated by the process of writing, typesetting and printing. In those days, the
office had always smelled of fresh black ink, and Renzo
had loved the scent. He had loved, too, to play with the
blocks of type in various point sizes, as well as with the
compartmentalized wooden trays in which they had been
stored, before technology and Joe's profits, reinvested in

the newspaper, had made them obsolete. Nowadays both type and trays were sold at antique stores, a collectible reminder of a bygone era. In his apartment in Washington, D.C., where he had lived for the last few years, Renzo had had one of the trays, filled with type, hanging over his desk. The type had been arranged so people had had to study it for a moment to realize it had spelled out *Butterfly*. Now the tray, like everything else he owned, was packed away in a moving van en route to his hometown.

Once, Renzo had never intended to return here. But that was before he had happened to view a piece that had run on CNN's *Headline News*, a sixty-second clip of a campaign fund-raiser for former governor J. D. Holbrooke, who was now vying for a seat in the United States Senate. At first, seeing the film, Renzo had thought his eyes were playing tricks on him. So, because *Headline News* was broadcast every thirty minutes, he had watched the tape again. And then again, until he had been certain beyond a shadow of a doubt that it was Sarah Kincaid he had spied on Bubba Holbrooke's arm, the two of them standing just behind J.D., who was speaking from a podium.

Renzo had felt gut-wrenchingly sickened and angered by the sight. Surely when he had fled from town all those years back, it wasn't Bubba Holbrooke whom Sarah had wed barely three months later! Renzo couldn't believe that. He didn't *want* to believe it. That she could have turned so quickly from him to Bubba, of all the men she might have chosen, seemed incredible, agonizing. The pain of Sarah's betrayal, which Renzo had thought he had buried finally and forever long after receiving his mother's letter more than a decade ago, had once more welled like a flood tide inside him, bursting through the barriers he had so carefully and deliberately erected around his heart.

He had known no peace after that.

At last, he had forced himself to call his mother, to confront her, and the way Madonna had stammered and hesitated on the telephone at his questions had done more than stir up Renzo's desire to learn the simple facts. It had aroused his suspicions, for his finely honed investigative reporter's instincts had told him his mother was lying to him, that she had probably lied to him in her letter when she had claimed Sarah had married and moved away from town to parts unknown.

So Renzo had come back. Because he couldn't bear not knowing the truth. Because no matter how hard he had tried, how many women he had been through, trying to purge himself of the memory of Sarah Kincaid, he had never got her out of his system. Hardly a day had gone by in the past twelve years that he had not thought of her.

"May I help you, sir?" The newspaper's receptionist, a young woman scarcely out of high school, spoke, startling him from his reverie.

"No. Yes. Well, actually, I'm Renzo Cassavettes, Joe's son. So if it's all right, I'll just go on back." Renzo indicated the rear of the building, where Joe Martinelli's office was located and through whose windows Renzo could see his father hunched over the desk. "He...ah...doesn't know I'm in town, and I'd kind of like to surprise him."

"Renzo Cassavettes!" the receptionist exclaimed, wide-eyed. "*The* Renzo Cassavettes? The Racket Club... Whistle-blower...the—the Pulitzer Prize?"

"That's the one," he confirmed lightly, grinning at the young woman's awe as he strode past her desk and through the short, swinging door set in the wooden railing that separated the reception area from the rest of the newspaper office. He knocked on his father's door, then opened it. "Hello, Pop."

"Renzo!" As though he couldn't believe his eyes, Joe Martinelli got slowly to his feet. "Renzo." In a moment, the two men were exchanging bear hugs, clapping each other on the shoulders. Although in the more than a decade that had passed since he had left town, Renzo's parents had visited him more than once in the various cities in which he had lived, he still hadn't seen either his father or mother for the past two years. "Sit down. Sit down, Son," Joe urged, motioning toward a chair. "So. You've finally decided to come home, have you? To take me up on my offer, after all?"

"Yeah, Pop, I have."

"Renzo, are you sure?" Joe's eyes were searching as he gazed intently at his son. "I'd hate to think I pressured you into something you didn't want to do. Right now, you've got the world by the tail. You can write your own ticket, journalistically. Go anywhere. Be anything you want to be. Your mother and I . . . we're so proud of you, of all you've managed to accomplish. Who would have thought it? My son, a Pulitzer Prize winner!" The older man shook his head, as though he still couldn't quite believe it. "Coming back here, taking over the *Tri-State Tribune,* that's a long way from being a crackerjack investigative reporter in Washington. So are you sure this is what you want to do, Renzo?" Joe asked again.

"I'm sure, Pop. As the saying goes, I've been there, done that. So what's left? I figure managing my own newspaper's not a bad step up the ladder from where I am at the moment. Besides, I'm tired of big cities, Pop. My life in Washington is..." *Empty, solitary. I'm the proverbial soul alone in a crowd,* Renzo wanted to say. "Well, ever since the Racket Club, it's like I'm under a microscope, Pop. I made a lot of enemies by exposing such far-reaching political corruption—and not a few of those enemies are my own jealous, highly competitive colleagues, I'm afraid. They'd love nothing better than to watch me stumble and take a long, hard fall. And I just don't think I want to spend the rest of my days running on the fast track, trying to stay one step ahead of everybody who's breathing down my neck. I'd rather quit while I'm ahead. Besides, I don't mind telling you I've missed the slower pace of life in a small town, Pop. Being the editor and publisher of the *Tri-State Tribune* will give me a chance to take things easier for a while, time to try my hand at writing a book, time to enjoy life for a change. These past several years... well, all I've done is work, Pop. I couldn't have gone so far, so fast if I hadn't. But now, I'm tired. Tired? Hell. I'm just flat burned out. So by selling me the *Trib* so you and Mom can retire to Florida like you've always wanted, you're actually doing me a big favor."

"All right, then. I'll have all the necessary papers drawn up first thing next week," Joe declared, satisfied at last that this was indeed what Renzo really wanted, that he didn't just feel pressured and obligated to take over the newspaper. "Meanwhile, I've got a Sunday edition to finish up. How'd you like to help me, for old-time's sake?"

"I'd love to, Pop. What's doing? Lots of stuff about J. D. Holbrooke's senatorial campaign, I'll wager." Renzo's voice was carefully casual.

"Of course we're covering it. Having moved in a few political circles yourself these past several years, you're undoubtedly aware J.D.'s been news ever since he ran for governor and won. Everybody in town expected he'd serve at least two terms, especially since ZoeAnn obviously relished being the state's first lady. But then word got out that J.D. had cancer, a rumor he himself confirmed when he stepped down at the end of his term. It was pretty serious, and I think most people believed he wasn't going to live much longer. But J.D.'s always been a fighter and a survivor, and in the end, he licked the disease—just as he'll probably beat his opponents in the Senate race."

"So you think his chances of winning a seat are pretty good?"

"Yes, I do." Joe nodded. "He was a popular governor, and ZoeAnn was perceived as a gracious first lady, if a trifle distant. Well, are you ready to get to work, Son?"

"Sure, Pop." Renzo stood, cursing himself silently for suddenly being unable to ask the question that was uppermost in his mind: Was it because Sarah Kincaid was now Bubba Holbrooke's wife that she had been on his arm at J.D.'s fund-raiser?

Renzo realized then that part of him was afraid to learn the answer, afraid of what he would feel, of what he might do if the answer was yes. So he didn't ask. Instead, he worked alongside his father until the Sunday edition was put to bed. Then they went home, where Madonna Martinelli greeted her son happily but nervously and served his favorite supper. And still, Renzo did not ask the question that haunted him.

In the back of his mind lingered the knowledge that, no matter what, he loved his parents. He didn't want to have an unmendable breach between them and him, and he wasn't certain how he would feel toward them if he discovered they had lied to him and, in doing so, had cost him Sarah Kincaid. Or perhaps he had foolishly lost her himself that day at the quarry, when he had taunted Sonny Holbrooke—and that, too, was something that even now, after all these long years, Renzo didn't want to face.

Like Sarah herself, Sonny had also haunted him. Renzo remembered that strange, tentative, unexpected offer of friendship on the top of the high rock, and he felt that his life had been somehow diminished because that friendship had been so abruptly snatched away from him before it had ever really begun. There was, as well, the fact that as Renzo had grown older and the shock, pain and disbelief of that fatal day had worn off, Papa Nick's casually spoken words in the long, sleek black car had returned to him: that his shoulder had displayed what had appeared to Papa Nick as a flesh wound from a bullet.

In later years, those words had come to trouble Renzo distinctly whenever he thought of them. Now he felt that Papa Nick had been trying to tell him something—and that he had not understood what it was. Sometimes he would touch his shoulder, where the wasp—or had it been a bee?—had stung him, and he would be transported back to the quarry. He would hear the summer stillness broken by the blaring music, the backfiring of Junior Barlow's clunker, and in Renzo's mind, the sound would become a gunshot, and he would wonder if someone had, in fact, tried to kill him. But why? Had Papa Nick's words been a warning? Of what nature? Why would anyone have wanted to kill him, Renzo Cassavettes, a twenty-two-year-old who had known blessedly little of the shadowy circles his mobster father and sluttish mother had moved in? The only crime he had ever committed had been the taking of Sarah Kincaid's innocence—a crime in the eyes of the law, technically, since she had been just seventeen. But neither he nor she would have called it that. At least, not then.

Did she look back on that day now with regret and re-sentment, he wondered, seeing him as nothing more than a callous seducer and herself as his trusting victim? Deep down inside, Renzo feared she probably did. The thought made him sick inside. He had loved her. If he were honest with himself, he must admit he loved her still. Otherwise, he wouldn't give a damn whom she had married. He wouldn't ever have come back here to this town.

Temporarily installed in his old room at the Martinelli bungalow on Elm Street, Renzo lay in bed that night and thought of Sarah lying in Bubba Holbrooke's arms—and fantasized about torturing his old enemy to death very slowly or pumping him full of bullet holes.

At three in the morning, Renzo awakened gasping and in a cold sweat, his heart pounding horrifically. It was his old, familiar nightmare that had held him in its terrifying grip, the interminable, dusty road beneath his bare feet a monstrous, writhing serpent, maw gaping, venom-drip-ping fangs poised to strike. It had bitten him on the side of his shoulder, a sharp, puncturing sting, and then had swallowed him whole. Inside the road-snake, he had tumbled endlessly down into the dark, cold acid of its stomach, where he had spied a body floating in a tangle of half-digested bones and other hideous debris. Only this time, when he had gingerly rolled the corpse over, the face hadn't belonged to Sonny Holbrooke.

It had been Bubba's.

Twelve

Bubba

"Say, boys! if you give me just another
        whiskey I'll be glad,
And I'll draw right here a picture of the
        face that drove me mad."

The Face upon the Floor
—Hugh Antoine D'Arcy

Bubba Holbrooke took another long swallow from the glass of whiskey he held in his hand. It was late, and he was tired—not to mention thoroughly bored by the discussion currently taking place in his father's study. Were it not for the fact that if J.D.'s race for the Senate were successful, he and ZoeAnn would pack up and move to Washington, D.C., Bubba wouldn't have volunteered to pass out so much as a single campaign flyer. But if J.D. won, Bubba would be left in charge of Field-Yield, Inc. again, as he had been when his father had been installed in the state's governor's mansion in the capital. Of course, J.D. would undoubtedly leave Evie behind once more, to manage those things he didn't trust Bubba to deal with at the fertilizer plant. But Bubba hadn't paid any heed to Evie's looking over his shoulder before—and he wouldn't this time, either. Besides which, the campaign allowed Bubba to spend a great deal more time with Sarah Kincaid than she would normally have permitted.

Bleary eyed, he gazed at her now, wondering what her reaction would be if she knew he was seeing not all the various campaign materials, but her naked body spread out on the massive old desk that dominated the study. In his mind, she was sweating and writhing frantically beneath him, and he was inside her, making her beg and scream for more. Not that that was likely to happen anytime soon, Bubba told himself disgustedly. Ever since she had started working for Field-Yield, Inc. five years ago and he had first really noticed her, Sarah had held him at arm's length. And the harder she had tried to keep him at bay, the more determined Bubba had grown to possess her. He hadn't been able to believe this beautiful, cool, poised woman was the same little "Coal Lump" Kincaid his sister, Evie, had used to tease so unmercifully at school.

Adding to Sarah's attraction had been the air of mystery, the touch of scandal that had clung to her. She had borne a child out of wedlock, and so far as Bubba knew, she had never named the father. That she just didn't seem the type had further fascinated him—to say nothing of the fact that, inexplicably, his notoriously demanding and tightfisted father had not only hired her, fresh out of college, to head up the entire advertising-and-promotions department at Field-Yield, Inc., but at an extremely generous salary, besides.

At first, Bubba had been struck by the horrible, jealousy-arousing suspicion that Sarah was his father's mistress, that her illegitimate son was none other than J.D.'s little bastard. But several weeks of spying on his father had finally convinced Bubba that while J.D. did, in fact, discreetly maintain a mistress, it wasn't Sarah Kincaid—which had made his father's actions all the more bewildering and Sarah herself all the more intriguing.

In the beginning, she had deftly turned aside Bubba's flattery, eluded his passes and refused every single one of his invitations, putting him off with one excuse after another: her child, her widowed mother, the fact that he was her boss. It had taken him two and a half years of carefully concealing his frustration and impatience, of cooling himself down with endless cold showers, just to persuade her to go out to dinner with him. And then she hadn't even let him kiss her good-night at the door! No woman had ever treated Bubba Holbrooke like that. All his life, women had fallen all over themselves to go out with him, to go to bed with him. But neither his blond good looks, the fact that he had been a star quarterback in high school, his position as manager of Field-Yield, Inc., nor his being J. D. Holbrooke's son and heir had carried one bit of weight with Sarah Kincaid. She had been maddeningly unimpressed. For the first time in his life, Bubba had found a woman who hadn't literally dropped to her knees to please him—and it had driven him crazy with wanting her.

Despite that they had dated more or less steadily after that, she had kept him dangling for another two and a half years now—obstinately refusing to share his bed. He had alternately cajoled, pleaded and threatened, all to no avail.

"Look, I was young and foolish once, Bubba," she had told him, "and I made a bad mistake. And although I don't regret it, since it gave me my son, I'm not so stupid as to repeat it, either. It's taken me a long time and a lot of hard work to live down the shame, the scandal and the stigma of my having borne an illegitimate child in this town, and I don't intend to throw away everything I've gained just because you want to go to bed with me."

"Well, you don't need to worry about any of that, Sarah honey. Really. I'm not an irresponsible boy. When the time comes, I'll protect you, I swear!" Bubba had insisted.

"Yeah, right," Sarah had replied with uncharacteristic curtness and sarcasm, her lip curling. "You know something, Bubba? That's exactly what Alex's father said. And that's why I'll never believe or trust another man again where there's a bedroom involved."

Nothing Bubba had said or done had moved her from this rigid stance. He had broken up with her more than half a dozen times over it. Sarah had merely shrugged, unconcerned, unaffected, and told him coolly that he must suit himself in the matter, that she certainly understood if he no longer wished to go on dating her.

Finally, it had belatedly occurred to Bubba that she was holding out for a wedding ring. After much long, hard contemplation, he had decided it was worth giving up his freedom to have her—besides which, no woman in her right mind expected a man to be faithful, anyway—and he had asked her to marry him. But to his total shock, Sarah had politely but firmly rejected his proposal.

"I have to think about Alex and what's best for him—and to tell you the truth, Bubba, I'm afraid he doesn't really much like you," she had said.

"Shit, Sarah! He doesn't even hardly know me! If you'd just give me a chance with the boy, I know I could win him over. But, no, you won't let me take him anywhere. I have practically to twist your arm off just to get you to invite me over to supper with him. I never saw a woman protect a kid so damned much. And that's exactly what's wrong with him—the boy's been mollycoddled by you and your mother all his life. He needs a man around to teach him a few things. But you won't move in with me—or let me move in with you. Hell, after two and a half frigging years, you still won't even go to bed with me, no matter that I've done everything I can think of to show you how serious I am about you, Sarah. Jesus Christ! I don't know any man worth being called one who would hang around as long as I have without getting a single damned night of sex for it in return! It's enough to drive a man clean off his rocker!"

"Are those the kind of things you want to teach Alex, Bubba? All about swearing and sleeping around?"

"Well, no, darlin', of course not." Bubba had realized his mistake immediately. "But for heaven's sake, Sarah! You just can't go on sheltering the boy from reality like this. It ain't healthy, and that's a fact. Besides, what did it ever do for you, get for you out of life? You just sneaked around behind your parents' backs, anyway, no matter how strict they were. In fact, you probably did it precisely *because* they were so damned strict! And as a result, you wound up spreading your legs for some no-good young bum who left you high and dry and pregnant! And if you ask me, that's the whole damned reason you've got this unnatural hang-up about sex! I'm beginning to think the bastard must have raped you or something and that's why you're so frigging frigid! Hell, I can even understand what drove the poor guy to do it. I'm so nuts from your behavior that I'm half tempted to force you myself, damn it!'' Bubba's voice had been harsh with anger and desire, his breathing labored, and his narrowed blue eyes had gleamed in a way that had made Sarah take a hasty step back from him, her own eyes wary.

For a long moment, silence had stretched tautly between them. Then, her throat working with emotion, she had stated quietly, "Bubba, it's not your fault. It's mine. I'm just not cut out for the kind of relationship you want to have with me. I knew that, and I should never have agreed to go out with you in the first place. I really think it's best if we don't see each other anymore.''

That idea had scared him so badly that he had apologized profusely, declaring that there was no excuse for anything he had said, that he was the world's biggest idiot and heel and that he ought to be horsewhipped. He had barely managed to placate her, and he had left feeling as though he were a dumb cluck more henpecked than any other man in town. That thought had been absolutely humiliating!

Now, not for the first time, Bubba asked himself why he tolerated Sarah's mental abuse and cock teasing. Who in the hell did she think she was, anyway? She was Coal

Lump Kincaid, mining trash, at the best no virgin, at the worst an outright slut. He could do a hell of a lot better. His entire family had told him so on more than one occasion.

Yet, as he went on gazing at her in the glowing lamplight that illuminated the study, Bubba could not prevent the tightening of his groin. She was beautiful—not in the icy, classically lovely, blond fashion of his sister, Evie, but in a dark, haunting way that made him think of sunlit green meadows, shaded summer ponds and hushed woods long with cool shadows. In his mind's eye, he could see Sarah in those surroundings, laid out on the grass, sunbeams streaming through the leaves of the trees to dapple her naked body, flushed and dewy from his lovemaking. Bubba wondered if that was how she had looked, spread for her lover, and the thought filled him anew with jealousy and rage toward the unknown father of her son.

Who had the man been? Bubba asked himself for the umpteenth time. For more than a decade, Sarah had maintained her silence on that subject, had never revealed the man's name. Not knowing drove Bubba insane. He looked at every man in town and wondered: *Is he the one who had her?*

"Was this the one you liked, Bubba?" Sarah's voice startled him from his half-drunken reverie. He shook his head, trying to clear it, to rouse himself from his lethargy as she held up for his inspection a recently taken publicity photo of his father.

"Why waste your time asking Bubba's opinion?" Evie sneered, glancing at him with disgust. "He couldn't care less about Daddy's campaign. The only reason my dear brother bothers to do anything at all to help is because he's all hot and bothered about *you*, Sarah—although I confess the reason for that continues to escape me.''

"Evie!" J.D. spoke sharply, frowning and shaking his white-haired head like an old, woolly albino buffalo. "I will not tolerate that kind of talk from you."

"Now, Daddy—" taking her arm in his, Evie smiled up at him as flirtatiously as a child "—it's no less than what everybody else in town is saying, and what's more, you know it. Everybody else is just too polite to say it to your face, that's all."

"Look, it's late, and we're all tired," Sarah declared before J.D. could reply. She coolly ignored Evie. "And I promised Tiffany I'd be home by eleven at the latest." Tiffany Haskell was the young college girl who baby-sat Alex at night. Although Sarah thought that at age eleven, he was now old enough to stay by himself during the day, she still wouldn't leave him alone after dark. And despite Alex's insistence that he wasn't a child, that girls only a year older than he were baby-sitters themselves, Sarah had refused to budge on the issue. The farmhouse was relatively isolated, and if anything ever happened to Alex, she knew she wouldn't be able to bear it. "So I really need to be going. Why don't we finish the rest of this sometime tomorrow in your office, J.D.?" she suggested, beginning to gather up the campaign materials strewn across the desk.

"I'll drive you home, Sarah," Bubba announced, hauling himself with obvious effort from the burgundy leather wing chair in which he'd been sprawled, his tie loosened,

collar opened, legs stretched out on the matching otto-
man before him.

"There's no need for that. I've got my own car."

"Then I'll follow you home. You know I don't like you
out by yourself on the country roads after dark. Anything
might happen to you—a flat tire, an overheated engine.
God knows, it's hot enough outside to fry eggs on the
sidewalk."

"Bubba, you know Sarah carries her cellular phone in
her purse everywhere she goes." Evie grimaced at her
brother. "So it isn't as though she couldn't call somebody
for help if she needed it."

"Nevertheless, even in this day and age, it's still a mark
of a gentleman to see a lady home, Evie," J.D. observed,
pouring himself two fingers of whiskey from the Baccarat
decanter on the bar, then settling his bulk into the chair
Bubba had vacated. Reaching out to lift the lid of the
wooden box on the end table, J.D. extracted a hand-rolled
cigar. "So you go on, Bubba, make sure Sarah gets home
safely. We'll reconvene tomorrow afternoon in my office."

"Thank you, J.D." Sarah finished packing her black
leather portfolio, then picked up her handbag. She knew
that as much as J.D. liked and respected her, he still didn't
approve of her as his son's possible future wife. Yet J.D.
never failed to ensure that Bubba saw her home when the
hour was late. In fact, on those occasions when she and
Bubba had been quarreling and he balked at accompanying her, J.D. actually insisted on it. It was almost as though
he were terrified by the thought that some mishap would
befall her, and that puzzled Sarah no end. Although she

was extremely good at her job, it wasn't exactly as though either Field-Yield, Inc. or J.D.'s senatorial campaign would collapse without her. So she couldn't think of any logical reason why her well-being should be of such seeming importance to him.

As she glanced around the study to be certain she wasn't leaving anything behind, it was all Sarah could do to repress a shudder. She loathed J.D.'s study in the Holbrookes' old, white-columned mansion. It was paneled in wood turned so dark with age and cigar smoke that being in the room made her feel as though she were inside a mausoleum whose walls were closing in on her. Adding to this macabre effect was the fact that on practically every large, square oak panel were mounted the stuffed heads of various animals, some big, some small. In addition to skeet shooting, the Holbrookes had all hunted for sport for years, and they were all excellent shots. The animal heads were their trophies, and the sight of so many dead, glassy eyes staring down at her from the walls gave Sarah the creeps. She always felt as though the beasts were silently condemning her for fraternizing with the enemy, and she was relieved to be escaping from the study.

After bidding both J.D. and Evie good-night, Sarah drove home slowly enough that Bubba, even in his inebriated state, had no difficulty following her. As she glanced at his headlights in her rearview mirror, she sighed, half wishing he would lose his way on the dark, country roads. She even toyed with the idea of abruptly speeding away from him, making an unexpected turn and killing her own headlights, so he couldn't find her. But that was childish and would only prove fruitless in any event, since he knew where she lived.

If only Bubba would be content with seeing that she got safely inside the house. But Sarah knew from experience that in his current condition, he would insist on coming in, on having another drink and on once more pressuring her to sleep with him. She had had a long, exhausting day, and all she was interested in was a shower and then bed. Instead, she would be compelled to entertain Bubba and fend off his advances, she thought wearily.

Why had she ever agreed to go on dating him? she asked herself, cursing the weakness that had led her to become involved with him in the first place. But he had been so persistent, and she had been so lonely, especially these last few years. Her mother's arthritis had grown increasingly debilitating—Iris Kincaid had never truly been right mentally since her husband's death, besides—and finally a few years back, Sarah had been forced to sell her parents' house and to place her mother in a nursing home. Since Mama's Social Security payments didn't amount to much, Sarah was grateful her father's pension was enough to cover all the medical expenses, although she had been startled to learn how much her mother received monthly from the Genovese Coal Mining Co. Initially fearing there had been some sort of mistake and that she would eventually wind up having to repay much of the money when the error was finally discovered, Sarah had made an appointment with Papa Nick Genovese to explain her concerns. But to her surprise, Papa Nick had assured her the pension amounts were, in fact, correct.

"Your late papa...he was one of my best and hardest workers, Miss Kincaid, and he was a smart businessman, besides. *Capisce?* He put away as mucha money as he coulda in his retirement plan and boughta stock in Genovese Coal Mining, too, every time we offered that option. So you donna havva to worry none about your sick mama. She'll be taken real good care of in that nursing home, and it wonna cost you an arm and a leg, neither. It belongs to a friend of mine, and he ain't in the business of ripping off poor, ailing widows or their families." Papa Nick had paused for a moment, then continued, abruptly changing the subject. "How's that young son of yours doing, Miss Kincaid? I see him sometimes. Looka like a real fine, strong, handsome boy. You oughta be right proud of him."

"I—I am, Mr. Genovese," Sarah had replied, nervous, as she always was, when anyone mentioned Alex. "Very proud."

"Papa Nick. Everybody calls me Papa Nick. Well, that'sa good you're so proud of your son. That'sa just fine, then. Some women wouldna been. They'dda been ashamed. But you got not'ing to be ashamed of. So you hold your head high, and you make that boy of yours do the same. You bringa him outta to the Chicken Coop sometime. I gotta small interest in that restaurant, on accounta it's owned by a couple of Mama Rosa's cousins. Mama Rosa...that'sa my wife, the best woman in the world—present company excepted, of course." Papa Nick had winked at Sarah broadly, chuckling. "We been married more 'n fifty years now, and I love her even more today than I did alla those years ago on our wedding day.

There ain't not'ing in life to take the place of *amore,* Miss Kincaid, because life ain't not'ing without it. You remember that now, you hear?''

"Yes, I will, Papa Nick," she had said quietly.

But that had been a lie, because she didn't want to remember, Sarah told herself now as, from the golden-oldies station on the Jeep radio, the strains of Jimmy Ruffin's "What Becomes of the Broken Hearted" drifted. The song brought sudden tears to her eyes. Amore, she thought dully. *You didn't say what one does when it goes out of your life forever, Papa Nick. When your heart's been broken so badly that no matter what you do, you just can't seem to put the pieces back together.*

"Forget it, Sarah. You're tired, that's all," she muttered aloud to herself. "And having to spend the evening in J.D.'s dead-animal trophy case always upsets you. Besides which, seeing Renzo Cassavettes again has thrown you for a loop—not to mention that the last thing you need tonight is to have to deal with Bubba in a drunken stupor!" She reached irritably to switch off the radio, only to draw her hand back at the last minute, letting the tune continue to play, reveling in the music, despite its melancholy lyrics. These days, except for Boyz II Men, there was no one around who equaled Motown in its finest hour, she thought. It was as though the song spoke only to her, telling her that happiness was just an illusion, filled with sadness and confusion.

Sighing heavily, Sarah hit her turn signal, wheeling the Jeep on to her gravel drive, pulling slowly to a halt in front of the farmhouse.

"Bubba, it's late, and I know you've got to be at the office early tomorrow morning for that meeting with the distributors," she called to him as he parked behind her and got out of his car. "So why don't you just go on home? There's no need for you to come inside. Really."

"Nonsense. I've got to see that you and Alex are locked up all nice and tight, don't I? You know the kind of nuts who're running around these days, even in a small town like ours, what with all the damned white trash, niggers, and dagos all over the place. I suspect it's just a matter of time before we're inundated with Columbian drug lords, Jamaican gangs, Chinese tongs, Russian mobsters and just plain old ignorant boat people, too. Jesus! Nobody's safe anywhere anymore, and that's a fact."

"Bubba, you know how I feel about talk like that. It's ugly and bigoted."

"Yeah, well, just because you don't like to hear it doesn't mean it ain't all true, darlin'. Whole damned country's going to hell in a handbasket. America, the Promised Land. Crooks in Congress, wimps in the White House, the wretched refuse of every teeming shore taking over the entire United States. Ought to rip that plaque off the Statue of Liberty and put up one that reads 'No Vacancies, So Go Home or Go to Hell!' " He walked toward her, stumbling a little and sloshing whiskey from the glass he had brought from home and now carried in one hand. "Gimme your key, honey. And while you're at it, why don't you gimme your heart, too? Or have you still got that locked up as tight as your damned thighs?"

"Bubba, go on home. You're drunker than I thought— and insulting. The mood you're in, we're only going to wind up having another fight, and I'm just not up to it tonight.''

"The Snow Queen has spoken, and her loyal subject must heed her icy dictates or be banished forever from her wintry realm. Very well. I promise to be good. There. Are you satisfied now? Gimme your key, damn it!''

Too exhausted to argue further, Sarah let him have it, so he could open the front door, hating herself for not trying harder to send him packing. He wasn't the man she wanted in her life and never would be. She knew that. It was deceitful and despicable of her to go on seeing him for no better reason than that she felt she should attempt to get on with her life and provide a father figure for Alex. Not that Bubba was an ideal candidate, by any means. But in a town this size, there just weren't a whole lot of choices available, especially for an unwed mother from Miners' Row, who, as Lucille had observed that day at Shear Style, wasn't getting any younger and wasn't likely to get any better offer, either. Regardless of his many faults, Bubba was considered *the* prime catch in town. So despite her misgivings, Sarah kept telling herself how lucky she was to have attracted his attention, hoping to convince herself of that fact. But it wasn't working.

Tiffany greeted them in the living room. "Alex is upstairs asleep, Sarah. I fed him supper and helped him with his homework for summer school. Then he practiced his saxophone lessons for a while, and after that, we played a couple of board games. Everything went fine, no trouble at all. Oh, I also cleaned up the kitchen for you and did a few loads of laundry, so you'll need to check the clothes drier before you go to bed.''

"Tiffany, you're a doll. Thank you so much! Honestly, I just don't know what I'd do without you," Sarah said with heartfelt sincerity and gratitude, taking the appropriate amount of cash from her billfold and handing it to the younger woman.

"Hey, no problem. I figure it all evens out, what with my eating supper here so much and doing my own homework at your kitchen table. Besides, since I'm majoring in child psychology at the university, Alex is kind of a case study for me, anyway."

"Yeah, I'll bet," Bubba muttered, taking another gulp of whiskey before he staggered toward the tea wagon on which Sarah kept her limited supply of liquor. "Kid's going to wind up in prison or a padded cell!"

"I'm sorry, Sarah." Her eyes stricken, Tiffany bit her lower lip, embarrassed. "I—I didn't mean it like that...like Alex needs a psychological evaluation. All children just interest me. You know that."

"Yes, I do. So please don't pay Bubba any mind. He's drunk and in one of his mean moods, besides."

"All right, then. Good night, Sarah, Mr. Holbrooke."

"Good night, Tiffany. Thanks again, and drive safe." Sarah closed the front door behind the baby-sitter, then turned angrily to confront Bubba. "What's the matter with you? Don't you have any manners at all? You were rude to me, rude to Tiffany. There's just no excuse for it! You're not *that* drunk. So I can only think it's something more than just the whiskey talking tonight, isn't it?"

"No. Yes. I mean... Oh, hell! If you must know, yes. I'm so pissed off that I'm ready to explode! I've kept it bottled up inside me all day, and I guess it's just spilling out onto you, since I couldn't bring myself to tell the old man or Evie, either one. And I'm depressed something awful on top of it, besides." Bubba flung himself onto the goose-necked couch, abruptly stripping off his loosened tie and unbuttoning his shirt halfway down to reveal his muscular, tanned chest matted with fine blond hair.

"Do you want to talk about it, to tell me what's troubling you?"

"Sure, why in the hell not? There's no reason for it to matter to you one way or another—except that I still can't believe you defended him that day."

"Defended who? What day? What are you talking about, Bubba?" Puzzled, Sarah joined him on the Victorian couch, slipping off her heeled sandals, rubbing her aching feet and then tucking them up under her.

"I'm talking about Renzo Cassavettes, damn it! After all these years, that son of a bitch has actually dared to come back here! I saw him today in town. The nerve of that bastard! Can you believe it?" Bubba's words came tumbling out. "He murdered my little brother, ran off to escape the justice he deserved, got away scot-free and now has the unmitigated gall to show his face in this town again! Well, some of us haven't forgotten what he did. We'll *never* forget! And one way or another, I'm going to make that fucking wop pay! I should have killed him years ago, when I had the chance. Then Sonny'd still be alive. He was the best of the Holbrookes. My God. My father worshiped the very ground Sonny ever walked on. He always called him the 'golden boy,' said Sonny was brilliant, that he was going to be president of the United States someday, another JFK. Hell, if you want to know the truth, I think that's the only reason the old man ever went into politics to begin with—some twisted way to honor Sonny's memory. Evie and I were never enough for him. We've spent our entire lives trying to measure up—and failing. Because how could we ever win? We were competing with a damned ghost! Poor Evie. There's nothing more pathetic than a daddy's girl who doesn't have Daddy's love and approval. Why do you think she's such a bitch, been married and divorced twice already and is even now working on a third trip to splitsville? Parker Delaney wasn't dear old Daddy. Tommy Lee Archer wasn't dear old Daddy. And Skeets Grenville ain't dear old Daddy, either.''

"Sonny's death was an accident, Bubba. A terrible tragedy," Sarah insisted, not caring about Evie's marital woes, but focusing on his remarks about Renzo instead, a tiny, sudden flame of fear licking through her at the thought that what had happened that day at the quarry should all be raked up again.

"That's what you said that day, too," Bubba observed. "I'll never forget it. Shit. Knowing you, how you always root for the underdog, you probably even believe it. But it's just not true, Sarah. Renzo Cassavettes deliberately shoved my little brother off that rock, murdered him as sure as I'm sitting here right now."

"I know that's what you think, Bubba, but it was ruled an accident at the inquest." Sarah wanted desperately to believe the inquest finding, because even now, she didn't want to admit to herself that deep down inside, she had always harbored a tiny but terrible doubt about Renzo's innocence that day at the quarry.

"Yeah. But let me tell you, there was something real funny about how that inquest turned out, about my father's behavior that morning."

"Funny? In what way? What do you mean?"

"Well, at first, the old man was totally out of his mind with grief over Sonny's death, was absolutely convinced it had been murder, pure and simple. He was so loony and in such a towering rage that he smashed the glass in the gun case—didn't even bother to unlock it—and hauled out his thirty-aught-six and loaded it for bear, yelling that he was going to blast Renzo Cassavettes full of bullet holes, make him regret the sorry day he'd ever been born, and so forth. Then, when he found out Renzo had fled, the old man lit into Sheriff Laidlaw, punched him in the nose and shouted that if he ever wanted to win another damned election in this town, he'd better get off his fat, doughnut ass real quick and track Renzo down and bring him back to stand trial. But of course, that didn't happen. And then, the morning of the inquest, Papa Nick pulled up to our house, in that long black car of his, with that bull-necked chauffeur, Guido, at the wheel. Papa Nick said he'd come to pay his respects and offer his condolences on Sonny's death. Right after that, at the inquest, my father stood up and apologized for all his recent actions and accusations, claimed he'd been crazed with grief, that he knew Renzo had never murdered Sonny, that it had all been an accident."

"And you think Papa Nick somehow forced J.D. to say that?"

"Damned straight I do! Hell, everybody in town knows what Papa Nick is. He probably told my old man he'd find himself wearing a pair of cement shoes and being pitched in a quarry if he didn't lay off Cassavettes.''

"Still, why would Papa Nick threaten your father, Bubba? Renzo wasn't anything to Papa Nick—at least, not so far as I ever heard tell.''

"Well, you know how it is, Sarah. All those guinea bastards are related one way or another, and they all always hang together, anyway, no matter what. Besides which, it was always rumored that Cassavettes's father— his *real* father, not Joe Martinelli—was a small-time mobster in the big city. Maybe he used to do Papa Nick's dirty work or something, so Papa Nick felt he owed Cassavettes a favor. I don't know. What I *do* know is that whatever Papa Nick said to my old man that morning caused him to back off big-time. So I don't care what was decided at the inquest. Renzo Cassavettes murdered my little brother—and for that, he's going to pay.''

Silence descended at that. Even though Sarah tried to convince herself it was the whiskey talking, Bubba's remarks nevertheless worried her. Seeing Renzo again had stirred up old, painful memories for them both. What else might his coming back to town incite? She had a sudden, bad feeling about all this, a strange foreboding as she remembered the dust devil she had seen dancing on the horizon the day of Renzo's return. In retrospect, it now seemed an ominous portent, somehow. A fragment from the Book of Hosea echoed in her mind: *They have sown the wind, and they shall reap the whirlwind.* She shivered at the thought, for might it not be said that twelve years ago at the quarry, she, Renzo, Bubba and all the rest had sown the wind? Would they now reap the whirlwind?

"Why're you shivering? It's so hot outside that I know you can't possibly be cold," Bubba murmured huskily in her ear, his arm sliding around her shoulders, pulling her near. Obviously, now that he had vented his spleen, his thoughts had turned amorous. "Except that you're always cold . . . cold and cruel to me, Sarah, when you know how crazy I am about you. What more must I do? I've done everything but stand on my head for you. . . ."

His mouth closed over hers, his tongue thrusting between her lips, tasting of whiskey. It wasn't the first time he had ever kissed her. But tonight . . . tonight was different, somehow. Sarah was tired, and her guard was down. So instead of pulling away, she let him kiss her, feeling strangely as though dark, powerful, fatal forces over which she had no control were even now rushing to take hold of her, dragging her down into something terrible and terrifying. She clung to Bubba as though to prevent herself from being sucked under by the fearsome, unknown thing, and he set down his whiskey glass and tightened his grip upon her. He was rich and handsome. He would keep her safe, if not happy, if only she gave him the chance, she thought. If only she could respond to him . . .

Unbidden, Renzo's dark, dangerously good-looking image rose in her mind, and suddenly, it was he who was kissing her, entwining his fingers roughly in her mass of long hair, sliding his palms over her breasts and up her stockinged legs, unbuttoning her jacket and pushing her skirt up about her thighs.

"Sarah . . . sweet Sarah," Bubba groaned.

His words—an echo from the past—jerked her abruptly, sharply, back to her senses. Good God! What was she thinking of? What was she doing? The buttons of her short-sleeved suit jacket were halfway undone; her lacy, front-closing bra was unfastened; her breasts were bare. Crying out softly, she shoved Bubba away and scrambled up from the sofa, her face ashen, her eyes huge, one trembling hand crushing the edges of her jacket together tightly, the other tugging down her skirt.

"Damn you, Sarah!" Bubba rasped, stumbling to his feet and taking an ominous step toward her, his eyes narrowed with anger and glinting with desire. "Damn you!"

Warily, she backed away from him, stretching out her hand to hold him at bay. "Please, Bubba. Please go. You're drunk, and I—I don't want you to do anything we'll both regret later. I'm sorry. I shouldn't have encouraged you. I—I don't know what got into me—"

"Well, I do, damn you to hell and back! I'm not so frigging drunk that I don't know when a woman is kissing me and thinking of somebody else! There were three of us on that couch a moment ago, when there ought to have been only two. Who is he, Sarah? Alex's father? Yes...yes, of course. That's it, isn't it? My God! How could I have been so blind, so stupid? After all these years, you're still carrying a torch for him, aren't you? I thought you were cold, frigid, frightened of a man's touch, and just needed some time. But that's not it at all, is it? There's fire in you, after all. It just doesn't burn for anybody but him." Without warning, his reflexes as quick as those of a snake striking despite his inebriated condition, Bubba reached out and grabbed her, giving her a rough little shake, making her gasp and quiver with apprehension. "Who was he?

Is he? Do you still see him? Damn you! Tell me his name, Sarah!''

''No, I won't tell you anything! It was over a long time ago between him and me, and it's none of your business, besides! Let me go, Bubba. I want you to leave. Now.''

''Fine. I'm leaving. But I'll be back, Sarah. So don't think I won't. And one of these days, I'm going to find out who he was ... *is* ... and when I do, I'll kill him. Then it'll be ended at long last, and I'll drive him from your heart and mind if it takes the rest of our lives for me to do it!''

With that Parthian shot, Bubba grabbed up his discarded tie and stormed from the house, slamming the door behind him. His Corvette spewed gravel in its wake.

Her hands still shaking, Sarah quickly turned the dead bolt, then leaned weakly against the door, feeling as though her knees were about to give out from under her. She blamed herself for what had just happened. She blamed Renzo Cassavettes, for had he never come back to town, had she never seen him again, she wouldn't have thought of him while Bubba had kissed her. She would have emptied her mind instead, forcing herself to think of nothing at all, as she had always done before.

Finally, after a long moment in which she struggled for composure, she poured herself a glass of red wine, turned off the lamps and trudged upstairs, pausing only to look in on Alex. To her relief, he hadn't been wakened by her altercation with Bubba, but was still asleep, his long, thick black lashes crescent smudges against his still-chubby cheeks, his beautifully shaped mouth parted a little. He suffered from seasonal allergies, so his turned-up nose always had a tiny crease across it from where he rubbed it.

The sound of his gentle snoring filled the room. As always, the sight of him sleeping brought a smile of love and tenderness to Sarah's face. No matter what, she would never regret having her son. The joy he had brought into her life far outweighed the pain. Gently, she tucked the top sheet more closely around him and settled his raggedy old teddy bear, which he still refused to part with, more firmly in his grasp. Then she continued on down the hall to her own room.

There, she stripped and showered, then drew a long, sleeveless nightgown of diaphanous, lace-edged lawn over her naked body. Pulling aside the lacy white sheers that covered the bank of windows and pair of French doors that ran the length of one wall of her room, she stepped outside onto the deck beyond, as she did every night, regardless of the lateness of the hour. This was her quiet time, her moment of reflection and introspection, treasured and as carefully guarded as her heart. Suspended from the overhanging roof was the collection of wind chimes she had started before Alex was born, refusing to admit to herself that they reminded her of the woods at the abandoned quarry and of bluebottle-fairies dancing on the wind while Renzo had made love to her. The wind chimes tinkled now as the night air stirred sluggishly. Moonlight slanted down, and from the shadowy edge of the yard, where honeysuckle vines sprawled in riotous profusion, the sweet perfume of their tiny white blossoms floated, and fireflies flashed in the dark.

Bubba was crazy, she thought as she slowly sipped the sweet red wine she had poured herself earlier. A madman. Still, wasn't it a madness she could understand, that she could relate to, that she suffered from herself? His accusing words still rang in her ears: *After all these years, you're still carrying a torch for him, aren't you?* If she were honest with herself, Sarah knew she must admit she was. And wasn't that crazy? What woman in her right mind went on loving a man who, until this summer, she hadn't even seen, hadn't even heard from for more than a decade, a man who didn't even know or care if she still existed somewhere on this earth—to whose very ends she once would have followed him?

But that was the road not taken. She would never know where it would have led her, to what far horizon. Her world was bounded by the limits of the small town in which she had stayed behind, only its sky infinite, stretching above her to places she would never see, would never know, could only imagine as she gazed at the starry firmament.

There was nothing on earth like the Midwestern sky at night, she thought. The stars shone so brightly and hung so low that it was almost as though she could have stretched out her hand and plucked them one by one from the heavens. She had used to imagine that somewhere, unbeknown to her, Renzo was standing outside, too, staring up at the same black-velvet sky, the same pearl moon, the same diamond stars, and thinking of her, as she thought of him. Was he even at this moment standing in the yard of the Martinellis' white bungalow on Elm Street? she wondered now. Was he looking up through the branches of the ancient, towering trees that had bequeathed their name to the old, brick-paved avenue? Did he ever remember, as she remembered? Did he ever lie in his bed in the still of a summer's night and long to feel her naked body pressed close against his in the darkness?

Somewhere in the distance, an owl hooted and a solitary coyote bayed at the silver-glowing moon, lonesome, wrenching sounds that tugged at Sarah's heartstrings. Sighing heavily, turning to go back inside, she drew her hand idly across the strands of rainbow prisms that dangled near the French doors. The colored crystals of the wind chimes struck one another gently; their forlorn music soughed in the night, echoing the sad song in her heart.

Stepping inside, she drew the sheers shut and turned out her light. But she lay awake in bed for a long while afterward in the darkness, unable to sleep, yearning wistfully for the lost, halcyon days of her youth, when life had been simple and sweet, and Renzo Cassavettes had loved her.

Thirteen

Searching for Sarah

Does the imagination dwell the most
Upon a woman won or a woman lost?

The Tower
—William Butler Yeats

Since coming home, Renzo had been principally occupied with the newspaper and with his parents. They had put their Elm Street bungalow, in which they had lived for more than thirty years, on the market. And because the old house was lovely and well cared for, it had sold immediately, to the very first couple who had looked at it, a pair of hopeful Italian newlyweds, much as Joe and Madonna themselves had been so many long years ago when they had bought the place.

Renzo had contemplated purchasing the house himself from his parents. But as much as he had loved it, he had known he would always associate it with them. It would never have felt as though it were his very own, but instead would have seemed theirs still—and empty and bereft without them. So the day the lawyers and bankers okayed the sale and transfer of the *Tri-State Tribune* from his father to him, he had started clearing out the loft over the newspaper office, then had remodeled it and moved into it. He was accustomed to lofts and apartments; it would serve adequately until he decided to buy a house of his own.

Over the years, his parents had saved frugally for the day when Joe Martinelli could take early retirement and they would move to Florida. In addition, Renzo had, over their protests, insisted on paying them a very handsome sum for the *Tri-State Tribune*.

"Pop, I've made a lot of really smart investments over the years. I've held good-paying jobs at more than one big-city newspaper and had nobody and nothing to spend my money on but myself. I bought a roadster, a watch, a couple of nice suits, that's all. I'm rich, Pop. I'm famous. Like you said, I can write my own ticket. And I want to do this for you and Mom, to make you this generous offer for the *Trib* to repay you for everything you've ever done for me. Because if you hadn't taken me in all those years ago, God only knows where I'd be now. Gunned down and lying dead in a ghetto gutter somewhere, no doubt—just like the man who fathered me. So let me do this for you, the both of you. Please."

The Martinellis had paid off the mortgage on their bungalow two years ago. With the proceeds from the sale of their house, which had escalated in value over time, they were able to buy a nice condominium in Florida. The money Renzo paid them for the *Tri-State Tribune*, he helped them invest in a portfolio of carefully selected stocks, bonds and mutual funds, so his parents would be able to live out the remainder of their lives in financial security, even if some unexpected mishap should befall him.

Yesterday a moving van had arrived to empty the bungalow of its contents. And now, after a last look at their home and after exchanging emotional good-byes and promises to visit with Renzo, his parents got into their car and began to back out of the driveway for the last time. They were halfway into the street when, at the last minute, Madonna suddenly flung open her door and ran to Renzo, hugging him tightly, fat tears rolling down her plump cheeks.

"Son, I just wanted to tell you that no matter what happens, if there should ever come a time when you should think your father and I . . . well, that we didn't do right by you, that we wronged you terribly somehow, please remember we always had your best interests at heart. *Always!*" she insisted fiercely, her big brown eyes filled with both love and anxiety as she gazed up at him intently, searchingly. "And we never really knew . . . that is to say, we could never truly be sure whether the . . . We *thought* so. Perhaps we even hoped so, for your sake . . . and I think that in our hearts, we always sensed the truth. And we would have helped, if ever we'd been asked, needed. . . . But it wasn't *our* place to ask, to offer, you see. We had foolishly given up any right to be a part of . . . So we could only watch from afar. And regret. Still, we would have told you if we'd ever been certain. We would have done whatever was necessary, whatever we could have to attempt to put things right. . . . I want you to know that, Son."

"Mom, Mom, I don't understand you. What're you trying to say to me?"

"Nothing. Nothing." Madonna shook her head, dabbing with her handkerchief at her eyes. "I'm a foolish, middle-aged woman, standing here rambling and weeping on your shoulder, while your father waits impatiently to hit the road before the day grows so hot that the pavement melts and the tires stick to the asphalt. Take care of yourself, Son. Be sure to eat right and get plenty of rest. And always remember we love you."

"I love you and Pop, too, Mom." Renzo smiled down at her, although his eyes were puzzled and concerned at her earlier disjointed dialogue. He wondered if her words had had anything to do with Sarah Kincaid, but in the face of his mother's emotional turmoil, he couldn't bring himself to ask. So all his questions remained unanswered.

After a long moment, during which it had seemed she would speak again, Madonna finally turned away silently, climbing back into the car and fastening her seat belt as Joe finished pulling out onto the street.

"Did you tell him, Mama?" he asked as they drove away slowly.

Madonna glanced back over her shoulder, smiling tremulously and waving vigorously at Renzo, despite the tears that continued to stream down her cheeks. "No," she sobbed, facing forward at last. "Oh, Papa! How could I? It will break his heart! For so long as I live, I'll never forgive myself for what I did all those years ago, what I wrote to him. *Never!*"

"There, there, now. Don't cry, Mama. Please don't cry. You're just upset, leaving our happy home, this town where we have so many good friends and have spent so many wonderful years together. That's all.'' Joe patted her hand comfortingly. ''After all, we could never really be certain.''

''No, I'm sure. In here, Papa—'' she laid her hand on her heart ''—I'm sure. The boy is the spitting image of Renzo at that age. He's Renzo's son, *our* grandchild. I know it! I should have told Renzo. All these years, I should have swallowed my fear and told him. I should have called on Sarah Kincaid, too—instead of being so afraid that she would only curse me, spit on me and slam the door in my face. She loved him. She loved our son, Papa. She bore his child, and she kept the boy. She worked hard, and she held her head high in this town, regardless of her shame. Now, when it's too late, I would be proud to call her my daughter. Oh, Papa! What have I done? What have I done?''

''What you thought was best at the time, Mama,'' Joe said softly as the car swept forward on to the highway, leaving the town behind. ''And no one in this whole wide world can ever do anything more than that.''

''Morse, I've got to run over to the courthouse for a little while,'' Renzo announced as he stuck his head into the older man's office at the newspaper. ''I don't know how long I'll be, and I may have to go elsewhere afterward. You want to hold down the fort while I'm gone? Close up shop for me if I don't get back before six?''

''Sure thing, Boss. Will do.'' Morse Novak had worked at the *Tri-State Tribune* for several years and now held the position of managing editor. A Vietnam veteran, he had twenty-odd years ago been stationed in that war-torn country, where an explosion had left him a paraplegic and wheelchair bound. Physically deprived, Morse had ever since concentrated on developing his mental abilities. In addition to his job at the newspaper, Morse taught night classes in computer science at the local state university.

Since buying the newspaper, Renzo had, like his father before him, come to rely heavily on Morse, deeply appreciating his brains and talent.

"Thanks, Morse." Whistling, his hands jammed into the pockets of his trousers, Renzo strode from the newspaper office. With his parents safely dispatched to Florida and things at the *Tri-State Tribune* pretty much settled following his acquisition of it, he was now free to pursue his investigation into the past. Like any good reporter, Renzo trusted his gut instincts, and these told him the place to begin was the courthouse.

After a short walk across the square in the afternoon sun, he entered the cool halls of the huge old granite building, making his way to the Records Office. There, he informed the clerk who waited on him that he wanted to see a list of marriage licenses issued for the year Sonny Holbrooke had died at the quarry, the year that he, Renzo, had fled from town, leaving Sarah behind.

"Hmm. Let me think. That was before we got so darned newfangled and computerized," the elderly but efficient clerk declared. Putting on her reading glasses, she made her way down a series of metal shelves holding seemingly endless rows of record books. Pulling a volume from a shelf, she handed it to Renzo. "Look at it at that table over there, young man. Record books are town property and not to be removed for any reason whatsoever from the courthouse premises.''

"I understand. Thank you very much, ma'am." Out of long habit, because in his profession he never knew when somebody might be of use to him, Renzo flashed the woman the dangerously roguish, seductive grin with which he had wormed confidential information out of countless administrative assistants, secretaries, receptionists and office clerks over the years. "I promise I'll handle this book very carefully—the pages are yellowed, I see—and that I'll return it just as soon as I'm done."

He carried the volume over to the long wooden table she had indicated and sat down, opening the book and beginning to turn its pages slowly. He wasn't interested in the months of January through May, only those following that fatal summer. Just to be on the safe side, however, he decided to start with June and began to read the entries written on the ruled pages. More than an hour later, he had finished. He couldn't believe there were so many people in the town and surrounding countryside who had got married that year. But to his vast relief, none of them had been Sarah Kincaid or Bubba Holbrooke. Of course, Sarah had been underage, Renzo reminded himself, so it was entirely possible she had slipped across the county or even the state line to be wed. Still, he didn't think that was too likely. His mother had written that Sarah had got married and moved away from town to parts unknown. In that order.

Renzo closed the volume and returned it to the clerk. "Much obliged, ma'am."

"I hope you found what you were looking for, young man. If I can help you further, please don't hesitate to let me know."

As he left the courthouse, Renzo glanced down at his wristwatch, a gold Rolex, his one extravagance over the years, save for his roadster, a 1974 Jaguar XKE. It was just shortly after two. Earlier, he had checked the telephone directory, but had discovered no listing for any Kincaid, either Dell, Iris or Sarah. He had then called directory assistance, only to be told there was no number, not even an unlisted one, for a Kincaid with any of those first names. There was, however, an unlisted number for an S. B. Kincaid, the operator had informed him. But as the number was, in fact, unlisted, she could not, of course, give out it or the address.

S. B. Kincaid. Sarah Beth Kincaid. It simply *had* to be her, Renzo told himself now. He had found no marriage license for her—at least not for the year of Sonny's death. It was entirely possible, of course, that she had wed later— twelve years was a long time, after all—and that she was now divorced, or that she was using her maiden name for professional reasons. That was a momentarily depressing thought. He would make a run out to Sarah's old house, he decided now. But first, he'd go back to the loft, grab a quick sandwich—as was often the case, he had worked through lunch instead of eating—and change his clothes. An Italian in jeans and a workshirt would be a hell of a lot less conspicuous in Miners' Row than an Italian in an expensive dark suit, a crisp white shirt and a foulard tie. He didn't want anybody to think he was a mobster, checking up on Papa Nick's employees at the Genovese Coal Mining Co.

At the thought of his grandfather, Renzo frowned. He owed it to the old man, he supposed, to call on him at least once. Papa Nick was, after all, not only his grandfather, but also had helped him that day he had fled from town. Had, in fact, provided him with Hal Younger's name at the *Herald* and thereby given Renzo the first break of his career, which had eventually led to his winning the Pulitzer Prize. Besides, common decency dictated that he visit Mama Rosa, his grandmother. She had written to him several times over the years, and it was not her fault that her husband was a mafioso. He'd go see them both tomorrow, Renzo told himself. Right now, it was Sarah who was uppermost in his mind.

Thirty minutes later, Renzo stood in the big garage at the rear of the *Tri-State Tribune,* where the newspapers were bundled and loaded into the trucks that stocked the blue metal stands on various street corners in the business district and deposited the rest of the newspapers at the pickup locations for their routes. He had confiscated a small portion of the garage for his own use, parking both the Jaguar and the Harley there. Now, his dark brown eyes lighting with anticipatory pleasure, he slowly drew from the motorcycle the canvas tarp that covered it. Papa Nick had had someone restore the bike to mint condition, and Renzo's parents had kept it safe for him all these years. He hadn't ridden it or any other motorcycle since that fatal day at the quarry. But it was like so many other skills acquired in one's youth—once you learned how, you never forgot.

After wheeling the bike out into the alley behind the garage, Renzo climbed aboard, inserted the key into the ignition and started the engine. Moments later, he was speeding from the present into the past, the wind streaming through his long, shaggy black hair, countless memories assailing him.

And Sarah Kincaid was a part of every single one.

The acreage in which Lamar Rollins stood belonged to old "Farmer" Farnsworth, but that wasn't important to Lamar. All that mattered to him was that the field had long ago been left fallow and then had been forgotten. So the trees and tall prairie grass and wildflowers that had once been burned away to clear the land had gradually encroached again upon it, turning it as wild as it had been before Farmer Farnsworth's intrusion. All this had made it ideal for Lamar's purpose, however—which was the undetected growing of marijuana. Every year since he had turned thirteen, Lamar had searched the surrounding countryside for isolated, virtually abandoned acreage, where he had furtively planted the seedlings sprouted from seeds he had germinated in planter boxes a month earlier. In the fields, he nurtured, cultivated and harvested his illegal crop.

He had started out small-time and been such a rube that he had let the male plants proliferate, taking over his crop. As a result, he had wound up smoking much of his mediocre grass himself and made very little profit. Now, four years later, he knew to cut down the male plants before their pods burst, so his principal crop consisted only of the prized female plants. When they reached a height of approximately three feet, he clipped off their lower leaves to produce even stronger plants.

These days, he made pretty good money, peddling his pot all over town as well as selling it to the occasional buyer who hauled it to the big city, for resale. This end of the business was, however, something Lamar planned to take control of himself eventually, in order to expand his growing marijuana enterprise. This goal had been greatly aided last year when, after dropping out of Lincoln High School, he had reluctantly gone to work as a janitor at Field-Yield, Inc., under the supervision of his uncle Thaddeus.

At first, Lamar had hated the job and considered it beneath him. He wouldn't have taken it at all, except that his grandmother had badgered him constantly after he had quit school, asking him what he intended to do with his life now and calling him a no-account fool. Sick and tired of listening to her, relieved to escape from their tumbledown house at night, he had at last grudgingly agreed to join the labor pool at the fertilizer plant. Within days, he was glad he had—because at Field-Yield, Inc., he had discovered two things: fertilizer and computers.

Field-Yield Guaranteed Growth worked so well on his illegal crop that more than once, Lamar had been tempted to leave a letter to that effect on the desk of former governor J. D. Holbrooke, president of the company, or to drop a note in the suggestion box, offering to appear on one of Field-Yield, Inc.'s folksy, testimonial farming commercials. Yes, indeed. The fertilizer had been highly beneficial, increasing his grass yield several times over.

The computers had proved a revelation.

Now, whenever he could escape from Uncle Thaddeus—which was often, because his uncle was old and slow and not very bright—Lamar slipped into one of the offices at the fertilizer plant and sat down at its computer. At the monitor and keyboard, he had found his milieu. The way he had, within just a few nights, begun to grasp hardware, software, programming and cyberspace had been truly astounding. He was a natural, the proverbial whiz kid, speeding down the information superhighway, surfing the Internet. Via modem, a whole wide world previously unknown to him had opened up to Lamar. In many respects, it had given him a better and certainly a far broader education than any he would ever have received at Lincoln High School. And he had not been slow to perceive the possibilities. This was better, even, than having a computer of his own, because he could use the telephone lines and electricity at Field-Yield, Inc. for free, not to mention not having to explain to his grandmother how he had come to have the money to buy something so expensive as a personal computer.

Unbeknown to anyone at Field-Yield, Inc., Lamar had soon created a hidden directory in the company's computer system, in which he had begun to record every single one of his marijuana transactions: dates, times, places, clients, amounts bought and sold, and so forth. What he would ever do with all this information, he didn't know, except that he thought of it as insurance, in case he should ever be arrested or one of his customers should decide to get mean and ugly. Some of them were Italians, and he would indeed be the fool his grandmother called him if he didn't know they were connected to the Mob, and perhaps even to Columbian drug lords and Jamaican gangs, who were even nastier than the mafiosi. He had locked up his directory with a password known only to himself and, as an additional security measure, had made backup copies of his files on double-sided, high-density diskettes he had stolen from one of the office-supply storerooms at the fertilizer plant. He kept these concealed beneath a floorboard in his bedroom at home.

"Whooee! Y'all sho' are lookin' good, babies," Lamar exclaimed now as he examined the pot plants he was growing in Farmer Farnsworth's field. "Umm-hmm. Y'all sho' are gonna be some good smoke."

Striding among the plants, a bowie knife in hand, he ruthlessly cut down the males, tossing them into an ever-increasing pile. Later, he would hang them up to dry in the old, rundown wooden shed out back of his grandmother's house. Then he would crumble them up, mix them in with the least potent parts of the female plants and divide up the resulting grass, sealing it into sandwich bags. Lamar always used Glad bags; he got a kick out of that, telling himself it was only appropriate, since his bags made his clients so glad. He invariably sold the male mixture to school kids on the commons, because the majority of them couldn't tell if they were smoking pot or oregano. He saved the buds and upper leaves of the female plants—all the good stuff—for customers who knew better.

Lamar broke a heat-withered leaf off one of the male plants and, figuring it was dry enough to try, crushed it and sprinkled it into one of the thin white cigarette papers he took from the orange Zig-Zag package in his pocket. Carefully, he rolled the joint, licked the edge to seal it, then lit up, inhaling deeply. He held the smoke in his lungs for as long as he could, then blew it out, coughing and choking.

"Not bad shit," he observed to himself, wiping at his abruptly red, teary eyes. "Not good, either—but then, what do them dumb-ass whitey jocks at school know? Hell. The only letter they can read is the one on their letter jackets."

Popping the trunk on his rusty, beat-up old car, he began to load his haul, whistling cheerfully as he worked, cocking one ear as he heard the drone of a motorcycle in the distance, drawing steadily nearer. Lamar wasn't too concerned by the noise, as he had both a shotgun and an automatic pistol in his clunker. But it paid to be careful, even if the only two people he really had to worry about were Sheriff Laidlaw and Deputy Truett. And even they posed little threat. After all, they weren't for nothing routinely referred to behind their backs as Tweedledum and Tweedledumber.

Despite how hard he fought against the magnetic sensation as he traversed the dusty country roads, the grassy green meadows and the cool, shaded woods of his past, Renzo found he was like a criminal—inevitably, irresistibly drawn to the scene of his crime. He had intended to go straight to Sarah's old house. Really, he had, he told himself. But somewhere along the way, he had got lost in the past, been pulled to the old quarry where he had made love to Sarah and where Sonny had died that fatal day.

It was a weekday. At this hour, both summer school and summer classes at the university were still in attendance;

the Sideshow—the local amusement park—was in full swing; and there was a band playing an outdoor concert somewhere in one of the town parks. Perhaps all that accounted for the fact that this afternoon, the quarry was strangely deserted. Or, more likely, its emptiness was due to the large, authoritative signs that had never been here before, but that were now prominently posted in several locations and that, in bold black letters, read: **Positively No Diving or Swimming, By Order of Sheriff. All Violators Will Be Prosecuted to the Fullest Extent of the Law, Without Exception.** As a result, Renzo had the place to himself. He rolled the Harley to a halt and got off, staring at the rough-hewn diving platforms, at the top rock, from which he and Sonny had fallen. It was a long drop—just as far as he had recollected.

After several minutes of contemplation, Renzo, driven by some dark, unknown compulsion, slowly undressed, leaving his clothes where they fell, tossing his mirrored aviator sunglasses onto the pile. Then, naked, the gold St. Christopher's medal he always wore around his neck gleaming in the sunlight, he strode toward the rocks and began to climb. When he had reached the top, he paused, as though expecting to find something, anything, that would tell him what had happened that day. But there was nothing. He looked down, feeling momentarily giddy, as he had so many years before. His heart seemed to pound in his throat. His blood roared in his ears. A wasp buzzed around his head, and his hand lashed out to knock the insect away. In his mind, a gunshot sounded; the bullet grazed the side of his shoulder, the sudden, sharp sting startling him. He turned, saw Sonny standing beside him, heard Sonny's voice on the breeze that stirred lethargically.

Onward, Watson.

"Right, Holmes," Renzo answered quietly.

He closed his eyes, took a deep breath and launched himself strongly in a perfect swan dive from the top rock.

Down—

Down—

Down—

He seemed to drop forever. His last thought before he struck the cool, murky water was that he had gone crazy from sunstroke and would surely be killed. Against his eyelids, Sonny's image swam, melting into Sarah's as the surface broke at Renzo's impact and, like a knife into a target, he plunged deep, feeling the water close over him, engulf him, taking him inside like a welcoming woman. At long last, he opened his eyes, batting with his hands at the mass of long, thin, gnarled willow roots that reached out to embrace him in a death grip, as they had embraced Sonny. But Renzo was like a fish, twisting and turning, eluding the tangle that would have entrapped him. He kicked his feet hard, propelling his body toward the sunlight glinting above. His heart raced. His lungs felt as though they would burst inside him. He couldn't breathe. But he knew the terrible sensation would pass, that he would have more air in his lungs the higher he ascended, something to do with pressure or the lack of it, he thought, although he couldn't remember for sure.

He finally surfaced, swam toward shore and hauled himself from the water, his breath coming in hard, un-

even rasps. He rolled over, one arm flung across his eyes
to shield them from the glare of the bright, burning sun.

"Man oh man oh man! I ain't never in my entire life
seen nothin' like what you just done, dude! It was way
cool...totally *un-be-liev-able!*" His mouth hanging open,
Lamar Rollins stared down in sheer amazement at Renzo
lying on the ground, as though he weren't quite sure Renzo was actually real. "I heard your bike, man, and came
to investigate. And boy, am I ever glad I did! I wouldn't
have missed seein' that dive of yours fo' nothin' in the
world!"

"Who in the hell are you?" Renzo inquired tersely as he
got slowly to his feet to confront the young black man
standing there.

"Me? Oh, hey, look, I ain't nobody, dude...ah...
mister," Lamar said hurriedly, judging it prudent to take
a step back as his eyes absorbed Renzo's six feet, three
inches of lean, hard, powerful muscle. "My name's Lamar Rollins, and I'm cool. I'm cool. So just relax. Relax.
I ain't gonna report you to the sheriff or nothin' like that."

"I didn't think you were." Calmly, unembarrassed by
his nakedness, Renzo pulled on his briefs and jeans, then
shrugged on his blue chambray workshirt, letting it hang
open, the sun feeling good upon his wet flesh. Reaching
into his shirt pocket, he withdrew a pack of Marlboros, lit
one up and dragged on it deeply, then exhaled, blowing a
cloud of smoke rings into the summer air. All the while, he
never took his eyes off the young man. Unless he missed
his guess—and Renzo seldom did—Lamar Rollins was
stoned on pot and probably on the wrong side of the law

more often than not. And Renzo wasn't about to be knifed in the back for his Harley.

"You're him, ain't you?" Lamar asked suddenly. "You're that reporter dude who's taken over the *Trib*, the one who won the Poo-lit-zer Prize, the one who killed Old Man Holbrooke's fancy college boy out here some years back. I knowed it! I knowed it as soon as I seen you make that dive! I says to myself right then, 'Lamar, ain't but one dude ever made that dive and lived to talk about it, and that's him right there.' That's right, ain't it? Well, ain't it?"

"Yeah, that's right." Renzo wondered idly whether he should warn Lamar that all the while they had been talking, Sheriff Laidlaw had, on foot, been stealthily circumnavigating the quarry and was even now coming up on them. Then Renzo decided it probably wasn't Lamar the sheriff wanted, but him. "Hoag," he called out with feigned casualness, causing Lamar to pivot abruptly. "You been following me around, Hoag, spying on me?"

"There some reason why I should be, Renzo?" the sheriff countered just as easily, although his eyes, too, were alert. Then he said, "Just making my usual rounds, that's all. I saw you make that frigging dive, boy. What in the hell's the matter with you? Can't you read?" Hoag Laidlaw's normally pasty face was red from his exertions as he huffed and puffed his way to where Renzo and Lamar stood. Sweat ran down into the sheriff's eyes, and the khaki shirt of his uniform was practically soaked through. Grasping his wide leather belt, he hitched his trousers up around his girth, which was soft from lack of exercise and running to fat from too many glazed doughnuts at Fritz-

chen's Kitchen. "I can't believe you had nerve enough to
ever show your sly, ugly mug in this town again after what
you done, much less to come out here and make that dive
once more. What was you trying to prove, boy?"

Taking another long drag on his cigarette, Renzo reflected wordlessly that it didn't matter how high in life he
had climbed since leaving this town behind, that he had
broken one of the biggest news story of the decade, had
won a Pulitzer Prize, had sat down to dinner with the
president in the White House and had been addressed by
the nation's most powerful movers and shakers as "Mr.
Cassavettes." He had only to return here to be reduced
again to "boy"—a guinea bastard from the wrong side of
the tracks. His mouth twisted derisively. He would have
laughed aloud at the bitter irony, except that he knew neither Hoag nor Lamar would have understood the joke.

"Why, I wasn't trying to prove anything, Hoag, except
that I could do it."

"It ain't Hoag to you, boy. It's Sheriff Laidlaw—and
don't you forget it. 'Cause just in case you don't remember, we don't hold with uppity dagos in this here town. Nor
uppity niggers, neither," he added for Lamar's benefit.
"You know, Renzo, there're hell of a lot of folks in town
already upset about you coming back here. And I reckon
they'd be even more pissed off if they ever learned about
this little stunt you pulled out here this afternoon. They
might start to wondering what're the chances you made
that dive long before you supposedly ever made it the first
time, so you *knew,* you see, without a doubt, that you
could handle it that day you shoved Sonny Holbrooke to
his death. They might start to wondering what're the

chances you could ride out here after more 'n a decade and make that dive again just as cool as you damned well please."

"Uh-huh," Renzo drawled, in unconscious imitation of Papa Nick. "Well, I'm certain you'll be sure to tell them— *Hoag*." He deliberately used the sheriff's first name again. "And in case *you* don't remember, Sonny's death was ruled an accident at the inquest."

"Yeah, and as a result, you weren't never charged." Hoag's jaw was set with outrage at Renzo's insolence. "There wasn't never no trial. So double jeopardy don't apply. And there ain't no statute of limitations on murder, boy. Why, I could arrest you right now if I was of a mind to." The sheriff pointed toward the signs posted. "That dive of yours broke the law."

"Uh-huh. Well, feel free to run me in, Hoag. I'm sure it's probably a misdemeanor offense with a hundred-dollar fine, tops. And if you haven't already heard, that's less than I spend these days for one of my neckties. You want I should just pay you now and save Judge Pierce the trouble of convening court?"

"You attempting to bribe me, boy?"

"Why, no, Hoag. Lamar, you hear me attempt to bribe our fine, upstanding sheriff here?" Renzo's sarcastic tone made it clear he considered Hoag anything but.

"No, sir, I sho' didn't."

"If you know what's good for you, you'll shut your damned fool mouth, Lamar!" Hoag snapped heatedly. "You ain't a credible witness, boy. You ain't shit! You're as high as a kite most of the damned time and probably out this way to check on your pot crop. Bet if I was to do some more poking around out here, I'd find that clunker of yours with its trunk just stuffed chock-full of weed.''

"Don't count on it, Sheriff!'' Lamar retorted impudently. Renzo's tall, muscular figure and contemptuous attitude were making the young black man a good deal bolder and much more disrespectful than he would normally have been, facing up to the sheriff, who was notorious in Lamar's circles for being quick and vicious with a nightstick. ''I ain't as stupid as you think. And as I recall, the last time you and ole Tweedledumber went out lookin' fo' my pot fields, you mistakenly burned up several acres of Mr. Oakes's alfalfa, and he weren't none too happy about it at all."

At that, the sheriff's face flushed so bright with fury that an ugly blue vein popped out on his forehead, looking as though it might burst at any moment, spraying blood. His hand reached instinctively for the nightstick at his belt. Warily, Lamar took a hasty step back, but to his astonishment and admiration, Renzo never moved a muscle, never even flicked an eyelash.

"I wouldn't, Hoag, if I were you," Renzo uttered softly. "You're at least twenty-five years older than me—and you ain't exactly in prime physical condition, either. Could be you might accidentally take a long tumble into that quarry, too, get all snarled up in those roots underwater, just like Sonny did."

To Renzo's satisfaction and amusement, fear flickered in the sheriff's eyes. "You'd best not be threatening me, boy!" Hoag blustered nervously.

"You hear me threaten the sheriff, Lamar?"

"No, sir, I sho' didn't." Lamar grinned hugely, taking mean-spirited delight in seeing Hoag squirm, as he had made so many of the blacks in town squirm for years.

"I'm warning you. From now on, you'd better watch your step, Renzo. And you, too, Lamar. Or you're both going to find yourselves sitting in one of my jail cells—where I feel pretty damned confident you're liable to wind up as a couple of suicides or prisoners killed while attempting to escape!" With that Parthian shot, the sheriff stamped off, muttering angrily to himself.

His dark brown eyes narrowed and hard, Renzo watched him depart, thinking all the while that the Sheriff Laidlaws of the world were a good deal to blame for the Lamar Rollinses.

"Man, you sho' told him!" Lamar declared, awed. "I only ever heard two other people in town talk to old lard-ass Tweedledum like that, and that was Old Man Holbrooke and Papa Nick Genovese. You sho' is some cool piece of work, dude."

"Yeah, well, if there's one thing I've learned in this life, it's that money talks and bullshit walks. Lamar, it's probably best if you take off now, while I'm still around to watch your backside. I wouldn't put it past old Hoag to go off and hide in the bushes someplace, so he can lie in wait for you. And while you may think you're real bright, the truth of the matter is that you're just a poor, disadvantaged kid who's had the misfortune to grow up in the bad part of a town in which you and I both are the wrong color. So, you wind up dead in a ditch out here somewhere, and it won't warrant any more than a brief mention in one of the back pages of my newspaper. I know that isn't fair, that it isn't right. But unfortunately, that's the way life is— a hard row to hoe all the way around. So if you want my advice—and you probably don't, probably won't be smart enough to take it—you'll forget all about your pot crop and get yourself an education and a job, however hard you have to work to get 'em. Otherwise, you're headed for prison or worse, and that's a fact."

"If you say so," Lamar growled sullenly, perturbed that his idol of the moment had abruptly ruined everything by displaying clay feet. "Later, dude."

"Yeah, later." After buttoning his shirt, Renzo tucked the ends into his jeans, then hauled on his socks and boots.

Shortly afterward, he was bringing the Harley to a halt in front of the Kincaids' old house, a small white cottage that had once been neatly kept but that now was in a considerable state of dereliction, the paint peeling, the shutters hanging awry, the porch settling and the yard overgrown with weeds. Three young, grimy children—the eldest no more than four years old, he estimated—played in a patch of dirt beneath the shade cast by a tall old oak.

Renzo's heart sank at the sight of the house, of the kids. Something twisted inside his gut at the thought of Sarah— his bright, beautiful Sarah—living this way, sunk to this level of obvious poverty and hardship. He imagined her married to some brute who worked at the coal mines and regularly got drunk, raped and abused her, and he thought he would rather see her dead or wed to Bubba Holbrooke than to have fallen prey to a life such as this—a life he had known himself once, in his childhood. His face grim, Renzo parked the motorcycle on the verge of the sandy road and strode toward the cottage.

"Hey there," he called to the children as he approached. "Is your mama around?"

"She's inside," the oldest youngster, a little towheaded girl, replied. "You want I should go and fetch her for you, mister?"

"If you wouldn't mind. I'd sure appreciate it."

The child scampered into the house, and a few minutes later, a woman stepped out onto the porch, a baby in her arms and another one in her swollen belly. Her feet were bare and filthy, and she wore a faded old sundress. Loose strands of her dirty, sun-bleached hair, most of which was scraped back in a careless knot, fell around her thin, pinched face, which sported a black eye and a cut lip. Bruises, old and new, marked her arms and legs. To Renzo's everlasting relief, she wasn't Sarah.

"Can I help you?" she asked tiredly as she pushed a small bottle of what looked to be apple juice into the baby's mouth.

"I hope so, ma'am. I'm looking for the family who used to live here, the Kincaids. I'm an old acquaintance of theirs, been gone from town for the past twelve years and just came home, thought I'd look them up. Do you know what happened to them, why they sold their house, where they might have gone?"

"Well, lemme see now. Best I can recollect, the realtor who showed us this here place told Eddie—that's my husband—that Mr. Kincaid had died some years before, an unexpected heart attack, I think she said it was. That Mrs. Kincaid had been on her own for at least a couple of years before we looked at the house, but that since she was in ill health—and not all there in the head anymore, either—she was going into a nursing home. The Woodlands, I believe it was. You might try there."

"Thanks. The Kincaids had a daughter, Sary... Sarah Beth. She'd be twenty-nine now. Do you happen to know what became of her, by any chance?"

"Sarah Beth, you said? Hmm. Seems to me like she might be the one who bought the old Lovell farm up the road a piece some years back. But I really couldn't say for sure. Sorry I can't be of more help."

"No, that's all right. You've given me enough to go on. Thank you again, ma'am. I'm much obliged to you." Reaching into his back pocket for his black leather wallet, Renzo took out a crisp hundred-dollar bill and handed it to the woman. "For your trouble, ma'am. It's the least I can do. I'm sorry to have bothered you."

The woman stared at the money as though she couldn't believe it was real. "I—I can't take this," she said weakly, clutching it like a lifeline.

"Sure you can. I want you to have it—you and your kids, do you understand me?"

"Eddie... if Eddie finds out I hid money from him—"

"You ever read a book entitled *Gone With the Wind,* ma'am?"

"No, I—I don't read much."

"Well, the heroine of *Gone With the Wind,* Scarlett O'Hara, once needed to hide some money from a man in a hurry. And it just so happened that the only place handy also happened to be the one place no man would ever think about looking—in a baby's diaper. One more thing, ma'am—you tell your husband, Eddie, that an Italian gentleman called on you today, said to tell him he'd better take it easy on you and your kids from now on, or he won't be working at Genovese Coal Mining any longer—and that'll be the least of his worries!''

With that, Renzo got back on his bike and rode away, roiling rage at the unknown Eddie consuming him. It might have been Sarah who had come out of the Kincaids' old cottage, he thought, Sarah hungry, frightened, beaten black and blue and trying to take care of nearly half a dozen kids as best she could. Renzo knew that if the pitiful woman had, in fact, turned out to have been Sarah, he would, with his bare fists, have killed the brutish Eddie.

Realizing suddenly that he was hot and thirsty, Renzo abruptly pulled into the gravel parking lot, pitted with potholes, of the old country store that had sat at the crossroads for as long as he could remember, and then some. He was vaguely surprised to find it was still in existence. But then, change had always come slowly to town, when it had come at all. He stepped up on the wooden porch that ran the length of the front and boasted a couple of straight-backed, farm-table chairs that looked like refugees from a yard sale, and a modern Coke machine. A now antique, rusted metal advertising sign was nailed to the old-fashioned screen door. The interior of the store was relatively dark after the glare of the sunlight outside, and cool, too, from the original, metal-bladed fans that whirled against the ceiling.

Renzo bought a six-pack of beer from the cooler in back, along with a couple of salami sandwiches from the meat-and-deli counter. Outside, he sat down on the stoop, his back against one of the thin wooden columns that supported the overhanging roof. He popped the top off one of the beer cans and wolfed down the two sandwiches. Until now, he hadn't realized how hungry he was, how late it was getting. The sun was beginning to go down on the western horizon, a blazing ball that, as it descended in the sky, seemed to set the entire countryside aflame. Still, it wouldn't be completely dark for another few hours yet. He had time.

So he took it, guiding the Harley along the old, familiar route he had used to take through the trees to the meadow where Sarah's tree house had been. *The old Lovell farm.* The words rang even now like music in Renzo's ears. Sarah had loved the beautiful old Victorian farmhouse, had spent the happiest days of her life in the tree house her daddy had built for her in the tall, spreading sycamore that had stood in the Lovells' meadow. And did still, Renzo presently learned, surprised to discover the tree had not been struck and felled by lightning, that the tree house itself had not rotted away over the years, that the rungs nailed into the trunk, in fact, looked fairly new and were in good condition, so they easily supported his weight as he climbed into the gnarled branches and hoisted himself into the tree house.

He was vaguely startled to find it empty. Somehow, deep down inside, he had expected to see Sarah sitting here, waiting for him, as she always had. If he closed his eyes, he could envision her even now, could smell the fragrance of her honeysuckle perfume in his nostrils, could taste her mouth and skin upon his tongue. He hadn't known how just the sight of this place, how the thought of her here would affect him, causing his throat to close up tight with emotion and unexpected tears to sting his eyes.

Slowly, Renzo let his body slide down one wall of the tree house to the floor, where, sighing raggedly, he laid his head on his knees, feeling suddenly tired and old far beyond his thirty-four years, as though he were long dead and turned to dust inside. He sat there for a very long time, smoking and drinking and remembering, so darkness had fallen when he finally rose to descend from the boughs of the sycamore.

Of their own volition, his booted feet carried him toward the farmhouse, coming to a halt amid the moon-shadowed trees at the edge of the lawn, where masses of honeysuckle vines spread in tangled abundance, their sweet scent filling the night air, fireflies flashing among the tiny white blossoms. The house was almost as he remembered it, except that upstairs, where there had once been a single old door leading to the deck above the veranda, there was now a bank of tall, spacious windows and a pair of French doors. But the remodeling had been harmoniously accomplished, with a great deal of thought and care for the Victorian architecture, so the change seemed a natural part of the original structure, as though it had always been there.

A collection of wind chimes hung above the deck, tinkling melodically with each breath of the torpid night breeze. How like Sarah they were, Renzo reflected; how she would love them, *did* love them. For she *was* here. Somehow he knew that instinctively. He sensed her presence, grasped intuitively that the bedroom that lay beyond the wind chimes was her own.

Even as the thought occurred to him, the French doors opened and Sarah herself appeared, a vision in white, the lawn nightgown she wore so delicate and sheer that Renzo could see she was naked beneath it. He inhaled sharply at the sight. She was, if possible, even more beautiful than he remembered, with the moonlight showering down on her, casting a silvery halo about her dark brown hair, which spilled in a shining mass around her arresting face upturned to the night sky.

"Sarah," he whispered hoarsely. "Sarah."

Perhaps the night wind carried the sound of his low voice to her ears. Renzo didn't know. He knew only that she suddenly glanced from the stars toward the trees where he stood, concealed by the darkness. Her lips parted, as though in surprise or fear, and then she abruptly whirled and disappeared into the house.

As he lay in bed in the loft that night, she came to him in misted dreams. And Renzo buried himself inside her, making love to her until she trembled and shuddered violently and cried out softly in his arms. Afterward, he held her close and gently kissed the tears from her face, luminescent in the silvery darkness.

But when he awoke at dawn, she was gone. Not even the delicate, intoxicating scent of her lingered in the rumpled white sheets. And he knew then, aching and bereft, that she had never really been there at all.

Fourteen

The Grain Elevator

Journeys end in lovers meeting,
Every wise man's son doth know.

Twelfth Night
—William Shakespeare

Last night, Renzo Cassavettes had stood outside on her lawn in the darkness, watching her. Sarah had known it as surely as she knew her own name, as though, despite their years apart, the bonds they had shared since childhood were as strong and whole as ever. She had sensed his smoldering, impassioned eyes on her body, mentally stripping her naked, and she had felt as shaken, heated and erotically violated as she would have had she suddenly been forcibly seduced by someone about whom she had hitherto only dreamed darkly and fantasized endlessly. A terrible, tantalizing foreboding and excitement had gripped her—so fiercely that she had felt almost physically ill from the blind sensations. Her head spinning as though she had drunk too much of the sweet red wine she routinely poured herself a single glass of each night—she thought of it as her one sinful indulgence—she had lain down on her bed. Only to realize some minutes later, to her shock and horror, that she was running her hands sensuously over her body, tugging with rough impatience at her nightgown, insidiously stroking her breasts and thighs, the soft, moist heart of her, which had ached unbearably.

He had only had to stand there in the distance, looking at her, not even close enough to touch her, and it had been as though some dark, raw, primal thing had seized her in its fist, unleashing desires and needs no other man had ever stirred and that she had believed long securely caged—or even dead—inside her. That thought had terrified her. For more than a decade now, she had been in control of herself and her emotions. Last night had revealed that control to be only an illusion, smoke and mirrors, easily shattered.

This morning, in the wake of her distress, questions and another fear had assailed her. Why had Renzo been on her property, spying on her? If he had gone to all the trouble of tracking her down, it was only a matter of time before he learned about Alex, as well. Or perhaps he already knew. Perhaps that was why he had come to the house last night. He was a successful investigative reporter, with the same sort of instincts as a secret agent or a private detective. If he planned to try to take Alex away from her, would he not gather as much information beforehand as he could, ammunition to use against her in battle?

That was why Sarah had finally called her friend Liz Delaney, née Tyrrell. After graduating from Lincoln High

School, Liz had obtained her law degree and was now married to Eveline Holbrooke's first ex-husband, Parker Delaney, having determinedly snagged him on the rebound and proved herself a much more satisfactory wife than Evie had ever been. Both Liz and Parker were junior partners in his father's law firm of Delaney, Pierce & Langford. Liz's schedule today had been such that she was unable to work Sarah in. But having known her since grade school, Liz had recognized the urgency and desperation in Sarah's voice on the telephone and so had agreed to meet her after work, for drinks and supper at the Grain Elevator.

The Grain Elevator actually had been used as such at one time. But these days, cleverly remodeled to support its new role while retaining the facade of its old, it was the trendiest restaurant and club for miles around, the prime gathering place for the town's upwardly mobile young crowd, not so old-fashioned and stuffy as the country club and a considerable step up from the blue-collar Steak 'n' Baked, the sleazy Kewpie-Doll Lounge and the rambunctious Rowdy's Roadhouse, which was out off the highway and a haven for bikers, coal miners and cowboys. When making the reservation at the Grain Elevator, Sarah had requested one of the more private booths in the restaurant upstairs, so she and Liz could talk undisturbed, the noisy, swinging singles tending to congregate in the ground-floor bar.

Now, as Sarah sipped the pleasantly cold and tart Tom Collins she had ordered once she and Liz had finished their dinner, she wasn't quite sure how to begin. "I—I need some legal advice, Liz," she confessed at last to her smart, redheaded friend sitting across from her at the table. "It's about . . . my son."

"Alex! Oh, sweetie, has he got into some kind of trouble with the law?" Liz's carefully arched brows flew together in a frown of concern.

"No. Oh, no, it's nothing like that, thank heavens." Sarah managed a tremulous smile. "Alex himself is fine." Glancing around cautiously, she lowered her voice and leaned toward Liz. "It's his father who's worrying me. I'm—I'm afraid he . . . well, that he may be planning on trying to—to take Alex away from me!"

"What?" Liz exclaimed, her mouth gaping with astonishment. Then, to Sarah's shock, she abruptly burst into laughter. "Oh, Sarah . . . I'm so . . . sorry," she gasped between peals of merriment. "I can tell from that look of injury and indignation on your face that you don't find this the least bit funny. But honestly, sweetie, the very idea is preposterous! I mean—no offense intended—but you don't even know who Alex's father is, do you? I thought that on his birth certificate, you listed his father as unknown—at least, that was the rumor floating around town at the time."

"Yes, I did. But for heaven's sake, Liz! Please don't tell me even *you* believed me that shamelessly wanton and stupid! Back in high school you were my best friend. You still are. Have you ever had cause to think I was really and truly the slut people claimed? Because I'm not—and I never was. I've always known who fathered my son. I simply had good and valid reasons for not wanting the rest of the whole damned town to know, too, that's all."

"I'm sorry, Sarah." Liz's voice was now laced with sincerity, her face sober. "I didn't mean to hurt your feelings. Really, I didn't. Of course I knew most of the gossip all those years back wasn't the least bit true. And I should have realized this is no laughing matter to you, but one of serious concern. So let's take things point by point, shall we? Number one—is the boy's father aware Alex is his son?"

"Until recently, I would have said no. But now, I'm not so sure." Sarah stirred the slender striped straw in her Tom Collins thoughtfully, her brow knitted in concentration. "Something's happened within the last weeks that has made me think he may have learned about Alex—or will shortly. No, please don't pry, Liz. I don't want to say anything more than what I've already told you."

"All right. Fair enough," Liz stated, resolutely suppressing her own personal curiosity, reminding herself she was currently acting as an attorney, as well as a friend, in this affair. "We'll set aside the question of the identity of Alex's father, then, for the time being. In addition, we'll assume for argument's sake that the boy's father has indeed learned Alex is his son. But in order to make any attempt at all at taking Alex away from you, he'd first require some proof of paternity. Does he have any?"

"No." Sarah shook her head. "It would be his word against mine. Still, aren't there DNA tests these days that would provide him with the proof he'd need?"

"Yes, but he'd have to show reasonable cause to justify his believing himself Alex's father for such tests even to be considered. Could he do that?"

"Yes," Sarah admitted reluctantly, anxiously, thinking of how much Alex resembled Renzo as a child. "He probably could."

"All right, then. Let's say he managed to persuade a judge to order you and Alex both to submit yourselves for DNA testing. Even if paternity were proved beyond a doubt, Alex's father would still have to convince a court he had legitimate reasons for wishing to deprive you of custody of the boy. He'd have to demonstrate that you're an unfit mother, for example. And, Sarah, sweetie, that's just not going to happen. So the best advice I can give you, both as your lawyer and your friend, is not to worry about this anymore. You're upsetting yourself over nothing."

"Oh, Liz, are you sure?" Sarah's green eyes were dark and haunted by shadows. "Because I just couldn't bear to lose Alex."

"I know. And I'm sure. So put it from your mind, sweetie."

"Are we interrupting anything? I mean, the two of you look as though you're deep into some real serious girl talk over here. How you doing, ladies? Long time, no see, now that you've both moved out of Miners' Row and up the corporate ladder." Dody Carpenter's words were slightly slurred, and her voice held a hint of jealousy and bitterness, even as she smiled at Sarah and Liz. Since graduating from high school, Dody had worked as a secretary at the Genovese Coal Mining Co., never making it out of Miners' Row herself. She was still single.

"Hey, Sarah, Liz. Come on, Dody." Krystal Watkins tugged futilely on her friend's arm, clearly embarrassed by her demeanor. "It's getting late. We need to be going home, and you've had too much to drink, besides."

"Well, it ain't every day that either one of *us* can afford to splurge on a night out, especially at the grandiose Grain Elevator, is it now?" Mulishly ignoring Krystal, Dody, as overweight as ever, determinedly heaved herself in next to Liz on the banquette. "Oh, go on and sit down, Krystal! It ain't even quite nine o'clock yet, for crying out loud! We'll all have a drink together for old-time's sake. Krystal and I are out on the town tonight, partying in celebration," she announced with bright brittleness to Sarah and Liz. "Krystal got a raise today at the clinic."

"Oh, Krystal, that's wonderful news!" Sarah declared, genuinely glad for her friend. Following graduation from high school, Krystal had become a registered nurse and was now married to Junior Barlow, who managed one of the gas stations in town. "Liz and I were finished with our discussion, anyway...just some boring old legalities having to do with J.D.'s senatorial campaign," she lied, shooting Liz a warning glance that spoke volumes.

"That's right," Liz drawled affably in confirmation. "I have to keep Sarah on the straight and narrow about all those tiresome FCC rules and regulations concerning political ads on television and radio. So, Krystal, business at the clinic must be booming, huh?" Liz smoothly changed the topic of conversation, earning a smile of heartfelt gratitude from Sarah.

"Yes, fortunately for me, since that's why I got a raise. I've been working extremely hard, putting in a whole lot of extra hours just to keep up, because of course, we're always understaffed at the clinic," Krystal explained, while

Dody ordered another round of drinks from the waitress who had appeared at their table. "We just don't have the funding required to hire the additional personnel we need. I can't believe there're so many poor, sick people in a town this size, but there are. I see quite a few older patients who've got everything from cancer to inexplicable rashes, and children, especially, who are physically or mentally handicapped and sometimes both. It's so sad."

"Well, it's like I've told you before, Krystal—those kids' mothers are probably all drunks or dopers—or, worse, hookers with AIDS. I mean, most of the people you treat at the clinic are on Medicaid or welfare and food stamps, aren't they?" Dody asked dryly, plainly feeling as though government assistance were offered only to the miserably undeserving.

"Yes, a lot of them are," Krystal admitted. "Still, it kind of bothers me, you know. I just think that, statistically speaking, we seem to have an inordinately disproportionate share of diseases, deformities and other disabilities in this town. I know some of them can legitimately be put down to disadvantaged backgrounds. But I can't help but wonder... well, Genovese Coal Mining and Field-Yield, Inc. are the two largest employers in town, really, along with the dog-food factory, I suppose. I keep thinking it just can't be good for people, breathing all that coal dust and fertilizer and dead-animal stench every day. Besides which, heaven only knows what's being dug up out of the earth along with the coal, or what kinds of chemicals are being mixed up for crops, or what bacteria all those old cows and chickens and horses being ground up for dog food might be carrying."

"That's true, Krystal," Liz observed thoughtfully, the wheels in her legal mind obviously churning speculatively. "Still, industries have to conform to OSHA's rules and regulations, and companies are periodically inspected by government officials to be certain they're operating within the boundaries prescribed by law."

"I know Field-Yield, Inc., at least, has fairly strict controls," Sarah added as, with her straw, she poked idly at the ice in her second Tom Collins. "Employees who work in the factory and warehouse, for example, where they actually handle the fertilizers and other farm products day in and day out, are required to wear goggles, masks and gloves. As a result, Field-Yield, Inc. has a pretty good safety record, Krystal."

"It's the same way at Genovese Coal Mining," Dody reported. "Honestly, Krystal, do you think either Papa Nick or J. D. Holbrooke wants the government on his back for safety and health violations? Papa Nick'd probably wind up charged somehow under the RICO statutes, and J.D.'s running for the Senate, for God's sake! He'd be front-page news, his political career finished. He's a former governor, too. If there were any dirt to be dug up on him, somebody would surely already have done it by now, don't you think? And the worst thing I ever heard happened at the dog-food factory—other than that rumor about Jimmy Hoffa, of course—was that some guy accidentally got his thumb and a couple of fingers sliced off by a processing machine. And hell, any fool could do that while working with a power saw in his own damned backyard!"

"I suppose you're right," Krystal agreed slowly. "My job's probably just getting to me, that's all. It's so depressing to see the children, especially. We had one in today... a little girl by the name of Keisha Rollins, I think it was. Her grandmother brought her in for what turned out to be just a summer cold, nothing serious. Keisha is mentally retarded... eight years old and can't even speak her own name properly. The grandmother reckoned it was some kind of brain damage at birth, but she couldn't say for sure, since the mother probably used both drugs and alcohol while she was pregnant. Plus, I doubt if she had much, if any, prenatal care. Poor environment may certainly have played a role, too. The mother was unwed and the father unknown. Oh, jeez, Sarah, I'm sorry. I—I didn't mean that the way it sounded—"

"That's all right, Krystal," Sarah said quietly in the awkward little silence that had fallen. "I may be an unwed mother, but I don't think anyone could ever accuse me of not providing a decent home and upbringing for my son."

"No, they couldn't," Liz asserted firmly.

"Well, it really *is* getting late, and I really *do* have to be getting home." Krystal glanced with more interest than was warranted at her wristwatch. "Junior's not the world's greatest baby-sitter, so I hate to leave him alone with the kids for too long. They've probably destroyed the entire house by now."

"Yeah, all right, then. Krystal's driving," Dody explained as she slowly pushed herself from the booth and stood. "So unless I want to call a cab, which I don't, I have to go on with her, so she can drop me off." Clearly, Dody was hoping to be invited to stay on at the Grain Elevator and catch a ride home with either Sarah or Liz, but neither of them offered.

"I've got to run, too," Liz announced instead. "I promised Parker I'd go over some briefs with him tonight. So I'll walk out with you two. Sarah, what do I owe you?"

"Not a thing. You go on, Liz. Supper's on me." Picking up the small leather folder that contained their check, which the waitress had brought with the round of drinks earlier, Sarah smiled at her friend. "Thanks for all your advice. I really do appreciate it."

"It was nothing, sweetie—and since you bought my dinner, I'm not even going to bill you! See you later, Sarah."

"'Night, Sarah," Krystal and Dody called over their shoulders.

The three women departed, leaving Sarah alone at the table, searching in her handbag for her credit card. Because of work, she had run late for her meeting with Liz, so hadn't had time before supper to stop at an automatic-teller machine for any cash. She placed the card in the small leather folder and sat back to finish her Tom Collins while she waited for the waitress to collect the check, noting idly that the upper level of the Grain Elevator was nearly deserted now, since it was almost ten o'clock and supper wasn't served past nine. A few diehard customers remained in a couple of the banquettes, but that was all. She bent her head over her drink, not wanting any of the lone males to get the mistaken impression that she was interested in being picked up for the rest of the evening, that that was why she hadn't left with her friends. So she didn't really see the man who approached her booth, mistakenly thought it was only the waitress returning—until he spoke.

"Hello, Sarah."

A long, slow, unexpected shudder that made her feel as though she were about to swoon crawled insidiously through her body at the sound of his low, silky voice. It was a voice she would have known anywhere; she had heard it in her dreams for more than a decade. Her hands began to tremble, abruptly tightened so convulsively around her glass that she was surprised it didn't shatter. Her cheeks flushed with sudden heat, and her heart started to hammer painfully in her breast as, after a long moment in which she struggled desperately for control of her emotions, she forced herself to glance up at him. She wondered apprehensively how long he had been in the Grain Elevator, watching her. If he had overheard her conversation with Liz.

"Hello, Renzo," Sarah said quietly.

He was even more devastatingly handsome than she remembered, the intervening years having polished and refined the rough, awkward planes and angles of young adulthood, so that now, in his prime, his body had fulfilled its promise of long bones, hard muscle and sinuous grace. He moved with the awesome strength and natural suppleness of some sleek, predatory animal, dark and dangerous, she thought, shivering a little. His glossy black hair was still long and shaggy, framing a hawkish visage even more finely chiseled than she recalled. Faint lines etched the corners of his eyes; the grooves that bracketed his sulky, sensuous mouth had deepened, giving his good looks a provocatively seasoned edge. He wore an obviously expensive, pin-striped black suit cut in the European fashion and a crisp white shirt, sans tie and unbuttoned at the collar to reveal a glimpse of throat and chest.

"You haven't changed a bit, Sary—except to grow even more beautiful. And there's a distant, elusive quality about you that I don't remember, one that reminds me of the princesses in those fairy tales you used to love, as though you dwell not in the world of mere mortals, but in some enchanted tower of misted, far-off lands, listening... waiting... for what, Sarah? Prince Charming? Or a knight in shining armor?"

He had been the latter to her—once, long ago. Did he recollect their childhood game and deliberately seek to remind her of it? "I'm sure I don't know what you're talking about, Renzo." Sarah tried to shrug off his observations, hurting inside, hating the fact that after all this time, he should know her so well. For even now, she felt as though she had, like Briar Rose, slept for a hundred years, spellbound, and had only just awakened. She shouldn't have had that second Tom Collins, she told herself fiercely. It had plainly wreaked havoc upon her senses. Renzo Cassavettes was a cad—and regardless of her daydreams about him, his giddying effect upon her, she would be the world's biggest fool to think any differently.

"Do you mind if I join you?" he asked, the glittering intensity of his dark eyes as they surveyed her belying the lightness of his tone.

"Actually, it's late and I was just leaving," she insisted, fumbling for her handbag and silently cursing the waitress, who had yet to reappear to take care of the bill. Although Sarah had dreamed of this meeting for years, now that it was upon her, she found she perversely didn't want it, after all. She was tied up in knots inside, a nervous wreck—not at all the calm, cool, poised femme fatale she had planned and imagined. Her heart was still pounding at an alarming rate; her mouth was so dry that she could hardly swallow. "I don't know why that waitress hasn't returned. I'd better go find her."

But to Sarah's sudden panic, before she could get up, Renzo smoothly slid in next to her on the banquette, effectively preventing her escape and forcing her back into the corner. His arm rested along the back of the seat, almost but not quite touching her shoulders.

"Please don't tell me you turn into a pumpkin at midnight. I won't believe you."

"No, but I—" She broke off abruptly, biting her lower lip. Dear God, she was so rattled by him that she had nearly said, *But I have a son waiting for me at home.* "But I have to work tomorrow," she ended lamely, acutely aware of his proximity, of the heat and muscle of his thigh pressed against hers.

"Really?" Renzo lifted one thick, unruly black eyebrow with mocking skepticism. "And here I thought only workaholics and journalists labored on Saturday."

"Yes, well, since, in addition to my regular job at Field-Yield, Inc., I'm currently handling all the advertising and promotion for J. D. Holbrooke's senatorial campaign, my schedule is pretty hectic at the moment." To Sarah's relief, the waitress showed up at last, but she was carrying a small, round, cork-lined tray on which sat a Tom Collins and a glass of Scotch, neat. "Miss, I think you've made a mistake. I didn't order another drink."

"No, you didn't, but I did." Reaching into the inside pocket of his jacket, Renzo withdrew a long, elegant black leather wallet, from which he removed a credit card. Then, picking up the folder that held Sarah's dinner check, he casually took out her Visa card, returning it to her and replacing it with his own American Express. A platinum one, she observed. Even Bubba's was only gold. Closing the folder, Renzo then handed it to the waitress, saying, "Thanks. You can cash me out now whenever you're ready."

After the waitress had gone, Sarah, having had a moment to try to gather her wits and composure, inquired tartly, "What do you think you're doing, Renzo?" She didn't want to be beholden to him for even so much as supper. She wanted nothing whatsoever from him or to do with him, she insisted to herself. Not now, not ever. He had no right to walk casually back into her life like this, to entrap her in the booth and coolly pay for her meal—as though he owned her. She had loved him, trusted him, given him her innocence—and he had repaid her by callously abandoning her, leaving her pregnant and alone. As she thought of that, all her old anger and resentment flared inside her. "I can pay my own bill, thank you very much!" she snapped indignantly.

Extracting a pack of Marlboros and a gold lighter from another pocket, Renzo lit up, dragging on the cigarette deeply before he exhaled, blowing a stream of smoke from his nostrils. "Humor me," he said shortly. "I owe you a dinner, at least."

"For what?"

For an interminable moment, she thought he wasn't going to answer. He stared down at his drink, as though he were lost in the past or hadn't heard her question—or had and intended to ignore it. Then, lifting the glass, he took a long swallow of the smoky Scotch it contained, drew on his cigarette again. Finally, as though he had just fought some violent, inner battle with himself—and lost—he glanced at her nakedly and spoke.

"For being so damned foolish as to leave you behind twelve years ago." His voice was soft but raw with emotion, and a muscle worked in his jaw, as she remembered it always had whenever he had been enraged or upset or both. If he had suddenly slapped her, she couldn't have been more stunned or dismayed. She couldn't seem to think anymore, such was the impact of his words upon her. Of all she had thought he might say, this was the very last thing she had ever expected. She was even more startled and distressed when he went on, his words coming now in a low, harsh rush that rang with truth and sincerity. "Damn it, Sary! We were going to be married! I loved you! I thought you loved me! So why'd you disconnect your telephone and refuse to answer my letters? Did you finally come to believe I'd actually murdered Sonny Holbrooke, as everybody else in town claimed? Is that why you cut me off as though I were just so much dead weight?"

This wasn't happening, Sarah thought dumbly, utterly stricken now, cold and sick inside. This wasn't real, but the product of her wild imagination, fueled by too many Tom Collinses. He wasn't truly here, wasn't truly saying all these things to her. Because if he were telling her the truth, she couldn't live with what she had done to him, would never forgive herself for it. He simply *must* be lying, as he had once lied about loving her, about wanting to marry her. Well, no matter what, she wouldn't be a gullible, trusting fool again!

"I—I don't believe you! You're lying! Just as you lied to me all those years ago, so you could—so you could... I never received any letters from you. There *weren't* any letters!" she insisted desperately, mercilessly assailed by doubts despite herself, her heart thudding furiously, her mind racing at the terrible, unthinkable thought that perhaps she *had* been wrong all these years about him never trying to get in touch with her. "You—you *never* wrote! You never called! My God! Do you honestly believe that if you had ever written or phoned me—even just once—I would have—" Shocked, horrified by the words that had nearly tumbled from her mouth, Sarah bit them back so hard that she bloodied her lower lip. *I would have kept your son from you?* she had almost blurted out heedlessly. "I wouldn't have answered you?" she amended hastily.

"Damn it, Sarah!" Renzo's eyes, smoldering like embers, seemed to scorch her own, to burn right through her. "I *did* call. But all I got was a recording that said your number was no longer in service. I *did* write. I never heard back from you. And then my mother sent me a letter, telling me that barely three months after I'd fled from town, you'd got married and moved away to parts unknown!"

"That's not true! I never did!" Sarah's consternation grew with each new revelation.

"I know that—now. But what do you think I thought back then? How do you think I felt? Especially when I wrote you again and then again, and you still never replied?"

"I—I never got your letters, Renzo," she confessed, devastated, compelled at last to admit to herself that he was telling the truth. She wanted to bury her head in her hands and weep at the realization. "Honestly, I didn't. Please believe me. Oh, my God! Mama! My *own* mama must have intercepted them. She must have opened them up and read them, then torn them up and thrown them away without ever telling me about them." Sarah knew suddenly with sick certainty, even as she voiced this conjecture, that it was indeed what had happened, why she had thought Renzo had forsaken her. It was what Mama had wanted her to believe.

Dear God. All these years, she had kept their son a secret from Renzo—to punish him for leaving her behind, for never getting in touch with her. What a horrible wrong she had done him! He hadn't lied to her, not ever. He had loved her, wanted her—and she hadn't known. *She hadn't known!* All those lonely, empty years wasted, when she might have been happy, when they and their son might have been a family! Sarah felt as though she were going to throw up, to be violently ill. But it was too late to put matters right. Renzo would hate her now; he would kill her, she thought dully. Yes, when he found out about their son, as he undoubtedly would, he would surely kill her. Italians set such store by family, by the eldest son, particularly.

"Why would your mother have done such a cruel thing, Sarah, not given you any of my letters? She didn't even know me!"

"Because..." *Because I was pregnant with your child,* she thought. *Because she blamed me for Daddy's death.* "Because we...had a lot of trouble after that day at the quarry, because I'd defended you. People started calling the house, harassing us, so we had to disconnect our telephone. And they—they sent us poison-pen letters, too." Sarah didn't explain to Renzo that both the hateful calls and mail had been directed at her, because she had been unwed and carrying his baby. She didn't tell him how often she had answered the telephone, only to hear unknown male voices saying things like, "Hey, Coal Lump, I got something real big and hard for you," and worse. How often she had opened envelopes, only to find notes inside, scrawled in unknown female handwriting, which had read, "You slut! You whore! God's going to punish you, Coal Lump Kincaid!" and worse, until she had ceased to open any mail addressed to her. "You of all people should know how hard and unforgiving this town can be, Renzo," she added, her voice ragged with the emotional turmoil that tore at her ruthlessly.

"Yeah, I guess I do." He sipped his Scotch, crushed his cigarette out in the ashtray. "People haven't exactly struck up the band and rolled out the red carpet for me since I've come home. You probably heard I bought the *Trib* from my folks and that they moved to Florida."

"Yes, word still gets around in this town, just as it always did."

"So you did know I was back, then. Tell me, weren't you the least bit...curious, even, to see me, Sary?"

"No," she forced herself to reply tersely, terrified as to where this discussion might be leading. She didn't want to know if he still loved her. She couldn't bear it. "Look, Renzo, twelve years ago we were just a couple of kids...in—" *In love,* she had nearly said. "Infatuated with each other, yes. But that's all. And now, it's just so much water under the bridge. You made a life for yourself elsewhere, and I made one for myself here, and just because you've chosen after all this time to return to town doesn't mean we're still the same two people. We're not."

"I know that. I know things have changed, and I'm not so foolish as to believe we can just pick up where we left off. But I..." *I never got over you,* Renzo wanted to say. "I never forgot you, Sary," he told her instead. "Call it *infatuation* if it pleases you." His mouth tightened with derision as he spoke the word, so she knew she had hurt him. "Whatever. I'd still like to see you again, to take you out if you'll let me."

"I'm—I'm sorry, Renzo." She swallowed hard, resolutely marshaling her defenses, compelling herself to continue calmly, coolly. Because what could she hope for, what could they have between them now, when it was too late? "But I'm afraid that's just not possible. I'm...involved with someone. We've been dating for over two years and he's...asked me to marry him." None of which was a lie exactly, Sarah assured herself, even if the way she had said it had been deliberately misleading. She still couldn't seem to think straight, to believe this entire conversation was actually taking place, to comprehend the hitherto unknown, unsuspected things he had told her. She knew only that she had wronged him terribly. She feared he knew it, too, and was playing some sort of horrible game with her.

"I see." Renzo's eyes were hooded, so she couldn't guess his thoughts. But the muscle in his jaw had started to twitch again, and she could feel the tension that coiled in his long, lean, hard body. His corded thigh was taut against hers. He drank the last of his Scotch, lit another cigarette. Then, after a moment, he glanced at her again and smiled—a smile that didn't quite reach his narrowed eyes, which glinted like shards in the dim lamplight of the Grain Elevator. "Congratulations. Anybody I know?"

She didn't want to tell him. He could see that plain upon her face, which had always been easy for him to read, he had known her so long and well, so deeply and intimately. And he hadn't needed to ask who the man in her life was. Renzo knew the name she was going to speak, even before she spoke it. His gut twisted inside him at the knowledge, roiled violently with rage and jealousy, even as he steeled himself to show no emotion outwardly, not even by the merest flicker of an eyelash, when she answered.

"Yes, you know him," Sarah admitted reluctantly. "It's Bubba . . . Bubba Holbrooke."

"Uh-huh," Renzo drawled.

Sarah's skin crawled at his response, so the fine hairs on her nape and arms stood on end. For in that moment, in the half light, he suddenly looked and sounded to her so much like Papa Nick that the resemblance was uncanny, frightening. Renzo despised Bubba. He always had. He certainly would not ever stand idly by and permit Bubba to rear Alex. She had made another awful mistake, she realized numbly, deceiving Renzo about Bubba. Who was it who had written, *Oh, what a tangled web we weave... ?*

"Look, Renzo, it's been ... good seeing you again, but I really *do* have to be leaving," she declared, gripped now by the same dark, unsettling sense of premonition that, like a serpent, had wrapped itself insidiously around her last night, when she had sensed him watching her from the trees at the edge of her lawn.

"All right. I'll walk you out to your car, then." Opening the folder the waitress had brought back to the table, he figured in the tip, then signed the credit-card slip and tore off his receipt, putting both it and his American Express card into his wallet. "Let's go."

"It really isn't necessary for you to see me to my Jeep," Sarah told him as they headed for the stairs that led down to the ground-level portion of the restaurant and club, she praying all that while that she wouldn't run into anybody she knew, Bubba himself or someone who would tell Bubba she had left the Grain Elevator in Renzo's company. She hadn't forgotten Bubba's wild threats, how he had said he would kill Alex's father if he ever learned his identity. "I assure you I'm perfectly capable of looking after myself."

"Yeah, I've noticed there's a hard, cold edge to you these days, Sarah, that you didn't used to have. I don't like it much," Renzo remarked as they stepped outside into the muggy night air, started toward the halogen-lit parking lot.

"Well, I don't really care what you like or don't like anymore, Renzo," Sarah lied. "That's my Jeep over there." She pointed to the British-racing-green vehicle, with its gold pinstriping, striding toward it quickly, having to force herself not to run, so he wouldn't know how scared she was, how much she longed to make good her escape from him before the dark, terrible, volatile thing she felt seething between them exploded. "Good night, Renzo. Thanks for supper," she called over her shoulder.

He caught her before she could get the Jeep door unlocked, abruptly spinning her around and pressing her up against the vehicle before she even realized what he intended, his eyes nearly black—and gleaming in a way she remembered only too well. It was the only warning she had before he fell upon her blindly, his strong hands tangling roughly in her mass of hair and his mouth seizing hers hungrily, his tongue inexorably forcing her lips apart and thrusting deep.

Wildly, Sarah fought him, pummeling him with her fists. But she was no match for his strength and determination. He captured her wrists easily, one hand pinioning them behind her back while the other imprisoned her by the hair again, holding her face still for his kisses. He took her mouth savagely, until at last, she was kissing him back feverishly, opening her lips pliantly to his, whimpering low in her throat with the desire and need that had like a wildfire erupted within her, setting her aflame. At that, his breath harsh and labored, Renzo released her. He stared down at her intensely, avidly, triumph and satisfaction glittering in his dark eyes as he drew the pad of his thumb slowly, tantalizingly, along her lower lip, bruised and swollen from his kisses, a single drop of blood from his teeth beaded there.

"You're not in love with Bubba Holbrooke, Sarah, my girl," he muttered thickly, one corner of his carnal mouth twisting into a mocking half smile. "Any more than I am. You couldn't have kissed me like that if you were."

Then he abruptly turned on his heel and left her standing alone in the darkness, tears seeping from her eyes to glisten like raindrops on her pale cheeks, one trembling hand pressed to her mouth to prevent herself from calling out his name, from calling him back to her.

Fifteen

Sad Songs

The music in my heart I bore,
Long after it was heard no more.

The Solitary Reaper
—William Wordsworth

He shouldn't have left Sarah standing there alone in the parking lot, Renzo thought fiercely. She had been crying. But if he had not got away when he had, he knew he would within the next few moments have been forcing her into her Jeep, forcing himself upon her, whether she had wanted him or not. But she *had* wanted him, had responded to him as passionately as she ever had. It was that realization that had nearly proved his undoing. It had been as though twelve years had not come and gone, as though all the old magic between them had merely been sleeping, biding its time, waiting to be reawakened. And by kissing her, he had stirred it to life again, roused it so it had once more sprung full-blown into being, engulfing him like the watery depths of the old quarry, so he had ached maddeningly to bury himself in the sweetness and light that was Sarah Kincaid.

She wouldn't have struggled against him for long, if she had even struggled at all. Why hadn't he just taken her? Because anyone might have happened upon them in the parking lot? He could have compelled her into his car and driven her to his loft. It was only the pain in her eyes that had stopped him, the tears streaking her cheeks. He had hurt her once, a long time ago, and the wound had gone deep, plainly never healing. Tonight, heedless of the agony to them both, he had brutally scraped off the scab, wanting, needing somehow to hurt her once more, to make her feel something—anything—for him again. She had just been so cool, so distant—calling their love an infatuation, taunting him with Bubba Holbrooke, telling him she didn't care what he, Renzo, liked and didn't like anymore.

She had infuriated him, prodded and provoked the devil in him, so he had unleashed it in order that it could collect its due. He just hadn't known how doing so would shake him up as badly as it had shaken her. How badly it would hurt him, as it had hurt her. He had behaved no better than a ravaging beast, he reflected, angry at himself for letting his violent emotions get the best of him. He hadn't meant his and Sarah's first encounter to go as it had.

Disgusted, Renzo stamped on the Jaguar's accelerator, speeding recklessly along the half-deserted streets of town, not caring if Sheriff Laidlaw or Deputy Truett pulled him over and ticketed him. He was spoiling for a fight, anything to rid himself of the unbridled turmoil churning inside him. He almost headed for the highway, intending to seek out someplace like Rowdy's Roadhouse and get rip-roaring drunk. But he knew that if he did, he'd only wind up in the end at Sarah's farmhouse, standing out on her lawn, shouting out to her like a damned fool. Or kicking her door down. And he wasn't that far gone. At least, not yet. So instead, he veered down the dark alley behind the newspaper building, pulled into the garage and killed the roadster's engine.

Minutes later, Renzo was upstairs in the loft, stripping off his clothes in the moonlit darkness, tugging on a pair of shorts to cover his nakedness. The skylights and windows were all open—he didn't see any point in running the huge air conditioner when he was usually gone most of the day, anyway—and the six old, metal-bladed ceiling fans original to the place whirled steadily, so the loft was cool enough, if a trifle humid. The Roman shades were all half drawn; beneath them, moonbeams filtered in to dance diffusely on the highly polished wood floor. From atop the antique sideboard that sat against one wall, he took a bottle of Scotch and a glass. Flinging himself down in a chair, he poured a drink, downed it. Then he grabbed his pack of cigarettes, lit one, inhaled deeply.

He was a fool. He should never have come back here, Renzo told himself wrathfully. He had accomplished nothing—except to drive himself crazy over Sarah again. It didn't matter that he had never got her out of his system. At least in Washington, D.C., he had been able to live with himself, to block her out of his mind for long periods at a time. Since he had returned to town, he hadn't stopped thinking about her. She was an obsession, pure and simple. He wished to hell he had never seen her on the

CNN news clip, had never imagined her lying in Bubba Holbrooke's arms, in Bubba's bed. If she married Bubba, Renzo knew he wouldn't be able to stand it, would be driven to some utterly rash and terrible act.

He poured himself another drink, drew on his cigarette again. Then, reaching abruptly for his saxophone, which sat in its stand to one side, he began to play.

The music that wailed into the night was wild and savage—and achingly sad, the blues as Sarah had only rarely ever heard them played. To her, they were always provocative, plucking deeply responsive, emotional cords within her. But these blues were something else, something *more*—raw, atavistic pain and need, gut wrenching, soul stirring, crawling not just inside her skin, but her very bones, her very essence, turning her inside out, clawing and ripping at her heart, rending it to shreds.

What on earth had ever possessed her to come here? she wondered, still dazed from the Tom Collinses, still reeling from the night's disclosures. She must be mad. The summer heat did that to people. She remembered Renzo reading a short story to her once, so many years ago that she could no longer even recall its title or who had written it. She knew only, vaguely, that it had been about a man who had dreamed that on a certain day, he had been murdered by a butcher. Happening by chance upon the butcher, the stricken man had recounted to him this tale. The poor butcher had been equally horrified, because he, too, had suffered a nightmare in which he had seen himself, on that very same day, a prisoner in chains, standing upon the transport docks. As a result, the two men had agreed to sit that particular day out together, so they could be absolutely certain nothing untoward would occur. The story had ended with the man watching the butcher sharpening his knives on the agreed-upon day, which was hot enough to drive a person mad. Even though the tale had ended there, Sarah had known the butcher had gone crazy from the heat and stabbed the man to death.

Now she thought that if she got out of her Jeep and went up to Renzo's loft, she would, like the hapless men in the story, be bringing her own fate upon herself, that something equally violent and terrible would happen. If Renzo's savage, demanding kisses had not warned her of it before, the saxophone music now was enough to tell her that, to let her know what kind of a dark, wild, yearning mood he was in. Yet, instead of driving home after leaving the parking lot at the Grain Elevator, she had inexplicably come here, to the town square, as though drawn by some irresistible, magnetic force. Was this what Renzo had felt last night, when he had stood upon her lawn in the darkness? She didn't know, could only guess.

Involuntarily, Sarah touched her fingertips to her mouth. It still burned from his kisses. Her body still ached from the emotions and tumult he had ignited within it. He had wanted her—and she him. She still wanted him, would only be lying to herself if she chose to believe otherwise. Was it possible that after all this time, Renzo actually still loved her? She thought again of all the horrifying, heartbreaking revelations this night had so unexpectedly offered up, of the wrong she knew in hindsight that she had done him. She was tempted, so very tempted to go up to the loft and tell him everything, the whole sad truth, and fling herself on his mercy, no matter how rough, how cruel.

Perhaps that was why she had come here.

But even now, fear and shame held her back. She had nothing left but her son, not even the forlorn hope, the impossible dream that Renzo would someday return and they would become a family.

Tears brimming once more in her eyes, Sarah started the Jeep and pulled slowly away from the curb, resolutely shutting her ears against the music of the weeping saxophone, which echoed in the dark.

On Monday, when Sarah returned home from work, it was to discover that Alex sported a black eye and a split lip from yet another fight at school, which had resulted in him receiving an automatic three-day suspension, the years having failed miserably to mellow the authoritative Mr. Dimsdale. Still the principal, he continued to enforce discipline as vigorously and stringently as he ever had in Sarah's day.

"Do you want to tell me what happened, Alex?" she asked her son after she had read the note from his teacher, which had accompanied him home from school.

"Well, what do you think happened?" he rejoined sullenly, fidgeting with the various condiments that sat on the kitchen table, refusing to look her in the eye. "Cash Archer and some of the other boys were hanging around the commons when summer school got out today. And they started in on me, as usual, calling me a bastard again, that's what!"

"Alex, we've had this conversation several times before," Sarah said wearily, feeling as though she should just record their discussion on tape, so she could play it when needed. "So I know you're fully cognizant of the fact that you are *not* to be fighting on school property—or anywhere else, for that matter—regardless of what the other children may say or do to provoke you."

"I know, I know. Sticks and stones may break our bones, but words can never hurt us," he droned in a smart-aleck, singsong voice. Then his face abruptly crumbled, and tears filled his eyes. "But it's not true, Mom! Words *do* hurt! I hate being called a bastard! I hate *being* one! Even if their parents are divorced, all the other kids at least know who their fathers are. It isn't right, it isn't fair that I don't! Why won't you ever talk to me about him? Why won't you at least tell me who he was . . . is? Or is it really true what people claim, that you don't even know yourself? Is that why my birth certificate says, 'Father Unknown' on it?"

"How do you know it says that?" Sarah queried sharply, mortified.

"Because when you never would let me see it, I wrote off to the capital for a copy of it," Alex confessed, wiping angrily at his eyes, ashamed of his tears. "I got the address from a book at the library, and I used six dollars of my allowance to pay the fee."

"Even though I understand why you did it, it still wasn't a very nice thing for you to have done, Son," Sarah insisted gently. "Especially your going behind my back like that. I kept your birth certificate from you for a very good reason—because I knew what it said about your father would hurt you. But since you've seen fit to pry into this matter before I felt you were old enough both to discuss and understand it, I'll tell you that what you read isn't true. I *do* know who your father is. I've always known."

"Then why did you say you didn't on my birth certificate?"

"Because I didn't want everybody else in town knowing, too, that's why."

"Why? Is my dad someone really awful, then? Like a—a serial killer or an armed robber or a—a lunatic? Is he locked up in prison or a nuthouse or something? A stinking old nursing home, like Grandma?"

"Good heavens, no! Of course not. Whatever gave you such bizarre ideas?"

"Well, that's what the kids at school say—and worse, Mom. They say you went through high school flat on your back until old Dimwit kicked you out for being pregnant with me. They say you slept with the entire football team, that you were the team mascot—Randy Dandy, the Lincoln Lie-on. I just can't bear it when they say such terrible things about you, Mom! And if you must know, that's why I keep on getting into fights at school and all."

"Oh, Alex, I'm so sorry...so very sorry." Deeply stricken, Sarah sat down beside her son at the kitchen table and put her arm around his shoulders, hugging him close and stroking his tousled black hair. "I guess I should have realized . . . But I just never dreamed people still said all those horrible things behind my back, or that if they did, you'd hear them."

"I didn't want to hurt your feelings, Mom. That's why I never told you before."

"That's okay, Alex. I've had a long time now to grow accustomed to it, to learn how to deal with the pain. It doesn't hurt me at all the way it used to. I'm just sorry it's hurt *you*. Because I wouldn't ever let that happen, not for anything in the whole wide world, if I could prevent it. But I can't. I can tell you, however, that none of that awful talk you've heard is true—not one single word of it! Your father's not anybody you'll ever have to be ashamed of, Alex. In fact, he's someone you can be extremely proud of. I loved him very much, and he was the *only* man I ever had anything to do with for practically my entire life. And the only football player I've ever even so much as kissed is Bubba Holbrooke."

"You're not going to marry big, bad Bubba, are you, Mom?" Alex inquired sourly, grimacing. "I mean, if you truly want to, I suppose I could force myself to be nice to him at least. But I don't really like him all that much, even if all the other kids *do* think he's way cool. He doesn't know anything about the classics or comic books or motorcycles. He hates to fish, and he insulted my saxophone playing once after supper, when you were in the kitchen, washing up. He said I sounded like a screech owl and ought to be arrested for disturbing the peace! That wasn't nice of him, Mom, was it?"

"No, it wasn't. And no, I don't think I'm going to marry Bubba. There are worse fates, I suspect, than winding up an old maid."

"You're not old, Mom. And maybe...well, maybe someday you and my dad will get back together again. Because I think you must still be in love with him, Mom. That's what Heather Thurley says, anyway—and she's the smartest girl in school, even if she *is* kind of silly about romance and always has her nose stuck in one of those Sweet Valley High novels. Mom, are you ever going to tell me who my dad was...is? I mean, he's not dead or anything like that, is he? I *am* going to get to meet him someday, aren't I?''

"No, he's not dead, and yes, you're going to get to meet him someday. Perhaps even sooner than you think and sooner than I ever intended, actually. And since that's the case, I probably should explain some other things to you now, as well, Alex—why your father hasn't been a part of your life all these years. I hope you won't ever blame him for that, because it's not his fault. You see, the truth is that I... Well, I never have told him about you, Alex. Something tragic happened that caused us to break up a long time ago, even though I didn't want to, and afterward, I was angry and hurt and going through a very difficult time in my life. My own daddy, your grandfather, had an unexpected heart attack and died then, too, which was terribly hard, especially since my mama, your grandmother, blamed me for it and said all the scandal and strain I had brought upon my family had caused it. It wasn't until years later, when I had to put Grandma in the nursing home, that I learned from one of the doctors there that my daddy had what was called a 'balloon heart,' which nobody knew how to treat very well back then, so one day, it had just swollen up and burst. It might have happened at any time. At any rate, through all that, I felt as though your father had abandoned me, and at a time when I desperately needed him most, so I wanted to punish him.''

"And that's why you—why you never told him about me?"

"Yes, that's right."

"Well, that was pretty mean and horrible of you, Mom," Alex asserted soberly, his dark brown eyes sad and accusing. "I mean, what if my dad had stolen me out of the hospital or something after I was born, so you never even saw me or knew anything about me? How would you have felt?"

"Oh, Son. I'd never have got over it. You're the light of my life, the one thing that's made all the pain and loneliness bearable all these years. And that's why I know how hurt your father's going to feel when he finds out about you, how angry he's going to be with me."

"Is he—is he going to be mad at me, too, Mom? To—to hate me?" her son asked anxiously, his eyes suddenly haunted by shadows.

"Oh, no, Alex. Regardless of whatever he may feel toward me, I know your father will love *you* with all his heart. That's the kind of man he is. So from now on, when the kids at school start teasing you, I want you not to fight with them anymore. I want you to hold your head high instead, to look them square in the eye and tell them your father is a man you can be proud of. And don't worry about what they say about me. I can take it. Do you understand me?"

"Yes, Mom."

"Good. Now, I'll tell you what. How about my taking as much time off as I can these next three days while you're suspended? We'll wade in the creek, go fishing, cook our catch over a fire, maybe even camp out in the tree house or the tent or something. What do you say to that, pal?"

"I say it's a deal. And, Mom...thanks for telling me that stuff about you and my dad, and all. I feel a whole lot better now, almost as I though I actually know him. Maybe I'll even recognize him if I ever run into him now! Do you think I might? I'm real glad he didn't turn out to be a convict or a crazy chump or anything, like I was half afraid he would. Do you think *he'll* like my saxophone playing, Mom?"

"Oh, yes, Son," Sarah replied quietly, remembering Renzo's wild, heartrending playing last Friday night. "I think he'll like it very much indeed."

Sixteen

The Interview

Be thy intents wicked or charitable,
Thou com'st in such a questionable shape
That I will speak to thee.

Hamlet
—William Shakespeare

The following morning, Sarah told J.D. that because of Alex having been suspended from summer school, she absolutely had to have some time off to spend with her son. As she had known he would, J.D. grumbled and groused at some length about both his senatorial campaign and his fertilizer plant. But eventually, he told her to go on home, and that since she was taking Tuesday, Wednesday and Thursday off, she might as well take Friday, too, making a week of it with her boy.

"Thank you, J.D. I surely appreciate it."

"Well, I don't," Bubba complained peevishly the minute they had left J.D.'s office, Bubba carrying a handful of reports that had required his father's signature. "I need you here, Sarah. Advertising and promotion for FYI have been in the toilet ever since you started working on that damned senatorial campaign. Nora just doesn't have your style, your flair." FYI was short for Field-Yield, Inc., while Nora Oliver was the assistant director of the fertilizer plant's advertising-and-promotions department, and had temporarily assumed several of Sarah's duties.

"Bubba, I'm sorry, but I just can't help it. Part of the reason Alex has so many problems is because I'm hardly ever around anymore—since I'm working all the time for you and J.D. both. And I just can't afford to keep on doing that, especially now."

"What do you mean, 'especially now'?" Bubba asked, puzzled and curious.

"Just—just Alex's suspension, that's all." Sarah's face flushed at the half truth, because what she had really meant was that if and when he found out about Alex, Renzo might use her job situation, all her overtime hours, to say she wasn't taking proper care of their son. "Alex is going to have to repeat the sixth grade if he doesn't do well in summer school—and he can't do well if he can't attend, can he?"

"That kid's more trouble 'n he's worth!" Bubba growled. Then, seeing the expression on Sarah's face, he hastily changed his tune. "But I'll tell you what—how'd you like me to come out sometime this week, play a little touch football with the boy or something? Part of the trouble, as I've told you before, Sarah, is that Alex needs a father. Now, maybe you don't think I'm exactly cut out for that role—and maybe I'm not—but the fact of the matter is that I've always offered, at least been willing to give it a try. You're the one who keeps on refusing to give me a chance, and that's not hardly fair, Sarah."

She sighed heavily, knowing his accusation was on target. "Maybe you're right, Bubba. Why don't you plan on coming to supper Wednesday night, then, and we'll see how it goes?"

"Okay," he agreed slowly, surprised but pleased. "That sounds good. I'll be there. You want me to bring some steaks? I can cook 'em on your grill for us."

"That'd be real nice, Bubba." It was hard for Sarah when he was on his best behavior, because then she knew he wasn't really as bad as he pretended. As she always had in the past, she wavered in her feelings toward him at times like these, telling herself that even if she wouldn't be happy with Bubba, she would at least be content, comfortable and cared for—which was actually a good deal more than a lot of wives could say. Bubba had a roving eye, and if she ever married him, or even slept with him, the sharp edge of his interest would dull and he would stray. He probably wouldn't be as fastidiously discreet as J.D. was about cheating on ZoeAnn, but Bubba wouldn't flaunt his women in Sarah's face, either—unless she drove him to it. He had money, and he wasn't cheap, wouldn't begrudge her any luxuries that wouldn't put him on the road to financial ruin. He would be a well-meaning but inattentive father, showering love and presents carelessly on their children, expecting that to make up for his absences.

Not for the first time, Sarah told herself she could, in fact, do a whole hell of a lot worse than Bubba Holbrooke, and she wondered what was wrong with her that she was so reluctant to settle for what he had to give. Was it possible she had in her youth seen Renzo Cassavettes through a pair of rose-colored shades? Had she, as a young, imaginative woman in the throes of her first love, scripted a romantic fairy tale for herself—and then put him in a suit of shining armor, whether or not it had fit? Had she, over the years, taken the best of him and magnified it in her mind, so he had loomed larger than life to her and she had conveniently forgotten the fears and flaws that had made him human? If their relationship had not been so suddenly, ruthlessly and tragically severed, would the sense that he had been the other half of her soul gradually have faded with time, to be replaced with the proverbial familiarity that bred contempt? Had she, all these years, loved only a dream? Or was it really and truly that regardless of what a person called it—love, infatuation, animal attraction, magic, fireworks, butterflies, bells, chimes, pheromones or chemistry—Renzo was the one and only man who had, in the words of so many love songs, ever thrilled her, sent her, turned her on, done it for her? The one and only man who ever would?

Sarah didn't know. She knew only that something deep inside her rebelled at settling for contentment in a world where ecstasy also existed, at reconciling herself to the commonplace when the rare was infinitely more precious. She would, she thought with a wry smile, rather be dead than dull. And if she were honest with herself, she must admit that the plain, simple truth of the matter was that Bubba just didn't excite her. And how did any woman ever explain that to a man without injuring his pride and deflating his fragile male ego? There was no way possible that she knew of—and because she also knew what it was to be hurt, Sarah found it difficult to hurt others. So she shuffled along with Bubba, offering him hope—when, in the end, it would have been kinder to be cruel.

Still, the supper she and Alex shared with Bubba passed pleasantly enough, if a trifle stiltedly, with both the boy and the man on their best behavior, studiously polite. But the best time of all was that which Sarah spent with her son alone, tramping through the meadows, creeks and woods, showing him all the secret, wondrous places that had been special to her and Renzo in their youth and recounting to Alex one story after another about his father—although she was careful never to mention Renzo by name. In that week, Sarah found at least a part of the loving little boy she had lost somewhere along the way—as she had lost his father, too—and she and her son grew closer than they had been in quite some time.

She realized then that in working so many long, hard hours to provide him with the financial security and material objects she had never had as a child, she was depriving him of the far more important intangibles, the things that would mold the boy someday into the man.

She returned to Field-Yield, Inc. the following week, fiercely determined somehow to cut her hectic schedule down to more manageable proportions—only to discover her desk stacked high with paperwork that had accumulated in her absence and Renzo Cassavettes comfortably ensconced in a chair in her office.

"What are *you* doing here?" she asked, startled.

"I believe it has something to do with the mountain coming to Muhammad."

"Yes, well, as you can plainly see, I already have a mountain!" She motioned toward her beleaguered desk. "And I don't need another one. So will you please leave so I can get on with my work?"

"Sarah, my girl," he drawled as he stood and began one by one to close the miniblinds that shielded the interior windows in her office from the hallway beyond. "I *am* your work—your nine o'clock appointment, to be precise." With a sharp little click, he firmly shot home the dead bolt that locked her office door.

"What—what do you think you're doing, Renzo?" Sarah stared at him, aghast, at once horrified and excited by his actions. "Have you completely lost your mind? This is my place of employment! Open those miniblinds and my office door immediately, and then get out!"

"Not a chance. Sit down, Sary. Supper didn't work, so this time, I've brought breakfast instead." Reaching down, he lifted from the floor a woven picnic basket she hadn't noticed earlier and set it in the middle of her desk, flipping back the lid and removing the tablecloth nestled inside to reveal an assortment of fruits, cheeses, breads and a bottle of wine.

"I am calling security," Sarah insisted, picking up the receiver on her telephone and punching the intercom. To her shock, the line was totally dead.

"I believe you require this in order for a telephone to work," Renzo observed as he reached casually into the inside pocket of his suit jacket to withdraw the slender cord that attached the telephone to its outlet in the wall. "And if I were you, I wouldn't even *think* about screaming, Sary. There are one or two things besides a handkerchief with which I would most certainly choose to silence you—and I would find them extremely pleasant myself, I assure you." His eyes raked her licentiously, in case his words had not made his meaning plain.

Sarah could feel the surge of crimson heat that rushed to stain her cheeks at that, and she sat down abruptly in her chair, stricken and panicked. She didn't know how to deal with this Renzo Cassavettes who had returned to town, she thought—in his expensive dark suits, his crisp white shirts and his foulard ties; this Renzo who was so smooth, so polished, so well-traveled and so experienced in the ways of the world and women. She simply couldn't believe he had any real interest in her anymore, feared that for reasons of his own, which were as yet unknown to her, he was merely amusing himself at her expense. And she had already suffered once that way at his hands.

"Why are you doing this to me, Renzo?" she asked quietly.

"Because it...pleases me to share your company."

"Even if I don't wish it?"

"You did once."

"That was before...that dreadful day."

"I asked you that night at the Grain Elevator, and you never answered me. So now, I'm asking you again, Sarah—do you believe I deliberately shoved Sonny Holbrooke off that rock?"

"No, I know it was a terrible accident."

"Then I don't understand. Why won't you go out with me?"

"I told you Bubba and I—"

"You don't give a damn about Bubba—not in your heart, anyway! No, there's something else, something you're not telling me, Sarah. I can feel it. I just can't quite put my finger on what it is." His dark brown eyes glittered avidly with perplexity and speculation as he watched the color slowly drain from her face.

Still, "There's nothing else," she insisted, shaking her head, her heart thudding fiercely at the frightening thought that he had learned about Alex at last and now, instead of confronting her, was playing some terrible cat-and-mouse game with her.

"Very well. We'll leave it—whatever it is—for now." Renzo spread the tablecloth on the floor, set upon it the single plate he had filled, the single glass of wine. "Come. Sit down here beside me," he demanded softly as he settled himself on the floor. "You can bring me up to date on J.D.'s senatorial campaign. I'll even turn on my tape recorder, so you can be certain I really *am* planning to write an article for the *Trib*." He laid a voice-activated, pocket tape recorder on the tablecloth as, not knowing what else to do, Sarah obediently went and sat down beside him.

To her surprise, Renzo actually did conduct an interview, ignoring, however, her statements to the effect that she was only handling advertising and promotions for the campaign, that he really needed to speak to J.D. or Taggart Evanston, J.D.'s campaign manager, if he wanted his questions answered. All the while Renzo talked to her, he fed her from the lone plate they shared, pressed upon her sips of wine from the solitary glass. He stroked her lightly—her hair, her face, her hands—nothing more. Yet she felt as heated and aroused as though he were making feverish love to her, as headily intoxicated as though she had drunk too much of the wine—although she knew she had consumed hardly any. Her mind and body reeled from the feelings and sensations that assailed her, besieged her, filling her with confusion. Her breath came far too rapidly and shallowly, as though she had run a long way and now could not get enough air into her lungs.

And then, when Renzo glanced at his wristwatch and saw that his allotted hour was up, he calmly packed everything away into the picnic basket and returned her telephone cord to her. Cupping her chin in his hand, he tilted her face up to his and brushed her mouth lightly with his own, saying, "You see? You've nothing to fear from me, Sarah." Then he opened the miniblinds, unlocked the door and left her.

Sarah was so flustered that she didn't know what to think, what to make of his behavior. She somehow felt as seduced by him as she had that summer's day at the old quarry. Renzo was wrong, she thought at last. She had everything to fear from him. Knowing that, she instructed her secretary, Kate Alcott, not to book any more appointments for Renzo Cassavettes.

Despite the wide-open window that was surely playing havoc with Field-Yield, Inc.'s air-conditioning system, Bubba Holbrooke's office reeked of marijuana smoke. In the luxurious, burgundy leather manager's chair sat Lamar Rollins, his feet propped up on the large, drawerless, steel-and-smoked-glass desk, the computer to one side humming. Lamar took another drag on his joint, his eyes closed, his head moving in time to the rhythm of the hip-hop music that drummed from the compact stereo on Bubba's credenza. Lamar was supposed to be cleaning the office this evening. But since Uncle Thaddeus was clear at the other end of the building and it would be a long while before he managed to shuffle up this way, Lamar had chosen this opportunity both to grab a smoke and to update the files in his directory secreted on Field-Yield, Inc.'s computer system. The sound of the vacuum cleaner would warn him of Uncle Thaddeus's approach. At that time, Lamar would hurriedly shut down the computer, close the window and spray around some of the Glade Potpourri air freshener he carried on his janitorial cart. As he now rapped along to Salt 'n' Peppa's latest hit, he opened his eyes to check on the programs he was currently running.

"Hellooo! What's this?" he asked himself, abruptly sitting bolt upright in the chair, his eyes widening, adrenaline beginning to pump through his body. For months, he had, through Field-Yield, Inc.'s computer system, hacked into various other systems around town and elsewhere, as well as into the fertilizer plant's own files, amusing himself by finding out, among other things, how much money the Holbrookes and everybody else who worked at Field-Yield, Inc. earned. So Lamar knew he was the lowest-compensated employee on the entire payroll. He used that information to justify the time he spent on the computer instead of sweeping up, not to mention the diskettes, fertilizer and other items he pilfered from the company.

During his hacking forays, he had discovered a mysterious hidden directory not dissimilar to his own. Intrigued, he had attempted to break into it. But like his own, it was protected by a password, and so far, nothing he had tried had worked. Since he had no idea to whom the directory belonged, the usual clues to the password—people generally chose words or numbers they could easily remember and that had some significance to them—weren't available to him. So Lamar had developed a deciphering program that utilized the various dictionaries installed on Field-Yield, Inc.'s system. It appeared that tonight he had finally found the key that would unlock the cryptic directory.

Quickly, he opened it, scanning the list of files, a puzzled frown knitting his brow. The file names were obscure. He didn't recognize any of them.

"Okeydoke. Let's just see what y'all babies is." He highlighted the first file and started to scan the information that appeared in chunk after chunk. For a moment, he couldn't make heads or tails of what he scrolled through on the screen. Then at last understanding dawned. "Shit! Oh, shit, man!"

What he read was so unbelievable, so dangerous to know that Lamar pushed himself away from the desk so fast that the rolling chair nearly toppled over backward. He only saved himself from falling by grabbing on to the edge of the desk. Briefly, he wished he had never seen what he had just viewed. But he had—and since he had, he might as well use the terrible information to his advantage. It would be worth a hell of a lot of money to him from someone to keep his mouth shut about it, he thought. Trembling then with excitement instead of fear, he fumbled around for the box of formatted diskettes he had taken from one of the storerooms earlier. He tore off the plastic wrapper, ripped off the lid and jammed the first diskette into the A: drive. Then, his heart racing, he began to download all the files in the directory.

Seventeen

Wicked Deeds

There is a method in man's wickedness—
It grows up by degrees.

A King and No King
—Francis Beaumont and John Fletcher

After that day in her office at Field-Yield, Inc., it seemed that Sarah ran into Renzo everywhere in town, that she spent much of her time trying to avoid him and, failing that, to escape from him. He unnerved her. She continued to refuse to believe he was serious about wanting to go out with her again, and even if he were, she knew there wasn't any future for them together. Because he turned up so often wherever she happened to be, she thought he must be spying on her, and that notion made her frantic, even though she knew with certainty that, realistically, it was only a matter of time before he finally did learn about Alex, if he didn't already know. More than once, she told herself that since that was the case, the sensible course of action would be to make an appointment with Renzo in his own office at the *Tri-State Tribune*—where he might be less likely to do her some violence—and tell him about their son.

But despite Liz's reassurances that night at the Grain Elevator, Sarah still harbored a gnawing fear that Renzo would attempt to take Alex away from her. Renzo didn't necessarily have to demonstrate that she was an unfit mother, she thought, disheartened, only to show he could provide Alex with many more advantages in life than she could, which was undeniably true. And perhaps a judge would be swayed not only by that, but also by the fact that Renzo had been deprived of his son for eleven long years. A sympathetic judge might rule that Renzo was now entitled to custody of Alex to make up for that deprivation.

Mentally, Sarah had begun to steel herself against these potentialities, to admit to herself that it was possible she would lose her son, even though she would fight tooth and nail to hold on to him. She hoped Renzo would not prove so cruel as to try to wrest the boy from her. But then, it had doubtless never occurred to Renzo that if he had left her pregnant, she herself could be so cruel as to keep their child from *him*. In such an event, he had probably expected to be informed in no uncertain terms, to be hit up by her for money for an abortion. Wasn't that both the risk and the responsibility all decent men assumed when they slept with a woman? But then, of course, decent men didn't casually take a seventeen-year-old girl's innocence, carelessly impregnate her and then callously abandon her, either. After all, she had only Renzo's word and her own gut instinct to tell her he had spoken the truth to her that night at the Grain Elevator, that he really *had* tried to get in touch with her all those years ago. And if he were lying to her, how could she trust her own intuition, when it would have played her false before where he was concerned?

Obviously, for her own peace of mind, she should drive over to the Woodlands Nursing Home and speak to her mother, Sarah told herself. She would do it today, on her lunch hour, even though it wasn't her regular day to visit. Still, Sarah hoped that maybe it would prove to be one of Iris Kincaid's increasingly rare, "sensible" days. Because if it had only been arthritis from which Mama suffered, Sarah would never even have considered putting her in a nursing home. That had become necessary when the doctors had diagnosed her mental decline as a result of Alzheimer's disease. At first, it had been only little things, like Mama forgetting what she had intended to take out of a cupboard or the refrigerator. But then she had not been able to remember her own telephone number—or where she had lived for over twenty-five years. She had begun to do bizarre things like putting silverware in the freezer and the ice trays in the silverware drawer. Now, on her more lucid days, she frequently believed her husband, Dell, was still alive and that Sarah was still a child.

Mama didn't remember Alex at all, even though she had practically reared him until he was seven and Sarah—feeling then that she and Alex had needed their own home, away from all of Mama's anger and bitterness, and away from Sarah's own unhappy memories, too—had bought the old Lovell place when it had come on the market. Sarah didn't blame Mama anymore for the anger and bitterness. She understood now how loss and grief could cause a person to do terrible things to someone she loved.

Sarah took a bouquet from the Flower Garden to the nursing home. But much to her disappointment, Mama was having an especially bad day and only looked at her blankly, bewildered, when asked about Renzo's letters, whether or not he had ever written. After an hour, Sarah left the Woodlands, knowing no more than when she had arrived and thoroughly saddened and depressed by her mother's condition.

In the Jeep, Sarah noticed lying on the floor a tiny white flower that had fallen from Mama's bouquet. The bloom made her think suddenly of the delicate white orchid Renzo had sent her on prom night so many years ago, of the white organza gown Mama had worked so hard to make for her to wear that evening and of Daddy with his Polaroid camera, snapping pictures of her and teasing her gruffly about her secret admirer. And sitting there in the nursing-home parking lot beneath the fierce, hot sun, Sarah abruptly laid her head on the steering wheel and cried.

Initially, the fact that the battery in his Rolex wristwatch was dead had been a source of great annoyance to Renzo. But now, as he stood grimly at the glass counter in Goldberg's Fine Jewelry, listening to Bubba and Mrs. Goldberg discuss the merits of various diamond engagement rings, Renzo could only count the dead battery as a blessing. Because until this moment, he had not, in his heart, truly believed Sarah Kincaid was going to marry Bubba Holbrooke.

"I declare, Bubba," Gladys Goldberg said, shaking her head and beaming jovially. "I'll bet you're just plumb tickled pink that that pretty little gal of yours is finally going to walk down the aisle with you after all this time!"

"Well, Sarah hasn't exactly said yes yet, Mrs. Goldberg," Bubba confessed a trifle reluctantly. "Still, she's softening. Yes-siree-bob, she is definitely softening, leaning in my direction." The smug smile on Bubba's face made Renzo's fingers itch to throttle him. "That's why I thought an engagement ring might just do the trick. You know. Might show her I really do mean business, that I really am serious about her. I'm just not sure which one of these she'd like the best." Bubba gazed uncertainly at all the diamond solitaires in the display case.

"Renzo," Mrs. Goldberg called. "Why don't you come on over here a minute and give us another opinion, while Isaac's popping the back off your watch to replace that battery."

"Well, I would, Mrs. Goldberg," Renzo answered politely, "except that I can't imagine my opinion would be of any interest whatsoever to Holbrooke there."

"Oh, now, you never know, Cassavettes," Bubba rejoined carelessly, much to Renzo's surprise, and smiled contemptuously. "It might. In fact, I expect it would prove real amusing, actually, to find out just what sort of ring a man from your side of the tracks would choose from out of this case—and for what sort of female. Just exactly what kind of taste you have."

"In rings—or women?" Renzo lifted one eyebrow coolly, a mocking half smile—which didn't quite reach his hard, narrowed eyes—playing about the corners of his mouth.

Bubba shrugged nonchalantly. "Both."

"Now, why should either be of any interest to you?"

"Oh, I don't know. Just plain old curiosity, I reckon."

"I do believe that's what killed the cat," Renzo drawled softly. "Ah, Mr. Goldberg, you're done with my wristwatch, I see."

"Yes, I am." Isaac Goldberg nodded. "It's running just fine now, Renzo. Do you want to wear it out of the shop?"

"Please." Renzo chatted congenially with old Mr. Goldberg long enough to observe Bubba pick out an engagement ring, pay for it and have it gift wrapped, telling Mrs. Goldberg he planned to give it to Sarah this coming Saturday night.

On Thursday afternoon, while Sarah was visiting the nursing home and after both Renzo and Bubba had departed from Goldberg's Fine Jewelry, Lamar Rollins was at the town square, choosing a public telephone from which to place his all-important call. He had got the unlisted number he needed from a Rolodex at Field-Yield, Inc., and he knew from what had been written on the card that the line was a private one that rang directly into the office of the person he wanted to reach, bypassing the switchboard. Lifting the receiver and dropping a quarter into the slot, he punched in the number. For a long moment, he thought no one was going to answer.

"Come on, come on," Lamar muttered to himself, cursing under his breath as the ringing continued to resound in his ear.

"Yes?" The single word was low, quietly spoken, so that with all the noise in the town square, Lamar hardly heard it. Perhaps using a pay phone hadn't been such a good idea, after all. But he had had some bizarre notion that his call might somehow be traced otherwise.

"Don't talk," he ordered tersely, nervously. "Just listen—and get all this straight, 'cause I'm only gonna say it one time. I know 'bout the quarries...what you been dumpin' out there. And I got me copies of them secret files of yours to prove it. So if you don't want me to turn 'em over to the Feds, it's gonna cost you. It's gonna cost you big time, man!

"Now, you'd probably like to tell me I don't know what I'm talkin' 'bout, but you'd be a fool, tryin' to jive me. And just in case you don't believe me, you go on ahead and try and access those files yourself. 'Cause you won't be able to... will find yourself locked out of your own directory. 'Cause, you see, I changed your password, so you'd know I ain't lyin' 'bout all this and that I mean business.

"So here's the deal. In exchange fo' my password and my copies of your files—not to mention me keepin' my mouth shut 'bout all this—I want twenty-five grand to start. Now, I reckon you might think that's too much money—'specially seein' as how it's just a little down payment, so to speak. But, hey, it's gonna cost you a helluva lot more 'n that if I talk to the law. 'Cause if that happens, you be goin' away fo' a long, *looong* time, man! To a place where they ain't too nice to fish, if you get my drift—and if you don't, fish is green inmates in the pen, fool, nice, fresh meat fo' all them big, mean homeboys.

But then, you *do* got connections, so maybe it won't be too bad. With time off fo' good behavior, you might even get out in, say, fifteen or twenty years—if you is still alive by then, that is. So I figger you is gettin' off cheap, payin' me.

"Now, I ain't a fool. So I know it ain't take long fo' you to get me my money. Hell. You probably got that much stashed in your safe. And if you don't, if you have to go to the bank, cash in some bonds or CDs or somethin', you do it tomorrow mornin', first thing. You get small, ole bills, nothin' larger than a twenty—and they better not be marked or have none of that dye shit on 'em, neither!

"Then you meet me out by the railroad tracks on the ole town road tomorrow night, at midnight. That way, I can see you comin'. And you best be by your lonesome self, man! 'Cause I be watchin' you, and if you ain't come alone, if I see any sign of that asshole Sheriff Laidlaw or that dumb Deputy Truett, I won't hang 'round to get caught. And I'll turn those files over to the Feds fo' sho'. And not only to them, neither!

"So don't you go gettin' any bright ideas 'bout gettin' rid of me, permanent-like. 'Cause I have taken myself out a little insurance policy, you see. I made copies of those files of yours and mailed 'em to a friend of mine, along with a note, sayin' as how if anythin' happens to me, he's to open the envelope I sent him and take a look at what's on them diskettes inside. I figger that if anybody will, he'll know what to do with your files. So you just think 'bout bein' spread out all over the TV and newspapers! You'll be front-page headlines, man! For all the wrong reasons!

"Now, did you get all that, fool?"

"Yes."

"Then, like the man says, be there or be square. Later, dude." Grinning with elation, Lamar abruptly severed the connection.

The party at the other end listened furiously to the resulting dial tone that buzzed from the receiver. And in that moment, Lamar Rollins was already a dead man.

He just didn't know it yet.

Eighteen

The Storm

And I was desolate and sick of an old passion,
Yea, I was desolate and bowed my head:
I have been faithful to thee, Cynara! in my fashion.

*Non Sum Qualis Eram Bonae Sub
Regno Cynarae*
—Ernest Dowson

For the first time in a long while, Bubba wasn't around to see her safely home after dark, and perversely, as Sarah pulled the heavy glass front doors of Field-Yield, Inc. shut behind her and securely locked them, she wished he were here. But he had been called away from the office earlier, just before closing, and had got tied up in a neighboring town and never returned.

"Sarah honey, I'm sure sorry," he had said to her on the telephone more than an hour ago. "But it looks like I'm not going to make it back home until real late tonight—if I get back at all. I might have to wind up checking into a motel here and driving back first thing tomorrow morning. So I'll see you sometime tomorrow afternoon, at the office. You're still planning on working half a day tomorrow, aren't you, darlin', even though it's a Saturday?''

"Yes," she had confirmed. "I've just got to take care of some of this stuff for FYI that Nora hasn't handled properly. The copy she's written for that new radio jingle we're going to start running in a few weeks needs work—and the music she okayed for it is just dreadful. She must have had flirting instead of farming on the brain at the time." After chatting with Bubba about business for a few more minutes, Sarah had hung up, feeling strangely depressed.

Under normal circumstances, she would have looked forward to spending a Friday night alone with Alex, playing Nintendo with him or popping corn and watching a movie together, which they would have rented from the video outlet at the Farmers' Market grocery store.

But her son had called earlier to ask if he could spend the night at Mickey Thurley's house. Mickey was Alex's best friend—even though Sarah suspected Alex liked Mickey's sister, Heather, equally as well. Jimmie Dean, Mickey and Heather's father, had offered to collect Alex in the Thurleys' new pickup truck and to bring him home in the morning. So, thinking she would be spending most of the evening with Bubba, Sarah had agreed that Alex could go.

Now, as she walked out to Field-Yield, Inc.'s halogen-lit parking lot to her Jeep, Sarah wished she had told Alex he had to stay home. But of course, that wouldn't have been fair to him. Still, the thought of going home alone to her dark, empty house was dispiriting. There was a storm coming on, too, she realized as she glanced up at the night sky, where lightning flashed against the far horizon. The temperature must have dropped by at least twenty degrees since its high of over a hundred this sweltering afternoon, because the air was considerably cooler and the wind had picked up. The rain would be welcome after the endless dog days of summer, because of which the town was experiencing a water shortage and the water-treatment plant had been strained to its utmost. Its equipment was so old and inadequate that it simply hadn't proved up to the task of meeting the town's demands this summer. As a result, water rationing was in full force, and people who didn't have access to a well had been put on a strict schedule for watering their lawns.

Still, despite that they needed the rain, Sarah hoped she wouldn't lose the electrical power at her old farmhouse, as she sometimes did during storms. She had better hurry home, just in case, to check that her flashlight had batteries, that her supply of candles hadn't been depleted by the last outage and that she had matches handy.

At this late hour, the parking lot was practically deserted, only a few cars remaining besides her own—and they probably belonged to the night watchman and the janitorial staff. Not for the first time—especially since her week spent with Alex—Sarah felt a stab of resentment that in addition to her regular job, J.D. had burdened her with the advertising and promotion for his senatorial campaign, even though he had increased her salary handsomely to compensate for it. And of course, it wasn't as though he had singled her out. Evie, who was her father's personal assistant at Field-Yield, Inc., had seen her own workload double, too. But since there wasn't anything she wouldn't do for her dear old daddy, Evie didn't mind all the extra labor. Sarah wished J.D. would hire more professionals to run the different aspects of his campaign, but she knew that was unlikely to happen. J.D. didn't like working with anybody he hadn't known and trusted for years. He and FYI's people had built the fertilizer company into one of the largest in the Midwest, he frequently bragged. They had put him in the state's governor's mansion. They could damned well put him up on Capitol Hill, too.

Personally, Sarah thought it was J.D.'s folksy, down-home appeal that had peddled so many bags of his fertilizer, pesticides and other farm products to thousands of farmers across the Midwest, and that had won him four years in the governor's mansion and that would win him at least one term in Washington, D.C., as well. That—and the fact that so far, nobody had ever managed to dig up any dirt on J.D. If there were any skeletons in his background, he had buried them as deep as it was rumored Papa Nick buried his.

Unlocking her Jeep, Sarah got in and started the engine, then turned on her headlights. In moments, she was on her way home, driving faster than usual, hoping to outrun the storm before it broke upon her. She was about a mile or so from her destination when some small animal suddenly darted out from the brush into the road, its eyes gleaming, terrified, in the glare of her oncoming headlights. Slamming on her brakes, Sarah swerved sharply to avoid hitting the startled creature, and as she did so, her front tire struck something—a good-sized stone, an old, broken beer bottle, a nail in the road—which caused her to have a blowout. Fortunately, she wasn't traveling so fast that she couldn't bring her vehicle safely to a halt. But as she slowly got out to inspect the damage, that wasn't much comfort. She stared in dismay at her flat tire and then at the horizon, where lightning continued to flare, accompanied by the distant rumble of roiling thunder.

"Damn!" She kicked the punctured tire angrily. How many times in the past had Bubba warned her something like this was liable to happen? Which was why he had always insisted on following her home. Only tonight, when she actually needed him, would actually be glad to see him pulling up behind her, he wasn't here!

Sarah didn't know what to do. She wasn't that far from home. She could walk, try to beat the storm. Or she could attempt to change the tire herself, which would be a slow and grubby process, during which she would surely wind up being pelted by a furious downpour. Or she could, on the cellular telephone she carried in her purse, call Junior Barlow and have him come change her tire and take the flat to the gas station he managed. She punched in his number, but to her dismay there was no answer. He and Krystal must have taken their kids and gone out for the evening. Seeing no other practical choice, Sarah finally decided to walk, reasoning that that was the quickest route home. She took her handbag but left her portfolio in the Jeep, then locked the vehicle. She was just about to start for her old farmhouse when a pair of headlights appeared behind her on the road.

As all of Bubba's words about drug lords and gangs, tongs and mobsters and nobody being safe anywhere anymore returned to haunt her, Sarah felt a sudden blade of fear knife through her. What if the approaching car belonged not to anybody she knew, but to some stranger who would knock her in the head, rob, rape and then kill her? She was, after all, a woman totally alone on a dark, relatively isolated country road illuminated only by the lightning. Then she realized how low slung the headlights were, and she thought with relief that perhaps they belonged to Bubba's Corvette.

She had almost been right, she reflected moments later, her heart slamming painfully in her breast as the long, sleek red Jaguar rolled to a halt alongside her, its powerful V12 engine idling like the purr of the large, predatory cat after which the car had been christened. Orange-glowing sparks flying away in the wind from the lit cigarette dangling from the corner of his mouth, his dark glance raking her in a way that made her shiver in the night air, Renzo Cassavettes drawled coolly, "Well, don't just stand there, baby. Get in."

After a long moment, as though in a trance, Sarah slowly opened the passenger door and slid into the seat beside him. Neither she nor he mentioned the fact that he hadn't offered to change her tire for her—which he could easily have done. Dragging on his cigarette, Renzo slid the gearshift into First and let out the clutch, propelling the roadster forward.

"How—how did you come to be out this way at this hour?" Sarah inquired, to break the silence that lay heavily between them.

At first, she thought Renzo didn't intend to answer. His eyes appraised her lingeringly again. Then, glancing back at the road, he drew another long puff from his cigarette into his lungs, holding it briefly before slowly exhaling, blowing a stream of smoke from his nostrils. After that, mindful—as most everyone who had grown up in the Midwest was—of setting the tall prairie grass, parched by the summer sun, on fire, he carefully ground the cigarette out in the Jaguar's ashtray. Then he took a long swallow from the long-necked bottle of beer he held between his legs as he drove. Only after all that did he at last speak.

"Earlier today, I telephoned FYI to follow up on my interview with you about J.D.'s senatorial campaign. You weren't taking any calls at the time, so just out of curiosity, I asked to speak to big, bad Bubba. The switchboard operator was kind enough to inform me that he had been called out of town and wasn't likely to return until tomorrow morning. So after I closed up shop for the evening, I decided that since you were going to be all by your lonesome self tonight, I'd just head on out your way." A strange, mocking smile curved Renzo's mouth. "And wasn't it fortuitous for us both that I did, Sarah?" he asked softly.

A tremor of fear—and something else—shot through her at his words. Briefly, she longed to strangle Jolene McElroy, the young, perky receptionist at Field-Yield, Inc., who blabbed everything she knew. For if not for Jolene, Renzo probably wouldn't have been out on this country road tonight, wouldn't have been around to pick Sarah up. And she was beginning to feel uneasily that she would have been better off walking. Unnerved, she wondered how many beers Renzo had drunk before driving out here. He had always held his liquor well, so there was no telling—but tonight he was obviously out on some reckless edge, brash with whatever it was that had seized him in its grip.

Although, earlier, Sarah had wished she had told Alex to stay home, she now thanked God she had given him permission to spend the night at the Thurleys'. Otherwise, the boy would have been at the old farmhouse when Renzo dropped her off—and there would have been hell to pay. Because the only reason Renzo had thought she would be all by herself tonight was that, miraculously, he had yet to learn about Alex. Sarah didn't know which prospect was worse: the fact that but for the twists of fate, Renzo might finally have found out about their son, or the fact that she was truly going to be all alone tonight—and that Renzo Cassavettes was not only driving her home, but also behaving in a way that made her think he was, like the night sky, charging himself up to unleash something dark and wild and violent.

"What kind of follow-up did you want to do regarding J.D.'s campaign?" Sarah inquired, trying hard to sound calmer than she actually felt and ignoring his earlier question.

"Nothing that can't wait." He dismissed her own query as easily as she had his.

Somehow she knew instinctively then that whatever he had planned to ask her about J.D.'s campaign had been only a pretext—that Renzo's real reason for calling Field-Yield, Inc. had been to find out whether or not she was seeing Bubba tonight. And because of Jolene's big mouth, Renzo had managed to accomplish what Bubba would have termed an "end run" around Sarah and Bubba both.

"Well, good," Sarah declared, silently cursing the nervous little quiver in her voice. "Because I've had a very long, exhausting day, so I'm way too tired tonight to sit up and discuss J.D.'s campaign with you."

Renzo shot her an insolent, knowing glance, his mouth twisting again with that strange, mocking smile, unsettling her. One hand lighting a cigarette, the other spinning the steering wheel easily, he abruptly turned on to her winding drive. The gravel crunched loudly beneath the tires of the Jaguar. The rising wind streamed through Sarah's long hair, loosed a shower of bright sparks from the tip of Renzo's cigarette and rustled the leaves of the tall old trees that lined the drive. In front of her house, he pulled to a stop and killed the engine.

"When are you going to stop avoiding me, running away from me, Sarah?" he asked as he drank the last of his beer, tossed the long-necked bottle onto the floor of the roadster.

"I—I don't know what you're talking about, Renzo."

"Of course you do, Sarah. You're like a skittish doe every time I even come near you, attempt to get close to you. I've tried to be patient. I really have. But now, I'm damned sick and tired of waiting. You must know I'm not just going to stand idly by while you make the worst mistake of your life by marrying Bubba Holbrooke!"

"I don't see what else you *can* do, Renzo. If that's what I choose to do, you can't stop me—and it's none of your damned business who I marry, anyway! So there. Now, just leave me alone! What in the hell did you ever come back here for, anyway?" she cried.

"You." The word was low, fierce, harsh with emotion; Renzo's eyes were dark with naked passion and glinting with determination as he spoke it.

Sarah's breath caught in her throat at the sight. Then, shaking, panicked, she fumbled at the handle, flung open the car door, not bothering to close it as she ran toward the house. She could hear Renzo cursing and calling her name, then the nerve-racking sound of his own door swinging wide as he came after her. Her heart pounded with fear and something else she did not want to acknowledge as she stumbled on to the veranda. Her hand shook as she wrenched open the screen door so hard that it was caught by the gusting wind and slammed against the house, then smacked back against her shoulder. But she scarcely felt the pain as she jammed her key into the front door's lock, twisted it and pushed frantically against the door itself. It gave way so suddenly from the force of her weight that she staggered across the threshold, nearly falling. Reaching out, she seized the screen door, jerked it shut and fastened its latch, then backed slowly away.

Her green eyes were huge and wary in her pale face as she stared at Renzo through the black mesh. Even blacker than the screen was the night sky against which his tall, lean, hard-muscled figure was silhouetted. Behind him, the lightning that had grown steadily wilder slashed and shattered the distant horizon, alternately illuminating his dark visage, then casting it into shadow. His long, shaggy black hair streamed in the wind. The fine material of his stark-white, short-sleeved shirt rippled and flattened against his powerful, bronzed body. The butterfly tattooed on his right forearm seemed to flutter its wings, so she had a sudden image of him as a pagan warrior—savage and untamed. His dark eyes glittered with raw sensuality and desire as they raked her, making her shiver like the leaves of the trees as the wind snaked through them, on its wings the rumble of thunder and the electric scent of the coming storm. On the deck above the veranda, her wind chimes clinked and clanged discordantly, frenzied fairies dancing in the dark.

As usual, no matter how many times Sarah had reminded him, Alex had forgotten to shut off the stereo before leaving the house earlier, and now from the speakers, the song "Lily Was Here," from Candy Dulfer's *Saxuality* CD, drifted, guitar lilting and saxophone wailing in sultry counterpoint to each other—a duet that was somehow at once a duel and a mating ritual. The guitar ran and teased lightly; the saxophone gave chase, echoing and taunting back forcefully, then suddenly caught up, taking over—until at last, in the end, the saxophone dominated and the guitar submitted, twining with it sinuously. As Renzo's own playing had years ago, the sensuous, bluesy music seemed to crawl insidiously inside Sarah's very skin, stirring old memories, the steady, primitive drumbeat echoing the hammering of her heart, the flutter of the pulse at the hollow of her throat.

Renzo stretched out a strong, slender hand. Grabbing the screen door's steel handle, he tugged on it sharply, making the hook jiggle ominously in the eyehole.

"Unlock it, Sarah," he demanded softly, arrogantly. "Let me in."

She took another step backward, mutely shaking her head and crossing her arms over her breasts, as though to defend herself against him.

"If you don't open this door, Sarah, I will," he insisted, the words both a threat and a promise, unmistakable steel underlying the silk of his voice.

Still, she didn't speak, didn't act, made no move to close the solid front door, to turn its dead bolt, which would, perhaps, have kept him out. Instead, she only watched and waited, knowing with certainty that he had meant what he'd told her. Even so, she gasped and flinched, startled, when, with a grated oath, a muscle throbbing in his set jaw, he abruptly yanked so hard on the screen door that the hook ripped the eyehole from the wooden frame. The door creaked menacingly on its hinges as he flung it wide, then stepped inside. And still, Sarah said nothing, did nothing, rooted where she stood, only her eyes pleading with him—for mercy...for something more.

In two long, predatory strides, Renzo inexorably closed the gap between them, stood there staring down at her for an interminable instant as atavistic and highly charged as the night sky alive with the lightning that continued to explode in the distance, splintering the heavens. Then, with a low growl that echoed the seething, rolling thunder, he snarled his fists in her hair, compelling her face up to his, his mouth swooping to imprison hers—hard and hungry, taking her breath. And as he kissed her ravenously, devouring her, Sarah knew dimly, in some dark corner of her mind, that despite herself, some terrible, treacherous part of her had wanted this, wanted him, that she had been only half alive until this moment.

Of their own volition, her arms coiled around his neck, fingers tightening upon him. Her lips softened beneath his, yielded pliantly to the swift, deep, relentless invasion of his tongue. And she did not care that there was no gentleness in him, only a desire so savage, a need so primal that it drove him to roughness and urgency, sweeping her along ruthlessly in its brutal wake. It was as though he had dreamed of nothing but her for the past decade and more, had been starved for her and now could not get enough of her as his mouth took hers feverishly again and again. His teeth grazed her lower lip, so she tasted blood, coppery and bittersweet, upon her tongue, and she gasped and moaned against him, shuddering violently, irrepressibly, in his embrace. Both fright and excitement rushed through her dizzyingly as she felt the strength of him, the powerful muscles that bunched and quivered in his arms and back as he bent her over, his lips at her throat, her breasts, hot and demanding, torturing and arousing her wildly. She felt weak and vulnerable in comparison—and as dazed as though she were drunk or drugged. Her head spun. Her thoughts floated in her mind, disordered, senseless, scattered by his mouth, his tongue, his teeth, his hands.

They moved on her expertly, as though they had every right to do so, remembered every soft, sensitive place they had ever explored and wakened and possessed. Every insistent kiss, every searing lick, every branding bite, every clever caress sent shocking thrills through her, as though the lightning that blazed beyond the screen door erupted within her, too, scorching her body and melting her very bones. Her knees weak and trembling, she clutched him, clung to him, gave herself up to him as, tearing impatiently at her clothes, ripping and dragging them from her, Renzo pressed her down on the Persian rug that covered the hardwood floor where they stood. She lay naked beneath him then, giddy, breathless, aching—and abruptly, painfully aware that she was no longer seventeen, and that she had borne a child. At the thought, Sarah turned her head away, made a shy, halfhearted attempt to cover herself. But this, Renzo would not permit, capturing her wrists and pinioning them above her head to hold her still for him.

"You're even more beautiful than I remembered," he muttered hoarsely against her mouth before he kissed her fiercely again, his tongue twining with hers, tasting, taunting.

Sarah wanted to protest, to insist she wouldn't be his again so easily as this. But she couldn't seem to form the words in her head, much less speak them aloud as his teeth scraped her throat lightly, then sank erotically into her shoulder, causing an unbearable jolt of electricity to shoot through her clear down to her toes. He found her burgeoning breasts, pressing them high for his covetous, carnal lips, his teeth and tongue wreaking further havoc upon her senses. Her nipples flushed, became engorged. A low whimper of wanting and need escaped from her parted mouth, moist and bruised and swollen from his kisses. Beneath him, she writhed and bucked helplessly, her head thrashing, and at last, Renzo rolled to one side to unbutton his shirt.

Roughly, he hauled it off and cast it aside, revealing his broad chest finely matted with dark hair. Sarah inhaled sharply at the sight, recalling the feel of him lying atop her so many years ago, that chest pressed against her own. Her skin sizzled at the memory and from the way he continued to kiss and caress her. She was a mass of sensation, every nerve raw, taut, expectant. She burned at the very core of her being. Rearing back, his eyes smoldering like twin embers, he watched her as his hand fell deliberately to his belt buckle, terrifying and tantalizing her. It had been so long, so very long since she had lain with him that day at the quarry. But such was her longing in that instant to touch his sleek, bare, bronzed skin once more, to feel it pressed against hers, to know him again as intimately as she could that moments later, when he, too, was naked and poised over her, his sex hard and throbbing, she willingly opened herself to him.

Groaning her name, Renzo drove into her so suddenly and forcefully that Sarah gasped, then cried out softly, a sound he swallowed with his mouth as he felt her sweet, slick heat close around him, envelop him, taking him deep. His breath rasped, catching on a serrated edge. She was as tight as though she were still a virgin. His eyes flew open in surprise to meet hers, then narrowed abruptly, gleaming drowsily with passion and triumph. A smile of satisfaction curved his lips. In that moment, Sarah knew his thoughts as well as her own—that she had kept herself for him alone. Sudden, hot anger and anguish for all the lost, empty years she had waited for him welled up in her, and for an instant, she wished vehemently that during Renzo's absence, she had given in to Bubba and taken him to her bed, had taken a dozen men—a hundred!—instead of none. Then, closing his eyes, his breath a long, ragged sigh of deepest desire and blind need, Renzo began to move inside her. And Sarah ceased to think of the past.

She ceased to think at all.

They drowned together as the gathering storm beyond where they lay broke without warning, brutally splitting the night sky asunder and catching them up in the fury of its sudden onslaught, mercilessly lashing them both to a frenzy. The rain pelted down as Renzo thrust into her urgently, savagely, again and again. And Sarah reveled in it, gloried in it, arching her body to meet his own, straining against him frantically, clawing his sweat-sheened back, spurring him on. He rode her roughly and high, so the climax that seized her came swiftly and violently, ripping through her like a thunderbolt and shattering her senses. She went rigid beneath him, her back bowed, her head thrown back, her fingers interwoven tightly with his, so their nails dug into each other's flesh. Her high keening rent the air as the seemingly infinite tremors rocked her, wave after wave so powerful that Renzo felt them, too, felt Sarah's muscles clenching tightly around him, maddening him. His body quickened exigently against hers as his own release came just as suddenly and violently, an explosion born of more than a decade of wanting her, of dreaming of her, of remembering her lying like this beneath him, begging him, sobbing his name. The orgasm tore wildly through his body, making him shudder long and hard against her, and his cry mingled with hers, a low sound dark and harsh with emotion—although not fulfillment or satiation.

Because even as he spilled himself inside her, Renzo wanted to go on making love to her—to fuck her until they were both utterly drained and spent and had nothing left to give.

Afterward, he swept her up in his strong, corded arms and carried her up the steep, narrow staircase in the foyer, pausing when he reached the shadowy landing at the top.

"Which way?" he asked, uncertain for a moment from which direction the wind chimes that would have guided him sounded.

"Left," Sarah whispered tremulously, her face buried against his shoulder. "Through the door at the end of the hall."

Renzo bore her into her room, laid her down upon the bed, his mouth and hands already moving possessively on her again, wakening her still-throbbing body afresh, such was his desire for her. But now he took his time, kissing and caressing her endlessly, and Sarah learned that this, too, brought its own brand of desperation and devastation. She quivered uncontrollably in his embrace, still shaken and overwhelmed by his earlier taking of her, by the unexpected ferocity and completeness of her response. It was as though when he had touched her, she had lost all control of herself, eagerly surrendering to him so he might do with her whatever he had wanted, however it had pleased him to do it. That thought terrified her. Over the years, she had worked hard to overcome her innate shyness, to cultivate a cool, distant composure and competence with which she had mastered her job and held the world at bay. Yet tonight Renzo had stripped all that from her as easily as he had divested her of her clothes.

Now, as he bent over her, she could feel the flood tide of emotions and sensations once more rising within her. And because she didn't know where this night would lead, what tomorrow morning would bring, she wanted to halt the fearsome, exhilarating swell. But it was so powerful, so relentless that she might as well have stood on a beach somewhere and tried to turn back the inrushing sea. She had loved Renzo Cassavettes since she was seven years old. With all her heart. Come what may, she belonged to him utterly—body, mind and soul.

His mouth was on hers, drinking long and deep, tongue tracing the outline of her lips before insinuating itself inside, searching, savoring. Outdoors, the rain still came hard, and the wind chimes suspended from the overhanging roof of the deck pealed dissonantly in the storm. From the stereo downstairs, music continued to waft. Dimly, Sarah realized it wasn't the radio running at all, as she had thought earlier, but a cassette Alex had assembled of songs in which the saxophone predominated, and that he must have the tape deck set on its continuous-loop mode. Now she recognized the strains of James Last's "The Seduction" and didn't know whether to laugh or weep at the irony. Because this time, Renzo was definitely seducing her—and with a superior skill and surpassing sensuality that left her as breathless and burning as had his rough rapacity before. His warm breath fanned her skin erotically as his lips found her ear, her throat, her breasts. He laved and sucked her nipples, sending thrilling tingles coursing through her, eliciting soft mewls and moans of pleasure from her compliant mouth. Helpless to stop his onslaught upon her senses, the churning tide within her growing ever stronger, she tried to draw him to her. But he resisted, his eyes dark and blazing beneath lazy lids as he appraised her.

"No...not yet...." he murmured huskily, deliberately trailing his long, elegant fingers down her taut, quivering belly as he bent his head once more to kiss her. "Be patient...wait...."

His teeth nibbled at her lower lip. His tongue plunged deep as his hand found her downy softness, brushed against her, fingers sliding tauntingly along the delicate, wet seam of her, coming to rest at the tiny nub that was the key to her delight. For a moment, they stilled there, and a low, pleading cry of torment issued from her throat. Then they began to move, circling and stroking languidly. The tempestuous tide surged and ebbed within her as he brought her to the brink of orgasm again and again—only to leave her unsated, unfulfilled, longing wildly for release. And then, just when Sarah was certain she couldn't take any more, he used his mouth, spreading her thighs wide and taking her with his tongue.

In its wake, dark, tumultuous emotions she had not known she possessed rushed to engulf her—along with fright, anger that Renzo should have such power over her, that he should be so skilled. How many beds had he lain in since leaving hers? She didn't know—knew only the fierce hurt and desire for revenge that welled inside her even as the flood tide did, so she longed to shake his certainty that she had been faithful to his memory. But the Pyrrhic, bittersweet taste of that triumph eluded her, for he was far stronger than she and in far better control, she thought dizzily, even though his breath came in harsh pants.

He held her down, ignoring her cries of protest, goading her on until her hands clenched spasmodically in his hair and she clutched him to her, gasping and whimpering, arching against him frantically. She was mindless, knew nothing but him, claiming her, taking her to a place that was wild and misted, and the wind was a breath primeval, howling down the corridors of time. Her blood roared in her ears, roiled through her body. She felt as though the storm outside had torn open the French doors of her room and come inside to grab her in its fearsome, feral grip, so she was aware of nothing but the maelstrom that swirled around her, its convulsive center the very heart of her. And she was powerless against it, against Renzo, shamelessly begging him for release as his lips and teeth and tongue had their terrible, glorious will of her.

"Yes, my love... now... now, I'll give you what you want," he rasped against her. "Because you *do* want this, don't you, Sarah... my sweet, sweet Sarah?"

"Yes... yes! Oh, please, Renzo!" she cried helplessly, imploring, sobbing.

His hot breath scorched the wet, opened petals of her. It was all the warning she had before, finding the pulsing, aching bud of her again, his tongue stabbed her with its heat, over and over. And while it lapped her, spurred her on toward the dark and madding abyss that frothed and yawned before her, his fingers drove deep inside her, pushing her over the edge.

She fell and fell, the climax that seized her blinding, bursting, seemingly boundless as it tumbled her into the void. She could do nothing but let it take her, sweep through her, claiming every part of her while she cried out her surrender to it, body and soul. Then, just when she thought she had struck bottom and could fall no farther, Renzo caught her, wrapping her hand around his hard, potent sex, so she knew in some giddy corner of her mind that she was only fleetingly suspended in midair. Kneeling over her, his voice low, serrated with desire, he demanded thickly, "Put me inside you, Sarah," wanting everything from her, even that.

And when she had done it, his hands gripped her hips tightly and he began to rock her against him. Their eyes locked in the darkness illuminated only by the lightning that scintillated jaggedly and erratically beyond the French doors. Sarah was the first to look away, fingers clenching the headboard convulsively, as though she would otherwise be swept away by the powerful waves that surged and broke again inside her. And even as the orgasm engulfed her, Renzo felt the sweet, wild force of his own jetting into her and thought dimly that in the end, in conquering her, he had defeated himself, as well, that he belonged as wholly and irrevocably to her as she ever had and still did to him.

Afterward, sensing her devastation, he was gentle with her. Cradling her against him, he crooned to her comfortingly and stroked her soothingly, until she ceased to tremble and weep in his arms, and sleep at last overtook her. Only then, when he knew she slumbered deeply and would not soon awaken, did he slip from the bed they shared and leave her.

* * *

Lamar was so afraid of being double-crossed that he arrived nearly an hour early at the rendezvous he had arranged. Pulling his clunker gradually to a halt at the railroad tracks on the old town road, he killed his headlights. Then he just sat there for a moment, glancing around warily. The swift summer storm that had raged earlier had died away, and now the moon was visible and nearly full, encircled by misty rings, so its silvery light illuminated the damp road hazily and eerily, making it shimmer. Even so, he didn't see anything to alarm him, so at last, he got out of the vehicle and closed the door, leaning against it. In his hand, he held a pair of night-vision binoculars he had heisted from Drucker's Sporting Goods. Tucked into his belt at his back and concealed beneath his T-shirt was the Saturday-night special—a cheap Llama .380 pistol—he had bought some time ago for fifty bucks from ''Porkchop'' Isley. Porkchop ran a pawn shop in the black part of town and turned a tidy profit on the side, selling various and usually stolen items out his back door.

The night was quiet, the silence broken only by the chirring of locusts and crickets, the croaking of frogs, the dripping of raindrops from the leaves into the grass. Lifting the binoculars to his eyes, Lamar scanned the surrounding area. He never spotted the figure hiding in the shadows of the woods some distance away, rifle in hand. So the only warning he had that his life was in danger was the loud reports of the shots. By then, however, it was too late. The bullets had already struck him, slamming him violently against his car, so he looked like a puppet gone haywire, arms flailing, legs shaking. Blood spurted from the wounds in his chest as he fought for breath, struggled futilely to remain upright. Dropping the binoculars on the wet road, he slid slowly to the ground, slumping forward and then toppling to one side, his face pressed in a mud puddle.

He lay still, no longer moving or breathing when his killer reached him and kicked him twice—hard—to be certain he was really dead. A rapid but thorough search of Lamar's vehicle revealed a manilla envelope tucked into the glove compartment. The envelope itself contained the damaging diskettes, which the killer carried away, smiling superciliously with satisfaction at Lamar's stupidity.

The time was surely well after midnight, Sarah mused dazedly as she slowly swirled up from her state of deep somnolence to one that was half awake and groggy. Something had roused her, teased even now at the edges of her mind, dragging her toward consciousness. What was it she had heard? The sound of a car door slamming? Abruptly, the night's events came rushing back to her. *Renzo!* She reached out for him, but he wasn't beside her. He had gone, left her, she thought, sitting bolt upright in bed, clutching the sheet to her naked body as she glanced around wildly in confusion, wondering if she had, in fact, dreamed the entire dark, stormy sequence of him making love to her so savagely and erotically.

No, it had been real. It had happened, she realized as she observed that the French doors that led to the deck beyond her bedroom were wide-open, their lacy sheers billowing inward. Renzo stood outside, smoking a cigarette beneath the wind chimes that now tinkled softly, melodically, in the breeze, which had been cooled by the storm.

"Renzo?" she called quietly.

At the sound of her voice, he half turned, glancing over his shoulder at her. After taking a last, long drag from his cigarette, he flicked it down onto the lawn, knowing the grass was wet enough to extinguish it. Then, silently, he strode inside, slowly unbuttoning his jeans as he came toward her, his eyes so dark that they seemed almost black in the moonlight that streamed inside to dance diffusely on the hardwood floor. She shivered as his gaze swept over her, his desire for her plain as he shucked off his jeans.

"I—I thought I heard a car door slam," she said, still holding the sheet to her trembling body, as though it would offer some protection against him, against the dark, spellbinding sorcery with which he had bedeviled her this night.

"You did. I went downstairs to get a pack of cigarettes out of the roadster," Renzo explained as he slipped into bed beside her, the mattress settling with his weight.

"I thought...I thought you were gone, that you had left me."

"No, I'm never going to leave you again, *cara*. Not so long as I live. *Never!*" he insisted fiercely as he determinedly tugged the sheet from her grasp, then drew her inexorably into his arms, his mouth silencing her own passionately, his hands pressing her down, weaving their diabolic magic.

Nineteen

Alex

It is a wise father that knows his own child.

The Merchant of Venice
—William Shakespeare

"Hoag?" Deputy Dwayne Truett spoke into the microphone of his patrol car's radio. "I think you better get on out here to the ole town road. We got us a problem."

"What kind of problem we talking about here, Dwayne?" The sheriff's voice came back through the radio, static crackling.

"Lamar Rollins. He's out here with his ole car, at the railroad tracks."

"So what's the problem? Is he drunk? Doped up? What?"

"He's dead, Hoag."

"Come again, Dwayne. I don't think I heard you right. Did you say Lamar's dead?"

"Yep. That's a roger. Dead as a doornail—and it ain't a purty sight, neither. I done puked up my breakfast all over the place."

"Well, how'd he die? Alcohol poisoning? Drug overdose? What?"

"Try murdered. He's got two bullet holes pumped in his chest. Now, I ain't no expert, so I can't be sure, and I expect we ought to wait for the county coroner and an autopsy. But if I had to make a guess, I'd say he was shot from long range, that the wounds are from a hunting rifle, most likely a thirty-aught-six. I've brought down enough deer myself with one that I reckon I oughta know. Still, like I said, I can't be certain. From the looks of him, I'd guess poor ole Lamar's been here half the night and all morning."

"Jesus!" The sheriff continued to curse and mutter for some minutes. Truth to tell, he wasn't really certain what all he needed to do in such a situation. Compared to the big city, death from unnatural causes was relatively rare in his small, rural town. Murder was virtually unheard of, except for the occasional Saturday-night brawl that wound up resulting in a shooting or stabbing—usually with several witnesses present. "Well, Dwayne," Hoag said finally, "call the coroner, for Christ's sake, and then seal off the crime scene. Don't let anybody touch anything—and don't you mess with nothing, neither, you hear? I'll be there just as soon as I can."

Toward morning, drowsy with sleep, only half awake, really, Renzo made love to Sarah yet again, this time slowly and lazily exploring anew all he had charted last night so

urgently, in hot, blind passion. Afterward, she slipped
from the bed they shared and, gathering her clothes quietly so as not to disturb him, crept into the bathroom to
dress.

She was shocked to see herself in the mirror—the wild
tangle of her dark hair, the smoky crescents under her eyes
from lack of sleep, her still-swollen mouth, the faint but
unmistakable bruises of passion that marked her body. It
was as though in a single night she had sought to make up
for her self-imposed celibacy of more than a decade. Sudden shame swept through her. Through hard work and
sheer determination, she had carefully built a life for herself. Now she felt as though she had permitted it to be
rocked on its very foundations, as she herself had been.
Renzo had used and abandoned her once before. Why
should this time prove any different?

Tears stinging her eyes at that thought, Sarah dressed
hurriedly. Finding that Renzo had shut off the stereo last
night and gathered up her torn garments that had been
strewn all over the floor, folding them neatly alongside his
own on the old church pew that sat in the foyer, she made
coffee. Then she left the house, stealing away into the
breaking dawn. Perhaps when she returned, Renzo would
be gone. Yet, despite herself, her heart tore at the notion—because she did not think she could bear losing him
a second time.

When Renzo awoke, Sarah was gone, and for a long
moment as he lay there alone in bed, he thought he had
only dreamed last night. Then, slowly, he became aware of
his surroundings and realized he was in her bedroom. It

was beautifully decorated in the Victorian style and, like Sarah herself, a mixture of sensibleness, softness, sweetness and sensuality. Yet despite this evidence of his whereabouts, Renzo still hardly believed he was here, in her bed. Last night had been so incredible that he couldn't stop thinking about it. Even now, he wanted her again.

But at last, when he recognized that she wasn't going to come back to bed, he rose, pulling on his jeans and calling her name. She was nowhere to be found. Downstairs, the aroma of fresh, hot coffee led him along the hall stretching back from the foyer to a swinging door that gave way to a big, old-fashioned country kitchen.

Still, there was no sign of Sarah.

She had fled from him, Renzo realized. Sharp pain lanced through him. He knew in his heart that the reason she had run away was because she had feared he wouldn't stay, that she would be left behind again. Spying her stoneware dishes through the glass-paned doors of the white cabinets, he removed a cup and filled it with coffee from the coffee maker on the tile counter. Renzo sipped the rich black liquid unhurriedly, savoring its taste. Doubtless, Sarah believed he would leave before she returned. Well, she wasn't going to be rid of him so easily—especially after last night. He wandered through the spacious rooms of the lovely old house to what he would have called the living room but that Sarah probably referred to as the "parlor." He glanced through the front windows. To his consternation, her Jeep wasn't parked on the circular gravel drive. Then he remembered it was sitting alongside the road, with a flat tire, and relief swept through him. She couldn't have gone very far.

Suddenly, at that realization, he knew where she was. Returning to the kitchen, setting his half-empty cup down on the counter, Renzo opened the back and screen doors to step outside. He inhaled deeply. The early morning air was fresh and sweet from last night's rain, the rich, dark earth ripe and lush with the storm's fragrant scent. The trees and grass still shimmered with raindrops and dew, which would be burned away by the sun before too much longer. But for now, it looked as though thousands of rainbow prisms dripped from the boughs and covered the ground. He could see why Sarah loved this old farm. It was beautiful—quiet and peaceful—a place to put down roots, to grow old with someone you loved. It occurred to Renzo that he could be happy here, with her.

But first, he had to find her, to convince her he had come home—to her—for good.

The meadow was hushed, the silence broken only by the soft cooing of mourning doves from the old barn in the distance, the crowing of a rooster somewhere, the drone of insects, the soughing of the rustling trees and rippling grass stirred by the breeze. The tree house itself was still. Even so, Renzo knew instinctively that Sarah was there. He walked slowly toward the huge old sycamore, laying his hand against the trunk and glancing up into its spreading green branches. He stood there for a moment, lost in the past and wondering if she sensed his presence, as he did hers.

Then, a smile of fond remembrance, tenderness and caring curving his mouth, he spoke, his voice low but strong, echoing in the morning quiet. "Sarah, sweet Sarah, let down your oak-brown hair!"

* * *

She should have run farther, faster, Sarah thought in some obscure corner of her mind, her heart hammering painfully. She should have known Renzo would remember the tree house and would come here in search of her. Perhaps that was why she had come here herself, because she had wanted him to find her. Maybe if she sat very still and didn't answer, he would go away, she told herself. The trouble was that deep in her heart of hearts, she knew she didn't want him to leave. She wanted him to join her in the tree house, to stay with her for always. At last, of its own volition, her hand reached out tremulously, grasped the thick, sturdy rope that lay coiled in one corner, tossed it over the edge, down to him. Whether or not he could—or would—still make the long ascent was up to him.

"Damn it, Sarah!" Renzo swore softly. "You don't intend to make it easy for me, do you?" Shaking his head when she didn't reply, he took hold of the rope, knowing, even if she didn't, that thanks to the fact that he lifted free weights and had taken up karate to stay in shape, he still possessed the upper-body strength of his youth. Determinedly, he began to climb.

A few minutes later, Sarah heard him pulling himself up, hoisting himself into the tree house. Her heart was now thudding so violently that she felt as though it wouldn't be able to sustain the pace, would simply jerk abruptly to a halt. Still, she didn't look at him, didn't want him to see the tears that seeped from her eyes—for so many reasons that, in her emotional upset and confusion, she didn't even begin to understand them all herself. She wept, perhaps, for lost youth, regrets and what might have been; for last night, that she loved Renzo still, that she had wronged him, had hurt him in a way he had yet to discover; for the uncertain future, fear that whatever they shared wasn't enough to overcome the past, to hold them together—that perhaps he didn't even want that, had never intended it, despite what he had said last night.

Even though Sarah was turned away, staring out a window of the tree house, her long hair falling forward and her hand against her cheek to conceal her face from him, Renzo knew she was crying. She was huddled against the wall, curled up in a fetal position. She wore jeans and a green shell, and her feet were bare, so she hardly looked any older, he thought, than the seventeen-year-old girl she had been when he had first taken her—fragile and ethereal, vulnerable and easily bruised. At once, he saw that the hard, cold edge he had that night at the Grain Elevator accused her of possessing was only a protective shell she had built around herself, and that last night, he had succeeded in smashing it, so that now she was like a wounded animal, hurt and afraid. He knelt beside her, gathered her trembling, unresisting figure in his embrace, pulling her close against him, tightening his arms around her, rocking her and stroking her mass of silky hair.

"Sarah, oh, Sarah," he whispered fiercely against her ear. "Don't you know you're the only woman in the world for me? That it's always been you? Only you. I love you. I love you...."

One by one, he kissed the tears from her cheeks. Then at last his mouth took hers, and the taste of her was sweet, wild honey melting on his tongue as, whimpering a little, she opened her lips to him and wound her arms tightly around his neck. And Renzo knew then that he had won, that she was his for as long as he wanted her—and he wanted her for as long as she would have him.

There was an old blanket in the tree house, and he spread it on the floor beneath them, taking his time, undressing her slowly, kissing and caressing her all the while. But when she was naked and he began to divest himself of his own jeans, she caught his hands in hers, saying softly, "No, let me. I want to do it." Then her palms flattened against his chest, fingers tensed and splayed, pushing him down on the blanket. She knelt over him, lowering her mouth to his, her tongue outlining his lips, then insinuating itself between them, touching, tasting, twining, as light and delicate as a butterfly. Her thick, shining mass of hair fell over him, curtaining his face, soft against his jaw. He wanted to wrap his fingers in the strands, as rich and dark and fragrant as the earth. But she pressed his hands against the floor, holding him prisoner. He realized then that she was seducing him, as he had seduced her last night. He could easily have overpowered her, wasn't helpless against her—as she had been against him. But as that thought occurred to him, Renzo understood what drove her—her need to claim him, as he had needed to claim her last night. And sensing its importance to her, he lay still and let her have her will of him.

Slowly, Sarah drew her mouth down his throat, at once shocked by her own bold wantonness and glorying in the power she knew instinctively that she possessed over him at that moment. She recognized then that far from being in complete control of himself last night, Renzo had been as excited by the things he had done to her as she had been.

Because now she was arousing herself as much as she sensed she was arousing him. But she no longer had the strength or will to go on fighting her feelings for him. She loved him, wanted him—no matter the cost. Somehow she would bewitch him, as he had bedeviled her, she thought, unable even now, despite his impassioned words of love, to quite believe he was truly hers. She would make certain; she would bind him to her forever and ever—as he had bound her.

His bronzed flesh tasted of sweat, smelled of cigarettes and potent masculinity. She would know the salty taste of him, the smoky, musky scent of him anywhere, Sarah reflected as she kissed him at the hollow of his throat. Even in a roomful of men and with her eyes closed, she would be able to pick him out. She licked his skin, sank her teeth gently into his shoulder, her hands circling and rubbing his chest, tracing the fine mat of dark hair that covered him there, tapering down his firm, flat belly to disappear enticingly into his jeans. She moved one hand lower. Still, she didn't touch him where he had thought—hoped—she would, but instead slid her fingers along the insides of his thighs, kneading and stroking, teasing him until a low groan escaped from his lips and he stirred restively beneath her.

"Shh. Be still...." Sarah silenced him with her mouth, her tongue wreathing his once more before she bent her head to capture one of his nipples between her teeth, nipping him tenderly. Her long hair trailed over him. Her full breasts, their dusky crests taut, brushed against him. Unable to restrain himself, he captured them with his palms, but his thumbs had barely begun to stimulate her nipples before, again, she took hold of his hands and pushed them insistently to the floor. "Be patient...wait...." she murmured, echoing his own words of last night.

Moments later, her hands were at his bulging fly, shaking with nervous excitement as she fumbled at the buttons, releasing them one by one, each feathery brush of her fingers against his arousal agony to Renzo. By now, he was so hard and hot for her that he was half afraid he would come the minute she freed him. But as though she sensed that, she tormented him still further by concentrating instead on slowly tugging his jeans from his body and casting them aside. Her hands glided up his legs, his hips, to his chest, tightened to fists in his hair as she claimed his lips once more. And while she kissed him, she spread her thighs and taunted him with her moist, dark softness, rubbing against his sex provocatively. He thought he would go mad with desire for her then. He wanted to feel her impaled upon him, riding him into oblivion. He reached out, clenching her buttocks to pull her to him, but once again, Sarah thrust his hands away.

"No...not yet...." she insisted—his own words of last night, tossed back at him once more. Beneath drowsy lids, her green eyes gleamed with passion and wicked mischief as she glanced down at him. A faint, beguiling smile curved her lips.

"I'll get you for this, witch," Renzo muttered hoarsely. "You know I will."

"Will you?" Her hands found his sex as she spoke, closed around him, so his only response was a sharp, strangled hiss of excitement as he jerked against her. She stroked him slowly at first, tracing slick, heated grooves and ridges, taunting sensitive, responsive flesh, drawing her nails lightly along the length of him, shivering at the sudden, raw passion that blazed in his eyes, the way his breathing became rough and uneven, so she thought that at any minute, he would cease to lie there passively, would grab her and finish them both himself. "Will you?" she whispered again seductively. "Get me?"

Then, before her words goaded him to resistance and action, she kissed her way down his chest and belly sheened with sweat, her breath warm against his flesh, against his hardness as she imprisoned him with her mouth. A low, ragged oath broke from him as she enveloped him, her tongue swirling and teasing, while her hands continued to move on him tantalizingly. Groaning deeply with pleasure, Renzo snarled his fists in her hair, and this time, Sarah didn't push him away. Gripping her tightly, he thrust himself between her lips, reveling in the warm, wet softness of her mouth. He had dreamed of her doing this, thought he must be dreaming still as, seeming to sense his need, she increased the pressure of her lips, the rhythm of her hands, until his body was screaming for release and he knew he couldn't hold back any longer. He tried—half-heartedly—to tug her away, but she wouldn't be drawn, and then it was too late. His climax seized him violently, blindingly, so he could only hang on to her fiercely, crying out, while she took all he had to give.

And still, it wasn't enough for her. For even afterward, Sarah went on pressing him down, stubbornly refusing to let him touch her, kissing and caressing him everywhere she could reach, exploring every hard plane and lean angle of his body, each strong and beautifully defined curve of muscle. Her fingers tunneled through his hair, twisting, tightening, as she wrapped herself sinuously around him. The musky taste of him was on her insidious tongue as it danced with his in a mating ritual as old as time, traveled the length of his throat, licked the sweat from his chest once more, savoring the sharp tang of salt. And then, when he had recovered—so rapidly that Renzo could scarcely believe he was already hard and eager for her again—she impaled herself on him, taking him deep inside her.

Sunlight streamed into the tree house, turning her body, glistening with sweat, to golden flame as she rocked him, rode him. Now he would no longer be denied, and his hands were on her everywhere, tangling in her hair, cupping her breasts, teasing their tautly furled buds, sweeping down to close over her hips, to seek the mellifluous petals of her, to stroke their heart as she moved upon him urgently, harder and faster. Her orgasm came swiftly and so strongly that she arched wildly atop him, her head thrown back. The soft keening of her pleasure rang in the morning air before she fell forward, her nails digging into his shoulders, her body still sliding on his. Grasping her buttocks tightly, Renzo thrust into her again and again, quickening against her feverishly, making her cry out once more as a second climax assailed her, taking her breath. Hard on its heels, his own release came, and he held her close as he shuddered powerfully beneath her, spurting into her until he had nothing left to give.

"Tell me you love me, *cara*," he murmured afterward as they lay quiet and entangled on the old blanket, he stroking her hair and smoking a cigarette from the crumpled pack of Marlboros he had taken from the pocket of his discarded jeans.

"I thought I just did." A small, mysterious smile of contentment curving her lips, Sarah glanced up at him tenderly from beneath passion-heavy lids, her green eyes drowsy with satiation in the morning light.

"Hmm. So you did—and very pleasantly, too, I might add. Still, I want to hear you say it. I *need* to hear you say it. You haven't—not once since I came back."

"I love you," she breathed, snuggling closer in his embrace, her head resting on his shoulder. "I love you. I always have. I always will."

"You'd better, because I warn you, I don't intend to lose you a second time." Renzo's voice, although low, was fierce with determination, rough with emotion. "So of course, you're going to send big, bad Bubba packing, aren't you?"

"Yes, if that's what you want."

"Do you still doubt it?" A serrated edge crept into his tone; his arm tightened around her, his hand snarling in her hair, forcing her face up to his. His hooded eyes smoldered hotly with possessiveness and jealousy. "If you don't get rid of him, I will, Sarah. Christ! Of all the men you could have chosen in this damned town, why in the hell did you ever take up with him?"

"I—I was lonely," she confessed softly, "and he wanted me."

"Did you sleep with him?"

"No. You know I didn't. You knew last night that there hasn't been anyone but you."

Triumph and satisfaction flared in Renzo's dark brown eyes at that. "Yes, I knew. Did you hate me very much for that, Sarah, for spoiling you for all other men?"

"Yes, sometimes."

Taking a last, long drag from his cigarette, he crushed it out against the floor. "I'll make it up to you, I swear!" he muttered thickly as he rolled her over, his mouth swooping to claim hers, his dark, bronzed body sliding covetously to cover her own pale one.

Like a madman, Renzo chased her all the way back to the house, kissing her, tickling her, strewing wildflowers in her hair, so Sarah was laughing helplessly and pleading with him for mercy when the screen door to the kitchen finally banged shut behind them.

"Don't think you can escape from me, wench, because you can't," he insisted, grinning roguishly as he caught hold of her, spinning her around and pressing her tightly against the refrigerator. His lips teased hers. His hands roamed over her boldly, tugging at her clothes. "I knew it was a mistake to ever let you get dressed!"

Still laughing, she tried to push him away, to hold him at bay, her cheeks flushed, her heart thudding wildly with excitement. "Don't you think you've had more than enough?" she inquired tartly as he bent his head to kiss her again.

"I'll never get enough of you, *cara*," Renzo declared, his voice abruptly low and husky, his molasses-brown eyes gleaming as his mouth captured hers, his tongue plunging deep.

"M-M-Mom?" The single, tremulously spoken word fell, exploded like a bombshell into the silence, and in that moment, at its impact, Sarah felt her entire world suddenly shatter into a million pieces. *Alex!* Dear God. How could she have possibly forgotten all about her son? *Renzo's* son?

As Renzo jerked his lips from hers and half turned to glance over his shoulder to see who had spoken, his strong, slender hands involuntarily tightened so painfully upon Sarah's arms that she knew she would have bruises there tomorrow. Time seemed to stop, frozen for an eternity, before at last it lurched again into motion, appearing strangely slow and out of kilter. She was simultaneously aware of the myriad expressions that crossed both the man's and the boy's faces as they stared at each other wordlessly: shock and disbelief, followed by dawning recognition, comprehension and pain...so much pain. Then naked, murderous rage such as she had never before witnessed darkened Renzo's handsome visage. The muscle in his jaw began to throb alarmingly, and all of a sudden, he released her and stepped back from her, folding his arms across his chest tightly, as though he feared that, otherwise, he would do her some terrible violence, would kill her. As though sensing the threat to her, Alex took a protective step toward her, wariness mingling with the confusion and eager hope that filled his own countenance.

"Mom?" he said again, in his eyes as he glanced at her the same question that burned like a dreadful, dark flame in Renzo's own gaze as it raked her ruthlessly—demanding an answer, an explanation.

Still, Sarah couldn't seem to speak, could only think, stupidly, how she must appear, with her hair in unaccustomed disarray, wildflowers tangled in its strands, and her lips bruised and swollen from Renzo's kisses. She tried to swallow, but her mouth was so dry that she couldn't. She couldn't force down the lump of trepidation and pain that had lodged in her throat, either. Her heart beat erratically in her breast. With hands that trembled, she combed desperately at her hair, thinking dully that she mustn't appear before Alex like some wanton fresh from her lover's bed—even if she was. The wildflowers fell to the hardwood floor at her feet, wilted and forlorn. The silence was deafening, ominous, horrible. Tears stung Sarah's eyes. She forced herself to blink them back, to draw a deep, ragged breath, to speak. The truth—because there was no point in attempting to lie. In her heart, she knew that, knew with certainty that both father and son were already sure of the answer to their unspoken question.

"A-A-Alex, this is—this is Renzo Cassavettes... your—your father," Sarah said quietly.

She heard her son's tiny gasp of acknowledgment in response, Renzo's sudden, harsh, sharply indrawn breath. It was the boy—who, unlike his father, had had some inkling at least that this day would come, some preparation for it—who recovered first. Sarah had never been prouder of Alex than she was in that instant, and she bit her lower lip hard in fear that his gesture would be rejected when, in the manner she had taught him to do when meeting an adult for the first time, he manfully stuck out his hand and, suddenly shy, uncertain, stammered, "How—how do you do, sir?"

After a long, tense moment, Renzo slowly took the boy's outstretched hand in his, gripping it tightly. Then, unable to restrain himself, he abruptly pulled Alex into his strong arms, hugging him close. Sarah could hear her son sobbing now with joy and relief against his father's broad chest, could see Renzo's shoulders shaking with silent emotion; and instinctively, she turned away, knowing somehow that this moment belonged to father and son alone, was too special and private even for her to share. She stared quietly out the screen door, blinded by the tears that now streamed, unchecked, down her face. She didn't know how much time passed before at last Renzo spoke.

"Alex . . . Son," he said gently as he stared, marveling, down into the boy's good-looking face, a smaller, paler replica of his own. Smiling falteringly, Renzo drew his arm roughly across his eyes, then brushed Alex's own tears from the boy's cheeks. "Would you mind very much going outside for a little while? Why don't you . . . why don't you wait for me in your tree house?" Because, of course, Renzo realized now—so much made clear to him—that was why the tree house was in such good condition, why Sarah had kept it up. It belonged to their son, just as it had once belonged to him and her. "I need to talk to your mother alone."

"Are you—are you very angry with her? Are you—are you going to hurt her?" Alex demanded bravely, suddenly fearful for his mother. "Because you've already hurt her enough! And she still loves you—I know she does!—and she knows it was wrong not to ever tell you about me. She told me so."

"Did she? Well, she was certainly right about that. But no, I'm not going to hurt her, so you don't have to be afraid. Now, please, run on along, Son. I'll join you outside in just a bit, I promise."

"Mom?"

"It's all right, Alex. I'll be fine." Sarah reached out to stroke her son's shaggy black hair, kissed him gently on the forehead. "Please, do as your father says."

Worriedly, the boy glanced from her to Renzo, and then back at her again. Finally, biting his lower lip, Alex nodded and reluctantly slipped out the screen door, leaving the two of them alone in the silence. It stretched as taut as a thong between them. Despite his reassuring words to their son, Sarah still half expected Renzo to do her some violence, and she shivered irrepressibly at the thought, at the menacing, turbulent thing that seethed and roiled like a thunderstorm between them, as though it would explode at any moment, tearing them asunder.

"You had no right to keep him from me, Sarah." Renzo spoke at last, his voice low, hard and deadly with emotion. The muscle in his jaw flexed fearsomely, warning her of the murderous rage that continued to assail him. "No right at all! My God! How could you have done such a thing to me? He's my son, too! *Mine,* Sarah! And you stole *eleven years* of his life from me! Were you *ever* going to tell me about him?"

"Yes ... yes, of course."

"When? Damn it!"

"Before you—before you came back here to this town? When he was ... when he was old enough to make his own decisions." Which meant that Alex would by then have been a young man, eighteen, or perhaps even twenty-one, at least.

"Jesus Christ! Damn you to hell and back for that!" Without warning, unable to restrain any longer the dark, savage thing that coiled within him, Renzo reached out, grabbed her, and shook her roughly. Of its own volition, his right hand shot up to smack her backhanded across the face, then froze in midair, fingers clenching and unclenching, making the powerful muscles in his arm tauten frighteningly as he stared down at her. Sarah's face was ashen; she trembled with fear, and tears spilled from her huge, haunted eyes. Still, she did nothing to fight him, to stop him from striking her, spoke no word of protest against him. Renzo understood then that she wouldn't, that she actually intended to stand there acquiescently and let him beat the hell out of her, to kill her, if that was what he wanted. And that realization made him so furious that it was all he could do to prevent himself from doing just that. He was abruptly sick and ashamed that he had nearly slapped her. This was Sarah, the woman he loved, the other half of his soul. Sarah, who only a short while ago in the tree house, had made love to him with every ounce of emotion in her body, heart, and soul. "Oh, God, Sarah...Sary, I am so sorry! I would never hit you, hurt you!"

Somehow she was in his arms then, and he was kissing her feverishly, sweeping her up, carrying her to one of the kitchen chairs, where he sat down, cradling her against his chest. She was sobbing uncontrollably now, and hysterical words were tumbling from her lips, all about her father dying and her mother blaming her for his death, about the horrible, hateful telephone calls and mail she had received, how she had thought Renzo had abandoned her, had never loved her, had only used her and then callously cast her aside. He felt deeply angry and ill as he listened silently, comprehending finally some of what Sarah had lived through—alone—in his absence. He thought of how hurt and terrified she must have been—just seventeen years old at the time—and of the quiet courage she had always possessed, which had seen her through what would have broken another, lesser woman. And he ached for her, wanted to weep for her. To wrap himself around her and tell her fiercely that so long as he lived, nothing and nobody would ever hurt her again. He stroked her hair soothingly, rocked her gently in his embrace, his terrible, brutal rage at her draining from him at last.

"Shh. Sary, sweetheart, hush. I'm not mad at you anymore. I know what you thought, that it wasn't your fault, that it was your mother and mine who were to blame for what happened between us, for why you never told me about Alex. Hell. Now, I realize my own parents knew about him and didn't tell me, either! My poor mother tried.... She just couldn't get the words out. She was afraid, too—just as you were.... Alex is what you were hiding from me, isn't he, Sarah? He's why you wouldn't see me, wouldn't go out with me when I came back here?"

"Yes ... yes! Oh, Renzo, I was so terrified you'd hate me! So terrified you'd try to take him away from me—and he was all I had!"

"I don't hate you. I could never hate you. And I wouldn't dream of trying to take Alex away from you, not ever. I just want to be a part of your lives, for you never to shut me out again. That hurt me, Sary. You'll never know how much that hurt me—especially when I thought you'd turned to Bubba. Just thinking of you lying in his arms made me want to kill him! It was that damned news clip of you hanging on Bubba at J.D.'s fund-raiser that brought me back to town. I saw it on CNN, and I went crazy! I couldn't eat or sleep for thinking about you.... Please, Sarah, I can't bear for you to cry like this. You're making yourself ill.''

Still, she continued to sob, albeit more quietly now, against his chest. And when he made out the muffled words she gasped softly between sniffles, he swore violently, cursing himself. Because she had said anxiously, ''Oh, Renzo, what if—what if I'm pregnant again now?'' He realized then that in his overwhelming desire last night and this morning to possess her, to be inside her, a part of her once more, he had never given a single thought to protecting her from the consequences of their actions. His hand swept down to her belly; he imagined his child growing there, as Alex had, and a wild, savage yearning for that suddenly filled him. Perhaps, subconsciously, it always had.

''Well, if you are, I certainly hope you'll tell me this time,'' he rejoined lightly.

''Oh, Renzo, how can you—how can you joke about it?''

''What do you want me to say? Damn it! It's done now, and I can't undo it. And honestly, Sarah, if you want to know the truth, if you keep hanging on me this way, I'm very much afraid I'm actually going to be compelled to do it again!''

She gasped at that, trying to scramble from his arms and wiping the tears from her eyes in a hurry. But he held on to her, kissing her deeply, running his hands over her body and beneath her shell and bra to fondle her breasts, aroused by the hardening of her sensitive nipples, the way she quivered and shuddered his embrace.

"Renzo, don't. Please, don't. Alex is waiting for you at the tree house," she reminded him gently. "And if you don't go out to him, he'll grow anxious and come back here."

"The boy has to learn sometime about the birds and the bees. Or does he already know?" Deep pain shadowed Renzo's eyes as he asked the question. Sarah knew it was because he was realizing how much he didn't know about his son, how much had been lost to him through the years—because of her.

"He already knows," she told him quietly. "Kids today have access to so many avenues of information we never had, it seems. PG-rated movies that would have got an R years ago, in our day. Sophisticated electronic games, computers, the Internet...." Her voice trailed away. Tears brimmed in her eyes again. "Renzo, I *am* sorry...so very sorry. I'll regret what I did to you and Alex for the rest of my life! If I had it all to do over again—"

"Shh. Hush, Sary. I know. But you don't, and it's done now. And there's nothing either of us can do to change that. We can only go on from here. So why don't you fix us all something to eat, while I go out and get to know my son?" Renzo spoke these last two words marvelingly, as though he still couldn't quite believe them.

"All right."

He let her up then and stood. At the screen door, he glanced back at her, his eyes dark and serious, all trace of lightness gone. "Sarah, you do realize, I hope, that we still have a lot of things to discuss between us, don't you?"

She nodded wordlessly, biting her lower lip nervously. Because even though he had said they would go on from here, she still didn't know yet where it was that they were going.

The screen door banged shut behind Renzo. For a long moment, Sarah watched him as he strode toward the meadow. She imagined herself in his place and wondered what he was thinking, what he and Alex would say to each other in the tree house. But she never did know. They never told her, and she never asked, feeling that it was, perhaps, only fitting; there was so much she and Alex had shared that Renzo would never know. She grieved deeply for that now, when it was too late—when she witnessed the happiness on her son's face as he and Renzo at long last walked back from the meadow toward the house, and she realized it wasn't just Renzo she had robbed of so much that could never be replaced. All these years, Alex had been hungry, desperate for a father. Bubba had been right about that. That had been a great deal of the problem all along, Sarah thought now, the cause of all of Alex's fighting on the school grounds, part of the reason why he had had trouble learning his schoolwork. She had always believed that the fact that he had been diagnosed by psychologists as suffering from Attention Deficit Disorder— Inattentive Type—had never been wholly to blame for his lack of concentration and effort.

It would take time, of course. But whatever had been said between them, father and son had made a good beginning, she reflected as she gazed through the screen door at them. Renzo's arm was slung about Alex's shoulders; Alex's own arm was around Renzo's waist. The two of them were talking and laughing. Even as Sarah watched, Alex broke away from his father, yelling gaily and running, while Renzo bent down and scooped up the boy's football from where it lay on the grass. The football flew from Renzo's hands—as good a pass, Sarah thought idly, as any Bubba had ever thrown in his days as a high-school star quarterback—and Alex jumped up and caught it in midair, beaming with pride.

"Gee! That was great, Dad!" he shouted, the name for his father coming easily and naturally to his lips. "Now, you catch!" Even as he spoke, Alex threw the football back, not a half-bad pass, and Renzo plucked it from the air and began to run forward. Joining wholeheartedly into the game, Alex tackled him, and they both went down in a tangle of arms and legs, Alex squealing as Renzo, much the way he had done with Sarah earlier, tickled him unmercifully. Finally, spying her watching them from the screen door, Renzo rose and hauled Alex to his feet.

"I see two sweaty guys who had better wash up before they come to the table," Sarah called through the screen door. "And one who'd better get a shirt on, too!"

"Come on, Dad." Alex tugged on his father's hand. "There's a pump. I'll show you."

A few minutes later, when father and son stepped, dripping, into the kitchen, Sarah had two towels and Renzo's shirt waiting. Then the three of them sat down at the kitchen table to eat the brunch she had prepared.

"Mom!" Alex spoke in a rush, bubbling over with excitement and enthusiasm. "Did you know Dad owns a motorcycle—a Harley-Davidson!—and a comic-book collection, and that he's read all the classics and likes to fish and plays the saxophone, too?"

"Yes, Son, I did." Her eyes met Renzo's, and she knew he understood then that this much at least, she had done for him—she had encouraged their son in interests Renzo shared, so that if and when the two of them had ever met, they would find common ground.

Naturally gregarious, Alex continued to talk all through the meal, his spirits only briefly dampened when the subject of his attending summer school, and why, arose and Renzo declared soberly, looking him square in the eye, "Your grades will have to come up by the end of the summer, Alex. No, don't look to your mother to defend you—because I'm sure she's told you the same thing. So we aren't going to have any debate about it. Your mother and I will help you if you need it, but the rest is your responsibility, and I think you know that. So either your grades come up, or repercussions follow. Is that clear?"

"Yes, sir." Alex swallowed hard, glancing again at Sarah for support.

But wisely, she held her tongue and kept her own counsel, knowing that to interfere would be to challenge Renzo's authority, to drive a wedge between him and her, which would anger and hurt him, and which Alex would take clever advantage of and manipulate to his own ends. Whether he realized it or not, Alex needed Renzo's firm but gentle hand and guidance— and Sarah wanted the boy to have them.

"I told Alex the TV and Nintendo set would come out of his room for the entire year if he has to repeat the sixth grade," she explained to Renzo, wanting him to know she had already set the terms of the consequences herself.

"Fine," he replied, nodding his approval. "Then that's what'll happen, Alex, should you fail to start the seventh grade, come fall."

Their son was silent for a little while after that. It was a new experience for him, Sarah thought—doing her best to repress the smile that tugged at her lips—to have *two* parents laying down the law. Plainly, he had not previously considered this aspect of the situation.

Finished eating, Renzo pushed away his plate and lit a cigarette, drawing on it deeply, then sipping his coffee. A faint smile played about the corners of his mouth, too, although his eyes were shadowed and uncertain as he wondered if he should have tried to be Alex's friend before becoming his father.

"You see, Alex, even though you might not have realized it until just now, there *are* some disadvantages to having a father around," Renzo observed lightly.

"Yeah, so I see." The boy sighed. "Are you always going to be just as strict as Mom?"

"Stricter," Renzo insisted, grinning to take the sting from the word. Crushing his cigarette out in a saucer, since there wasn't an ashtray handy, he stood, picking up his plate and cup to carry them to the counter. "Come on, big guy. Let's help your mother clear away these dishes and get them scraped off in the sink."

"When Bubba ate here, he never helped with the cleaning up afterward," Alex announced blithely, plainly bemused by his father's action. "He said dishes were women's work."

"Uh-huh," Renzo drawled in the way that made Sarah think strangely of Papa Nick and sent a shiver down her spine. "Well, number one, when a woman holds down a full-time job outside of the home, the way your mother does, the dishes are everybody's work. And number two, I am *not* Bubba Holbrooke!"

"Thank heavens for that!" Alex exclaimed with obviously heartfelt gratitude, causing Renzo to burst into laughter. At that, the boy regained his equilibrium, joining in his father's mirth. "I take it you don't much like big, bad Bubba, either, do you, Dad?"

"No." Renzo shook his head, still smiling. "I don't. And I've already told your mother she's to tell *him* to hit the road, Jack, and not to come back no more, no more."

"Good." Alex's eyes danced with mischievous delight at this.

"Now, who's the one outnumbered here?" Sarah inquired archly. "Is this what's referred to as a 'male conspiracy'—or just a 'guy thing'?"

"Both." Renzo kissed her lightly on the mouth as she rose to begin loading the dishwasher. "I'm going to put my socks and boots on, stroll down the road and fix your Jeep, then drive it back here for you. Where are your car keys, *cara?*"

"In my purse. I'll get them."

"Dad, you *are* going to come back, aren't you?" Alex asked anxiously as he and Sarah accompanied Renzo to the front door.

"Oh, Son, of course I am." The man reached out tentatively to ruffle the boy's hair tenderly. "You help your mother finish wiping down the kitchen table, and I'll be back here before you know it, I promise."

But after he had walked out the front door and disappeared down the gravel drive, Renzo didn't return. And presently, it became clear to Sarah and Alex that he wasn't going to, either.

Book Three

Dust Devil

Youth on the prow, and Pleasure at the helm;
Regardless of the sweeping whirlwind's sway,
That, hushed in grim repose, expects his evening prey.

The Bard
—Thomas Gray

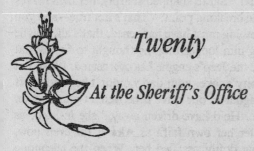

Twenty

At the Sheriff's Office

The terrible grumble, and rumble, and roar,
Telling the battle was on once more.

Sheridan's Ride
—Thomas Buchanan Read

A Small Town, The Midwest, The Present

"Dad's not coming back, is he, Mom?" Alex asked dully after more than two hours had passed and, still, Renzo hadn't returned. Tears started in the boy's eyes. Angrily, he dashed them away. "He lied, didn't he? Everything he said was a lie—and I hate him! I *hate* him! I hope he never comes back here! I hope he's dead on the road someplace, run over by a Mack truck and squashed as flat as a possum!" Opossums, which came out at night, were always being struck and killed by cars on the country roads, along with rabbits, squirrels and the occasional raccoon, coyote, and deer.

"Hush, Alex!" Sarah snapped sharply, her own nerves stretched to the breaking point. "That's not true—and you know it! Something must have happened, that's all. Maybe it's just taking him longer than he thought to fix my flat tire. Or maybe the Jeep's engine has overheated. It's so hot outside. For pity's sake, your dad wouldn't have gone off and left his Jaguar in our drive if he weren't planning on returning here. He'd have driven away," she insisted, as much to bolster her own faith as Alex's, for even now, fierce, gnawing doubt assailed her. When the telephone suddenly rang, she practically jerked the receiver from its box on the kitchen wall. "Hello."

"Sarah? It's Liz."

"Oh, hi, Liz," Sarah greeted her friend, swallowing her dread and disappointment.

"Listen, Sarah, I called FYI, but you weren't there."

"No, it's—it's Saturday. I—I wasn't planning on going in until later this afternoon."

"That's what I figured, so I guess you probably haven't heard what happened last night."

"Last night? No, I haven't, Liz. Why? What's up?"

"A young black man by the name of Lamar Rollins was murdered out by the railroad tracks on the old town road. Dwayne Truett found the body this morning. It had two bullet holes pumped into it, apparently from a thirty-aught-six. Lamar was known to have grown marijuana in several isolated fields in the country, so everybody reckons his killing is drug related. Now, here's the reason I called, Sarah, why I'm telling you all this. Hoag Laidlaw is claiming he saw Renzo Cassavettes out at the old quarry—the swimming hole—earlier this summer and that Renzo was standing there with Lamar Rollins, that they were having a secret meeting. The way Hoag's got it figured is that Renzo and Lamar were involved in some kind of drug deal together, which went sour, and so Renzo murdered Lamar."

"That's impossible!" Sarah cried, stricken, her heart pounding furiously, her mouth dry with sudden fear, her hand sweating on the receiver. "Renzo's father—his *real* father, not Joseph Martinelli—used drugs. Marijuana and cocaine. Because of that, Renzo *hates* drugs. He would never—*never!*—have anything to do with them, Liz!"

"Well, that may be. I'm just telling you what Hoag's saying. He's raked up all those old accusations about Renzo deliberately shoving Sonny Holbrooke off that rock out at the quarry that summer, too, and insisting that except for an occasional, drunken, Saturday-night shootout at Rowdy's Roadhouse, or a hot-tempered stabbing down in the Italian or black parts of town, there hasn't been a killing here since Renzo left town more than a decade ago. And now, since Renzo's come back, Lamar Rollins is suddenly brutally shot to death out on the old town road, just some weeks after he was seen in Renzo's company."

"Liz, Liz, what're you saying to me? If Renzo were going to kill a man, he'd take a knife to him—or use his bare fists. That's the kind of man he is. He wouldn't do it with a thirty-aught-six! Oh, God, what am I saying? He wouldn't do it at all! Good God! Why would he? He's got no reason at all to murder anybody! He's rich and famous, a Pulitzer Prize-winning investigative reporter, for

God's sake! Besides which, he was here with me last
night...all night!'' Sarah blurted out, determinedly
pushing away the memory of Renzo standing outside on
the deck, in the darkness, so she had wondered if he had
left her while she had slept. "Why would he even be mixed
up with somebody like this Lamar Rollins?"

"I don't know. Maybe Lamar was some kind of a news
source or something, like that Whistle-blower person.
What I do know is this—Hoag's either arrested Renzo or,
at the very least, has taken him in for questioning about
last night. He's got him over to the jail, even as we speak.
I'm not real sure what all's happening over there, except
that when Hoag and Dwayne got there with Renzo, they
sent Wanda on home, so she wouldn't be privy to anything." Wanda Greeley was the dispatcher. "But J.D.,
Bubba and Forrest's daddy, Judge Pierce, are all over
there. Hoag called 'em all after he'd brought Renzo in,
figuring the Holbrookes would have an interest in the case
because of what happened to Sonny out at the quarry, and
that the judge's presence would lend everything credibil-
ity, I guess. Hoag may not be the world's smartest sheriff,
but he's bright enough to know that these days, Renzo's
got money and connections both. Forrest called Parker
here at home to tell him about it, which is why I know all
this. I thought... Well, look, Sarah, I don't mean to pry
or anything, but ever since that night at the Grain Elevator, I couldn't help but be curious, you know. And so I
started thinking, and a lot of little things over the years
began to add up for me, and then I thought about Alex—
what he looks like, or, rather, who—and that's when
everything suddenly fell into place for me. It's Renzo

Cassavettes, isn't it, who's Alex's father? That's why I called you, why I thought you'd want to know what's happened. Am I wrong, Sarah?"

"No...no... Oh, God, Liz, I've got to go! I've got to get into town right away! If Hoag's arrested Renzo, he's got to let him go! I can alibi Renzo, and I'll swear in a court of law to his whereabouts last night if I have to—"

"Sarah, if you need my help, if Renzo needs an attorney, call me back. I'm not afraid of this town. I won't be afraid to defend him, for your sake and Alex's."

"Thank you, Liz. Thank you for that. You're a true friend, the best one I've ever had, except for Renzo." Tears seeping down her cheeks, Sarah hung up the phone.

"Mom? Mom, what's wrong?" Alex's face was white; his eyes were huge with fright. "It isn't true, is it? That Dad killed somebody last night? You said he was here! All night! And he must have been! I mean, I saw your and Dad's clothes on the pew first thing this morning when I came home, after Mickey and Mr. Thurley dropped me off in their new pickup truck. That's how I—how I knew you and—and Dad...well, you know what I mean, Mom...that you had spent the night together."

Sarah's cheeks became stained with color. She had realized earlier this morning that Alex must have recognized that she and Renzo had slept together last night. But she was embarrassed to hear their son put it into words. She had always tried to set such high standards, and she supposed that sleeping with a man who wasn't her husband—even if she did love him and had borne his child— didn't particularly qualify as a good example for her son.

"Alex..."

"It's all right, Mom. I know Dad's special to you. Has he—has he really been arrested, Mom? Is that why he never came back? Is that why we're going into town?"

"Yes." Sarah was already yanking on her leather sandals, gathering up her handbag and sunglasses. "Oh, my God, I don't have a car!" She grasped the fact abruptly, dismayed. "Maybe Renzo left the keys in the Jaguar." Once she and Alex got outside, she saw that Renzo had, in fact, forgotten his keys in the roadster's ignition last night. But it didn't help. The Jaguar didn't have an automatic gearshift, and Sarah didn't know how to drive anything else. "We'll have to walk down the road to the Jeep, Alex, and hope your father had time to fix the flat tire before Sheriff Laidlaw and Deputy Truett showed up."

"If Dad didn't, I can help you fix it, Mom. I'm big and strong enough to do that."

"I know you are, Son." Sarah smiled at him tremulously, taking his hand in hers, squeezing it reassuringly. They walked down the road that way, hand-in-hand in the hot sun and silence, until they reached the Jeep. To her relief, Sarah saw that Renzo had indeed managed to put the spare on and the flat tire in the back before being hauled away. Her keys were in the ignition. He must have been about to start home when Sheriff Laidlaw and Deputy Truett had cruised by, spotted him and taken him into custody. At gunpoint, no doubt.

She and Alex got into the vehicle. Moments later, they were headed toward town.

"Hoag, I'm warning you. You'd better either charge me or take these damned cuffs off me right now and turn me loose." Renzo's voice was low and steely with menace. His eyes were narrowed and hard, belying the seemingly casual way he slouched in his chair.

"Don't get smart with me, boy. I know the law—and it says I can hold you for up to twenty-four hours without charging you. Ain't that right, Judge?" Hoag inquired as he chewed vigorously on the wooden toothpick in his mouth.

"Yes," Judge Pierce confirmed dryly as, with a big white handkerchief he pulled from his pocket, he carefully cleaned his wire-rimmed bifocals. "But, Hoag, you know damned good and well Renzo's got a right to an attorney if he wants one, and to make a telephone call."

"That's right," Renzo insisted grimly. "I'm an investigative reporter. I know the law, too, Hoag—and you'd better listen to the judge. Besides which, every single one of you present—including you, Judge Pierce—" he glanced one by one at all the men assembled in the sheriff's office, at the judge, Deputy Truett and the Holbrookes, before returning his piercing gaze to the sheriff "—are witnesses to the fact that I wasn't Mirandized, either, before old Hoag and Dwayne there hauled me in. In fact, Hoag *still* hasn't read me my rights!"

"Well, so what? I ain't officially charged you with nothing—yet. Just brung you in for questioning, is all. And I don't have to Mirandize you for that. So if you don't want to wind up sitting back there in one of my jail cells—" Hoag jerked his thumb toward the rear of the small building that had been the town's sheriff's office for nearly a century "—you'd better wise up and start talking, and I mean real fast, boy. 'Cause I don't mind telling you that it don't look good for you, refusing to tell us where you was last night."

"Like I told you before—it's none of your damned business!" Renzo grated, obstinately continuing to withhold the information that would have provided him with an alibi for last night. After all Sarah had been through in this town because of him, he wasn't about to see the good name and reputation she had worked so hard over the years to reestablish dragged through the mud again.

"You fucking wop!" Bubba snarled, abruptly leaning forward in his own chair and staring furiously at Renzo. "I don't care what in the hell my daddy claimed and Judge Pierce ruled at that goddamned inquest all those years ago! You murdered my little brother, Sonny, just as sure as I'm sitting here. And now, you think you can come back here to this town and get away with killing that poor, dumb nigger! Well, you aren't going to get off scot-free this time. We're going to nail your frigging dago ass to the barn door, Cassavettes!"

Coolly, Renzo ignored Bubba. "Hoag, I want to make my telephone call."

"Hoag, you'd better take those cuffs off that boy and let him make his call," Judge Pierce warned soberly. "Because you sure don't want to do anything that might prejudice this case if you wind up arresting him and it goes to trial."

"All right, all right. If you say so, Judge." The sheriff grumbled under his breath as he fumbled in his trouser pocket for the key to the steel cuffs that bound Renzo's hands behind his back. "Just a precaution," Hoag had called it earlier, causing Renzo to laugh shortly, harshly, an insolent, mocking sound that had let the sheriff know just exactly what Renzo had thought of him.

After much dilatory searching, Hoag finally produced the key to the cuffs. But before he could begin removing them from Renzo's wrists, the door to the sheriff's office opened and Sarah stepped timidly inside.

Startled at the sight of her, Bubba hurriedly leaped from his chair and strode toward her solicitously. "Sarah honey. Why aren't you over at FYI? I thought you were going to work at least half a day today. What's wrong? What're you doing here?"

She shrank from him, tried futilely to draw her hands from his, turned her face from his kiss so his lips brushed her cheek instead, eliciting a low growl from Renzo. She trembled at the sound, refusing to look at Renzo. She hadn't realized he would be present; she had thought he would be locked up in a cell. She had hoped, too, that Bubba and J.D. would be gone by now, that she would be able to speak to Judge Pierce alone—because she had never liked Hoag Laidlaw and didn't trust him as far as she could throw him.

"I—I need to talk to the judge. Privately," she said, stubbornly pretending not to see the sharp glance of concern, comprehension, and forbidding that Renzo directed at her. Forrest's daddy at least, she thought, wouldn't be bent or bribed, the way she suspected the sheriff and his deputy might be.

"About what, darlin'?" Bubba inquired, as though to a confused child. "We're in the midst of something real important here, Sarah. Can't it wait?"

"No, it—it has to do with what's going on here."

"Shut up, Sarah!" Renzo demanded abruptly, a muscle working in his taut jaw.

"You're the one what'd better shut your damned mouth, boy!" Hoag retorted, grabbing hold of his wide leather belt and hitching up his trousers. Then he ran his hands through his thinning hair, preening as he strutted pompously toward Sarah. "Now, then, missy. If you've got something to say, if you know anything at all about what happened last night, you'd best spit it out right now. 'Cause, as you appear to have heard, we got us a real nasty little murder on our hands at the moment—and even if the damned fool what was killed was only a worthless, dope-peddling black sonuvabitch, I still got the law to uphold and a job to do."

Finally, Sarah managed to pull her hands from Bubba's, the sheriff's disrespectful attitude toward Renzo and bigoted remarks providing precisely the impetus she needed to collect herself, to remind herself it didn't matter what anybody in this town thought of her when Renzo's freedom—and perhaps even his very life—might well be at stake.

"Well, then, Sheriff, I guess you'd better get on out and start beating the bushes again," she uttered, surprising even herself by how cool and composed she sounded, so only Renzo sensed how flustered and frightened she was beneath her now outwardly calm demeanor. "Because you've got the wrong man in custody."

"What?" Hoag snorted, then guffawed loudly with disbelief. "What're you talking about, missy? Everybody in town knows that guinea bastard sitting over there is a killer, that he's been one ever since he shoved J.D.'s poor young Sonny off that rock out at that old quarry where all your crowd used to swim as kids. Why, the first thing that frigging wop did when he come back here was to ride out on that hog of his to the scene of his crime—and make that very same dive again just as cool as you please, proving he could do it. I saw him with my own two damned eyes, missy! And right after Renzo hauled his ass out of the water was when Lamar Rollins showed up. And the two of 'em was deep in conversation by the time I got around the quarry to where they was standing. You should of heard 'em when I confronted 'em. First, that dago there tried to bribe me. Then he threatened me—said he was gonna drown me in the quarry, same as he had Sonny—and then, on top of all that, that uppity nigger, Lamar, had the nerve to boast to me about his pot fields. So, now, missy. What in the hell would make you waltz in here and try to tell me I got the wrong man in custody?''

''Don't answer that, Sarah!'' Renzo growled, attempting to rise from his chair, only to be slammed back down by Dwayne Truett—who was built like a professional wrestler, the kind who put on ridiculously absurd shows in the ring, for a crowd that howled with malicious delight and pretended it was all real fighting, not fake.

''Because Lamar Rollins was murdered *last night*,'' Sarah replied to Hoag's question, ignoring Renzo as though he hadn't spoken, although she quivered with apprehension at the thought of his black rage being unleashed on her again. ''And so Renzo couldn't possibly have done it. You have to let him go, Sheriff.''

''Sarah...what are you saying, Sarah?'' Bubba's voice was taut with emotion and suspicion as he glanced from her to Renzo and then back at her again, as though he had begun to grasp dimly some inkling of where she was headed—and couldn't believe it, didn't *want* to believe it. "What're you trying to tell us, darlin'?"

"Judge, please, could I just speak to you privately?" Sarah entreated, turning to Forrest's daddy. "I—I really don't want any trouble, and I'm afraid there's going to be some—"

"No, not here, there won't!" Hoag ostentatiously patted the big, heavy revolver in the leather holster at his hip. "Not in my office, I assure you. No-siree-bob. So you go right on ahead, missy, and speak your piece. And while you're at it, quit your damned hemming and hawing around, and get to the point if you've got one! 'Cause either you know something relevant to these here proceedings or you don't—and in that case, you're wasting our time! Now, which is it?"

Realizing then that there was no help for it, that the sheriff was bound and determined to hear what she had to say, Sarah took a deep breath and went on in a rush, before her courage could desert her. "I'm trying to tell you Renzo couldn't have murdered anybody last night. Because he was with me...*all night.*" She emphasized the last words, flushing scarlet at the admission. "He never left until this afternoon."

"What?" Bubba cried, stunned, stricken, even though he had sensed in his heart of hearts that this was what was coming. "No, that's a lie! Tell me that's a lie, Sarah, goddamn it!"

But before she or anybody else could speak, the front door opened, and Alex—to whom she had given stringent instructions to wait outside in the Jeep—stepped anxiously into the sheriff's office. At the sight of her son, Sarah didn't know whether to laugh or cry, knew only that his timing couldn't have been more ironic—or apropos. It had somehow been so all day, she reflected idly.

"Mom? You took so long.... Is everything all right?"

"Well, now, that explains a great deal, which I confess has mystified me for many a long year." J.D., who had until now been strangely silent, spoke, his blue eyes sparking with fascinated interest and comprehension as they flicked alertly from Alex's tanned face to Renzo's dark visage.

"Yeah, well, you always were quicker on the uptake than Bubba and the rest of these clowns, old man," Renzo drawled insolently. "So, Bubba, I guess now you know my taste in women—what it is and what it always was!"

Understanding suddenly dawned in everybody's eyes then. And that was when all hell broke loose. With a fierce, strangled cry of outrage and hatred, Bubba sprang from Sarah's side, grabbing for Renzo's throat. But Renzo had clearly been expecting this and was prepared for it. In one swift, smooth movement, he rolled from his chair to the floor, bringing his hands down and under his legs as he did so. In moments, he was on his feet, his cuffed hands now in front of him, so he could defend himself against Bubba. As they had all those years ago on the commons, the two men went at it vehemently, fists and elbows pummeling, feet hooking and kicking, chairs roughly shoved aside and skidding wildly across the floor.

"Bubba! Here, Bubba! Stop this right now!" J.D. roared, cursing mightily.

"Punch him in the nose, Dad!" Alex shouted with glee, and he would have run to his father's aid had Sarah not hastily seized him, hauling him back by the collar.

"Hoag... this isn't going to look real good for any of us—especially if it ever winds up being brought out in a courtroom," Judge Pierce declared, moving to a corner, distancing himself from everybody present. "You'd best do something, Hoag."

But for all his big talk earlier, the sheriff was useless himself, jumping up and down excitedly and bawling like a stuck pig, "Well, hell's bells, Dwayne, you fool! Don't just stand there like a complete dumb shit! Get in there and break that up, goddamn it!"

At that, drawing his nightstick, Deputy Truett waded into the melee, to try to put a halt to it, only to find himself the recipient of a hail of violent blows from both sides, which sent him reeling. As Dwayne staggered back, Bubba jerked the nightstick from the deputy's hands and hit him hard over the head with it, so Dwayne slid slowly down the wall, coldcocked. Then, weapon held at the ready, Bubba took after Renzo with it. By now, Sarah's nerves were so shot that, to her utter mortification, she was suddenly gripped by such a wild, crazy urge to laugh hysterically at the entire scene that it was all she could do to restrain herself. She couldn't remember the last time she had witnessed such pandemonium. It was, she thought dully in some dark corner of her mind, unreal, like something out of a movie—except that there was nothing funny about the deadly seriousness that etched both Renzo's and Bubba's faces.

Plainly, the two men meant to kill each other. Renzo's nose was bleeding profusely, and one of Bubba's brows was gashed open on the ridge, his eye even now bruising and swelling shut. But despite that Renzo's hands were cuffed and Bubba had possession of the nightstick, the latter was clearly getting the worst of the fight, Renzo using his feet in a fashion that made Sarah think he must, during his years away from her, have studied some form of martial arts or something. The way he moved reminded her of the combatants on Alex's Street Fighters and Mortal Kombat games. Bubba had boxed in college and still did at the local gym—a dubious, rundown old place not far from the university. But Sarah remembered Alex telling her once that a kickboxer could take a regular boxer every time, because boxers didn't know how to use their feet. Apparently, that evaluation was true.

"Hoag, if you can't handle so much as a frigging brawl, you aren't going to be winning any more elections in this town—and that's for damned sure!" J.D. bellowed, his steely blue eyes flashing sparks.

"J.D.," the sheriff whined plaintively. "What in the hell do you expect me to do? For Christ's sake! You saw what happened to Dwayne! Oh, shit!"

Renzo had somehow managed to grab the nightstick from Bubba and had broadsided him in the stomach with it, so Bubba was now doubled over. But before Renzo could bring the weapon crashing down on Bubba's head, Hoag finally moved into action. Drawing his revolver, he fired it wildly at the ceiling, which rained plaster at the impact. Everybody in the room froze at the unexpected blast.

"Now, you better toss that nightstick aside, boy," the sheriff ordered Renzo angrily. "Or the next thing I shoot is gonna be you! Bubba? Hey, Bubba, you all right?"

"Yeah, fine," Bubba muttered between gritted teeth as, clutching his abdomen, he stumbled to one of the over-turned chairs, righted it and sat down, panting hard.

Renzo's own breathing was equally labored. He had pitched the nightstick down on the floor, and now he stood tiredly but warily, his nose still bleeding, so bright splotches of red splattered his torn shirt. Finishing rip-ping away the lower half himself, he pressed the fine cot-ton to his nose in an attempt to staunch the flow of blood.

"Are—are you okay, Dad?" Alex asked in the tense si-lence that had fallen.

A low, agonized groan issued from Bubba's split lips as he heard Alex acknowledge Renzo as his father. Renzo himself nodded tersely, throwing down his makeshift towel and sniffing to hold back the blood that still trickled from his nose as he strode toward the sheriff.

Stretching out his cuffed wrists, Renzo demanded fiercely, "Take 'em off, Hoag! You've got no cause to hold me here any longer or to charge me, either."

"Do as he says, Hoag," Judge Pierce instructed warn-ingly. "Renzo's right. He's got what would appear to be an ironclad alibi, and unless you can prove Miss Kincaid is a liar, you've got no call to hold him further."

Muttering hotly under his breath, the sheriff reluc-tantly unlocked the cuffs. "This ain't by no means the end of this affair, boy—not by a long shot!" he blustered, motioning curtly toward Alex, who stood at Sarah's side, both of them trembling in the aftermath of the violence.

"I reckon we can all see plain as day why that there fucking wop's whore lied for you!"

Renzo's head jerked up sharply at that. His eyes narrowed, glinted as hard as nails in the sunlight that streamed in brightly through the windows of the sheriff's office. It was the only warning Hoag received before Renzo abruptly backfisted him smack across his pasty, leering face. The impact of the powerful blow was such that the sheriff went down like a poleaxed steer, falling heavily to the floor, to lie there in a crumpled heap, moaning. After that, turning wordlessly to his family, Renzo put one arm around Sarah's waist, the other around Alex's shoulders. Together the three of them began to walk out of the sheriff's office.

"Sarah!" Bubba hollered hoarsely behind them. "Sarah! You leave here with that fucking guinea bastard, and we're through! We're through, do you hear me? Sarah! I had you an engagement ring, damn it! I was going to give it to you tonight! Sarah honey, please! Goddamn it, Sarah! You're fired!"

"Shut up, Bubba!" J.D. snapped disgustedly. "You're making a total cake of yourself!"

Sarah ignored Bubba and J.D. both, leaning against Renzo, her arm wrapped tightly around his waist as they and their son stepped outside onto the sidewalk, to make their way to the Jeep. All around the square, people were staring at them, whispering. The three of them got into the vehicle, Renzo in the driver's seat. His nose had finally stopped bleeding, Sarah observed as, after fumbling in her purse, she withdrew her car keys and handed them to him. He inserted the proper one into the ignition. After that, he just sat there for a long, silent moment. Then, without warning, turning in his seat, he reached out and yanked Sarah to him, tangling his hands in her hair and kissing her deeply, feverishly. In the backseat, Alex gazed out the window, tactfully pretending his interest was absorbed by something across the square.

After a while, Renzo reluctantly released Sarah, his eyes staring into hers intently, searchingly, gleaming with love and wonder that a woman such as she should belong to him. Because more than anyone, he knew what it had cost her to come here, to publicly acknowledge their relationship—and him as the father of her child. He combed her dark brown hair back from her face, laid his hand gently against her cheek. Then, without speaking, knowing she already understood all he might have said, he started the Jeep and backed slowly away from the curb, into the street.

Twenty-One

The Homecoming

The days may come, the days may go,
But still the hands of memory weave
The blissful dreams of long ago.

Sweet Genevieve
—George Cooper

To fill the silence on the way home, Renzo turned on the Jeep's radio, punching the buttons until he found a station he thought everybody could live with. Soon the mellow strains of Kenny G.'s saxophone crooning "Forever in Love" drifted from the speakers. The music was not only apropos, but also slow, lilting and soothing, Renzo thought, something they all three needed right now, this having so far proved to be a momentous day in more ways than one. It didn't seem possible to him that it was only half over. He couldn't imagine what might happen next, could hardly repress the urge that assailed him to take his small family home and lock all the doors and windows up tight against whatever else might come. He suspected that by now, the news about him and Sarah and Alex was all over town. Renzo's jaw set grimly, a muscle pulsing as he remembered what Hoag Laidlaw had called her, and all the hateful telephone calls and mail she had received when he, Renzo, hadn't been here to protect her, as he should have been.

"Sarah, is that old garage out back empty?" he asked as he turned on to the gravel drive that led to the farm-house.

"Yes, why?"

"I'm going to put the Jeep and the Jag away. Under the circumstances, it just seems a sensible precaution. Alex, are you strong enough to open those heavy wooden doors for me?"

"I don't know. But I'll sure try, Dad."

"All right, why don't you hop on out here and get started on 'em, then, while I drop your mother off up at the house?" Renzo pulled the Jeep to a halt so Alex could get out, then drove Sarah on around to the front door. "Sary, I know you have an unlisted telephone number, but first thing Monday morning, I want you to get it changed. Bubba has it, I'm sure, and there's no telling who he may give it to—and I'm not having you go through all over again what you did before. When you get inside, you call that secretary of yours…the one you told not to make any more damned appointments for me." At the memory, Renzo eyed her with mocking accusation, his mouth turning down wryly at the corners, so she flushed with guilt. "What's her name? Kate Alcott. You ask her to go into FYI and box up all your personal possessions in your office, because you're not going back there. Even if Bubba hadn't fired you, I wouldn't have let you go back there after today. No, don't argue with me about this—and if you say one word to me about you not having any job now and no way to support yourself and Alex, my black temper's really going to be provoked. You know damned good and well that I intend to marry you, that I have intended to marry you since I was twelve years old, and that I would have done so long before now if my mother and your own—however well-intentioned they may have thought themselves—hadn't seen fit to meddle in our business after that day at the old quarry!"

"I—I don't even know if you ever married anybody else, Renzo," Sarah murmured, her heart beginning to pound fiercely in her breast at his words. "If you're divorced—"

"No, I didn't, so I'm not. That's one of the things we would have talked about today if Hoag and Dwayne hadn't hauled me away. One of the things we *will* talk about. Look, sweetheart, I know you must know I haven't exactly lived like a monk these past twelve years, that one of the ways a man tries to forget one special woman is with a string of other women who don't mean a damn to him. And none of 'em did mean a damn to me, either. I know, too, how it must hurt you to know I wasn't as faithful as you. But you have to remember that until this summer, Sarah, I thought you had got married and moved away barely three months after I fled from this town. If it helps the hurt at all, however, I will tell you this—if I had known, if I'd had even an *inkling* of the truth, of what was really happening to you here, *nothing*—not even the thought of being charged with murdering Sonny Holbrooke—would have kept me from coming back to this town for you. I hope you believe that, *cara,* because I mean it with all my heart."

"Oh, Renzo..." Sarah began. But of course, by then, she was sobbing so hard that she couldn't go on. But that didn't matter, because he had her in his arms, cradled against his broad chest, and he was crooning to her, stroking her hair and kissing the tears from her cheeks.

"Shh. Hush, baby, hush. Because I'm afraid that if you don't stop all this crying you've been doing since last night, Cooper Northrup'll be hotfooting it over here next—trying to make off with you so he can fill up his damned water tower!"

Cooper Northrup managed the water-treatment plant. Rumor had it he was so desperate for rain to take the pressure off the plant and the tower both that he did a rain dance in his boxer shorts every morning in his backyard. The idea of him dragging her up to the water tower to fill it with her tears couldn't help but make Sarah laugh.

"That's better," Renzo declared, tilting her face up to his and smiling gently before his mouth brushed hers. "Go on inside now and do what I told you."

Nodding wordlessly, Sarah got out of the Jeep and went into the house. She called Kate, saying only that she and Bubba had quarreled, that they were through and that he had fired her as a result. Kate was upset, but finally realizing nothing she said was going to persuade Sarah things would all blow over, as they always had before, the secretary agreed to clean out Sarah's office. Then, feeling hot, sweaty and dirtied by the way Hoag Laidlaw had leered at her earlier, by what he had called her in his office, Sarah trudged upstairs to take a shower. She had just finished washing and dressing, and was seated before her vanity, brushing her long hair, when Renzo appeared in her bedroom. He carried a black leather overnight bag—a fact that momentarily took her aback and roused her indignation.

"Now, now, Sary," Renzo said placatingly before she could speak. "Don't go getting on your high horse, thinking I came out here last night expecting to spend the weekend with you—even if I did," he added cockily, grinning. "The truth is that over the years, in my profession, I've never known where an assignment might take me or for how long, is all. So I've just got into the habit of carrying a few essentials with me in the roadster at all times."

Unzipping the case, Renzo began to unpack it, laying its contents on the bed—a change of clothes, a razor, a bottle of cologne and various other items. To Sarah's shock and dread, the very last thing he removed was a huge automatic pistol. With obvious skill and familiarity, he slid the magazine from the grip, then checked to ensure that the chamber was empty.

"My God, Renzo!" she cried, blanching. "What—what are you doing with that?"

"Protecting my family, if need be." His face and tone were grim, determined

"N-n-no. I mean, why do you—why do you even have it in the first place?" Despite herself, Sarah shivered as she stared at him, unable to prevent herself from thinking of that summer's day at the old quarry, and of last evening, of the slamming of his car door in the dead of the night. That Lamar Rollins had been shot with a 30-06 rifle could only be conjecture until an autopsy was performed, or unless shell casings had been recovered from the crime scene, she thought—horrified, ashamed, hating herself for even thinking Renzo might be capable of murder. Still, he had been capable of taunting Sonny Holbrooke into a dangerous—ultimately deadly—game; of ripping open her screen door last evening and taking her in ways that had had a darkly erotic edge; of nearly beating Bubba to death in the sheriff's office today.

"Look, Sarah, ever since the Racket Club, there are a lot of people, in Washington and elsewhere, who are in prison or who will be there shortly, thanks to me—and a lot of 'em just aren't the kind of people it pays to cross."

"You—you mean they might—they might try to—to *kill* you?"

"It's probably not likely, baby. They don't usually assassinate reporters—at least, not in this country. But I'd certainly be a damned fool if I hadn't considered that possibility, now, wouldn't I?" Renzo opened the drawer of the nightstand, put the gun and clip away inside it, so they would be within easy reach at night. Then he motioned toward the rest of his belongings. "Are you going to make room for me someplace?"

She recognized then that of course he planned to stay here, in her house, in her bed. "Renzo, I—I don't know if this is such a good idea, such a—a good example. Alex—"

"Knows I'm his father and how he got here, both. So please don't tell me I can't sleep with you, Sarah. After last night and this morning, I won't stand for that—and you know it," he insisted softly.

No, of course he wouldn't, she realized, a dizzying, frightening tremor of excitement shooting through her as she glanced at the bed and thought again of all he had done to her in it last night, of sharing it with him once more. He wasn't Bubba; he wouldn't be held at bay, the way Bubba had been. Renzo had known her too long and well, too deeply and intimately for that—and because she loved him, wanted him, it wasn't in her to resist him, anyway. Determinedly, Sarah thrust from her mind her terrible suspicions that he might be capable of murder, reassuring herself that they had no basis in reality.

"I mostly use the armoire. The dresser's practically empty," she told him.

"Fine, I'll take it, then. I'm going to shower, too, and get cleaned up." He hauled off what remained of his torn, bloody shirt, tossed it in the wastebasket. "I phoned Morse, told him to handle things today at the *Trib*. Did you call your secretary, Kate?"

"Yes. She's going to drop my things off Monday, on her lunch hour. It—it just seems so strange . . . the idea that I don't have to think about getting up for work in the mornings now, that I don't have a job anymore. I mean, I've worked since I was seventeen years old."

"And that's my fault, I know." Renzo's mouth tightened with anger at himself.

"Oh, Renzo, I'm so sorry. I didn't mean that the way it sounded. Really, I didn't," Sarah asserted quietly. "I just meant that my schedule has been so hectic lately that I'm having a hard time adjusting to the fact that it isn't going to be like that from now on."

"Well, if you miss it, you can come to work at the *Trib* if you like. If you want to stay home full-time, that's fine, too. Meanwhile, it isn't going to hurt you to have some time off for a change, until you decide what you want to do. I know your life hasn't been easy or much fun for you these past several years, Sarah, and I can't help but blame myself for that. I want to make that up to you, to take care of you and Alex both. I *will* take care of you both."

"Where *is* Alex, by the way?" she inquired curiously.

"He'd better be down the hall, cleaning up that pigsty he lived in until he showed it to me so proudly." Renzo smiled wryly, shaking his head. "Somehow I got the impression that my reaction wasn't precisely what he had hoped for. Sary, you know you've spoiled him rotten. I understand why you did it, but it's got to stop now. The boy has to learn that nobody in this life hands you anything on a plate, that you've got to earn it yourself, through hard work and determination, that you've got to take responsibility for your actions, either to reap the rewards for them or to suffer the consequences."

"I know that. Don't you think I've tried to teach him that?"

"I know you have. But I'm here now—and I'm not going anywhere, either. So he no longer needs a bunch of material objects to make up for him not having a father. He *does* have one, however belatedly I may have arrived on the scene."

Before Sarah could respond, the telephone rang. She jumped, startled, her face draining of color as she stared at the instrument on the nightstand as though it were some kind of monster—and she were just seventeen again. Seeing that, Renzo growled a low imprecation and picked up the receiver to answer.

"Yes?" After a long moment, he drawled coolly, "You're drunk, Bubba. Go sleep it off." Renzo paused, holding the receiver a little away from his ear as a tirade of abuse clearly followed. Then he continued. "Bubba, I'm not going to argue with you, and I'm not going to put Sarah on the phone, either. You said it yourself. The two of you are through. And that's all there is to it—so don't call back here." Then he replaced the receiver in the cradle.

"Why didn't you just hang up on him?" Sarah asked nervously, biting her lower lip.

"Because, believe it or not, I'm sorry for him. I know how the poor bastard feels, losing you." Abruptly, Renzo strode over to the vanity, where she still sat. He wrapped one hand gently in her hair, tilting her face up to his, gazing down at her soberly. "*Cara*, you're going to have to keep out of his way from now on—or at least until he cools down considerably—and I mean that. He's angry and hurting, and so, while he may have played the part of a gentleman before, it may be that he won't now."

"What makes you think that?"

"Trust me. I know. I'm a man, and that's the nature of the beast. Whether we like it or not, Sarah, emotions are volatile, primal, an inborn part of us. My father told me that once, and I've since learned he was right. Under the right circumstances, any one of us can be driven to sloughing off the trappings of civilization and reverting to the wild, the savage." Lowering his mouth to hers, Renzo kissed her deeply, lingeringly, silencing anything else she might have said, releasing her only when the telephone rang again insistently. This time, instead of answering, he unplugged it from the wall. Then he disappeared into the bathroom to take his shower, leaving Sarah sitting there, staring at the nightstand drawer, where his automatic pistol lay—and shuddering at the sudden, chilling thought that murder was undeniably the most savage act of all.

Surprisingly, given the day's events, the evening passed quietly. Discovering that Sarah's cupboards and refrigerator held the makings for spaghetti, a Caesar salad and garlic bread, Renzo cooked supper, much to Alex's bemusement. As Renzo did so, he entertained the two of them with tales of his life as an investigative reporter, how he had over the years worked his way up the journalistic ladder from one big-city newspaper to another, until he had finally reached Washington, D.C., where, based on a tip he had received from the source known to him only as the Whistle-blower, he had broken the Racket Club story, in the end winning the Pulitzer Prize.

The three of them ate by candlelight in the dining room, Renzo opening a bottle of Lambrusco from Sarah's wine rack and, over her protests, pouring three glasses—although Alex's held no more than a few sips' worth.

"It's not going to hurt the boy to have just a taste, Sarah." Renzo raised his glass. "To us—all three of us," he said simply, and they all drank, Renzo and Sarah unable to repress smiles at Alex's grimace when he swallowed the wine. "It's an acquired taste, Son," Renzo explained. "Now, let's eat." He dished up the meal, handed Sarah and Alex their plates.

"Gee, Dad, this is great!" Alex consumed his spaghetti with gusto. "You'll have to teach Mom how to cook it this way. Hers isn't nearly so good!"

"That's because she doesn't have an Italian mother." Then, seeing the shadows that haunted Sarah's eyes, knowing she was remembering that summer's day at his parents' bungalow, Renzo smoothly changed the topic of conversation. He told himself he was going to have to speak to his parents eventually, to make them understand that he had never stopped loving Sarah Kincaid and that he was going to marry her—come hell or high water.

After dinner, Alex played his saxophone, Renzo giving him pointers to improve his technique and applauding enthusiastically when he had finished, much to the boy's delight. Then Renzo played, and Alex knew he was hearing a master, and Sarah thought it was perhaps this more than anything else that impressed him most deeply about his father.

Finally, it was Alex's bedtime, and the boy retired to his room. That was when Sarah opened one of the doors in the entertainment cabinet to reveal a row of videocassettes to Renzo.

"I made these over the years," she told him quietly. "Oh, Renzo, it was the strangest, most incredible thing. I've never got over it. Even now, I still can't believe it when I think about it. One day this big box addressed to me was delivered to the house, and when I opened it up, there was a video camera inside, along with a typewritten note that said, 'For the baby and its father—because you will have your memories.' That was all. It wasn't signed or anything. So I didn't have any way to return the camera, and

I had to keep it. At first, I thought you had somehow learned I was pregnant and sent it. But later, I realized that couldn't possibly be so. To this day, I still don't know who gave it to me, who I have to thank. But I used the camera to record Alex's life, because I realized what the card had said was true—that I would have my memories, but that Alex would be too little to remember his early life and that you would never know about it at all without these video-cassettes. Oh, Renzo, who do you imagine could possibly have done such a thing? The only people I could think of were your parents, but somehow, deep down inside, I don't believe it was them."

"No, I don't think it was them, either, Sarah." Renzo stared down at his wineglass, realizing belatedly that of course, there had been someone besides his parents who had known about him and Sarah, someone else who could have told him about his son. Papa Nick. Why hadn't his grandfather ever let him know? Renzo wondered with anger, bitterness and deep sorrow. But even as the question occurred to him, he knew the answer: Papa Nick had wanted him to make something of himself, something to be proud of, and he couldn't have done that in this small, prejudicial, rural town. Renzo recognized then that the price he had paid for that seemingly simple, innocent favor given in the long, sleek black car on the old town road that summer's day had been far higher than he had, until now, ever known.

"I know you can't watch all these videocassettes this evening, Renzo. Maybe you don't even want to see any of them tonight—or ever. But I wanted to let you know they were here." Sarah paused for a moment, watching him draw silently on his cigarette, take a long swallow of his wine. She wondered what he was thinking. But she was intuitive and sensitive enough not to ask. "I'm going to go on upstairs now, take a bath, read for a little while, talk to the fairies . . . my wind chimes," she elucidated, flushing a little with embarrassment at his inquiring glance. "That's how I imagine they speak to me—the butterflies, the blue-bottles and the fireflies, I mean. Oh, I know it probably sounds silly, but somehow I've just always thought of them as fairies."

To her surprise, Renzo nodded, understanding. "You never did know this before, but that's what I thought you were the first time I ever saw you, Sary." His voice was low, soft, husky with emotion at the memory. "A fairy child. I'll never forget it. It was long before that day at school when Evie confronted you over that old lunch box. It was an Indian summer, stretching even then toward fall, and you were in the meadow, dancing and singing—that song about the tallyman and the bananas. You wore a shabby, faded pink sundress, and your long brown hair hung down your back, almost to your knees, and your feet were bare. You had a bouquet of flowers clutched in one grubby little fist, and all of a sudden, you dropped them, stretched out your hands and closed your eyes as though you were whispering a spell of enchantment. And then the most magical thing happened. A big yellow butterfly came to light in your palms. And that was the moment I fell in love with you, Sarah Beth Kincaid . . . that I somehow knew that when I grew up, I was going to love you for the rest of my life. . . ." Renzo's voice trailed away into silence. He smoked his cigarette, drank his wine, watched the glisten-

ing tears drip like raindrops from her green eyes to slip
soundlessly down her pale cheeks.

After a long moment, utterly unable to speak for the
lump in her throat, for all the love and emotion that welled
in her heart, filling it to overflowing, Sarah turned and
went wordlessly up the stairs. And Renzo—understanding that, too—slowly rose to take from the shelf the first
tape, labeled in her seventeen-year-old hand *Sarah, Pregnant*.

He pushed it into the VCR, punched the Play button.
The TV screen flickered briefly, and then the images began to unroll before him—all the things he should have
seen, and never had, never would, except here, in the vi-
gnettes Sarah had captured for him for all time. She had
set the camera up on a stand, he realized, using the battery pack to record the videocassettes herself, because she
sat in their meadow, beneath their sycamore tree. Her soft,
sweet, smoky voice spoke to him, telling him the date and
what was happening.

"Today the doctor did the sonogram. Oh, Renzo, we're
going to have a son! I'm so happy, so excited! I so wanted
a little boy, one who will look just like you! That probably sounds strange to you, I know. But the truth is . . . the
truth is that even though you're not here, I can't seem to
stop loving you, to stop wanting a part of you that will be
mine forever and ever. Mama and Daddy wanted me to
have an abortion. But I wouldn't do it! Now, they want me
to put our baby up for adoption. But I won't do that, either! I wish you were here—to help me be strong. But
you're not, so I just have to go on the best I can. It's—it's
so hard, sometimes. Because you see, you weren't just the

boy I loved. You were my best friend. I don't know if you'll ever even see this tape—or any of the others I'll make. I have to hide the camera and videocassettes, so Mama and Daddy won't find them. I—I got expelled from high school, for being pregnant. It was so awful! Mr. Dimsdale said he was so terribly disappointed in me. So I'm working as a waitress at the diner, and with the money I'm making, I bought a small steel locker, and I put it in our tree house. That's where I keep the camera and tapes. It's the best I can do at the moment.''

In silence, Renzo watched as the months passed, as Sarah's belly grew round and swollen with their child, her face so luminescent that it made all the more visible beneath her eyes the dark, crescent smudges born of her solitary struggle and fragility. Then, finally, after more than two hours had passed, there was nothing on the TV screen but snow and only static came from the speakers. By then, the ashtray was full of cigarette butts and he had finished the bottle of wine he had opened earlier. Getting to his feet, he put the videocassette away carefully, closed the entertainment cabinet and shut off the lamps one by one. Then Renzo slowly climbed the stairs to the woman he loved.

She was asleep, a fairy woman-child in a long, sleeveless nightgown of delicate, diaphanous, lace-edged lawn, bathed in the silvery radiance of the moonlight that streamed in through the French doors and windows. He undressed in the semidarkness, slid into bed beside her, slipped the nightgown from her naked body, watched it float like a white cloud on the wing to the floor. His tender mouth and gentle hands woke her, and when, at long last, he sank into her, winding himself like the ribbons of moonbeams around her, her soft keening of wonder and splendor echoed in the summer night, to mingle dulcetly with his own low, profound cry.

Twenty-Two

Lamar's Legacy

There is a strange charm in the thoughts of a
good legacy, or the hopes of an estate, which
wondrously alleviates the sorrow that men would
otherwise feel for the death of friends.

Don Quixote
—Miguel Cervantes

The package had been delivered to the *Tri-State Tribune*
on Saturday afternoon, but as he had left Morse in charge
of the newspaper over the weekend, Renzo didn't receive
the big manilla envelope until Monday morning, after he
had driven into town and dropped Alex off at summer
school. Although the package was addressed to Renzo, he
didn't recognize the handwriting, so he examined the manilla envelope carefully—having, since exposing the Racket
Club, been wary of receiving a letter bomb. But he saw
nothing about the package to alarm him, so at last, with
the letter opener on his desk, he slit it open to pull a single

piece of stationery and another, smaller manilla envelope
from inside. The missive had been composed and printed
out on a computer, on Field-Yield, Inc. letterhead.

Dear Renzo Cassavettes,
You was rite about what you said that day at the ole
quarry, about me not bein smart enuff to take yore
advice—except that it ain't that I ain't smart enuff, it's
that I just don't see the point when I have thought of
a plan to get rich in a hurry. And the man ought to
pay anyway fo what he's done. But just in case somethin should go wrong, I am sendin you these diskettes. If I should turn up daid, you'll know what to do
with them, seein as how you are a Poolitzer Prize-
winnin reporter and ain't afraid of ole lard-ass
Tweedledum.

                                              Later, dude.
                                              Lamar Rollins

As Renzo stared down at the small package that had accompanied the letter, he was of two minds. Part of him
knew that he should take everything over to Judge Pierce
immediately, as Hoag Laidlaw could not be trusted with it
and it was plainly evidence in Lamar's murder. Another
part told Renzo to open the envelope himself, as Lamar
had trusted him to do.

In moments, Renzo was using his letter opener to cut
through the brown string tied around the envelope and to
slice the packing tape that sealed it. There were several
diskettes inside, all neatly labeled in numerical order.

Renzo knew without a doubt that whatever information they contained was what Lamar had been killed for.

Turning to the computer on his desk, Renzo shoved the first diskette into the A: drive and attempted to access its files. ENTER PASSWORD flashed on his screen.

"Damn!" he swore softly. "How did you expect me to help you, Lamar, if you didn't even trust me enough to give me your password? But I guess this was your way of stalling me in case I tried to read the information on these diskettes while you were still alive, huh?" At random, Renzo typed in a few different words that came to mind, but none of them allowed him access to the files. At last, picking up the receiver on his telephone, he pushed one of the intercom buttons. "Morse, could I see you in my office a minute, please?" Morse Novak knew more about computers than anyone else Renzo could think of in town.

"On my way, Boss." Presently, Morse wheeled himself into Renzo's office. "What's up, Boss? Something I didn't handle to your satisfaction this weekend after your little dustup with Hoag, Dwayne and Bubba?" Morse grinned hugely, wishing he had seen it.

"No, nothing like that. You're a top-notch journalist, Morse—even if that article you wrote about my brush with the law *was* terribly slanted. I'll bet old Hoag was fit to be tied when he read it!" Renzo grinned back at Morse before explaining the situation to him, saying, "Take a look at this first diskette and tell me what you make of it."

"Hmm. It's asking for a password, isn't it? Well, that's a relatively simple security device," Morse observed as he studied the monitor thoughtfully. "The trouble is that the password could be anything—a word that had some meaning to Lamar, a random series of letters, a combination of letters and numbers. All those, as I'm sure you're aware, are used to access online accounts like America Online, CompuServe and GEnie, for example, or to lock up files in various word processing, database and spreadsheet programs, and the like."

"Right. So my question is, how do we figure out Lamar's password?"

"Well, you could just sit there for however long it takes, Boss, entering words and so forth off the top of your head, hoping to get lucky," Morse announced cheerfully, obviously knowing this wasn't the answer Renzo was after.

"Actually, I *was* hoping for a little better solution than that, Morse."

"Why don't you let me work on the diskettes for a while, then? Having done my fair share of hacking over the years, it may be that I have a couple of programs of my own at home that will help us find out what's on these babies."

"Good. And, Morse, I'm sure I don't need to tell you that none of this is to go beyond you and me. You've got to know I'm withholding evidence in a crime, breaking the law by not immediately turning these diskettes over to Hoag, particularly since Lamar's note to me makes it clear he believed his life was probably in danger."

"So you think whatever's on these diskettes is what got him killed, Boss?"

"Yeah, I do. Unquestionably, he was using whatever information's contained in those files to blackmail somebody here in town—which means the stuff must be pretty damned explosive. Because I sincerely doubt that anyone would have murdered Lamar just because he had found out some bored housewife is slipping over to the Rest-Rite Motel every time her old man's out of town.''

''No, I don't think so, either,'' Morse agreed whole-heartedly. ''All right, then. I'll take these home with me tonight to work on them and let you know what, if anything, I discover. I hope you're not counting on a quick answer, however. It'll take me some time.''

''Thanks, Morse. I appreciate it.''

That same Monday morning, at Field-Yield, Inc., the first thing Jolene McElroy did when she sat down at her switchboard in reception was to get out the purchasing order she had filled out the previous Friday, before leaving work. In addition to answering the telephone lines at the fertilizer plant, it was Jolene's job to see that the office-supply storerooms remained properly stocked. Since, when she wasn't answering the phones, Jolene was generally yakking on one herself, she never paid sufficiently close attention to the storerooms, so as a result, Field-Yield, Inc. was always running out of stationery or staples or Scotch tape—much to everybody's annoyance. Late Friday afternoon, however, Jolene had finally unglued her headset from her ear long enough to traipse down the hall to the storerooms, where she had, much to her surprise, discovered that the plant was—in addition to various other items—totally out of the double-sided, high-density diskettes used in its computer system. Jolene hadn't believed how quickly the company had gone through the cases she had ordered the last time, and she had speculated to herself that more than one employee must be pilfering a box here and a box there, taking them home to use on their own personal computers or to sell them.

Now, smacking her gum as she gazed at her purchase order, Jolene slipped on the headset to her switchboard and punched in the number of De Fazio's Computers & Electronics.

"Mr. De Fazio? This here's Jolene McElroy, over to FYI. I need you to send me over a couple of cases of double-sided, high-density diskettes."

When she had finished placing her call, Jolene trotted down the hall to Bubba Holbrooke's office. After she had knocked on the door, she stepped inside.

"Oh, excuse me, Bubba. I didn't know you were occupied," she said as she spied J.D. and Evie sitting in the office, as well.

Obviously, the three were having some kind of a family quarrel, Jolene thought—and she'd be willing to wager a week's pay that it had something to do with the fracas over at the sheriff's office this past Saturday afternoon. Even this morning Bubba still looked like hell, sporting a black eye and a cut lip—and suffering a pounding hangover, too, unless Jolene missed her guess. She smiled inwardly at all the gossip she'd have to report later to everybody she talked to on her switchboard—unless, of course, Bubba made it worth her while to keep silent.

That was the great thing about always blabbing everything you knew. People usually went out of their way to do you favors or buy you things, so you wouldn't tell all you were privy to about *them!* In the past, whenever Sarah Kincaid had got him all hot and bothered, only to leave him hard and hurting, Bubba had come to Jolene to ease the pain. And he had always given her something real nice afterward. Last time, she had got a bracelet she had admired at Goldberg's Fine Jewelry. Nothing *too* fancy or expensive; still, she'd bet he had spent at least a hundred dollars on it.

"I'll come back later, Bubba, when you're not so busy," Jolene announced.

"It's all right, Jolene honey," Bubba replied as he massaged his forehead, groaning a little at the pain stabbing behind his eyes. "What can I do for you this morning?"

"I just wanted to let you know about the office supplies. I know people are stealing 'em, Bubba. I ordered two cases of double-sided, high-density diskettes only a short while back, and last Friday afternoon, when I checked, they were already gone. Why, if I didn't know better, I'd think old Thaddeus Rollins and that poor, dumb nephew of his who got murdered out on the old town road last Friday night were taking 'em—except that I can't imagine why, unless it'd be to sell 'em on the side. I don't believe Thaddeus can hardly even write his own name, much less use a computer, and Lamar was a high-school dropout."

"All right, I'll check into it later," Bubba told her. "And, Jolene honey, would you mind getting me another cup of black coffee—and a couple of aspirin, too, if you can find some? My poor head's just about to split wide-open!"

"Sure thing, Bubba." Taking the coffee cup he handed her and blowing a bubble with her gum, Jolene sashayed from his office, thinking about the darling little dress she had seen last week in the window of the Fashion Boutique.

"Your head wouldn't be pounding like a sledgehammer, Bubba, if you hadn't got drunk all weekend, pissing and moaning in your beer over that sluttish piece of coal-mining trash Daddy and I both warned you not to take up with in the first place!" Evie gibed disgustedly. "My God! I never thought I'd live to see the day when my brother would make a complete, idiotic ass of himself over stupid little Coal Lump Kincaid!"

"Shut up, Evie!" Bubba growled angrily. "At least I ain't been married and divorced three times already—and you ain't even thirty yet! Why in the hell don't you just screw 'em instead of marrying 'em all the damned time? 'Cause at the rate you're going, by the time you're dead, you're going to have had more husbands than Elizabeth Taylor!"

"Yeah, that's right." Evie's voice was frosty, disdainful. "Enough for pallbearers, anyway—which is more than you'll have whenever you finally keel over. Lord, at the rate *you're* going, we'll have to cremate you and hope you at least have a decent girlfriend to carry away the urn full of ashes! Because let me tell you something, Brother—unlike your little lump of coal-mining trash, my husbands have all been perfectly respectable. And I'll tell you another thing, too, Bubba Holbrooke. They weren't sneaking around behind my back, fucking any goddamned dagos on the side, either!"

"Evie!" J.D. roared, his face turning scarlet with fury at her language—since although he considered it perfectly acceptable for gentlemen, he didn't hold with ladies swearing.

"Evie, you bitch!" Bubba cried fiercely, jumping up from his burgundy leather chair and clenching his fists as though he were preparing for a boxing match. "You'd better get her out of here, Daddy! I'm warning you. You'd better get her out of here right this minute—before I strangle her!"

"Daddy, you'd better settle down...just settle down now." Coolly ignoring her enraged brother, Evie patted her father's arm soothingly. Her brow knit anxiously as she saw how a big blue vein had popped out on his forehead, so she feared he might have a stroke. "I'm sorry for talking so unladylike. Really, I am. But Bubba had no cause to insult me like that—and you know it, Daddy. After all, I'm not the one who's brought scandal and disgrace on this family and our good name! And I tried hard to make my marriages work, Daddy. Truly, I did. But Parker and Tommy Lee and Skeets, well, not one of them was half the man you are, Daddy. Why, they couldn't get themselves elected to a garbage detail if their lives depended on it! Come on, Daddy. Let's leave big, bad Bubba here to cry in his beer. Taggart Evanston ought to be here by now, and we can get on with planning your senatorial campaign. I've got some great ideas for advertising and promotion, Daddy. I never did know why you listened to that stupid little Coal Lump instead of me. She never had your best interests at heart, Daddy, the way I always have! Why, at the rate we're going, one of these days we'll be living in the White House, and people will be addressing you as 'Mr. President.' Won't that be something, Daddy? Won't that be fine?"

"It would have been a whole helluva lot finer if I'd lived to see Sonny in the White House, missy!" J.D. declared gruffly. "But I'll get there for him—the Good Lord willing. Although I doubt even that'll help, that I'll ever get over burying that boy... my golden boy, moldering in his grave. While you and Bubba continue to thrive like a pair of damned-nuisance weeds!" J.D. snorted with derision and disappointment. "Why, I'd trade you both away tomorrow to have Sonny back again. He was a thoroughbred, worth ten of either of you two pack mules! So quit your fussing and hanging on me, Evie! I don't need you to mollycoddle me like some old mother hen. Now, I'm going down to my office, and I don't want to be bothered for a while. So you'd best get on out of here and leave Bubba alone. Because I don't care if the two of you do kill each other. I'm not going to come running back down here again to put a stop to your arguing!"

With that Parthian shot, J.D. stalked from Bubba's office, leaving both his children standing there hurting—and silently cursing their dead brother.

In the big, plush, semidark office, the computer screen glowed brightly. From the burgundy leather chair, a pair of capable hands stretched out to fall upon the keyboard, while the wheels of the brain that directed the hands churned furiously. Lamar Rollins had not proved so stupid as originally thought. The diskettes in his car had *not* contained the deadly files; instead, they had all been blank—although clearly, at one time, they had held some sort of information. For, gazing at them, Lamar's killer could see traces of adhesive backing where old labels had been peeled away from the black plastic.

So if Lamar had used the diskettes himself before erasing them, whatever files they had held and that he had deleted could still be reconstructed—provided, of course, that he hadn't written over and erased them a couple of times or used a program like Norton Utilities on the diskettes themselves, which, short of a bulk eraser, were the only sure methods of preventing recovery.

Fortunately for the killer, Lamar had done none of those things, merely deleted his files.

In the silence of the summer night, the killer worked painstakingly, clever mind—so much more clever than anyone had ever suspected—continuing to direct competent hands on the keyboard, until, finally, the monitor flashed, darkened momentarily, then brightened again, and all the information Lamar had ever recorded about his dope deals began to scroll by on the screen. At the sight, the killer's face lit up just as the monitor itself had, glowing with a purely wicked smile.

What a stroke of luck! the killer thought, a perfect complement to the stroke of genius that would wreak havoc on Lamar's files and the town itself before the killer was through.

Twenty-Three

The Investigation

Attempt the end, and never stand to doubt;
Nothing's so hard but search will find it out.

Hesperides: Seek and Find
—Robert Herrick

"What did you find out, Virgil?" Renzo asked, glancing up from his desk at the young black man who had entered his office at the newspaper. Virgil Bodine was a journalism major at the university. After Renzo had taken over the *Trib,* he had given Virgil a job as a summer intern.

Virgil flipped open his small notepad, reading back the notes he had made to himself during the investigation Renzo had instructed him to undertake. "One Lamar Rollins, black, aged seventeen. Mother, Tonette Rollins, current whereabouts unknown. Father, unknown. Lamar lived with his grandmother, Mabel Rollins, in a rundown cottage outside the town limits, in what's commonly referred to by a name that isn't any nicer than what your part of town is called, Boss. I have the address and a telephone number. Mrs. Rollins may or may not have a phone currently, however, as it's periodically disconnected due to her inability to pay the bill. Other members of the Rollins family include Thaddeus Rollins, Mrs. Rollins's brother-in-law, and Keisha Rollins, the deceased's mentally retarded little sister. Mrs. Rollins used to be employed at the dog-food factory but was forced to quit work some years back, due to ill health. She currently receives government assistance. Mr. Rollins has been employed at Field-Yield, Inc. for a number of years, as the head janitor, and lives with his dead brother's wife.

"After dropping out of Lincoln High School at age sixteen, Lamar was employed at FYI, as well, as a janitorial assistant. In his daylight hours, he was known to have grown and marketed marijuana. Some of his more major customers are rumored to have been friends from your side of the tracks, Boss.

"When he wasn't engaged in peddling pot, Lamar spent most of his spare time hanging with various and assorted homeys at Zeke Folsom's pool hall and Porkchop Isley's pawn shop, from whom—it is gossiped—Lamar purchased the cheap Saturday-night special he was carrying the night he was killed. Also in his possession that unfortunate evening was a pair of night-vision binoculars he had apparently heisted from Drucker's Sporting Goods.

"His gun had not been fired. Autopsy report showed he was shot twice from long range—both times in the chest—with a hunting rifle, definitely a thirty-aught-six, as shell casings were recovered at the crime scene. Said shots were, in fact, the cause of death. It had been speculated, however, that Lamar might have drowned in the mud puddle in which he was found facedown alongside his clunker, but there was no edema of the lungs or foam present in the airway. A number of partial prints were recovered from Lamar's old car. But it is not known whether these will ultimately prove of any use, as the killer may have worn gloves.''

"Virgil, I'm *very* impressed!'' Renzo grinned broadly. "If you keep on like this, you'll be a fine investigative reporter by the time you've graduated from college.''

"Thanks, Boss.'' Virgil beamed with pride, reminding Renzo of himself as a young man who had worked eagerly on his first big assignment.

"Now, give me Mrs. Rollins's address and telephone number. Then get on one of the computers and get those notes of yours typed up neatly for me, please.'' Renzo was sure that Virgil had his own form of shorthand, as he himself did. Most journalists did, and usually, nobody could read or understand it except themselves. Sometimes it was even indecipherable to the reporter who had written it. "After that, check in with Morse to find out what's doing.''

"Right, Boss.''

"Oh, and, Virgil, close the door for me on your way out, will you?''

The young black man nodded. Once Renzo was alone, he picked up the receiver on his telephone to place a call to his grandfather. They had a fairly lengthy and rather heated discussion, which ended with Papa Nick snorting skeptically and growling, "Renzo, getta real. That Rollins boy's death may well be drug related, I donna know and I donna care. But I will tell you this. Nobody in the business hadda it outta for him. I mean, when was the last time you ever hearda anybody in the business making a hit with a thirty-aught-six, for Christ's sake? No, for this, they woulda used a handgun, a twenty-two... two shots to the backa the head—and dumped him in a quarry afterward. But of course, I can't speak for alla these new boys on the block. They donna got the same kinda rules we hadda in my day. So far as I can tell, they donna got no rules whaddasoever! Be that as it may, however, your brain's still backa in Washington. So you're barking uppa the wrong tree. Looka someplace else...someplace closer to home."

With those mysterious words, before Renzo could even thank him, Papa Nick hung up on him. As he had come to believe about the conversation that had taken place between them in his grandfather's sleek black car that long-ago summer's day, out on the old town road, Renzo now suspected Papa Nick had again been trying to tell him something. Unfortunately, he hadn't a clue as to what it was, and before he could ponder the matter further, Sarah knocked upon the window in his office door, then stepped inside.

"Are we still going to lunch together?" she asked, smiling.

"Hmm. I don't know." Renzo's dark eyes traveled appreciatively over her French braid, the simple sundress she wore, her bare legs and sandals. She looked just as she had that summer's day he had first made love to her, he thought. "Maybe I'll just close the blinds here in my office, and we'll think of some other way to entertain ourselves." He stood as he spoke, and stalked her, pressing her up against the door and kissing her lingeringly.

"Renzo!" she gasped against his mouth. "Your employees can see us!"

"Well, if they don't like it, they're fired. Come on. I've changed my mind about going out to lunch. We'll eat upstairs in the loft. I'll make us a couple of salami sandwiches."

"Dining in today, are we, Boss?" Morse called casually, smirking as Renzo led Sarah down the hall to the stairs that would take them up to the loft.

"I'd dine in, too, Boss, if I had me a woman as pretty as that one," Virgil added.

Sarah flushed crimson with embarrassment at their teasing, but Renzo only grinned, knowing how much Morse and Virgil liked her and that they didn't mean anything disrespectful.

"I am just mortified!" Sarah hissed, once she and Renzo had reached the loft.

"Oh, they didn't mean any harm, baby," he insisted. "Besides, I'll bet you ate with big, bad Bubba in *his* office more than once."

"He didn't have a bed in his!"

"Well, I always did say he was a damned fool." Catching her in his arms, Renzo tossed her down on his bed. "But I'm not. And that's precisely why I plan to keep the loft just as it is, sweetheart—at least until we decide what furniture we do and don't want." He had her pressed into the mattress now and was kissing, caressing and undressing her as he spoke, his hands deftly unbraiding her hair, tangling and spreading it about her. Presently, they were both naked and Sarah was moaning softly with desire and need, drawing him down to her urgently.

"No...like this...." Renzo rolled her over, positioning her on her knees, so her face was against the big, fluffy pillows. "Because I know you don't want my employees to hear your cries of delight, my love," he whispered impudently in her ear before he thrust into the warm core of her from behind, one hand wrapped in her mass of hair, the other upon her mound, rubbing, stroking as he drove into her, drove them both to mindless, breathless excitement and fulfillment.

Afterward, in the loft's small bathroom, he made love to her once more against the shower wall, while the water sprayed endlessly upon them. "Probably driving old Cooper Northrup's water-treatment plant nuts," Renzo murmured, laughing softly against Sarah's sweet, pliant mouth, her slender, bared throat. Then, when they had dressed, he actually did fix her a salami sandwich.

"You want to take a ride with me?" he asked as they ate.

"Wasn't that what I just did?" she inquired archly.

"You keep on like that, and we'll be taking that kind of ride again before we leave here." His gleaming eyes roamed over her insolently. A smug, arrogant smile curved his lips, letting her know he was well pleased with himself. And with her. "No, I mean a ride in my car, baby. I'm going out to talk to Lamar Rollins's grandmother—and she might talk easier to you than to me."

"Why do you want to talk to her at all?" The happy light in Sarah's eyes darkened abruptly. "Oh, Renzo, why? I don't understand why you're mixing yourself up in all this. You know Hoag still thinks you're guilty of murdering Lamar, that I lied for you that day in his office. So, why?''

"Because, for whatever reason, Lamar trusted me, Sary—and I don't imagine there were ever too many people he trusted in his entire young life. Because he counted on me to do the right thing if he were killed. Because if not for the strange twists of fate, if not for my parents taking me in all those years ago, I might have wound up just like poor Lamar. You know I might have, *cara*. Maybe I owe the Lamar Rollinses of the world something for that—because I got out, and they didn't. Besides, you know that damned fool Hoag isn't out there beating the bushes, trying to find the real killer, that he isn't going to be satisfied with pinning Lamar's murder on anybody but me. Don't you grasp what that means, Sarah? It means there's a killer on the loose somewhere in this town, walking around scot-free, probably laughing up his sleeve at all of us! A killer who may kill again!''

That thought had not previously occurred to Sarah, and now, as it did, she shivered. "All right," she said quietly. "I'll go with you."

Lamar Rollins had lived in what was contemptuously referred to by some in town as "Niggerville." It huddled just beyond the town limits, in a cluster of small, old, derelict houses that formed the community's only real slum. There were, of course, other lower-class sections, like Miners' Row and Dagotown, composed principally of blue-collar workers, both white and Italian. But those who lived in the black ghetto were, for the most part, truly poor, the majority subsisting on welfare and food stamps.

The Rollinses' house was no different from its neighbors, a two-bedroom cottage that hadn't seen better days for at least a couple of decades. The once-white paint was grimy and flaking so badly that the worn wood showed through in big patches. The front porch had settled, so the overhanging roof sagged at one end, shingles loose or gone entirely. Shutters hung askew or were missing altogether. Windows were cracked and shattered, boarded up in places. The tiny yard was overgrown with weeds where there had once, long ago, been flower beds, and what had once been lawn was now gravel and dirt, home to discarded beer cans, empty cigarette packages, old newspapers and other trash.

Before coming out here, Renzo had taken his automatic pistol out of the Jaguar's glove compartment, tucking it into his belt at the back so it was concealed by his suit jacket. Sarah had been horrified by his action. But now, as they got slowly out of the roadster, she knew why he had wanted the gun, and she realized this was not the first time he had ever had cause to come into a neighborhood such as this one.

"Watch your step," he cautioned as he took hold of her arm firmly, guiding her through the littered yard and up the single, sunken concrete step to the porch.

There, a plump little girl sat. She wore a frayed sundress that was too tight and too short for her, showing chubby arms and legs, a thick waist. Her black, nappy hair had been plaited into several braids that stuck out at odd angles all over her head, their ends fastened with bright, cheap, plastic barrettes. She played quietly with a filthy old rag doll that lacked one arm and whose own head was nearly bald, displaying only a few fuzzy tufts of black yarn. Renzo's eyes were grim and distant, lost somewhere in the past, as he gazed down at the child, and on his dark visage was a peculiar expression Sarah had never seen before.

It was as though he had known once what it was to live in a place like this, she thought. And then she realized that of course, he had. He spoke to the little girl, but she didn't even glance up at him, her face strangely vacant and uncomprehending as she rocked the rag doll and sang to it tunelessly, the words gibberish. Suddenly, Sarah recognized that this was the child Krystal Watkins had mentioned that night at the Grain Elevator. When the little girl went on ignoring him, Renzo knocked on the dilapidated screen door with its mesh half torn away.

"Hello? Anybody home?" he called.

Despite how badly she wanted Lamar's real killer identified, so Renzo would no longer be under suspicion, Sarah hoped no one would answer the door. She was vividly conscious of how conspicuous she and Renzo were in the slum, of how his bright red Jaguar XKE convertible stood out, of the uneasy quiet that filled the summer air and of how dark eyes watched them covertly, hostilely, from behind shabby curtains. But at last, a heavyset, elderly woman with greying hair lumbered to the door. Her faded, flower-print dress didn't quite conceal the rolled-down tops of her thick support hose. On her feet were worn, fuzzy slippers.

"What you want?" she asked, peering at them suspiciously through the screen and her bifocal glasses.

"Mrs. Rollins? I'm Renzo Cassavettes, from the *Tri-State Tribune*. And this is my friend, Sarah Kincaid. We'd like to talk to you about your grandson, Lamar, if we may."

"What fo'? He's daid, ain't he?"

"Yes, ma'am, and you have our deepest sympathies for that. But before he died, Lamar contacted me, asking me for my help if anything should happen to him. So I'd like to find out who killed him, Mrs. Rollins. I thought you might know something, anything, that might be of assistance. It could be some small piece of information you're not even aware you know."

For a long moment, Mrs. Rollins was silent. Then, finally, she opened the door and stepped outside, sighing heavily as she settled into the battered old rocker on the porch.

"I cain't stand up fo' long periods of time," she explained tiredly. "My po' ole ankles swell sumpin' fierce, 'specially in this heat. I got high blood pressure, too. 'Sides, you don't want to come inside and leave that there fancy au-to-mo-bile of your'n sittin' out there in the road. Won't have half its parts or the radio or hubcaps when you get back." Since this was probably the truth, and there were no other chairs, Renzo and Sarah sat down on the stoop. "I already done tole the sheriff all I know, which weren't much. Lamar...he didn't confide in me none. He wouldn't listen to me, neither. He dropped out of high school, got mixed up with a bad crowd—Porkchop Isley, Zeke Folsom and that bunch—had a run-in now and then with the law."

"The sheriff seems to think Lamar both used and sold drugs, Mrs. Rollins," Sarah said gently, knowing from the careworn expression on the black woman's face that no matter how resigned she appeared to her grandson's death, she nevertheless grieved for him. "Do you think that's true, that his murder was drug related?"

Mrs. Rollins shrugged. "Mighta been. I found some bags of that there marijuana once in his bedroom. But there weren't none when the sheriff come here. He didn't find nothin' 'cept a loose floorboard in Lamar's room, with a hidey-hole underneath. Mighta been some of them bags hid in there at one time, but it was empty when the sheriff looked at it. If I tole Lamar once, I tole him a hundred times that that ole weed wouldn't lead to nothin' but trouble. But like I said befo', he wouldn't listen. You know how boys that age are. He thought he knowed everythin', that he was gonna live forever."

"In the last days before Lamar was killed, did he behave any differently, Mrs. Rollins?" Renzo asked. "Did he seem frightened or depressed?"

"No." The black woman shook her head, thinking back. "Fact of the matter is, he was real excited . . . like he was all keyed up 'bout sumpin'. Said as how there was gonna be some changes in our lives, that he was gonna get back some of our own, that Keisha, 'specially, was gonna have what she deserved in life, that he was gonna get it from the man."

"Keisha?" Sarah glanced inquiringly at the little girl on the porch.

"My granddaughter, Lamar's sister. Don't know who they fathers was, neither one. My daughter, Tonette, she weren't never too particular 'bout who she took up with.

She run off with some travelin' salesman what come through town a few years back. I ain't seen her since. She said Lamar was purt near growed and Keisha . . . well, she ain't never been right in the haid, po' lil' thing. Some kind of brain damage at birth, I reckon. She don't talk much, cain't even say her own name proper. Calls herself 'Kiss-Kiss.'" Mrs. Rollins smiled wanly, her mouth tremulous, her eyes tearful. "Lamar . . . he always thought that were so cute. If there was one thing in this world that boy ever cared 'bout, it were his little sister, Keisha. He thought the sun rose and set in that chile. Felt sorry fo' her, I guess."

"Well. We've taken up enough of your time, Mrs. Rollins." Seeing that the black woman had told them all she really knew, Renzo stood, pretending not to notice as, pushing up her bifocal glasses, she wiped at her eyes. He didn't try to offer her any money, knowing instinctively that for all her circumstances, she would be too proud to take it. "Thank you so much for talking to us. We appreciate it." He helped Sarah to her feet, led her to the car, while Mrs. Rollins rocked silently and Keisha played with her rag doll, still singing tunelessly, the idiopathic words making no sense at all.

"I don't mind saying that I'm relieved to be getting out of this neighborhood in one piece," Sarah remarked as they drove away. "I don't know how people live like this, why something more isn't done to help them."

And Renzo thought of a little boy, a ragged, one-eyed teddy bear and another concrete stoop, and for the first time in his life, he realized he did, after all, have something to thank Sofie and Uncle Vinnie for: the fact that they hadn't wanted him.

Twenty-Four

Unfriendly Fire

No man chooses evil because it is evil;
he only mistakes it for happiness, the
good he seeks.

A Vindication of the Rights of Men
—Mary Wollstonecraft

Lamar's killer sat again in the office, at the computer whose screen gleamed lucidly in the semidarkness, its modem hooked into the vast network that had grown to connect the world, so the modem was like the long, long leg of a spider poised upon a horrendous web. But tonight the spider didn't have far to creep, only into the *Tri-State Tribune* and the other places in town that were part of the linking web. So the spider crept, looking, seeking, slinking down one dark, cyberspace corridor after another, finding nothing here, nothing there. And the clever brain churned, and the capable hands tapped on the keyboard. *Click, click, click.* Somewhere the secret files Lamar had stolen—and given to a friend as insurance—would be found. There weren't that many computer systems or personal computers in town. PCs...now there was a thought. The spider abruptly pivoted, scuttled down a new track, poking, prying—suddenly sighing, *Ahh, poor Morse, you found the key. How bad for you, how good for me.*

*****GOTCHA!*****

Morse Novak stared at the message on his computer screen uneasily, not certain whether it was meant as a joke or not—and if it were, what kind of a joke. He glanced at his wristwatch. It wasn't too late, he decided, for Virgil to be still at the *Trib,* although these days, Renzo usually cleared out at five, to go home to his family.

Ever since returning to his own solitary house at the dead end of a country road, Morse had worked all evening again on the diskettes Lamar had sent to Renzo. Tonight the Vietnam veteran had finally learned the password with which Lamar had guarded his secrets. Having unlocked the directory, Morse had been about to take a look at the actual files themselves when he had realized his urine bag was full. So, leaving his computer running, he had wheeled himself into the bathroom to take care of his physical needs. After he had finished, he'd propelled himself from the bathroom into the kitchen, to grab another beer from the refrigerator. So he didn't know how long he had been away from his desk.

During his absence, however, someone had, via modem, accessed his computer. While this wasn't unusual, since he was tied into the *Trib*'s system, no one at the

newspaper had ever left him such a peculiar message before. He could only think it was Virgil playing some sort
of prank—or else, Morse reflected glumly, despite all his
precautions, some kind of virus might have got into his
computer, or into the entire *Trib* system, for that matter.

At that thought, he decided to run a quick virus check.
But it turned up nothing out of the ordinary. So, return-
ing to his starting point, Morse dispatched a message to the
Trib.

*******VERY FUNNY, VIRGIL. BUT WHAT IN THE HELL IS IT
SUPPOSED TO MEAN?*******

There was no reply. After a long moment, Morse's nape
began to prickle, his skin to crawl, some sixth sense warning him—as it had always done in Vietnam, when the enemy, the VC, had been hidden in the villages and jungle,
waiting...waiting. He had never cursed his wheelchair
more than he did in that moment, knowing that were it not
for that, he would have a fighting chance to save himself.
Still, he wasn't a coward, a quitter. He never had been. He
pushed himself from his desk and turned, intending to
wheel himself into his bedroom, where he kept his automatic pistol.

The bullet plowed through the front window of his small
living room, struck him right between the eyes, bored
through his brain to blow out the back of his head. His
body jerked at the impact, slumped heavily, and the
wheelchair toppled over, sending him sprawling.

Minutes later, Morse's killer was inside the house, moving swiftly, sparing hardly a glance for Morse's pitiful,

crumpled corpse. In one hand, the killer carried a bulk eraser, which was soon plugged into a wall and switched on to quickly wipe Morse's hard drive and diskettes free of all they had ever contained, destroying them. When that was finished, the killer unplugged the bulk eraser, then returned to the dimly lit back porch, where the diskettes containing the altered records of Lamar's dope deals had been left as a precaution. These, the killer concealed between Morse's fallen body and the cushion of his wheelchair, to make it appear as though they had been missed during the search and so not wiped clean like the rest. Wrapped around the diskettes was a typewritten note, secured with a rubber band.

Everything thus satisfactorily accomplished, the killer slipped from the house, laughing softly at the memory of the message sent earlier.

*****Gotcha!*****

As it had not been by Lamar's killing, the entire town was totally outraged and horrified by Morse's murder. That someone would cold-bloodedly shoot a Vietnam veteran, who had served his country honorably and with distinction—however unpopular the war—and been permanently confined to a wheelchair for his brave efforts, was a crime so heinous that it seemed unimaginable.

Realizing from the note wrapped around them that the diskettes discovered beneath Morse's corpse were of the utmost importance, Sheriff Laidlaw had hastily summoned one of Morse's fellow computer-science instructors, Professor Tully O'Neill. Although Morse had taught only the occasional night class at the college, he and Tully had been friends nevertheless. Shocked by his colleague's brutal murder, Tully at once offered to do whatever he could to help. Since Morse's hard drive was destroyed, Hoag escorted Tully and the diskettes to the sheriff's office, where the dispatcher's computer was used to read them.

Thirty minutes later, in a state of high glee, Sheriff Laidlaw and Deputy Truett drove first to the newspaper building, where they arrested Renzo for the murders of Lamar Rollins and Morse Novak. Then, after Renzo was securely locked up in jail, Hoag and Dwayne rode on out to Sarah's old farmhouse, where—because she had provided an alibi for Renzo the night of Lamar's killing—they arrested her, too, as an accessory to the murders.

Twenty-Five

The Nightmare

Between the acting of a dreadful thing
And the first motion, all the interim is
Like a phantasma, or a hideous dream.

Julius Caesar
—William Shakespeare

Renzo was fiercely angry and upset when Hoag and Dwayne brought Sarah back to the rear of the sheriff's office, where the jail cells were located. There was, Renzo knew, little she could do at the moment to help him, and he didn't want her to see him locked up the way he was, his hands still cuffed before him, he having by this time worked them under his legs, from behind his back. He saw that the sheriff and deputy must have already told Sarah the charges against him, because she was crying. But then he spied the handcuffs locked around her own wrists and realized Hoag and Dwayne had arrested Sarah, too. He went crazy then, swearing and shouting at them that they had better turn her loose.

"Why, we can't do that, boy." Hoag grinned wolfishly. "She alibied you that night you killed dumb ole Lamar. This here whore's your accomplice, and that's a fact. That being the case, I expect we'd better frisk her real good before we lock her up, don't you, Dwayne?"

"I reckon so, Hoag," Dwayne replied, leering and grinning as broadly as the sheriff.

"Don't you touch her!" Realizing their intention, Renzo went absolutely berserk even before they put their hands on Sarah lewdly, slowly and deliberately fondling her breasts through the thin material of her pink shell, sliding groping fingers over her jeans, squeezing her buttocks and the soft mound between her thighs. The whole time, she shook uncontrollably and wept and swayed on her feet as though she would faint, her face ashen, stricken. "Hoag, I'll kill you, you fucking bastard! I'll kill you! You and Dwayne are dead men! Do you hear me, Hoag? You're dead, you goddamned son of a bitch, Hoag!" Renzo yelled, kicking the bars of the cell so savagely and repeatedly that the sheriff grew afraid that they would actually give way from the violent blows.

Because of that, he and Dwayne at last released Sarah. Then, drawing the revolver at his hip, Hoag ordered Renzo to get back against the far wall of the cell. Knowing the sheriff would love nothing better than to shoot him and claim he had been trying to escape, Renzo furiously did as he was instructed, his blood boiling, his rage such that he feared he would explode. Then Dwayne opened the cell door, roughly pushing Sarah through it.

"Just consider her our little present to you, boy," Hoag declared before, laughing raucously, he and Dwayne headed for the front office.

Renzo cursed the cuffs that bound his wrists, so that he was forced to drop his arms down over Sarah's head even to hold her and could do little more than that as he pulled her trembling body against his, crooning to her, wishing desperately that he could stroke her hair, her face, to soothe her, comfort her as she sobbed hysterically against his chest. He did manage somehow to get them seated on the hard cot in the cell and her pulled into his lap. He was able that way at least to rock her like a child until, after a long while, she finally began to quiet down. He spoke to her then—softly, gently, although even that couldn't disguise the vicious note in his voice, borne of the brutal wrath that consumed him utterly.

"Sary, sweetheart, before you got here, did those two bastards...hurt you?"

Knowing what he was really asking, she shook her head, which was buried against his chest. Then, after a moment, she whispered tremulously, "But, oh, Renzo! They—they would have, if they hadn't been scared I'd...I'd tell Bubba."

A short, harsh, mocking laugh escaped from him at that. Anger and hurt that he hadn't been able to protect her, that she had been forced to turn to Bubba, assailed him mercilessly. "My God! I never thought I'd live to see the day when I was grateful to Bubba Holbrooke, glad you had gone out with him!" Swearing, tightening his arms around her, Renzo took her mouth savagely with his, as though to reassert his own claim on her, hating what she had endured because of him, the way she quivered and whimpered in his embrace even as her lips clung to his, yielded pliantly to the deep invasion of his tongue.

"Oh, Renzo, what's going to happen to us?" she asked fearfully after a long moment.

"I don't know." His voice was grim. "Did they let you make a telephone call?"

"No, you?"

"No. But sooner or later, they'll have to, Sarah. And when they do, I'll get some outside help into this town. That's what Hoag and Dwayne are afraid of, I know—that I'll drag my high-powered friends in Washington here. And I will. So don't you worry, *cara.* We're not totally alone, without any resources. I've got money and connections both. This town isn't going to railroad us through any kangaroo court and into prison! I'll see to that, I swear!"

In the end, Sarah and Renzo discovered that they did, after all, have friends in town, too, when Liz, her fiery redhead's temper in full force, her grey eyes snapping, was escorted by the sheriff into the small cell block.

"Get out, Hoag!" Liz snarled contemptuously. "I've got the right to consult with my clients privately—and I don't want to see your fat ass back here until I call you to tell you I'm done! No, don't even *think* about giving me any of your ignorant lip! Because I'll tell you what, Hoag. You'd best not forget that my father-in-law is Kingston Delaney and that I work for him and Judge Pierce—not to mention Wade Langford, Drew's daddy. So you get smart with *me,* Hoag, and they'll all be down on you like ducks on a june bug. You won't even know what hit you! Now, get on out of here!" Grumbling heatedly under his breath,

Hoag stamped off, and Liz turned to Sarah and Renzo. "Sarah, I came the minute I heard. What can I do to help?"

"Tell us what evidence Hoag's got, number one, that's led him to believe he can see me convicted of two brutal homicides I didn't commit!" Renzo exclaimed before Sarah could respond.

"He's got a set of diskettes—recovered from the crime scene. On 'em, they have a series of names and dates that make it appear as though you and Lamar were in cahoots, peddling pot to half this damned town! My God! Even Parker's down on the list as having bought grass from you! Hoag's talking about calling in the state bureau of investigation!" Liz went on to explain everything that had occurred since, concerned when Morse hadn't reported to work this morning and unable to reach him via telephone or computer, Renzo had sent Virgil out to Morse's house to check on him, and Virgil had discovered Morse's body.

Valiantly, Virgil had attempted to call Renzo, to warn him about what had happened to Morse. But by then, Renzo had left the newspaper office and gone over to the courthouse to look up some old records for an article he was researching, returning only shortly before Hoag and Dwayne had shown up to arrest him.

"I'll speak to Judge Pierce, see if I can't schedule a quick arraignment, so we can get bail set and get you both out of here," Liz continued.

Renzo nodded. "Thanks, Liz. Meanwhile, would you do one other thing for us? Will you go get Alex out of summer school right now? Tell him what's happened and

Rebecca Brandewyne

that I said for you to take him up to stay at Papa Nick's
house until Sarah and I can come for him."

"Papa Nick?" Sarah and Liz exclaimed jointly, startled.

"Yes, Sary," Renzo insisted, in a tone that brooked no
argument. "I want to be sure the boy's safe—and no offense, Liz, but it may be that you can't protect him. And
after what Hoag and Dwayne did in here a little while ago
to Sarah, I've just *got* to be concerned for my son, to be
certain he's in a place where they can't somehow get at
him."

"All right," Liz said slowly, the wheels in her sharp, legal mind obviously churning as she speculated upon what,
if any, relationship Renzo might have with Papa Nick—
and what possible bearing that might have upon the former's guilt or innocence with regard to the two murders, not
to mention the dope-dealing charges Hoag had tacked on
to the list against Renzo. "Sarah, I'm sorry . . . so terribly
sorry about what Hoag and Dwayne did to you. That was
totally uncalled for, and they had absolutely no right to do
anything like that! No right at all! And you can be sure I'm
going to tell Parker and Kingston when I get back to the
firm. This town's just *got* to stop looking the other way
where Hoag and Dwayne are concerned, to realize they've
been the sheriff and deputy for so damned long around
here that they've got to thinking they *make* the laws instead of just enforce 'em. They've gone too far, they've
overstepped the boundaries." With that observation, Liz
departed, leaving Renzo and Sarah alone together in the
cell.

* * *

At the arraignment, despite how Frank Bannister, the town's district attorney, argued strenuously against it, Judge Pierce ruled that neither Renzo nor Sarah, who both owned property in town, was a flight risk, and he set bail for each of them. Shortly after Renzo had put up the bail money, they were released from jail. They collected Alex from Papa Nick's big, red-brick house on the hill and returned home to begin planning their defense. Unfortunately, the only thing they possessed as evidence of their innocence was Lamar's note to Renzo—and without the accompanying diskettes, which had been destroyed at Morse's house, it was virtually worthless. As, unlike those of big cities, the town's docket ensured that Renzo and Sarah's trial would take place sooner rather than later, they didn't have a whole lot of time to prepare, to prove their innocence.

That night in bed, driven by a dark, powerful sense of fatalism, they made fierce, feverish love together, losing themselves wholly in each other, Sarah with a wild abandon and savage desperation to match Renzo's own. Afterward, she lay in his arms and wept soundlessly, while he held her close in the moonlit darkness, so drained and dispirited that for the first time, he had no solace to offer.

In the small hours of the morning, he awakened gasping and in a cold sweat from his old nightmare, the one in which he was bitten and swallowed by the road-snake. To his relief, Sarah slept on, so exhausted that she was undisturbed by his rousing. But Renzo lay there silently in the greying night, drinking the Scotch he poured for himself, smoking endless cigarettes and staring at the ceiling, sick with fear and despair at the thought that by coming back to this town, to her, he had, instead of renewing their lives, utterly destroyed them.

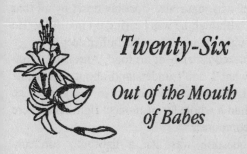

Twenty-Six

Out of the Mouth of Babes

Out of the mouth of babes and sucklings
hast thou ordained strength because of
thine enemies, that thou mightest still
the enemy and the avenger.

> *The Holy Bible*
> —The Book of Psalms, 8:2

In the end, it was Alex who solved the puzzle for Sarah. Always, there had been something about Lamar's diskettes that had bothered her. She just had never been able to put her finger on what it was—although afterward, she realized it was so obvious that she should have seen it from the very start.

She and Alex sat at the kitchen table, eating a subdued and solitary supper. Renzo was in town, at the *Trib*, his hours long and difficult now that he no longer had Morse to rely on and so many of the town's businesses had yanked their advertising, in light of the accusations against Renzo and Sarah. Alex was, naturally, horribly upset by all that had happened, although he was bearing up manfully. He had, Sarah thought, come to love his father deeply.

Now, as he picked listlessly at his food, Alex said, "You know, Mom, what I don't understand about this whole thing is...well, if Lamar lived down in the ghetto, he couldn't have had a whole lot of money, right? So where did he get the computer?"

Her son's question was like a lightbulb suddenly switching on in Sarah's brain. Where, indeed, had Lamar got the computer? She could think of only one place: Field-Yield, Inc., where he had worked as a janitorial assistant.

Sarah knew the murder and dope-dealing charges against Renzo were untrue, that he was being cleverly framed by some unscrupulous person in town. Now she asked herself slowly if it made good sense that, that being the case, the killer would have relied on Lamar's grass-transaction records as evidence against Renzo if the killer were somehow involved with Lamar's marijuana fields and pot peddling. And the answer was no. The killer would have had to suspect that with half the town being named as pot purchasers, Hoag would at least be forced to consider calling in the state bureau of investigation—which would have meant a real risk of eventual exposure for the killer, were Lamar's drugs at the bottom of the affair. Which meant that something else entirely must have been on the diskettes Lamar had sent to Renzo...something

Lamar had perhaps discovered in Field-Yield, Inc.'s computer system.

It would doubtless be in a hidden directory, Sarah thought, her heart beginning to pound horrifically as she suddenly remembered Krystal Watkins's words that night at the Grain Elevator—and Lamar's own words to his grandmother, about getting Keisha what she deserved from the man.

She had to get to Field-Yield, Inc., Sarah realized, to get into its computer system. Fortunately, after Bubba had fired her, so many things had happened so swiftly that she had never had a chance to return her master key to the fertilizer plant to him, even if it had occurred to her to do so. She still had access to all the company's buildings—and it was highly unlikely that Bubba had thought to alter the code for the alarm system.

Before leaving the farmhouse, Sarah placed three calls. No one answered at the *Trib;* Renzo must have gone over to Fritzchen's Kitchen or someplace else for supper, she thought. Tiffany Haskell wasn't busy and agreed to come right over to baby-sit Alex. Tully O'Neill, Morse's friend and Sarah's old professor in computer science at the university, was only too happy to give her instructions as to how to go about tracking down a hidden directory in a computer system. So that she wouldn't have to trust her memory or hastily scribbled notes, Sarah repeated them verbatim after Tully, recording them on Renzo's voice-activated, pocket tape recorder, which he had left on the nightstand that morning.

Then she told Alex where she was going and why, so he could inform Renzo. After that, she grabbed her purse and keys and left the farmhouse.

Sarah parked in the space at Field-Yield, Inc. reserved for J. D. Holbrooke, not only because it was the one closest to the front doors, but also because it was shielded from the highway by a row of tall, spreading quince bushes. Although she didn't spy anyone else around, she nevertheless got out of the Jeep furtively, closing the door as quietly as she could before striding quickly toward the front doors of the big building. Her hand trembled as she inserted her master key into the lock, pushed open one of the heavy glass doors. Once inside, she deactivated, then reset the alarm system, relieved that it accepted the code she punched in. Then she swiftly made her way past the switchboard-reception desk, down the long, dimly lit halls to Bubba's office. The whole time, her heart was racing and her mouth was so dry that she could hardly swallow, no matter how hard she tried to tell herself that this night was no different from any other when she used to work late at the fertilizer plant. It was. She had never before been a trespasser here, never before attempted to break into unknown areas of Field-Yield, Inc.'s computer system.

Nervously, she switched on the banker's lamp on Bubba's desk, dismayed by how shadowy and sinister everything once so familiar to her suddenly appeared in the dim light, as though it were somehow distorted, a scene from a nightmare.

"That's silly, Sarah. Get a grip," she muttered to herself in a futile attempt to bolster her faltering courage.

"You're letting your wild imagination run away with you, is all." Still, her fingers itched to turn on the overhead fluorescent lights. But that would undeniably announce her presence here. She was taking a big enough risk as it was, without flagrantly attracting attention to herself. The soft glow of the lamp probably would not be spied from the highway, especially with the blinds drawn, and if it were, she hoped it would be put down to Bubba himself working late or to the janitorial staff doing their nightly cleaning.

That she wasn't totally alone in the building mitigated Sarah's fear a little, comforting and reassuring her. She determinedly pushed from her mind the knowledge that Thaddeus Rollins was old and slow, not very bright and slightly deaf, besides. If anything untoward were to happen, if she screamed, he would surely hear *that*, would have sense enough at least to telephone the sheriff or to go for Otis Krueger, the night watchman.

Sitting down in Bubba's burgundy leather chair, Sarah flicked on the computer. In the semidarkness, the light from the monitor seemed much brighter than usual as the machine warmed up and the screen came on in a burst of brilliant color. Once she was into the system, she pulled from her handbag Renzo's voice-activated, pocket tape recorder and began to play back the detailed instructions Tully O'Neill had given her for finding hidden directories and files in a computer system.

Her former college professor was undoubtedly an expert at it, but for Sarah, this exercise was a maddeningly slow and tedious process, made all the more nerve-racking by the fact that she didn't know exactly what she was looking for and was apprehensive about being discovered, so she jumped at the slightest sound. She had never before been so conscious of the vast emptiness of the building at night, of all the noises it made. There were things she had never been aware of before: the loud workings of the air-conditioning system, the whoosh and hiss of the cool drafts through the vents, the gurgle of the water cooler in the hallway, the ringing of a telephone line that went unanswered in some office, the distant drone of Thaddeus's vacuum cleaner somewhere beyond, the thud of june bugs against the office windows, attracted by the glow of the lamp.

More than a few times, Sarah made mistakes that forced her to backtrack in the computer system. Once, she became hopelessly lost somehow in a mass of warehouse-inventory files and was finally compelled to power down to purge the computer, and then start all over again. So it was more than an hour later when she at last managed to pull up a hidden directory that looked as though it might be what she was searching for. She requested a list of the files it contained, but instead of receiving that, ENTER PASSWORD flashed on the screen.

"Damn!" she said softly, now more than ever certain this was, in fact, the directory Lamar Rollins had somehow accessed and downloaded to the diskettes he had sent to Renzo, that the information it contained was why Lamar and Morse both had been murdered.

Making random guesses, Sarah typed in *Field-Yield* and then *fertilizer* and *Holbrooke*. When those failed, she tried several other words that occurred to her. Much to her despair, nothing worked. She couldn't even be absolutely certain this was the right directory. She might be wasting all her time and effort. Still, her gut instinct told her this was, in fact, the directory she needed to open. But how could she possibly hope to succeed where even Morse Novak, a computer scientist extraordinaire, had failed—at least, so far as she knew?

Sarah stared at the monitor, chewing her lower lip and thinking hard. Maybe she was going about this all wrong, she mused slowly. Somehow Lamar, the whiz-kid hacker, had got into this directory. He would have wanted to give his blackmail victim proof of that fact, she reasoned, while leaving the files themselves intact, in case he should ever need to access them again. Plus, he wouldn't have wanted his victim to be able simply to delete the files. How would Lamar have accomplished all that?

"Well, how would you do it, Sarah?" she asked herself quietly. Inspiration struck suddenly. "Of course. By changing the victim's password to one of my own, thereby locking him—or her—out of the directory, while still being able to access it myself."

But what password would Lamar have chosen? *Marijuana* and all its nicknames seemed too obvious, but Sarah tried them one after another, anyway, without success. Deeply frustrated and disheartened, she was just about ready to call it a night, to give up and go home, when, out of the blue—or out of sheer desperation, she thought wryly—she suddenly recollected what Lamar's grandmother, Mabel Rollins, had told her and Renzo that day they had spoken with her, about how Lamar had thought the sun rose and set in his little sister, Keisha, and what the child, unable to say her name properly, called herself.

Slowly, her heart pounding with excitement, Sarah typed in the words *Kiss-Kiss*. As she had hoped and believed, they proved to be the key that unlocked the directory. Once more, she asked for a list of files. When they came up, she highlighted the first one, opened it, and scanned its contents, absolutely sickened and horrified by what she read. This was exactly what she had, in her heart of hearts, begun to suspect. No wonder Lamar and Morse had both been murdered over this! Grabbing a DAT tape from one of Bubba's credenza drawers, she inserted it into the tape backup machine and began to download all the files.

Sarah was so engrossed in what she was doing that she never heard the whisper of a door opening and then closing in the distance, or the light tread of footsteps moving stealthily down the corridor beyond Bubba's office, in her direction.

Twenty-Seven

The Revelation

Time reveals all things.

Adagia
—Desiderius Erasmus

"**D**id you find what you were looking for, Coal Lump?"

At the softly but viciously sneered epithet, Sarah's skin crawled, so the fine hairs on her nape and arms stood on end, and she was suddenly just seven years old again, standing on the commons, terrified, the secondhand lunch box clutched to her breast.

"Evie!" she exclaimed, stricken as she glanced up and spied her childhood nemesis looming there in the doorway, holding a hunting rifle—a 30-06—almost casually in her hands. Like Sarah, Evie wore a shell, a pair of jeans and sandals. But incongruously, a string of pearls encircled her throat—as though she were on her way to the Grain Elevator or the country club. In the dim lamplight, the pearls seemed somehow alive, a lustrous, oyster-colored snake coiling and slithering around Evie's throat. A pair of surgical gloves encased her hands. Her icy blue eyes glittered with a cold, cunning light. "Have you gone mad?" Sarah cried—knowing that of course, that was the only possible explanation, that Evie was insane. "What do you think you're doing, Evie?"

"Oh, I think you already know the answer to that, Coal Lump. You got into the directory—just as Sonny and Lamar and Morse did. So now, I've got to kill you, too, the same way I killed all of them, so Daddy will be safe. He's a brilliant man, my daddy. He's going to be president of the United States someday, you know, and I'm going to live in the White House. And I won't let you stand in the way of all that. Not you, not anybody. Take the tape out of that backup machine. Then shut down the computer and get up out of that chair. Slowly, Coal Lump. No sudden moves, or I'll splatter you all over big, bad Bubba's office."

By now, Sarah's heart was beating so wildly and erratically in her breast that she thought it was going to explode. Somewhere inside her, a dam had burst, releasing a flood of adrenaline that gushed and churned through her shaking body. Her mouth was dry; her breathing was so rapid and shallow that she feared she was hyperventilating, that she would faint, that her knees would give out from under her, sending her tumbling to the floor. Her mind raced ninety miles an hour, spinning out of control, the way Alex's electronic car had done at the Penny Arcade that afternoon when Renzo had—like the dust devil that had danced on the distant horizon that day—swept back into town, his arrival proving a catalyst. Vaguely, she expected to see the words GAME OVER flash on Bubba's monitor.

She had to stop panicking and think, she realized, her survival instinct suddenly shifting into high gear—or Evie was going to kill her. Determinedly, Sarah licked her lips to moisten them and swallowed hard to force down the lump in her throat, which seemed to be cutting off her air. She had to play for time, to try to get Evie to talk. Abruptly, it dawned on her that Evie had confessed to *three* murders.

"Sonny?" Sarah murmured disbelievingly—for surely that couldn't be right, could it? "You said you killed your brother Sonny, Evie. Was he the first one, then, to discover what Field-Yield, Inc. was doing?"

"Yes." Evie's chillingly distorted face slowly softened, took on a trancelike, dreamlike quality as she remembered. "He had come home that summer from Harvard, stuffed full of idealism and righteousness, a gloriously burning ambition to change the world—as though anybody ever has. Or could. He was like a pure, shining golden flame. Sonny thought Man was a noble creature, blessed with a mind that could soar to infinite heights, envision boundless dreams—and then make them real. His head was always in the clouds. Books, poetry, music. He sought perfection, never realizing that even if it were possible to achieve it, it's not in Man's nature to endure it. He never understood that we're all savages under the skin, that the only true law is the law of the jungle, that the weak are always winnowed out, that it's only the strongest, the fittest of us who survive, those who're willing to fight for whatever they can, however they have to do it—like Daddy and me. Once he found the directory, Sonny couldn't live with it. He was going to make the files public, tear down everything Daddy had ever scratched and struggled to build. I couldn't allow that."

"So you killed Sonny. But how can that be, Evie? He died that summer at the old quarry. He fell off the seventh rock, plunged underwater and broke his neck in a terrible, tragic accident."

"No, it was no accident. I was there that day, remember? I had my hunting rifle in the trunk of my car, because Daddy and I had been skeet shooting earlier that morning. When Renzo began to taunt Sonny, goading him up the rocks, I realized then how I could kill him and nobody would ever know. They'd think it was an accident—or that Renzo was to blame. There wasn't any risk at all, because even if Renzo survived, who would believe him innocent, a Dagotown boy like him, with a mobster father? So I slipped away to my car. No one was watching me. Their attention was riveted on the diving. I took out my rifle, crept away to the edge of the woods, where I climbed a tree, so nobody would see me make the shot. I couldn't afford to leave a bullet in Sonny's body, of course. So at first, I wasn't sure exactly how I would do it. But then I saw how the two of them were standing, that if Renzo were startled, he'd probably lose his footing and fall, taking Sonny with him. So when I heard Junior Barlow driving up in his backfiring clunker, I pulled the trigger, grazing Renzo's shoulder. He and Sonny fell."

"And Sonny broke his neck and died."

"Yes. And then Renzo ran away, and everybody blamed him, just as I'd known they would. It was the perfect crime. Sonny was never half so clever as I. And neither are you, Coal Lump. I know what you're doing, how you think you can keep me talking, play for time until help arrives. But help isn't going to come—at least, not in time for you."

"You won't get away with it, Evie," Sarah insisted, her fear now a dull, gnawing worry at the pit of her stomach, no longer controlling her. "You won't be able to blame Renzo for my death."

"Of course I will. I only have to suggest that you'd grown frightened of him, that you were going to testify against him at the trial. I'll say you came to me, desperate, looking for Bubba, that Renzo had attacked you and tried to kill you, but you had managed somehow to escape and wanted Bubba's help and protection. Everybody in town knows what a jealous temper Renzo has—especially where you're concerned. Everyone knows how, that day in the sheriff's office, he tried to beat Bubba to death over you, and then knocked down Hoag for calling you a whore. Nobody will doubt my word. It's the big lie. If you tell it often enough, everybody eventually believes it. So you see, Coal Lump, I *will* get away with murder, just as I always have. Now, take the tape out of that backup machine, then shut down the computer."

While Evie had talked, Sarah had, with a start, realized Renzo's pocket tape recorder, lying by the computer, was still switched on and in the Stop-Record position. So because it was voice activated, it had recorded every word Evie had spoken. Now, as Sarah leaned forward to remove the DAT tape from the backup machine, she laid her hand unobtrusively over the tape recorder, hoping Evie wouldn't notice her action. At the same time as she pushed the button on the backup machine to release the DAT tape, she also popped the microcassette from the tape recorder, quickly slipping it into the pocket of her jeans.

"Just out of curiosity, what's Lamar's password?" Evie inquired casually as Sarah turned off the computer.

"Why should I make it easy for you by telling you? You're going to kill me, anyway."

"That's right, Coal Lump." Evie smiled in a way that sent an icy shiver crawling up Sarah's spine. "Now, toss that DAT tape over here to me. Then stand up and pick up your purse. It'll be easier for me if I don't have to come back here to clean up after you."

Silently, Sarah did as instructed, knowing the DAT tape wasn't important, that she could always locate the hidden directory and retrieve its files again, that it was the microcassette from the tape recorder that mustn't fall into Evie's hands. To Sarah's relief, Evie stayed in front of Bubba's desk and didn't notice the tape recorder, blocked from her view by Bubba's big, twenty-one-inch monitor.

"All right, Coal Lump." Evie motioned with her rifle toward the door. "Let's go."

For the first time, Renzo cursed the fact that Sarah had bought the old Lovell place, which was outside the town limits and on the opposite side of the community from Field-Yield, Inc. And every second was precious. The killer had proved too clever to make the mistake of underestimating the opposition, of not keeping a wary eye on the fertilizer plant, if that was the key to this entire business. Why in the hell had Sarah ever gone there? Renzo wondered, hating himself. Because in his heart, he knew the answer. She had done it for him, to prove his innocence. Oh, God, why hadn't he called home before leaving Fritzchen's Kitchen to head to the farmhouse? If he had, he would have learned everything from Alex then—and would already be at Field-Yield, Inc. Even now, Sarah could be dead. The very thought filled Renzo with mind-numbing fear and anguish.

The country roads brought more snarled oaths to his lips. He wanted to open the Jaguar up, to jam the accelerator to the floorboard and let the powerful V12 engine spring forward like the huge, predatory cat for which the car was named. But that would be foolish on the dark, dusty roads, where animals darted from the brush and loose sand caused the tires to shift and slide. He drove as fast as he dared—all the while haunted by a terrible sense of impending doom, as though it weren't fast enough, as though Sarah's life were hanging in a deadly balance and he weren't going to get there in time. He was absolutely frantic. The Jaguar growled ferociously as he urged it on savagely.

In the dark corridors of Field-Yield, Inc., knowing only that if she were going to die, she would not do so without a struggle, Sarah took her chance. As they passed the doorway of her old office, she knelt down on one knee, pretending that her sandal had come loose, and when Evie suspiciously stepped in closer to her, Sarah abruptly sprang up, slamming her handbag so hard into Evie's face that the purse went flying. Stunned, Evie staggered back, and before she could recover, could raise the rifle into position to fire, Sarah shoved her back into the office and yanked the door shut.

Then, knowing she had only moments before Evie would be hard on her heels, Sarah ran toward the heavy glass front doors of the fertilizer plant, jerking her keys from her pocket so they would be at the ready. As she had feared, the doors refused to budge as she slammed against them. She jammed her key into the lock, twisted it furiously, then raced outside toward her Jeep. Her heart sank as she saw that it sported a flat tire, courtesy of Evie and the rifle. Even knowing how sparks could fly up and set the gas tank on fire, Sarah was desperate enough to have driven the vehicle on the rim. But there was no time to make the attempt as, without warning, Evie barged out the front doors of Field-Yield, Inc.

Wildly, Sarah glanced around the halogen-lit parking lot. On the outskirts of town, the fertilizer plant occupied several acres of land and was surrounded by a high, chain-link fence. There was nothing else close, no place for her to go in search of help, other than the night watchman's booth. As she reached it, she observed to her despair that it was empty and that Otis Krueger was nowhere in sight. In some dim corner of her mind, she wondered if Evie had killed him. If she had killed poor old Thaddeus Rollins, too. If she, Sarah, were the only person left alive at Field-Yield, Inc.—and utterly alone with a madwoman who was bent on murdering her.

Evie must have been crazy for years, Sarah thought. Only, she had been so clever at concealing her madness that nobody had ever recognized that fact.

The fertilizer plant sprawled before Sarah like some huge, hulking alien spacecraft. Around the tall, white-glowing halogen lights that lit the grounds, moths flew, and june bugs droned and scuttled on the asphalt. She would have to go back inside, she realized, dismayed. Out here in the open, she would be like a deer caught in the cross hairs of Evie's scope. That thought had no sooner entered Sarah's mind than, some sixth sense warning her, she bolted from the security booth. It was the only thing that saved her life as Evie raised the rifle and fired. The bullet zinged in the darkness, seeming to buzz like a wasp or a bee in Sarah's ear before it drilled a hole in one window of the security booth, so the safety glass crackled, a giant spider web abruptly burgeoning across its smooth surface.

The tar that filled the cracks in the parking lot was still gooey from the day's heat and stuck to Sarah's sandals as she stumbled on, gasping with pain at the stitch that had begun in her side. A scream was torn from her throat as she reached the factory and saw Otis Krueger, the night watchman, slumped outside against the wall near the door. Quickly, she bent to check for a pulse. To her relief, he was alive but unconscious. Evie must have sneaked up behind him and coldcocked him with the butt of her rifle while he was making his nightly rounds, Sarah thought. For her own sake, she'd have to leave him there until she could get help.

She thanked God for her master key as she let herself
into the factory proper. Evie had deactivated the alarm in
the office building, so it hadn't gone off when Sarah had
opened the doors. Now her own failure to deactivate and
reset the factory alarm would cause it to sound—and the
alarm company would notify both the sheriff's office and
Bubba. Disheartened, she wondered if she could expect
assistance from either source. Hoag hadn't balked at
groping her, and Bubba managed Field-Yield, Inc. Even
though Sarah didn't want to believe it of him, she thought
that surely he had to know what was going on here, to be
as much a part of the hideous cover-up at the fertilizer
plant as his father and sister. But it was too late now to
worry about whether either the sheriff or Bubba would
come to her rescue—or whether they would prove more
than happy to let Evie kill her. Thirty seconds had passed
since Sarah had entered the factory; as a result, the alarm
had begun to blast deafeningly.

It would continue to do so for several minutes before
resetting itself. She needed to use that time to get as deep
into the factory as she could—while Evie couldn't hear her,
couldn't tell which way she was headed. Sarah ran through
the plant, the silvery moonlight that streamed through its
high, louvred windows of green glass illuminating it dimly,
casting processing machinery into macabre shadow, making her think, like a child, that monsters lurked in the dark.
And they did—in the shape of Evie and her murderous,
mad mind. By now, she must be inside the factory, coming up behind Sarah from the gloom at her back.

The alarm had stopped blaring now. Sarah's footfalls
echoed hollowly in the resulting eerie stillness as she hur-

ried on, slipping from one piece of machinery to the next, hoping to work her way through the plant to the warehouse and loading docks beyond, from where she could run outside to the parking lot again, should help arrive. She was sweating so profusely from fear and the heat that perspiration ran into her eyes, nearly blinding her as she continued on. Her top was almost soaked through, sticking uncomfortably to her skin, and her breath came in harsh pants that seemed to her to sound like a bellows in the factory, overly loud, betraying her position. Surely she wouldn't have to hide and flee much longer. Surely the sheriff and Bubba would presently arrive. Realistically, however, Sarah knew that how long it took them to get here would depend on where they were when their respective calls came through.

"Saaarrry. Saaarrry." Like the hiss of a snake, the stage whisper reverberated in the plant, appearing to come at her from all directions, so she glanced around frantically, attempting to pinpoint the source. "Saaarrry." Evie's voice soughed again, slinking and slithering through the entire factory, reminding Sarah strangely of the pearls at Evie's throat, coiling and twining, constricting. They seemed now to be wrapped around Sarah's own throat, squeezing, cutting off her breath. Her heart thudded in her breast. "Saaarrry." The sound was coming through the PA system, Sarah realized at last. Evie must be in the cubicle that was the foreman's office.

Crouched low to the floor to avoid being a bigger target than she had to be, knowing only that she had to keep moving, Sarah struggled on toward the warehouse.

* * *

It was actually Bubba who pulled into the parking lot of Field-Yield, Inc. first, the wide tires of his Corvette burning rubber as he wheeled off the blacktop and screeched to a halt before the office building. He pushed open the car's low-slung door, then got out a trifle unsteadily, having been on his third or fourth whiskey of the evening when the alarm company had telephoned to notify him that the alarm at the fertilizer plant was going off.

Belatedly, he remembered he had never followed up on Jolene's suspicion that office supplies were being pilfered from the storerooms. Now he thought hazily that it must be a gang of thieves at work and that tonight they had got brazen enough to attempt to make off with more than a couple of cases of diskettes. They probably had a truck parked out back and were even now inside, ripping off the computers and Lord only knew what else! Fuming at the very idea, Bubba stalked determinedly toward the office building.

He was so intent on throttling whomever he might find inside that he didn't notice Sarah's Jeep parked in the space reserved for his father, behind the tall, sprawling quince bushes. Much to his surprise, the heavy glass front doors of the office were unlocked and the alarm had been deactivated. Jolene's theory must be right, Bubba thought hotly, and it was old Thaddeus Rollins who was stealing from Field-Yield, Inc.! Bubba couldn't believe it. Thaddeus had worked for the company as its head janitor for over twenty years and was considered a valuable, trusted employee—and this was how he had repaid them! Bubba was fit to be tied.

"Thaddeus Rollins!" he called angrily as he strode down the corridors. "Hey, Thaddeus! Where are you? Get your damned black ass on out here! I know you're in here, trying to rip me off!"

The distant drone of a vacuum cleaner attracted Bubba's attention. He found Thaddeus sprawled on an office floor, unconscious, a big, nasty lump on the back of his head where he had been struck from behind. Bubba shut off the vacuum cleaner and picked up the telephone receiver to call an ambulance, now slightly ashamed of himself for suspecting Thaddeus as the thieving culprit.

Outside in the parking lot, Renzo stared down the long, blue barrel of Hoag's .357 Magnum revolver, knowing it was just a matter of moments until the sheriff pulled the trigger—even though Hoag, having driven in behind Renzo, was well aware of the fact that it wasn't Renzo who had broken into Field-Yield, Inc. Having spied both Sarah's car and Bubba's, Renzo was frantic at the idea that she was even now at Bubba's cold-blooded mercy, that Bubba would rape and then kill her.

"Come on, boy!" Hoag goaded, chewing furiously on the toothpick in his mouth. "You know you want to have at me so bad you can taste it! So come on. Think about me with my hands all over that sweet little whore of yours, and come on! Give me an excuse to shoot you right where you stand!"

"You don't need an excuse, you filthy bastard!" Renzo retorted hotly, his dark visage grim, enraged, a muscle flexing in his set jaw, his eyes narrowed and hard as he stared at the sheriff, his fingers itching to punch Hoag's

442   *Rebecca Brandewyne*

pasty face in again, to beat the hell out of him. "Now, get out of my way, damn you! It's Bubba who killed Lamar and Morse—and now, he's inside there with Sarah somewhere, and he'll kill her, too!"

"Yeah, right. Like I believe that shit, boy!"

"Hoag?" Bubba called as he exited the office building and spied Renzo and the sheriff standing toe-to-toe in the parking lot. "What in the hell's going on out here, Hoag?"

As the sheriff glanced instinctively toward the sound of Bubba's voice, Renzo made his move, swiftly kicking the revolver from Hoag's grasp and then attacking him with brutal vengeance. At that, growling an imprecation, Bubba came running; and in moments the three men were locked in a furious knock-down-drag-out, beating one another viciously.

The warehouse was darker than the factory had been, its windows higher and not quite so large as those of the plant. So it took Sarah's eyes a moment to adjust to the dimmer light, to the moonbeams that filtered in hazily, illuminating the swirling clouds of fertilizer dust stirred by the torrid breeze that whispered through the warehouse.

"I know you're in here, Coal Lump Kincaid." Evie's voice sounded from out of the shadows somewhere, echoing in the huge building. "I can smell the stench of coal dust and dago sweat, you slut! You know I'm going to get you in the end, so why don't you just save us both a whole lot of trouble and show yourself? I'll be quick if you do. I'll shoot you in the head, the same way I did Morse, so you won't even know what struck you, won't feel any pain at all, will be dead before you ever even hit the ground. But if you don't come out, I'll kill you like I did Lamar—and you won't die so fast or easy. You should have seen him! He looked like a little black puppet, dancing on its strings. Is that how you want to die, Coal Lump?''

Sarah didn't make the mistake of answering, knowing Evie was only trying to goad her into talking so her position in the warehouse would be revealed. As she huddled behind the stacks of fertilizer and pesticide bags that concealed her from Evie, Sarah's heart drummed horrendously in her ears and she was stricken by the horrible sensation that she was going to wet her pants. Adrenaline pumped furiously through her body, and she trembled violently. The pungent smell of the fertilizer and pesticides gagged her, so she felt as though she were going to throw up at any moment. Tears stung her eyes from the irritating dust, and from her fear. Worst of all was the fact that she could feel a sneeze building up in her nose. With every ounce of her will, she tried desperately to hold it back. But it wouldn't be contained, bursting from her in a small, noisy exhalation only partially muffled by her palm.

At the sound, Evie, creeping through the warehouse, whirled and fired. In that exact moment, some instinct warning her frantically, Sarah leaped to her feet and ran as hard as she could, her lungs filling with the fertilizer and pesticide dust, feeling as though they were going to burst. The bullet struck the voltage box that was mounted on the warehouse wall, boring through the steel casing and drilling into the thick wiring inside, causing a shower of sparks to erupt and spray violently from the box. On the floor, just to one side of the box, sat a hundred-gallon container of gasoline that was kept for emergency use at Field-Yield, Inc., to power the generator or in case one of the company's pickup trucks should somehow accidently run out of fuel on the road. As the temperature today had risen to well over a hundred degrees in the shade and was still close to that in the huge, sweltering warehouse, the gasoline in the can had vaporized, building up a tremendous amount of pressure. Now, as the sparks from the voltage box spat forth frenziedly, they ignited the gasoline vapors.

And when that happened, the warehouse exploded.

"Oh, my God! *Sarah!*" Renzo cried hoarsely, his head jerking up wildly, his heart in his throat as the big, heavy doors of the warehouse were suddenly blasted open to release a torrent of flames, smoke and debris into the night. *"Sarah!"* Involuntarily, his fists tightened savagely on Bubba's torn shirt as the two of them froze in midfight, their eyes locking, Bubba's widening in horror and disbelief as he abruptly understood.

Leaving Hoag where he lay sprawled, bleeding and groaning on the asphalt, the two men began desperately to run.

The explosion had knocked Sarah down, slamming her flat against the hard, concrete floor of the warehouse and ripping the breath from her lungs. Her ears rang horrendously from the blast, so she couldn't even hear the fire alarm that had started to shriek, and her head pounded sickeningly, making her feel imbalanced, as though she couldn't get her bearings and were going to vomit from the sensation. For a long minute, she could only lay where she had landed, numbly fighting the waves of dizziness and nausea that assailed her mercilessly, not quite certain what had caused them. In some obscure corner of her mind, she understood that she was in shock and hurting, that a portion of the warehouse had blown up and that flames were even now sweeping wildly through the rest, irrepressibly fueled by all the fertilizer present.

The heat was horrible, as though she had died and gone to hell and were being consumed by an inferno. The acrid, billowing smoke burned her eyes, nose and lungs. She coughed violently, realizing dimly that if she didn't somehow get to her feet, escape from the warehouse, she would rapidly be overcome by smoke inhalation. As the fumes rose to the rafters, the sprinkler heads in the ceiling spurted to life. Briefly, water showered down to combat the fire. At that insatiable, wholly unexpected demand, two miles away in Cooper Northrup's beleaguered water-treatment plant, the old, inadequate equipment wheezed and groaned and, with a last, ragged gasp, ground slowly to a pathetic halt. In the blazing warehouse, the sprinkler heads sputtered a few pitiful trickles of water, then dried up.

"Sarah! *Sarah!*" Like a madman, Renzo battled his way through the flames to reach her, his heart lurching horribly to a stop as he spied her prone, still figure. Then, to his everlasting relief, her eyelids fluttered open and a tiny whimper of disorientation and pain issued from her throat. "*Sarah!* Oh, thank God, you're alive!" Feverishly, he swept her up into his strong arms to carry her from the warehouse.

"Evie..." she moaned as her head lolled against his shoulder. "It was...Evie...all the time. You have to...save her, too...Renzo...."

"Bubba!" he shouted furiously at that, his voice rising above the roar of the fire as he strode swiftly through the crackling flames, spurred on by the ominous creak of the rafters above them. "Bubba! Evie's in here, too! Damn it, Bubba! Do you hear me? You've got to find your sister!"

To Renzo's relief, Bubba heard. Seeing Sarah in Renzo's arms, he turned, his face ashen and frantic as he disappeared into the blaze, in search of Evie.

Chaos and cacophony reigned in the parking lot of Field-Yield, Inc., which was now crowded with a multitude of vehicles that had appeared in response to the alarms and the raging inferno. The town's fire trucks and water trucks were out in full force, the firefighters rushing to hook up their hoses and begin dousing the blaze. Thaddeus Rollins and Otis Krueger had been discovered and were being treated by the paramedics who had arrived in the ambulance Bubba had summoned earlier. Dwayne Truett was yelling orders right and left, while Hoag, having finally dragged himself to his feet, slouched miserably in the backseat of his patrol car, still groaning from the beating he had received—and somehow knowing in his agonized gut that his days as the sheriff in this town were numbered.

J. D. Holbrooke had appeared on the scene and stood a little to one side, as though in a trance, unable to believe his eyes at the sight of the burning warehouse, at the thought that Bubba was inside. The media vans of Channels 5, 7 and 12 were disgorging their camera crews, so there would be film at eleven; and K-104 on the FM dial had a reporter calling in live reports from the parking lot, as did a few other radio stations. Virgil Bodine was speaking quickly but competently into his voice-activated, pocket tape recorder, making notes for the *Trib*. Hearing the news, Liz and Parker Delaney had come, together with a number of the town's other citizens, who continued to flock to the scene, drawn by a morbid curiosity inherent in Man. Additional officers and firefighters were attempting to prevent spectators from pouring into the parking lot, so that many of the cars were lined up along the highway.

It was into this confusion that Renzo bore Sarah, both of them to be set upon immediately by a barrage of television and radio reporters, who shoved cameras and microphones into their faces, spitting a stream of questions and demanding answers. Fearful that J.D., Hoag and Dwayne would somehow succeed in suppressing what she now knew, Sarah weakly but fiercely bade Renzo to stop, to let her speak. Then, clinging tightly to his neck, she cried, "It's toxic waste! Field-Yield, Inc.'s been dumping toxic waste into the old quarries! It's what's leaching up into everybody's backyards! It's poisoning us all! I have proof! I discovered it in FYI's computer system tonight! It's why Sonny Holbrooke, Lamar Rollins and Morse Novak were murdered! Evie Holbrooke killed them—all of them, including her own brother—so nobody would learn what her daddy was doing! I have it all on tape!"

The crowd went crazy at her words, the low, buzzing drone of anger and disbelief speedily growing to riotous proportions as people began dazedly to comprehend what

Sarah had said. The media rushed to confront a stunned, utterly destroyed J.D.—and then an equally stunned, incredulous Bubba, who came staggering from the burning warehouse, Evie in his arms, only moments before the hideously straining and groaning rafters at last gave way and the entire building collapsed with a thunderous roar.

High above the clamor rose Bubba's shouts of "I didn't know! Sarah, you've got to believe me! I didn't know!"

Evie's thin, eerie, childlike wails of "Daddy! I did it for you, Daddy! I did it all for you!" were almost lost in the cacophony.

Bubba's face held such a mixture of shock, disbelief and terrible sadness as he gazed at his poor, disconsolate, bewildered sister that Sarah knew he was telling the truth. Her heart welled with pity and pain for him. He *had* loved her, in his fashion.

"I'm glad, Bubba. I'm so very glad you didn't know," she said with heartfelt sincerity.

And understanding that, accepting it for what it was—her parting gift to Bubba—Renzo, his voice low, hoarse, throbbing with emotion, uttered, "Oh, Sarah . . ." The words trailed into silence as she kissed him wildly, fervently, in that way speaking all that was in her heart, crying and clinging to him for dear life as he carried her to the roadster and gently settled her inside.

The powerful engine roared to life. Then the Jaguar sprang forward into the summer darkness, hastening down the long, winding, dusty road toward home.

Twenty-Eight

The Last Good-bye

What though youth gave love and roses,
Age still leaves us friends and wine.

Irish Melodies: Spring and Autumn
—Thomas Moore

As Renzo watched the huge, spike-topped, wrought-iron gates swing open slowly before him, he was transported back to his childhood, back to the first moment he had ever seen the coal-black barriers, nearly thirty years ago now. He wondered idly what had ever become of Sofie and Uncle Vinnie, who had brought him here that day he had first come to town. He had been just seven years old then. It was hard now to believe so much time had passed. Where had it all gone? It seemed only yesterday that he had sat out front of these same gates, in Uncle Vinnie's flashy, two-toned convertible. Now it was his own roadster Renzo guided slowly up the long, serpentine drive, through the stands of trees to the big, imposing, red-brick house on the top of the rise.

He remembered how badly it had frightened him to spy it perched there like some predatory animal, as though it had been lying in wait for him, and his mouth twisted in an ironic half smile at the memory. How the years had cut the house down in size, so it no longer seemed nearly as large and intimidating to the man he now was as it had appeared to the boy he had once been.

He parked the Jaguar out front, got out, then strode to the front porch and rang the bell. To his surprise, his grandmother herself answered the door. Mama Rosa's face was wan and drawn; clearly, she had been weeping. Still, her eyes lit up with pleasure when she saw him standing there, and she managed a tremulous smile.

"Renzo, come in. Papa said we should expect you. He's out on the veranda, waiting for you. Are you hungry? Would you like something to eat?"

"No, thank you. Grandmama, how you doing?" He kissed her cheek and hugged her, dismayed by how small and frail she seemed. "You don't look so good. What's the matter? Are you ill?"

"No, not in the way you mean. There's nothing wrong with me, except that I'm old and tired, and my heart is breaking. Oh, Renzo!" Her voice caught on a ragged little sob, alarming him. "It's Papa! He—he pretends to me that he's all right... that it's nothing more than the summer heat that ails him. But I know. In here—" she laid her hand on her breast "—in here, I know the truth. He's dying, Renzo. Papa's dying."

"Grandmama! Are you... are you sure?" Renzo was surprised to find himself deeply stricken by this wholly unexpected news, as though he had received a stunning blow to his head or midsection. Until now, he had been certain he felt nothing toward Papa Nick but suspicion, wariness and contempt. Now he was shocked to discover that, impossibly, he also deep down inside harbored a hitherto unrecognized affection and gratitude toward the old man. Whatever else Papa Nick was, he was Renzo's grandfather and had in his own way watched over him, Sarah and Alex all these years. Did that not count for something? "Have you spoken to him, to his doctor, Grandmama?"

"No." Mama Rosa shook her head, smiling gently at Renzo's confusion. "Papa doesn't want me to know he's dying, Renzo. So for his sake, I've tried to be strong, to pretend as though there's nothing wrong. But we've been married for more than fifty years. Our love is such that there is a bond between us even death will not break, I think. And so I know he will soon be taken from me and that somehow I'll have to go on alone until my own time comes. But, please. Don't say anything to Papa about my knowing, Renzo. Let him go on believing he's protecting me, as I've always let him believe all these years. He is a man—and very proud."

"All right, Grandmama. If that's what you want."

"It is. Now, go on out to the veranda."

As he stepped outside, Renzo had another momentary sensation that time had somehow turned back on itself to come full circle and that he was seven years old again. For Papa Nick looked just as he had the first time Renzo had ever seen him. He sat deep in the shadows of the veranda, rocking, a glowing-tipped cigar in his mouth, his gnarled, age-spotted hands curled like talons over the silver-knobbed head of the malacca cane propped between his legs. Still, when Renzo spied his grandfather, his heart involuntarily sank and he knew his grandmother had spoken truly, that Papa Nick was dying. Some immensely powerful, vital spark had gone out of him. He was just a tired old man now, half asleep in his rocking chair, cigar ash spilling down the front of his white shirt. Suddenly torn and half ashamed of himself, not wanting to disturb his grandfather, Renzo turned to go back inside, only to be halted by the sound of Papa Nick's gruff voice.

"Where're you going, boy? Sitta down. I ain't dead yet, and I know you didn't come alla way uppa here in this heat just for a glass of Mama Rosa's lemonade." He indicated the small table beside him, on which sat a sweating pitcher filled with pale yellow liquid in which ice and lemon slices floated.

"No. But I didn't know you were ill, or I wouldn't have bothered you." Renzo sat down in the second rocker, the one that was his grandmother's. "Why didn't you let me know?"

"Whadda for? Ain't not'ing wrong with me but this heat and weariness and old age. I'm like an old grandfather clock whose mainspring is finally winding down for the last time. You t'ink you climbed so high in life that you can stoppa that, can winda me uppa again? Well, you ain't, and you can't. Nobody escapes from death, boy. Not you, not me. He comes for alla us in the end, that old Grim Reaper. But I've seen too mucha in my day to fear him.

Death and I...we're old companions. And that'sa why you're here, ain't it?''

"Yes. You've seen the morning paper, then, I take it?" At Papa Nick's nod, Renzo continued—a trifle defensively, much to his anger and disgust. "I transmitted that same article over the AP wire last night. It's breaking news now all over the country. And that's as it should be. You couldn't have expected me not to report a story like this, to cover it up—not even for your sake."

"I didn't. What'sa that old saying? A man's gotta do what a man's gotta do. You're an investigative reporter, Renzo, one of the best. I expect that before it'sa alla over, you mighta even win another Pulitzer Prize for whadda you and Sarah unearthed at Field-Yield, Inc."

"Maybe. But that's not why I wrote the initial article— or why I'll write the rest, either, as events unfold. I did it because it's my job and my duty, because innocent people have a right to know what's being done to them by those who're powerful and corrupt. It's only a matter of days— hours—now before the media and the appropriate government officials descend in full force upon this town. Before that happens, I want to know—for my own curiosity's sake, if nothing else—what, if anything, they're going to find in all those old, abandoned quarries besides Field-Yield, Inc.'s toxic waste?"

"Whadda you t'ink they're gonna find? Jimmy Hoffa's remains?" Papa Nick laughed shortly, the sound turning into a hacking cough and ending in a wheeze.

"That thought has crossed my mind," Renzo confessed soberly.

"I knew that . . . knew that'sa why you'dda come to see me. But I'm afraid whaddaever became of old Jimmy is gonna remain one of life's little unsolved mysteries, like who murdered them two little princes in the Tower of London. 'Cause I wouldn't wanna nobody to t'ink I was a whistle-blower, now, woulda I?" Papa Nick asked softly, intently.

Renzo's head jerked up sharply at that; his swiftly indrawn breath was harsh. He stared at his grandfather, dumbfounded, disbelieving. "It was *you!*" he accused. "Wasn't it? All that time, *you* were the Whistle-blower—and I never knew!"

Papa Nick smiled mockingly, his eyes like dark flames. "Was I? Now, whadda woulda make you t'ink a crazy t'ing like that? You got too mucha sun today, boy? Suffered some kinda heatstroke or somet'ing? Why woulda I wanna do anyt'ing like your Whistle-blower did?"

"Dying men often want to atone for their past sins," Renzo stated quietly. "And you still haven't answered my questions, not any of them."

"No—and I ain't gonna answer them, neither. Your Whistle-blower chose to give uppa his secrets. Fine. If those old quarries choose to give uppa their secrets, fine. But I'm taking alla mine to the grave, boy. You see, business in my day wasn't like it'sa now. Alla these people today, these upstarts, these Columbians and Jamaicans, these Chinese and Russians, whoever . . . they ain't got no sense of loyalty or honor. And as strange as it may seem to you, Renzo, in my day, we hadda code of ethics. People got mixed uppa with us, they knew whadda they were getting into. They knew they'dda be rewarded for following the rules—and whadda woulda happen to them if they broke 'em, too. In my day, we didn't gun down innocent women and children in the streets, didn't engage in these gang wars and drive-by shootings and such that, nowadays, are just for sport and ain't got not'ing whaddasoever to do with business. That ain't professional. It ain't smart.''

"And that was your justification? That made everything all right?''

From beneath his bushy brows, Papa Nick shot Renzo a sharp, penetrating glance. Then, his black eyes gleaming slyly, he drawled quietly, "You tell me, boy. Which is worse? An old Italian like me, who was whadda he was and never made no bones about it? Or somebody like J. D. Holbrooke, who passed himself off as a fine, upstanding citizen, while, alla the time, he was dumping toxic waste into those quarries, poisoning hundreds of innocent, unsuspecting people, leaving 'em crippled and deformed, mentally retarded, suffering from cancer and God only knows whadda other diseases, killing 'em, slow and terrible, young and old? You see, Renzo,'' Papa Nick continued gently in the face of his grandson's silence, "life donna come in black and white—only shades of grey. And every one of 'em's a hard choice, without any easy answer. Only once in a blue moon does a man come along who travels the high road, who achieves fame and fortune and power honestly, and who isn't corrupted by them in some way once he has them. You're one of those men, I t'ink. Sonny Holbrooke, if he'dda lived, woulda been another. But most of us, well, we just ain't that strong, ain't that courageous, donna havva the kinda unshakable faith in ourselves and our Maker that it takes to be one of the golden boys in this here life. It probably donna mean mucha to you, but for whaddaever it'sa worth, I'm proud of you, Renzo. You give me hope that wherever I'm going when I die, I'll havva at least one mark in my credit column.''

Papa Nick fell silent then, closing his eyes, his breathing slowing to the point that Renzo, in sudden alarm, thought his grandfather had abruptly died in the rocking chair. But before he could rise to check on the old man, Papa Nick spoke again.

''Pour us a glass of Mama Rosa's lemonade, boy,'' he directed. Then, with a hand that trembled a little—as it never had before—with weakness, he reached into his trouser pocket and drew forth two pieces of gold-foil-wrapped chocolate, handing one to Renzo. It was warm and half melted from the summer heat, so that after he had opened it, Renzo was forced to lick the chocolate from the inside of the wrapper. Still, it was no less sweet for that, in sharp contrast to the cold, tart lemonade with which he swallowed the chocolate down. ''Once, a long time ago, I told you that you wasn't never gonna owe me no favor, boy,'' Papa Nick declared as he sipped his lemonade, sighing with simple pleasure as the liquid trickled down his throat. ''But I lied. Now, there're two t'ings I wanna you to do for me after I'm dead and buried. One is that I wanna you to looka after Mama Rosa for me. We both got other family, but you're our only grandson, Renzo, the only flesh of our flesh and bone of our bones.''

''Of course I'll take care of her. You didn't need to ask.''

''No, I know that. Still, it eased my mind to hear you say it. She's a good woman, the best. I been lucky to havva her. I donna t'ink my life woulda been mucha without her. A man's born alone, and he dies alone, and if he finds one person, one beautiful, special woman in his entire life who loves him, then he's richer than most. You gonna marry that girl of yours, Renzo?''

"Yes, if she'll have me."

"Good. That'sa good. She's a fine girl, your Sarah, just like Mama Rosa. She donna know how I helped her alla these years, your Sarah, with her scholarship at the university—I sitta on the board of trustees there, you know—and with her daddy's pension and the nursing home where her poor, ailing mama is. I sent her that camera, too, and suggested to J.D. that he'dda be wise to hire her on at Field-Yield, Inc., once she hadda graduated from college. I t'ink maybe your Sarah didn't needa my help, that she'dda made it somehow on her own, anyway. But she loved you, and she was loyal. She understood about family, and she gave you a fine son...a son to be proud of. She deserved that I shoulda standa in your stead in your absence. So, this is the other t'ing I wanna you to do for me.'' Reaching down on the far side of his rocker, Papa Nick drew up an unopened bottle of wine and passed it to Renzo. ''I made it myself, from grapes from my own vineyards. After I'm gone, I wanna you and your Sarah to open that bottle and drink a toast for me . . . to *amore*. Because when alla is said and done, that'sa the only t'ing in the world that makes life worthwhile, Renzo, that makes it worth living. Because, otherwise, what'sa the point? What'sa it alla for, if you donna havva nobody to share it with?''

*   *   *

Papa Nick died quietly in his sleep that night. He was buried four days later in the old, grassy cemetery at the edge of town. Much to Sarah's surprise, as she stood with Renzo and Alex at the graveside, she observed that one of the many mourners present was J. D. Holbrooke. She hadn't seen him since that night at Field-Yield, Inc., when all hell had broken loose and Evie had been taken into custody for murder. Since then, a panel of three psychiatrists having judged her mentally incompetent to stand trial, Evie had been quietly packed off to a sanatorium, where she would in all likelihood spend the rest of her life. And of course, J.D. had withdrawn from the Senate race and was even now facing indictment on several counts for his crimes.

Now, as she gazed at him, Sarah thought J.D. looked as though he had aged twenty years in recent days, as though the rumor circulating around town—that his cancer had returned with a debilitating vengeance—were, in fact, true. Neither ZoeAnn nor Bubba accompanied J.D., and when the service had ended, he walked heavily and alone toward his car, speaking to nobody, and nobody speaking to him. It was the last time Sarah ever saw him alive. He died in a hospital bed barely six months later—leaving Bubba alone to clean up the horrible mess his father and sister had made. Like J.D., Evie hadn't trusted Bubba with the knowledge that Field-Yield, Inc. was dumping its toxic waste into the quarries. She had sensed that he, like Sonny, would draw the line at poisoning the town to spare the fertilizer plant the expense of properly disposing of its noxious refuse. So, from the time years ago when she had learned her father's secret, Evie had kept it, protecting and covering up for him.

"Alex, will you help Mama Rosa back to the limousine, please?" Renzo asked after they had all tossed their single red roses on to Papa Nick's elaborate bronze casket and the gravediggers had begun to make the necessary preparations for lowering it into the freshly turned earth, the rich scent of which filled the summer air, mingling lushly with the perfume of the roses and the rest of the flowers, the funeral wreaths. "Your mother and I will join you in a minute."

"Sure, Dad. Here, Mama Rosa." Alex slid his arm about her thin shoulders, which shook silently from her weeping. "Lean on me."

Tears stung Sarah's own eyes at the sight of her tall, sturdy, handsome son walking so slowly and patiently as he carefully assisted the frail old woman to the car. "It's as though he somehow knows she's his great-grandmother," Sarah remarked quietly, for at long last, upon Papa Nick's death, Renzo had revealed to her his relationship to the old man. "Even though we agreed he was too young to be told yet."

"Perhaps he doesn't need to be told," Renzo suggested. "Children are often wise beyond their years, knowing things by instinct that we adults don't give them credit for being aware of. I think perhaps I always knew on some level that Papa Nick was my grandfather, that I knew that first day I ever saw him and that it was something I simply buried in my subconscious, because I didn't want to know it, was afraid to acknowledge it. Sofie, my biological mother, had called him a 'big, mean old spider,' and that had frightened me horribly. *He* frightened me that day. I was only a little boy. It wasn't until this summer that I came to understand that there was great goodness, as well as great wickedness, in him, as strange as that may seem to you. Believe it or not, I'm going to miss that old man, Sarah. He stood for everything I've ever fought against my whole life. Yet, except for you, he understood me better than anyone else alive. He goaded me on, even when he knew my triumphs would prove his own defeats. In his own way, he loved me the way his son, Luciano, my real father, never did. If it hadn't been for Papa Nick, for him seeing that I grew up in the Martinelli household, I don't think I'd ever truly have known what love is. I don't think I'd ever have been the man I am today." Renzo paused for a moment. Then he said, "Walk with me a piece, Sarah. There's something else I need to do here before leaving the cemetery today."

"All right," she replied quietly, forcing herself to breathe calmly in order to still the sudden, painful, hopeful throbbing of her heart. Since that day when he had first learned about Alex, Renzo hadn't mentioned marrying her again; and at first, when he had requested she walk with him, Sarah had thought he intended to propose to her. Now she realized how crazy an idea that was. If and when Renzo asked her to marry him, he wouldn't choose a graveyard as the place to do it in, or hard on the heels of his grandfather's funeral as the time.

Renzo didn't speak further as they seemed to wander aimlessly among the old headstones, many of which were engraved with dates as far back as the late 1800s. But at last, beneath an old willow tree, he came to a halt, and as

Sarah gazed down at the marker they now stood before, she recognized that they had not, after all, been meandering through the cemetery, that Renzo had intended to come here all along.

Twelve years of sun and wind, of rain and snow, had dulled the once-polished grey granite of Sonny Holbrooke's elaborate headstone—but not his memory. In her mind's eye, she could see him as plainly as though he were still alive and standing there before them, a shock of his golden-blond hair falling carelessly into his blue eyes, his face studious and absent, as though he were perpetually lost in thought, heard in the distance a drummer different. To her surprise, Sarah now realized suddenly that it was the same expression she sometimes spied on Renzo's dark, handsome visage.

Reaching out, he rested one hand on the top of the granite marker, went down on one knee upon the grassy grave, his head bowed. For a long time, he was silent, and the only sounds were those of the gravediggers in the distance, burying Papa Nick, the soughing of the humid breeze through the trees, the drone of locusts and other insects. Then at last Renzo spoke softly, saying what to Sarah seemed a very strange thing.

"Right, Holmes," he murmured. Then he laid upon the grave the book he had carried all through Papa Nick's service, which, until this moment, Sarah had assumed was the Holy Bible. But it wasn't so at all, she recognized now as she read the title stamped in gold on the forest-green leather.

Her eyes were puzzled. Still, instinctively, she said nothing. It was one of those things about Renzo, she knew, that would forever remain a mystery to her, unless and until he chose to enlighten her. Perhaps he would some-day. Or perhaps he would not. And that was all right; that was something she understood in her heart. There were some things too private to share even with those closest to you, with those you loved, with the one who was the other half of your soul.

As Renzo was hers. Had always been hers.

Rising, he stared down at her intently, searchingly, for a long moment—marveling at the fact that, unlike most women would have, she asked no questions, but stood there waiting patiently for him. As she always had and al-ways would, he thought, his heart flooding, welling to overflowing with love for her. Without speaking, he took her hand gently in his. In silence, they strolled back to the limousine, the afternoon sun beating down brightly upon them and upon those who now slept forever in the dark, quiet earth . . . dust in the wind.

Epilogue

To Amore

A man travels the world over in search of
what he needs and returns home to find it.

The Brook Kerith
—George Moore

Twenty-Nine

Wind Chimes and Heartstrings

Now lies the Earth all Danaë to the stars,
And all thy heart lies open unto me.

The Princess
—Alfred, Lord Tennyson

An Old Victorian Farmhouse, The Midwest, The Present

As she always would, Sarah sensed Renzo behind her
even before he stepped quietly out onto the deck to join
her, a wine bottle and two glasses in hand. Still, she didn't
turn to acknowledge his presence, but went on staring at
the night sky, at the full silver moon, at the countless glittering stars that swirled across the heavens, like the fiery
trail of a flaming Catherine wheel captured at the height
of all its glory, forever poised in motion. Her piquant face
was upturned to the sultry, soughing wind, which ruffled

her long, dark brown hair, her diaphanous white nightgown, so she seemed like some beautiful, otherworldly
creature standing there, the woodland fairy princess he had
once called her years ago, Renzo thought.

Or a butterfly.

For after he set the wine bottle and glasses down on the
rail that bounded the deck, he reached out to stroke the
strands of her hair, and she trembled a little at his touch,
the way a butterfly's gossamer wings quivered lightly when
it was poised upon a flower. Her breath came quickly and
shallowly as he slowly slid his hands insidiously down her
bare arms, cupped and stroked her breasts sensuously, so
her nipples hardened and strained against his palms, ig-
niting a fire in him and her both. All around them, her
collection of wind chimes tinkled melodically, fairies frol-
icking to the music of the night.

"I like this evening ritual of yours, this quiet time of reflection and introspection," Renzo whispered against her
ear, his teeth nibbling her lobe, his lips caressing her silky
mass of hair—all a potent promise of what the night held
in store—before he reluctantly drew away for a moment to
pour the wine. It splashed in the glasses, as dark and red
and sweet as the heart.

"That's the wine Papa Nick gave you." She spoke at last
as she observed the antique-looking, private-stock label on
the slender, dark green bottle and recalled what Renzo had
told her the day he had brought the wine home, the dying
wish Papa Nick had expressed in its regard.

"Yeah, I thought we'd open it and share it tonight. It
somehow seemed appropriate to the occasion."

"And what occasion is that?" Sarah asked, striving to keep her tone light, despite the fever that burned in her blood, the way her heart had begun to hammer painfully, with sudden, wild hope, in her breast.

"Don't tease me, Sarah," Renzo replied softly, roughly. "Please. I just don't think I can bear it right now, not after so many long years without you, not after all that's happened this summer. And in your heart, you must know what I'm going to say. I love you. There's always been you—only you—for me. You know that. I want to spend the rest of my life with you, to grow old with you, to know you'll be lying next to me forever after we've gone ungently into that good night." He stared down at her, his dark brown eyes naked, intense, filled with deep longing and love for her, with pain and regret for all the lost, bittersweet days of youth that would never come again, for the empty, wasted years he and she had spent, lonely and apart, each aching for the other. Tenderly, he smoothed her hair back from her face, then laid his hand against her cheek. "We've never really had a chance these past several weeks to talk about us...to discuss where it is we're going together, you and I. And I don't think I ever really asked you properly before, all those years ago, or even that day in the Jeep, when I told you that from the time I was twelve years old, I had intended to make you my wife. But I'm asking you now, with all my heart. Sarah, will you marry me?"

"Yes, oh, Renzo, yes. You know I will," she answered fervently, her heart in her eyes as she went into his strong arms then, lifting her face eagerly and trustingly for his kiss.

With sweet, fierce passion and possession, his mouth claimed hers, tasting, savoring, drinking deep and long, as though even now, he feared she wasn't quite real, wasn't quite his, but an illusion that would evanesce into the peaceful, halcyon night if he didn't hang on to her tightly, hold her close forever and ever. But Sarah understood, for the same thought filled her own mind, so that even when Renzo finally broke the kiss, she didn't move away, but remained in his embrace, resting her head against his chest, listening intently to the steady, reassuring beat of his heart. This was where she belonged, where she had always belonged, she reflected, even as he thought, *Now, at long last, I have well and truly come home.*

After a moment, he reached into his pocket to withdraw the ring he had bought for her earlier today at Goldberg's Fine Jewelry—a ring Bubba had, that afternoon when Mrs. Goldberg had asked Renzo to give them his opinion, dismissed as not being stylish and elegant enough for Sarah, as being too old-fashioned. It was a band of dark old gold, an intricate garland of flowers, a single diamond at its heart. Wordlessly, Renzo slipped it onto Sarah's finger, and as she gazed down at it, tears of joy filled her eyes at how beautiful, how perfect it was.

"I've waited twenty-two years for you, Sarah. So I want to have our wedding ceremony soon—just as soon as we can arrange it," he insisted in the summer silence.

"Yes, I want that, too." Her voice was breathless, tremulous. "Not only because I love you, Renzo, but also because there's something I want, that I *need* to tell you. Something I never got a chance to tell you all those years ago. I know I can't make up for that now—" She broke off abruptly, biting her lower lip, anguished by memories. Then she went on. "But with all that's happened this summer, we never did talk about . . . we never did do anything about . . . Well, what I'm trying to tell you is that . . . we're going to have a baby, Renzo."

"Oh, Sarah . . ." His dark eyes leaped, flared like embers bursting into flame, gleamed with pride and happiness and wonder at the sudden mystery of her, of what they had made together. His indrawn breath was swift, sharp, serrated with emotion. "Oh, Sarah . . ." he breathed again, his hand sweeping down, coming to rest upon her belly.

Her own hand slipped down to cover his. Almost—although she knew it was yet too soon—she imagined the child stirred, as light as a butterfly, beneath their intertwined fingers.

After a long while, Renzo finally spoke again, his low voice hoarse with all the strong, deep feelings that continued to assail him. "I talked to my parents this evening. I told them I was going to marry you. They're going to come back here for the wedding. Pop got all choked up, and Mom cried. She said she'd done a horrible thing to us both and wanted to know if you'd ever forgive her. She also said to tell you she's bringing you copies of all her recipes, that she's going to teach you how to cook for me, that no daughter of hers is *not* going to know how to make Italian dishes!"

Even as a smile curved her lips at that, Sarah felt tears brim in her eyes again. "We all make mistakes, Renzo. Of course I can forgive her. I shall be proud to call her my mother-in-law. So she and your daddy, they're not upset about us getting married, then?"

"No... no, they know now that we've stood the test of time, Sarah, that we love each other—and always will. That you're the woman I want, that I've always wanted."

"And you're the man I want, Renzo, that I've always wanted, with my whole heart and every fiber of my being. But then, you know that. You've always known that." She paused, reflecting on how well and deeply and intimately he knew her, as though somehow, that long-ago day in the meadow, the butterfly's kiss upon her palms had marked her as his forever, the other half of his soul. Quietly, she continued. "Did you know your timing was apropos, too? Since earlier today, Alex asked me if you and I were ever going to get married."

"Indeed? And what did you say to that?"

"I said I hoped so, believed so. Then he asked me what I thought the chances were that you'd have him as your best man." Sarah glanced up earnestly at him, her heart turning over as she saw the sudden tears that came to his dark eyes, glistened on his thick black lashes. It was one of the things she had always loved most about him, that he was a man strong enough not to be afraid to show his emotions. "I told him he could count on it. I hope that was the right thing to have said."

"You know it was," Renzo murmured huskily, his throat once more choked with feeling. "Oh, Sarah, I *do* love you so!" His mouth took hers again, the impassioned kiss speaking for them both all that needed still to be said—and more. When, at long last, they drew apart, Renzo reached out slowly to lift the wine-filled glasses from the rail of the deck. He handed one to her. "To *amore*," he declared softly.

"To *amore*," Sarah echoed, touching her own glass gently to his.

They drank deep in the still of the summer night, while the wind chimes sang low and sweet, and among the white-blossomed honeysuckle vines that twined wild and forever at the edge of the old, moon-shadowed trees, the fireflies danced in the dark.

Author Note

Dear Reader,

I wanted to take this opportunity to thank you so very much for buying and reading my novel, Dust Devil. I hope you have enjoyed it. If you would like to write to me, you may do so at the following address: c/o MIRA Books, 225 Duncan Mill Rd., Don Mills, Ontario, Canada, M3B 3K9. Please enclose a stamped, self-addressed #10 envelope for reply.

I also want to thank my friends, Detectives Mauro V. Corvasce and Joseph R. Paglino, co-authors of Modus Operandi, who took the time and trouble to answer so many of my questions. If I have not got it right, it's not their fault, but mine.

Last but certainly not least, I want to thank all my wonderful friends at MIRA, including Dianne Moggy, Pam Lawson, and especially my editor, Tara Gavin, for being so very kind and patient as to give me the time and space I needed to write the book I really wanted to write.

Rebecca Brandewyne

To an elusive stalker, Dana Kirk is

FAIR GAME
JANICE KAISER

Dana Kirk is a very rich, very successful woman. And she did it all by herself.

But when someone starts threatening the life that she has made for herself and her daughter, Dana might just have to swallow her pride and ask a man for help. Even if it's Mitchell Cross—a man who has made a practice of avoiding rich women. But to Mitch, Dana is different, because she needs him to stay alive.

Available at your favorite retail outlet this March.

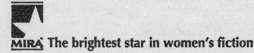

MIRA The brightest star in women's fiction

MJKFG

Take 3 of "The Best of the Best™" Novels FREE

Plus get a FREE surprise gift!

Somewhere over the

MIDNIGHT RAINBOW

love is waiting

LINDA HOWARD

Priscilla Jane Hamilton Greer had always been given the best by her daddy—including the services of Grant Sullivan. Grant, one of the government's most effective, most desired agents, was given two orders—to find this high-society girl being held captive in Costa Rica, and to bring her home.

Alone in the jungle, fleeing armed gunmen, the two battle fear and find a love that teaches them to put the demons of the past to rest—in order to face the demons of the present.

Available at your favorite retail outlet this May.

MLH3

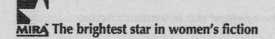